W9-BXC-956

PRAISE FOR NERO WOLFE

"It is always a treat to read a Nero Wolfe mystery. The man has entered our folklore. . . . Like Sherlock Holmes . . . he looms larger than life and, in some ways, is much more satisfactory."
—*New York Times Book Review*

"Nero Wolfe towers over his rivals . . . he is an exceptional character creation." —*New Yorker*

"The most interesting great detective of them all."
—Kingsley Amis, author of *Lucky Jim*

"Nero Wolfe is one of the master creations."
—James M. Cain, author of *The Postman Always Rings Twice*

AND FOR REX STOUT

"Rex Stout is one of the half-dozen major figures in the development of the American detective novel."
—Ross Macdonald

"I've found Rex Stout's books about Nero Wolfe endlessly readable. . . . I sometimes have to remind myself that Wolfe and Goodwin are the creations of a writer's mind, that no matter how many doorbells I ring in the West Thirties, I'll never find the right house." —Lawrence Block

"Fair warning: It is safe to read one Nero Wolfe novel, because you will surely like it. It is extremely unsafe to read three, because you will forever be hooked on the delightful characters who populate these perfect books."
—Otto Penzler

AND FOR ARCHIE GOODWIN

"Archie is a splendid character." —Dame Agatha Christie

"Stout's supreme triumph was the creation of Archie Goodwin." —P. G. Wodehouse

"If he had done nothing more than to create Archie Goodwin, Rex Stout would deserve the gratitude of whatever assessors watch over the prosperity of American literature. . . . Archie is the lineal descendant of Huck Finn." —Jacques Barzun

The Rex Stout Library

REX STOUT

Too Many Cooks

&

Champagne for One

Introduction to Champagne for One

by Lena Horne

BANTAM BOOKS

TOO MANY COOKS/CHAMPAGNE FOR ONE
A Bantam Book / May 2009

Published by Bantam Dell
A Division of Random House, Inc.
New York, New York

This is a work of fiction. Names, characters, places, and incidents either are the product of the author's imagination or are used fictitiously. Any resemblance to actual persons, living or dead, events, or locales is entirely coincidental.

ISBN: 978-0-553-38629-5

Printed in the United States of America
Published simultaneously in Canada

www.bantamdell.com

Too Many Cooks

FOREWORD

I USED as few French and miscellaneous fancy words as possible in writing up this stunt of Nero Wolfe's but I couldn't keep them out altogether, on account of the kind of people involved. I am not responsible for the spelling, so don't write me about mistakes. Wolfe refused to help me out on it, and I had to go to the Heinemann School of Languages and pay a professor 30 bucks to go over it and fix it up. In most cases, during these events, when anyone said anything which for me was only a noise, I have either let it lay—when it wasn't vital—or managed somehow to get the rough idea in the American language.

ARCHIE GOODWIN

1

WALKING up and down the platform alongside the train in the Pennsylvania Station, having wiped the sweat from my brow, I lit a cigarette with the feeling that after it had calmed my nerves a little I would be prepared to submit bids for a contract to move the Pyramid of Cheops from Egypt to the top of the Empire State Building with my bare hands, in a swimming-suit; after what I had just gone through. But as I was drawing in the third puff I was stopped by a tapping on a window I was passing, and, leaning to peer through the glass, I was confronted by a desperate glare from Nero Wolfe, from his seat in the bedroom which we had engaged in one of the new-style pullmans, where I had at last got him deposited intact. He shouted at me through the closed window:

"Archie! Confound you! Get in here! They're going to start the train! You have the tickets!"

I yelled back at him, "You said it was too close to smoke in there! It's only 9:32! I've decided not to go! Pleasant dreams!"

I sauntered on. Tickets my eye. It wasn't tickets that bothered him; he was frantic with fear because he was alone on the train and it might begin to move. He hated things that moved, and was fond of arguing that nine times out of ten the places that people were on their way to were no improvement whatever on those they were coming from. But by gum I had got him to the station twenty minutes ahead of time, notwithstanding such items as three bags and two suitcases and two overcoats for a four days' absence in the month of April, Fritz Brenner standing on the stoop with tears in his eyes as we left the house, Theodore Horstmann running out, after we had got Wolfe packed in the sedan, to ask a few dozen more questions about the orchids, and even tough little Saul Panzer, after dumping us at the station, choking off a tremolo as he told Wolfe goodbye. You might have thought

1

we were bound for the stratosphere to shine up the moon and pick wild stars.

At that, just as I flipped my butt through the crack between the train and the platform, I could have picked a star right there—or at least touched one. She passed by close enough for me to get a faint whiff of something that might have come from a perfume bottle but seemed only natural under the circumstances, and while her facial effect might have been technicolor, it too gave you the impression that it was intended that way from the outset and needed no alterations. The one glance I got was enough to show that she was no factory job, but hand-made throughout. Attached to the arm of a tall bulky man in a brown cape and a brown floppy cloth hat, she unhooked herself to precede him and follow the porter into the car back of ours. I muttered to myself, "My heart was all I had and now that's gone, I should have put my bloody blinders on," shrugged with assumed indifference, and entered the vestibule as they began the all aboard.

In our room, Wolfe was on the wide seat by the window, holding himself braced with both hands; but in spite of that they fooled him on the timing, and when the jerk came he lurched forward and back again. From the corner of my eye I saw the fury all over him, decided it was better to ignore realities, got a magazine from my bag and perched on the undersized chair in the corner. Still holding on with both hands, he shouted at me:

"We are due at Kanawha Spa at 11:25 tomorrow morning! Fourteen hours! This car is shifted to another train at Pittsburgh! In case of delay we would have to wait for an afternoon train! Should anything happen to our engine—"

I put in coldly, "I am not deaf, sir. And while you can beef as much as you want to, because it's your own breath if you want to waste it, I do object to your implying either in word or tone that I am in any way responsible for your misery. I made this speech up last night, knowing I would need it. This is your idea, this trip. You wanted to come—at least, you wanted to be at Kanawha Spa. Six months ago you told Vukcic that you would go there on April 6th. Now you regret it. So do I. As far as our engine is concerned, they use only the newest and best on these crack trains, and not even a child—"

We had emerged from under the river and were gathering speed as we clattered through the Jersey yards. Wolfe shouted,

"An engine has two thousand three hundred and nine moving parts!"

I put down the magazine and grinned at him, thinking I might as well. He had enginephobia and there was no sense in letting him brood, because it would only make it worse for both of us. His mind had to be switched to something else. But before I could choose a pleasant subject to open up on, an interruption came which showed that while he may have been frantic with fear when I was smoking a cigarette on the platform, he had not been demoralized. There was a rap on the door and it opened to admit a porter with a glass and three bottles of beer on a tray. He pulled out a trick stand for the glass and one bottle, which he opened, put the other two bottles in a rack with an opener, accepted currency from me in payment, and departed. As the train lurched on a curve Wolfe scowled with rage; then, as it took the straightaway again, he hoisted the glass and swallowed once, twice, five times, and set it down empty. He licked his lips for the foam, then wiped them with his handkerchief, and observed with no sign at all of hysterics:

"Excellent. I must remember to tell Fritz my first was precisely at temperature."

"You could wire him from Philadelphia."

"Thank you. I am being tortured and you know it. Would you mind earning your salary, Mr. Goodwin, by getting a book from my bag? *Inside Europe*, by John Gunther."

I got the bag and fished it out.

By the time the second interruption came, half an hour later, we were rolling smooth and swift through the night in middle Jersey, the three beer bottles were empty, Wolfe was frowning at his book but actually reading, as I could tell by the pages he turned, and I had waded nearly to the end of an article on Collation of Evidence in the *Journal of Criminology*. I hadn't got much from it, because I was in no condition to worry about collating evidence, on account of my mind being taken up with the problem of getting Nero Wolfe undressed. At home, of course, he did it himself, and equally of course I wasn't under contract as a valet—being merely secretary, bodyguard, office manager, assistant detective, and goat—but the fact remained that in two hours it would be midnight, and there he was with his pants on, and someone was going to have to figure out a way of getting them off without upsetting the train. Not that he was clumsy, but he had had practically no practice at balancing himself while on a moving vehicle, and to pull pants from under him as he lay was out of the question, since he weighed something between 250 and a ton. He had never, so far as I knew, been on a scale, so it was anybody's guess. I was guessing high that night, on account of the problem I was confronted with, and was just ready to settle on 310 as a basis for calculations, when there was a knock on the door and I yelled come in.

It was Marko Vukcic. I had known he would be on our train, through a telephone conversation between him and Wolfe a week before, but the last time I had seen him was when he had dined with us at Wolfe's house early in March—a monthly occurrence. He was one of the only two men whom Wolfe called by their first names, apart from employees. He closed the door behind him and stood there, not fat but huge, like a lion upright on its hind legs, with no hat covering his dense tangle of hair.

Wolfe shouted at him, "Marko! Haven't you got a seat or a bed somewhere? Why the devil are you galloping around in the bowels of this monster?"

Vukcic showed magnificent white teeth in a grin. "Nero, you damn old hermit! I am not a turtle in aspic, like you. Anyhow, you are really on the train—what a triumph! I have found you—and also a colleague, in the next car back, whom I had not seen for five years. I have been talking with him, and suggested he should meet you. He would be glad to have you come to his compartment."

Wolfe compressed his lips. "That, I presume, is funny. I am not an acrobat. I shall not stand up until this thing is stopped and the engine unhooked."

"Then how—" Vukcic laughed, and glanced at the pile of luggage. "But you seem to be provided with equipment. I did not really expect you to move. So instead, I'll bring him to you. If I may. That really is what I came to ask."

"Now?"

"This moment."

Wolfe shook his head. "I beg off, Marko. Look at me. I am in no condition for courtesy or conversation."

"Just briefly, then, for a greeting. I have suggested it."

"No. I think not. Do you realize that if this thing suddenly stopped, for some obstacle or some demoniac whim, we should all of us continue straight ahead at eighty miles an hour? Is that a situation for social niceties?" He compressed

4

his lips again, and then moved them to pronounce firmly, "To-morrow."

Vukcic, probably almost as accustomed as Wolfe to having his own way, tried to insist, but it didn't get him anywhere. He tried to kid him out of it, but that didn't work either. I yawned. Finally Vukcic gave it up with a shrug. "To-morrow, then. If we meet no obstacle and are still alive. I'll tell Berin you have gone to bed—"

"Berin?" Wolfe sat up, and even relaxed his grip on the arm of his seat. "Not Jerome Berin?"

"Certainly. He is one of the fifteen."

"Bring him." Wolfe half closed his eyes. "By all means. I want to see him. Why the devil didn't you say it was Berin?"

Vukcic waved a hand, and departed. In three minutes he was back, holding the door open for his colleague to enter; only it appeared to be two colleagues. The most important one, from my point of view, entered first. She had removed her wrap but her hat was still on, and the odor, faint and fascinating, was the same as when she had passed me on the station platform. I had a chance now to observe that she was as young as love's dream, and her eyes looked dark purple in that light, and her lips told you that she was a natural but reserved smiler. Wolfe gave her a swift astonished glance, then transferred his attention to the tall bulky man behind her, whom I recognized even without the brown cape and the floppy cloth hat.

Vukcic had edged around. "Mr. Nero Wolfe. Mr. Goodwin. Mr. Jerome Berin. His daughter, Miss Constanza Berin."

After a bow I let them amplify the acknowledgments while I steered the seating in the desired direction. It ended with the three big guys on the seats, and love's dream on the undersized chair with me on a suitcase beside it. Then I realized that was bad staging, and shifted across with my back to the wall so I could see it better. She had favored me with one friendly innocent smile and then let me be. From the corner of my eye I saw Wolfe wince as Vukcic got a cigar going and Jerome Berin filled up a big old black pipe and lit it behind clouds. Since I had learned this was her father, I had nothing but friendly feelings for him. He had black hair with a good deal of gray in it, a trimmed beard with even more gray, and deep eyes, bright and black.

He was telling Wolfe, "No, this is my first visit to America. Already I see the nature of her genius. No drafts on this train

5

at all! None! And a motion as smooth as the sail of a gull! Marvelous!"

Wolfe shuddered, but he didn't see it. He went on. But he had given me a scare, with his "first visit to America." I leaned forward and muttered at the dream-star. "Can you talk English?"

She smiled at me. "Oh yes. Very much. We lived in London three years. My father was at the Tarleton."

"Okay." I nodded and settled back for a better focus. I was reflecting, it only goes to show how wise I was not to go into harness with any of the temptations I have been confronted with previously. If I had, I would be gnashing my teeth now. So the thing to do is to hold everything until my teeth are too old to be gnashed. But there was no law against looking.

Her father was saying, "I understand from Vukcic that you are to be Servan's guest. Then the last evening will be yours. This is the first time an American has had that honor. In 1932, in Paris, when Armand Fleury was still alive and was our dean, it was the premier of France who addressed us. In 1927, it was Ferid Khaldah, who was not then a professional. Vukcic tells me you are an agent de sûreté. Really?" He surveyed Wolfe's area.

Wolfe nodded. "But not precisely. I am not a policeman; I am a private detective. I entrap criminals, and find evidence to imprison them or kill them, for hire."

"Marvelous! Such dirty work."

Wolfe lifted his shoulders half an inch for a shrug, but the train jiggled him out of it. He directed a frown, not at Berin, but at the train. "Perhaps. Each of us finds an activity he can tolerate. The manufacturer of baby carriages, caught himself in the system's web and with no monopoly of greed, entraps his workers in the toils of his necessity. Dolichocephalic patriots and brachycephalic patriots kill each other, and the brains of both rot before their statues can get erected. A garbageman collects table refuse, while a senator collects evidence of the corruption of highly placed men—might one not prefer the garbage as less unsavory? Only the table scavenger gets less pay; that is the real point. I do not soil myself cheaply; I charge high fees."

Berin passed it. He chuckled. "But you are not going to discuss table refuse for us. Are you?"

6

"No. Mr. Servan has invited me to speak on—as he stated the subject: *Contributions Américaines à la Haute Cuisine*."

"Bah!" Berin snorted. "There are none."

Wolfe raised his brows. "None, sir?"

"None. I am told there is good family cooking in America; I haven't sampled it. I have heard of the New England boiled dinner and corn pone and clam chowder and milk gravy. This is for the multitude and certainly not to be scorned if good. But it is not for masters." He snorted again. "Those things are to la haute cuisine what sentimental love songs are to Beethoven and Wagner."

"Indeed." Wolfe wiggled a finger at him. "Have you eaten terrapin stewed with butter and chicken broth and sherry?"

"No."

"Have you eaten a planked porterhouse steak, two inches thick, surrendering hot red juice under the knife, garnished with American parsley and slices of fresh limes, encompassed with mashed potatoes which melt on the tongue, and escorted by thick slices of fresh mushrooms faintly underdone?"

"No."

"Or the Creole Tripe of New Orleans? Or Missouri Boone County ham, baked with vinegar, molasses, Worcestershire, sweet cider and herbs? Or Chicken Marengo? Or chicken in curdled egg sauce, with raisins, onions, almonds, sherry and Mexican sausage? Or Tennessee Opossum? Or Lobster Newburgh? Or Philadelphia Snapper Soup? But I see you haven't." Wolfe pointed a finger at him. "The gastronome's heaven is France, granted. But he would do well, on his way there, to make a detour hereabouts. I have eaten Tripe à la mode de Caen at Pharamond's in Paris. It is superb, but no more so than Creole Tripe, which is less apt to stop the gullet without an excess of wine. I have eaten bouillabaisse at Marseilles, its cradle and its temple, in my youth, when I was easier to move, and it is mere belly-fodder, ballast for a stevedore, compared with its namesake at New Orleans! If no red snapper is available—"

I thought for a second Berin was spitting at him, but saw it was only a vocal traffic jam caused by indignation. I left it to them and leaned to Constanza again:

"I understand your father is a good cook."

The purple eyes came to me, the brows faintly up. She gurgled. "He is chef de cuisine at the Corridona at San Remo. Didn't you know that?"

7

I nodded. "Yeah, I've seen a list of the fifteen. Yesterday, in the magazine section of the *Times*. I was just opening up. Do you do any cooking yourself?"

"No. I hate it. Except I make good coffee." She looked down as far as my tie—I had on a dark brown polkadot four-in-hand with a pin-stripe tan shirt—and up again. "I didn't hear your name when Mr. Vukcic said it. Are you a detective too?"

"The name is Archie Goodwin. Archibald means sacred and good, but in spite of that my name is not Archibald. I've never heard a French girl say Archie. Try it once."

"I'm not French." She frowned. Her skin was so smooth that the frown was like a ripple on a new tennis ball. "I'm Catalana. I'm sure I could say Archie. Archiearchiearchie. Good?"

"Wonderful."

"Are you a detective?"

"Certainly." I got out my wallet and fingered in it and pulled out a fishing license I had got in Maine the summer before. "Look. See my name on that?"

She read at it. "Ang...ling?" She looked doubtful, and handed it back. "And that Maine? I suppose that is your arrondissement?"

"No. I haven't got any. We have two kinds of detectives in America, might and main. I'm the main kind. That means that I do very little of the hard work, like watering the horses and shooting prisoners and greasing the chutes. Mostly all I do is think, as for instance when they want someone to think what to do next. Mr. Wolfe there is the might kind. You see how big and strong he is. He can run like a deer."

"But...what are the horses for?"

I explained patiently. "There is a law in this country against killing a man unless you have a horse on him. When two or more men are throwing dice for the drinks, you will often hear one of them say, 'horse on you' or 'horse on me.' You can't kill a man unless you say that before he does. Another thing you'll hear a man say, if he finds out something is only a hoax, he'll call it a mare's nest, because it's full of mares and no horses. Still another trouble is a horse's feathers. In case it has feathers—"

"What is a mare?"

I cleared my throat. "The opposite of a horse. As you know, everything must have its opposite. There can't be a right

8

without a left, or a top without a bottom, or a best without a worst. In the same way there can't be a mare without a horse or a horse without a mare. If you were to take, say, ten million horses—"

I was stopped, indirectly, by Wolfe. I had been too interested in my chat with the Catalana girl to hear the others' talk; what interrupted me was Vukcic rearing himself up and inviting Miss Berin to accompany him to the club car. It appeared that Wolfe had expressed a desire for a confidential session with her father, and I put the eye on him, wondering what kind of a charade he was arranging. One of his fingers was tapping gently on his knee, so I knew it was a serious project. When Constanza got up I did too.

I bowed. "If I may?" To Wolfe: "You can send the porter to the club car if you need me. I haven't finished explaining to Miss Berin about mares."

"Mares?" Wolfe looked at me suspiciously. "There is no information she can possibly need about mares which Marko can't supply. We shall—I am hoping—we shall need your notebook. Sit down."

So Vukcic carried her off. I took the undersized chair again, feeling like issuing an ultimatum for an eight-hour day, but knowing that a moving train was the last place in the world for it. Vukcic was sure to disillusion her about the horse lesson, and might even put a crimp in my style for good.

Berin had filled his pipe again. Wolfe was saying, in his casual tone that meant look out for an attack in force, "I wanted, for one thing, to tell you of an experience I had twenty-five years ago. I trust it won't bore you."

Berin grunted. Wolfe went on, "It was before the war, in Figueras."

Berin removed his pipe. "Ha! So?"

"Yes. I was only a youngster, but even so, I was in Spain on a confidential mission for the Austrian government. The track of a man led me to Figueras, and at ten o'clock one evening, having missed my dinner, I entered a little inn at a corner of the plaza and requested food. The woman said there was not much, and brought me wine of the house, bread, and a dish of sausages."

Wolfe leaned forward. "Sir, Lucullus never tasted sausage like that. Nor Brillat-Savarin. Nor did Vatel or Escoffier ever make any. I asked the woman where she got it. She said her son made it. I begged for the privilege of meeting him. She said he was not at home. I asked for the recipe. She said no one knew it but her son. I asked his name. She said Jerome Berin. I ate three more dishes of it, and made an appointment to meet the son at the inn the next morning. An hour later my quarry made a dash for Port-Vendres, where he took a boat for Algiers, and I had to follow him. The chase took me eventually to Cairo, and other duties prevented me from visiting Spain again before the war started." Wolfe leaned back and sighed. "I can still close my eyes and taste that sausage."

Berin nodded, but he was frowning. "A pretty story, Mr. Wolfe. A real tribute, and thank you. But of course saucisse minuit—"

"It was not called saucisse minuit then; it was merely sausage of the house in a little inn in a little Spanish town. That is my point, my effort to impress you: in my youth, without a veteran palate, under trying circumstances, in an obscure setting, I recognized that sausage as high art. I remember well: the first one I ate, I suspected, and feared that it was only an accidental blending of ingredients carelessly mixed; but the others were the same, and all those in the subsequent three dishes. It was genius. My palate hailed it in that place. I am not one of those who drive from Nice or Monte Carlo to the Corridona at San Remo for lunch because Jerome Berin is famous and saucisse minuit is his masterpiece; I did not have to wait for fame to perceive greatness; if I took that drive it would be not to smirk, but to eat."

Berin was still frowning. He grunted, "I cook other things besides sausages."

"Of course. You are a master." Wolfe wiggled a finger at him. "I seem to have somehow displeased you; I must have been clumsy, because this was supposed to be a preamble to a request. I won't discuss your consistent refusal, for twenty years, to disclose the recipe for that sausage; a chef de cuisine has himself to think of as well as humanity. I am acquainted of the efforts that have been made to imitate it—all failures. I can—"

"Failures?" Berin snorted. "Insults! Crimes!"

"To be sure. I agree. I can see that it is reasonable of you to wish to prevent the atrocities that would be perpetrated in ten thousand restaurant kitchens all over the world if you were to publish that recipe. There are a few great cooks, a sprinkling of good ones, and a pestiferous host of bad ones. I

10

have in my home a good one. Mr. Fritz Brenner. He is not inspired, but he is competent and discriminating. He is discreet, and I am too. I beseech you—this is the request I have been leading up to—I beseech you, tell me the recipe for saucisse minuit."

"God above!" Berin nearly dropped his pipe. He gripped it, and stared. Then he laughed. He threw up his hands and waved them around, and shook all over, and laughed as if he never expected to hear a joke again and would use it all up on this one. Finally he stopped, and stared in scorn. "To *you?*" he wanted to know. It was a nasty tone. Especially was it nasty, coming from Constanza's father.

Wolfe said quietly, "Yes, sir. To me. I would not abuse the confidence. I would impart it to no one. It would be served to no one except Mr. Goodwin and myself. I do not want it for display, I want it to eat. I have—"

"God above! Astounding. You really think—"

"No, I don't think. I merely ask. You would, of course, want to investigate me; I would pay the expense of that. I have never violated my word. In addition to the expense, I would pay three thousand dollars. I recently collected a sizable fee."

"Ha! I have been offered five hundred thousand francs."

"For commercial purposes. This is for my guaranteed private use. It will be made under my own roof, and the ingredients bought by Mr. Goodwin, whom I warrant immune to corruption. I have a confession to make. Four times, from 1928 to 1930, when you were at the Tarleton, a man in London went there, ordered saucisse minuit, took away some in his pocket, and sent it to me. I tried analysis—my own, a food expert's, a chef's, a chemist's. The results were utterly unsatisfactory. Apparently it is a combination of ingredients and method. I have—"

Berin demanded with a snarl, "Was it Laszio?"

"Laszio?"

"Phillip Laszio." He said it as if it were a curse. "You said you had an analysis by a chef—"

"Oh. Not Laszio. I don't know him. I have confessed that attempt to show you that I was zealous enough to try to surprise your secret, but I shall keep inviolate an engagement not to betray it. I confess again: I agreed to this outrageous journey, not only because of the honor of the invitation. Chiefly my purpose was to meet you. I have only so long to live—so many books to read, so many ironies to contemplate, so many meals to eat." He sighed, half closed his eyes, and opened them again. "Five thousand dollars. I detest haggling."

"No." Berin was rough. "Did Vukcic know of this? Was it for this he brought me—"

"Sir! If you please. I have spoken of confidence. This enterprise has been mentioned to no one. I began by beseeching you; I do so again. Will you oblige me?"

"No."

"Under no conditions?"

"No."

Wolfe sighed clear to his belly. He shook his head. "I am an ass. I should never have tried this on the train. I am not myself." He reached for the button on the casing. "Would you like some beer?"

"No." Berin snorted. "I am wrong, I mean yes. I would like beer."

"Good." Wolfe leaned back and closed his eyes. Berin got his pipe lit again. The train bumped over a switch and swayed on a curve, and Wolfe's hand groped for the arm of his seat and grasped it. The porter came and received the order, and soon afterward was back again with glasses and bottles, and served, and again I coughed up some jack. I sat and made pictures of sausages on a blank page of my expense book as the beer went down.

Wolfe said, "Thank you, sir, for accepting my beer. There is no reason why we should not be amicable. I seem to have put the wrong foot forward with you. Even before I made my request, while I was relating a tale which could have been only flattering to you, you had a hostile eye. You growled at me. What was my misstep?"

Berin smacked his lips as he put down his empty glass, and his hand descended in an involuntary movement for the corner of an apron that wasn't there. He reached for a handkerchief and used it, leaned forward and tapped a finger on Wolfe's knee, and told him with emphasis: "You live in the wrong country."

Wolfe lifted his brows. "Yes? Wait till you taste terrapin Maryland. Or even, if I may say so, oyster pie à la Nero Wolfe, prepared by Fritz Brenner. In comparison with American oysters, those of Europe are mere blobs of coppery protoplasm."

12

"I don't speak of oysters. You live in the country which permits the presence of Phillip Laszio."

"Indeed. I don't know him."

"But he makes slop at the Hotel Churchill in your own city of New York! You must know that."

"I know of him, certainly, since he is one of your number—"

"My number? Pah!" Berin's hands, in a wide swift sweep, tossed Phillip Laszio through the window. "Not of my number!"

"Your pardon." Wolfe inclined his head. "But he is one of Les Quinze Maîtres, and you are one. Do you suggest that he is unworthy?"

Berin tapped Wolfe's knee again. I grinned as I saw Wolfe, who didn't like being touched, concealing his squirm for the sake of sausages. Berin said slowly through his teeth, "Laszio is worthy of being cut into small pieces and fed to pigs!—But no, that would render the hams inedible. Merely cut into pieces." He pointed to a hole in the ground. "And buried. I tell you, I have known Laszio many years. He is maybe a Turk? No one knows. No one knows his name. He stole the secret of Rognons aux Montagnes in 1920 from my friend Zelota of Tarragona and claimed the creation. Zelota will kill him; he has said so. He has stolen many other things. He was elected one of Les Quinze Maîtres in 1927 in spite of my violent protest. His young wife—have you seen her? She is Dina, the daughter of Domenico Rossi of the Empire Café in London; I have had her many times on this knee!" He slapped the knee. "As you no doubt know, your friend Vukcic married her, and Laszio stole her from Vukcic. Vukcic will kill him, undoubtedly, only he waits too long!" Berin shook both fists. "He is a dog, a snake, he crawls in slime! You know Leon Blanc, our beloved Leon, once great? You know he is now stagnant in an affair of no reputation called the Willow Club in a town by the name of Boston? You know that for years your Hotel Churchill in New York was distinguished by his presence as chef de cuisine? You know that Laszio stole that position from him—by insinuation, by lies, by chicanery, stole it? Dear old Leon will kill him! Positively. Justice demands it."

Wolfe murmured, "Thrice dead, Laszio. Do other deaths await him?"

Berin sank back and quietly growled, "They do. I will kill him myself."

"Indeed. He stole from you too?"

13

"He has stolen from everyone. God apparently created him to steal, let God defend him." Berin sat up. "I arrived in New York Saturday, on the *Rex*. That evening I went with my daughter to dine at the Churchill, driven by an irresistible hatred. We went to a salon which Laszio calls the Resort Room; I don't know where he stole the idea. The waiters wear the liveries of the world-famous resorts, each one different: Shepheard's of Cairo, Les Figuiers of Juan-les-pins, the Continental of Biarritz, the Del Monte of your California, the Kanawha Spa where this train carries us—many of them, dozens—everything is big here. We sat at a table, and what did I see? A waiter—a waiter carrying Laszio slop—in the livery of my own Corridona! Imagine it! I would have rushed to him and demanded that he take it off—I would have torn it from him with these hands"—he shook them violently at Wolfe's face—"but my daughter held me. She said I must not disgrace her; but my own disgrace? No matter, that?"

Wolfe shook his head, visibly, in sympathy, and reached to pour beer. Berin went on: "Luckily his table was far from us, and I turned my back on it. But wait. Hear this. I looked at the menu. Fourth of the entrées, what did I see? What?"

"Not, I hope, saucisse minuit."

"Yes! I did! Printed fourth of the entrées! Of course I had been informed of it before. I knew that Laszio had for years been serving minced leather spiced with God knows what and calling it saucisse minuit—but to see it printed there, as on my own menu! The whole room, the tables and chairs, all those liveries, danced before my eyes. Had Laszio appeared at that moment I would have killed him with these hands. But he did not. I ordered two portions of it from the waiter—my voice trembled as I pronounced it. It was served on porcelain—bah!—and looked like—I shall not say what. This time I gave my daughter no chance to protest. I took the services, one in each hand, arose from my chair, and with calm deliberation turned my wrists and deposited the vile mess in the middle of the carpet! Naturally, there was comment. My waiter came running. I took my daughter's arm and departed. We were intercepted by a chef des garçons. I silenced him! I told him in a sufficient tone: 'I am Jerome Berin of the Corridona at San Remo! Bring Phillip Laszio here and show him what I have done, but keep me from his throat!' I said little more; it was not necessary. I took my daughter to Rusterman's, and met Vukcic, and he soothed me

14

with a plate of his goulash and a bottle of Chateau Latour. The '29."

Wolfe nodded. "It would soothe a tiger."

"It did. I slept well. But the next morning—yesterday—do you know what happened? A man came to me at my hotel with a message from Phillip Laszio inviting me to lunch! Can you credit such effrontery? But wait, that was not all. The man who brought the message was Alberto Malfi!"

"Indeed. Should I know him?"

"Not now. Now he is not Alberto, but Albert—Albert Malfi, once a Corsican fruit slicer whom I discovered in a café in Ajaccio. I took him to Paris—I was then at the Provençal— trained and taught him, and made a good entrée man of him. He is now Laszio's first assistant at the Churchill. Laszio stole him from me in London in 1930. Stole my best pupil, and laughed at me! And now the brazen frog sends him to me with an invitation to lunch! Alberto appears before me in a morning coat, bows, and as if nothing had ever happened, delivers such a message in perfect English!"

"I take it you didn't go."

"Pah! Would I eat poison? I kicked Alberto out of the room." Berin shuddered. "I shall never forget—once in 1926, when I was ill and could not work, I came that close"—he held thumb and forefinger half an inch apart—"to giving Alberto the recipe for saucisse minuit. God above! If I had! He would be making it now for Laszio's menu! Horrible!"

Wolfe agreed. He had finished another bottle, and he now started on a suave speech of sympathy and understanding. It gave me a distinct pain. He might have seen it was wasted effort, that there wasn't a chance of his getting what he wanted; and it made me indignant to see him belittling himself trying to horn a favor out of that wild-eyed sausage cook. Besides, the train had made me so sleepy I couldn't keep my eyes open. I stood up.

Wolfe looked at me. "Yes, Archie?"

I said in a determined voice, "Club car," opened the door, and beat it.

It was after eleven o'clock, and half the chairs in the club car were empty. Two of the wholesome young fellows who pose for the glossy hair ads were there drinking highballs, and there was a scattering of the baldheads and streaked grays who had been calling porters George for thirty years. Vukcic and Miss Berin were seated with empty glasses in front of them, neither looking animated or entranced. Next to her on the other side was a square-jawed blue-eyed athlete in a quiet gray suit who would obviously be a self-made man in another ten years. I stopped in front of my friends and dropped a greeting on them. They replied. The blue-eyed athlete looked up from his book and made preparations to raise himself to give me a seat.

But Vukcic was up first. "Take mine, Goodwin. I'm sure Miss Berin won't mind the shift. I was up most of last night."

He said goodnights, and was off. I deposited myself, and flagged the steward when he stuck his nose out. It appeared that Miss Berin had fallen in love with American ginger ale, and I requested a glass of milk. Our needs were supplied and we sipped.

She turned the purple eyes on me. They looked darker than ever, and I saw that that question would not be settled until I met them in daylight. She said, with throat in her voice, "You really are a detective, aren't you? Mr. Vukcic has been telling me, he dines every month at Mr. Wolfe's house, and you live there. He says you are very brave and have saved Mr. Wolfe's life three times." She shook her head and let the eyes scold me. "But you shouldn't have told me that about watering the horses. You might have known I would ask about it and find out."

I said firmly, "Vukcic has only been in this country eight years and knows very little about the detective business."

"Oh, no!" She gurgled. "I'm not young enough to be such a big fool as that. I've been out of school three years."

"All right." I waved a hand. "Forget the horses. What kind of a school do girls go to over there?"

"A convent school. I did. At Toulouse."

"You don't look like any nun I ever saw."

She finished a sip of ginger ale and then laughed. "I'm not anything at all like a nun. I'm not a bit religious, I'm very worldly. Mother Cecilia used to tell us girls that a life of service to others was the purest and sweetest, but I thought about it and it seemed to me that the best way would be to enjoy life for a long while, until you got fat or sick or had a big family, and then begin on service to others. Don't you think so?"

I shook my head doubtfully. "I don't know, I'm pretty strong on service. But of course you shouldn't overdo it. You've been enjoying life so far?"

She nodded. "Sometimes. My mother died when I was young, and father has a great many rules for me. I saw how American girls acted when they came to San Remo, and I thought I would act the same way, but I found out I didn't know how, and anyway father heard about it when I sailed Lord Gerley's boat around the cape without a chaperon."

"Was Gerley along?"

"Yes, he was along, but he didn't do any of the work. He went to sleep and fell overboard and I had to tack three times to get him. Do you like Englishmen?"

I lifted a brow. "Well...I suppose I could like an Englishman, if the circumstances were exactly right. For instance, if it was on a desert island, and I had had nothing to eat for three days and he had just caught a rabbit—or, in case there were no rabbits, a wild boar or a walrus. Do you like Americans?"

"I don't know!" She laughed. "I have only met a few since I grew up, at San Remo and around there, and it seemed to me they talked funny and tried to act superior. I mean the men. I liked one I knew in London once, a rich one with a bad stomach who stayed at the Tarleton, and my father had special things prepared for him, and when he left he gave me nice presents. I think lots of them I have seen since I got to New York are very good-looking. I saw one at the hotel yesterday who was *quite* handsome. He had a nose something like yours, but his hair was lighter. I can't really tell whether I like people until I know them pretty well..."

She went on, but I was busy making a complicated discovery. When she had stopped to sip ginger ale my eyes had wandered away from her face to take in accessories, and as she had crossed her knees like American girls, without undue fuss as to her skirt, the view upward from a well-shaped foot and a custom-built ankle was as satisfactory as any I had ever seen. So far, so good; but the trouble was that I became aware that the blue-eyed athlete on the other side of her had one eye focused straight past the edge of his book, and its goal was obviously the same interesting object that I was studying, and my inner reaction to that fact was unsociable and alarming. Instead of being pleased at having a fellow man share a delightful experience with me, I became conscious of an almost uncontrollable impulse to do two things at once: glare at the athlete, and tell her to put her skirt down!

I pulled myself together inwardly, and considered it logically: there was only one theory by which I could possibly justify

17

my resentment at his looking at that leg and my desire to make him stop, and that was that the leg belonged to me. Obviously, therefore, I was either beginning to feel that the leg was my property, or I was rapidly developing an intention to acquire it. The first was nonsense; it was *not* my property. The second was dangerous, since, considering the situation as a whole, there was only one practical and ethical method of acquiring it.

She was still talking. I gulped down the rest of the milk, which was not my habit, waited for an opening, and then turned to her without taking the risk of another dive into the dark purple eyes.

"Absolutely," I said. "It takes a long time to know people. How are you going to tell about anyone until you know them? Take love at first sight, for instance, it's ridiculous. That's not love, it's just an acute desire to get acquainted. I remember the first time I met my wife, out on Long Island, I hit her with my roadster. She wasn't hurt much, but I lifted her in and drove her home. It wasn't until after she sued me for $20,000 damages that I fell in what you might call love with her. Then the inevitable happened, and the children began to come, Clarence and Merton and Isabel and Melinda and Patricia and—"

"I thought Mr. Vukcic said you weren't married."

I waved a hand. "I'm not intimate with Vukcic. He and I have never discussed family matters. Did you know that in Japan it is bad form to mention your wife to another man or to ask him how his is? It would be the same as if you told him he was getting bald or asked him if he could still reach down to pull his socks on."

"Then you *are* married."

"I sure am. *Very* happily."

"What are the names of the rest of the children?"

"Well . . . I guess I told you the most important ones. The others are just tots."

I chattered on, and she chattered back, in the changed atmosphere, with me feeling like a man just dragged back from the edge of a perilous cliff, but with sadness in it too. Pretty soon something happened. I wouldn't argue about it, I am perfectly willing to admit the possibility that it was an accident, but all I can do is describe it as I saw it. As she sat talking to me, her right arm was extended along the arm of her chair on the side next to the blue-eyed athlete, and in

18

that hand was her half-full glass of ginger ale. I didn't see the glass begin to tip, but it must have been gradual and unobtrusive, and I'll swear she was looking at me. When I did see it, it was too late; the liquid had already begun to trickle onto the athlete's quiet gray trousers. I interrupted her and reached across to grab the glass; she turned and saw it and let out a gasp; the athlete turned red and went for his handkerchief. As I say, I wouldn't argue about it, only it was quite a coincidence that four minutes after she found out that one man was married she began spilling ginger ale on another one.

"Oh, I hope—does it stain? Si gauche! I am *so* sorry! I wasn't thinking... I wasn't looking..."

The athlete: "Quite all right—really—really—rite all kight—it doodn't stain—"

More of the same. I enjoyed it. But he was quick on the recovery, for in a minute he quit talking Chinese, collected himself, and spoke to me in his native tongue: "No damage at all, sir, you see there isn't. Really. Permit me; my name is Tolman. Barry Tolman, prosecuting attorney of Marlin County, West Virginia."

So he was a trouble-vulture and a politician. But in spite of the fact that most of my contacts with prosecuting attorneys had not been such as to induce me to keep their photographs on my dresser, I saw no point in being churlish. I described my handle to him and presented him to Constanza, and offered to buy a drink as·compensation for us spilling one on him.

For myself, another milk, which would finish my bedtime quota. When it came I sat and sipped it and restrained myself from butting in on the progress of the new friendship that was developing on my right, except for occasional grunts to show that I wasn't sulking. By the time my glass was half empty Mr. Barry Tolman was saying:

"I heard you—forgive me, but I couldn't help hearing—I heard you mention San Remo. I've never been there. I was at Nice and Monte Carlo back in 1931, and someone, I forget who, told me I should see San Remo because it was more beautiful than any other place on the Riviera, but I didn't go. Now I... well... I can well believe it."

"Oh, you should have gone!" There was throat in her voice again, and it made me happy to hear it. "The hills and the vineyards and the sea!"

"Yes, of course. I'm very fond of scenery. Aren't you, Mr. Goodwin? Fond of—" There was a concussion of the air and a sudden obliterating roar as we thundered past a train on the adjoining track. It ended. "Fond of scenery?"

"You bet." I nodded, and sipped.

Constanza said, "I'm so sorry it's night. I could be looking out and seeing America. Is it rocky—I mean, is it the Rocky Mountains?"

Tolman didn't laugh. I didn't bother to glance to see if he was looking at the purple eyes; I knew that must be it. He told her no, the Rocky Mountains were 1500 miles away, but that it was nice country we were going through. He said he had been in Europe three times, but that on the whole there was nothing there, except of course the historical things, that could compare with the United States. Right where he lived, in West Virginia, there were mountains that he would be willing to put alongside Switzerland and let anyone take their pick. He had never seen anything anywhere as beautiful as his native valley, especially the spot in it where they had built Kanawha Spa, the famous resort. That was in his county.

Constanza exclaimed, "But that's where I'm going! Of course it is! Kanawha Spa!"

"I . . . I hope so." His cheek showed red. "I mean, three of these pullmans are Kanawha Spa cars, and I thought it likely . . . I thought it possible I might have a chance of meeting you, though of course I'm not in the social life there . . ."

"And then we met on the train. Of course, I won't be there very long. But since you think it's nicer than Europe, I can hardly wait to see it, but I warn you I love San Remo and the sea. I suppose on your trips to Europe you take your wife and children along?"

"Oh, now!" He was groggy. "Now, really! Do I look old enough to have a wife and children?"

I thought, you darned nut, cover up that chin! My milk was finished. I stood up.

"If you folks will excuse me, I'll go and make sure my boss hasn't fallen off the train. I'll come back soon, Miss Berin, and take you to your father. You can't be expected to learn the knack of acting like the American girls the first day out."

Neither of them broke into tears to see me go.

In the first car ahead I met Jerome Berin striding down the passage. He stopped and of course I had to.

He roared, "My daughter? Vukcic left her!"

"She's perfectly all right." I thumbed to the rear. "She's back in the club car talking with a friend of mine I introduced to her. Is Mr. Wolfe okay?"

"Okay? I don't know. I just left him."

He brushed past me and I went on.

Wolfe was alone in the room, still on the seat, the picture of despair, gripping with his hands, his eyes wide open. I stood and surveyed him.

I said, "See America first. Come and play with us in vacationland! Not a draft on the train and sailing like a gull!"

He said, "Shut up!"

He couldn't sit there all night. The time had come when it must be done. I rang the bell for the porter to do the bed. Then I went up to him—but no. I remember in an old novel I picked up somewhere it described a lovely young maiden going into her bedroom at night and putting her lovely fingers on the top button of her dress and then it said, "But now we must leave her. There are some intimacies which you and I, dear reader, must not venture to violate; some girlish secrets which we must not betray to the vulgar gaze. Night has drawn its protecting veil; let us draw ours!"

Okay by me.

2

I SAID, "I wouldn't have thought this was a job for a house dick, watching for a kid to throw stones. Especially a ritzy house dick like you."

Gershom Odell spit through his teeth at a big fern ten feet away from where we sat on a patch of grass. "It isn't. But I told you. These birds pay from fifteen to fifty bucks a day to stay at this caravansary and to write letters on Kanawha Spa stationery, and they don't like to have niggers throwing stones at them when they go horseback riding. I didn't say a kid, I said a nigger. They suspect it was one that got fired from the garage about a month ago."

The warm sun was on me through a hole in the trees, and I yawned. I asked, to show I wasn't bored, "You say it happened about here?"

He pointed. "Over yonder, from the other side of the path. It was old Crisler that got it both times, you know, the fountain pen Crisler, his daughter married Ambassador Willetts."

There were sounds from down the way. Soon the hoofbeats were plainer, and in a minute a couple of genteel but good-looking horses came down the path from around a curve, and trotted by, close enough so that I could have tripped them with a fishing pole. On one of them was a dashing chap in a loud-checked jacket, and on the other a dame plenty old and fat enough to start on service to others any time the spirit moved her.

Odell said, "That was Mrs. James Frank Osborn, the Baltimore Osborn, ships and steel, and Dale Chatwin, a good bridge player on the make. See him worry his horse? He can't ride worth a damn."

"Yeah? I didn't notice. You sure are right there on the social list."

"Got to be, on this job." He spit at the fern again, scratched the back of his head, and plucked a blade of grass and stuck it in his mouth. "I guess nine out of ten that come to this joint, I know 'em without being told. Of course sometimes there's strangers. For instance, take your crowd. Who the hell are they? I understand they're a bunch of good cooks that the chef invited. Looks funny to me. Since when was Kanawha Spa a domestic science school?"

I shook my head. "Not my crowd, mister."

"You're with 'em."

"I'm with Nero Wolfe."

"He's with 'em."

I grinned. "Not this minute, he ain't. He's in Suite 60, on the bed fast asleep. I think I'll have to chloroform him Thursday to get him on the train home." I stretched in the sun. "At that, there's worse things than cooks."

"I suppose so," he admitted. "Where do they all come from, anyway?"

I pulled a paper from my pocket—a page I had clipped from the magazine section of the *Times*—and unfolded it and glanced at the list again before passing it across to him:

LES QUINZE MAITRES

Jerome Berin, the Corridona, San Remo.
Leon Blanc, the Willow Club, Boston.

Ramsey Keith, Hotel Hastings, Calcutta.
Phillip Laszio, Hotel Churchill, New York.
Domenico Rossi, Empire Café, London.
Pierre Mondor, Mondor's, Paris.
Marko Vukcic, Rusterman's Restaurant, New York.
Sergei Vallenko, Chateau Montcalm, Quebec.
Lawrence Coyne, The Rattan, San Francisco.
Louis Servan, Kanawha Spa, West Virginia.
Ferid Khaldah, Café de l'Europe, Istanbul.
Henri Tassone, Shepheard's Hotel, Cairo.

DECEASED:

Armand Fleury, Fleury's, Paris.
Pasquale Donofrio, the Eldorado, Madrid.
Jacques Baleine, Emerald Hotel, Dublin.

Odell took a look at the extent of the article, made no offer to read it, and then went over the names and addresses with his head moving slowly back and forth. He grunted. "Some bunch of names. You might think it was a Notre Dame football team. How'd they get all the press? What does that mean at the top, less quinzy something?"

"Oh, that's French." I pronounced it adequately. "It means 'The Fifteen Masters.' These babies are famous. One of them cooks sausages that people fight duels over. You ought to see him and tell him you're a detective and ask him to give you the recipe; he'd be glad to. They meet every five years on the home grounds of the oldest one of their number; that's why they came to Kanawha Spa. Each one is allowed to bring one guest—it's all there in the article. Nero Wolfe is Servan's guest, and Vukcic invited me so I could be with Wolfe. Wolfe's the guest of honor. Only ten of 'em are here. The last three died since 1932, and Khaldah and Tassone couldn't come. They'll do a lot of cooking and eating and drinking, and tell each other a lot of lies, and elect three new members, and listen to Nero Wolfe make a speech—and oh yeah, one of 'em's going to get killed."

"That'll be fun." Odell spit through his teeth again. "Which one?"

"Phillip Laszio, Hotel Churchill, New York. The article says his salary is sixty thousand berries per annum."

"Which may be. Who's going to kill him?"

"They're going to take turns. If you want tickets for the

series, I'd be glad to get you a couple of ringsides, and here's a tip, you'd better tell the desk to collect for his room in advance, because you know how long it takes—well God bless my eyes! All with a few spoonfuls of ginger ale!"

A horseman and horsewoman had cantered by on the path, looking sideways at each other, laughing, their teeth showing and their faces flushed. As their dust drifted toward us I asked Odell, "Who's that happy pair?"

He grunted. "Barry Tolman, prosecuting attorney of this county. Going to be president some day, ask him. The girl came with your crowd, didn't she? Incidentally, she's easy on the eyes. What was the crack about ginger ale?"

"Oh, nothing." I waved a hand. "Just an old quotation from Chaucer. It wouldn't do any good to throw stones at them, they wouldn't notice anything less than an avalanche.—By the way, what is this stone-throwing gag?"

"No gag. Just part of the day's work."

"You call this work? I'm a detective. In the first place, do you suppose anyone is going to start a bombardment with you and me sitting here in plain sight? And this bridle path winds around here for six miles, and why couldn't he pick another spot? Secondly, you told me that a Negro that got fired from the garage is suspected of doing it to annoy the management, but in that case it was just a coincidence that he picked fountain pen Crisler for a target both times? It's a phony. You didn't show me the bottom. Not that it's any of my business, but just for fun I thought I'd demonstrate that I'm only dumb on Sundays and holidays."

He looked at me with one eye. Then with both, and then he grinned at me. "You seem to be a good guy."

I said warmly, "I am."

He was still grinning. "Honest to God, it's too good not to tell you. You would enjoy it better if you knew Crisler. But it wasn't only him. Another trouble was that I never get any time to myself around here. Sixteen hours a day! That's the way it works out. I've only got one assistant, and you ought to see him, he's somebody's nephew. I had to be on duty from sunrise to bedtime. Then there was Crisler, just a damn bile factory. He had it in for me because I caught his chauffeur swiping grease down at the garage, and boy, when he was mean he was mean. The nigger that helped me catch the chauffeur, Crisler had him fired. He was after my scalp too. I made my plans and they worked."

24

Odell pointed. "See that ledge up there? No, over yonder, the other side of those firs. That's where I was when I threw stones at him. I hit him both times."

"I see. Hurt him much?"

"Not enough. His shoulder was pretty sore. I had fixed up a good alibi in case of suspicions. Crisler checked out. That was one advantage. Another was that almost whenever I want to I can say I'm going out for the stone thrower, and come to the woods for an hour or two and be alone and spit and look at things. Sometimes I let them see me from the bridle path, and they think they're being protected and that's jake."

"Pretty good idea. But it'll play out. Sooner or later you'll either have to catch him or give it up. Or else throw some more stones."

He grinned. "Maybe you think it wasn't a good shot the time I got him in the shoulder! See how far away that ledge is? I don't know whether I'll try it again or not, but if I do, I know damn well who I'll pick. I'll point her out to you." He glanced at his wrist. "Jumping Jesus, nearly five o'clock. I've got to get back."

He scrambled up and started off headlong, and as I was in no hurry I let him go, and moseyed idly along behind. As I had already discovered, wherever you went around Kanawha Spa, you were taking a walk in the garden. I don't know who kept the woods swept and dusted off the trees for what must have been close to a thousand acres, but it was certainly model housekeeping. In the neighborhood of the main hotel, and the pavilions scattered around, and the building where the hot springs were, it was mostly lawns and shrubs and flowers, with three classy fountains thirty yards from the main entrance. The things they called pavilions, which had been named after the counties of West Virginia, were nothing to sneeze at themselves in the matter of size, with their own kitchens and so forth, and I gathered that the idea was that they offered more privacy at an appropriate price. Two of them, Pocahontas and Upshur, only a hundred yards apart and connected by a couple of paths through trees and shrubs, had been turned over to the fifteen masters—or rather, ten—and our Suite 60, Wolfe's and mine, was in Upshur.

I strolled along carefree. There was lots of junk to look at if you happened to be interested in it—big clusters of pink flowers everywhere on bushes which Odell had said was

25

mountain laurel, and a brook zipping along with little bridges across it here and there, and some kind of wild trees in bloom, and birds and evergreens and so on. That sort of stuff is all right, I've got nothing against it, and of course out in the country like that something might as well be growing or what would you do with all the space, but I must admit it's a poor place to look for excitement. Compare it, for instance, with Times Square or the Yankee Stadium.

Closer to the center of things, in the section where the pavilions were, and especially around the main building and the springs, there was more life. Plenty of folks, such as they were, coming and going in cars or on horseback and sometimes even walking. Most of those walking were Negroes in the Kanawha Spa uniform, black breeches and bright green jackets with big black buttons. Off on a side path you might catch one of them grinning, but out in the open they looked as if they were nearly overcome by something they couldn't tell you, like bank tellers.

It was a little after five when I got to the entrance of Upshur Pavilion and went in. Suite 60 was in the rear of the right wing. I opened its door with care and tiptoed across the hall so as not to wake the baby, but opening another door with even more care I found that Wolfe's room was empty. The three windows I had left partly open were closed, the hollow in the center of the bed left no doubt as to who had been on it, and the blanket I had spread over him was hanging at the foot. I glanced in the hall again; his hat was gone. I went to the bathroom and turned on the faucet and began soaping my hands. I was good and sore. For ten years I had been accustomed to being as sure of finding Nero Wolfe where I had left him as if he had been the Statue of Liberty, unless his house had burned down, and it was upsetting, not to mention humiliating, to find him flitting around like a hummingbird for a chance to lick the boots of a dago sausage cook.

After splashing around a little and changing my shirt, I was tempted to wander over to the hotel and look-to-see around, but I knew Fritz and Theodore would murder me if I didn't bring him back in one piece, so instead I left by the side entrance and followed the path to Pocahontas Pavilion.

Pocahontas was much more ambitious than Upshur, with four good-sized public rooms centrally on the ground floor, and suites in the wings and the upper story. I heard noises before I got inside, and, entering, found that the masters were having a good time. I had met the whole gang at lunch, which had been cooked at the pavilion and served there, with five different ones contributing a dish, and I admit it hadn't been hard to get down—which, since Fritz Brenner's cooking under Nero Wolfe's supervision had been my steady diet for ten years, would be a tribute for anyone.

I let a greenjacket open the door for me and trusted my hat to another one in the hall, and began the search for my lost hummingbird. In the parlor on the right, which had dark wooden things with colored rugs and stuff around everywhere—Pocahontas was all Indian as to furnishings—three couples were dancing to a radio. A medium brunette about my age, medium also as to size, with a high white brow and long sleepy eyes, was fastened onto Sergei Vallenko, a blond Russian ox around fifty with a scar under one ear. She was Dina Laszio, daughter of Domenico Rossi, onetime wife of Marko Vukcic, and stolen from him, according to Jerome Berin, by Phillip Laszio. A short middle-aged woman built like a duck, with little black eyes and fuzz on her upper lip, was Marie Mondor, and the pop-eyed chap with a round face, maybe her age and as plump as her, was her husband, Pierre Mondor. She couldn't speak English, and I saw no reason why she should. The third couple consisted of Ramsey Keith, a little sawed-off Scotchman at least sixty with a face like a sunset preserved in alcohol, and a short and slender black-eyed affair who might have been anything under 35 to my limited experience, because she was Chinese. To my surprise, when I had met her at lunch, she had looked dainty and mysterious, just like the geisha propaganda pictures. I believe geishas are Japs, but it's all the same. Anyway, she was Lio Coyne, the fourth wife of Lawrence Coyne; and hurrah for Lawrence, since he was all of three score and ten and as white as a snowbank.

I tried the parlor on the left, a smaller one. The pickings there were scanty. Lawrence Coyne was on a divan at the far end, fast asleep, and Leon Blanc, dear old Leon, was standing in front of a mirror, apparently trying to decide if he needed a shave. I ambled on through to the dining room. It ·was big and somewhat cluttered. Besides the long table and a slew of chairs, there were two serving tables and a cabinet full of paraphernalia, and a couple of huge screens with pictures of Pocahontas saving John Smith's life and other things. There were four doors: the one I had come in by, a double one to the large parlor, a double glass one to a side terrace, and one out to the pantry and the kitchen.

There were also, as I entered, people. Marko Vukcic was on a chair by the long table, with a cigar in his mouth, shaking his head at a telegram he was reading. Jerome Berin was standing with a wineglass in his hand, talking with a dignified old bird with a gray mustache and a wrinkled face—that being Louis Servan, dean of the fifteen masters and their host at Kanawha Spa. Nero Wolfe was on a chair too small for him over by the glass door to the terrace, which stood open, leaning back uncomfortably so that his half-open eyes could take in the face of the man standing looking down at him. It was Phillip Laszio—chunky, not much gray in his hair, with clever eyes and a smooth skin and slick all over. Alongside Wolfe's chair was a little stand with a glass and a couple of beer bottles, and at his other elbow, almost sitting on his knee, with a plate of something in her hand, was Lisette Putti. Lisette was as cute as they come, and had already made friends, in spite of a question of irregularity regarding her status. She was the guest of Ramsey Keith, who, coming all the way from Calcutta, had introduced her as his niece. Vukcic had told me that Marie Mondor's sputterings after lunch had been to the effect that Lisette was a coquine and Keith had picked her up in Marseilles, but after all, Vukcic said, it was physically possible for a man named Keith to have a niece named Putti, and even if it was a case of mistaken identity, it was Keith who was paying the bills. Which sounded like a loose statement, but it was none of my affair.

As I approached, Laszio finished some remark to Wolfe and Lisette began spouting to him in French, something about the stuff she had on the plate, which looked like fat brown crackers; but just then there was a yell from the direction of the kitchen, and we all turned to see the swinging door open and Domenico Rossi come leaping through with a steaming dish in one hand and a long-handled spoon in the other.

"It curdled!" he shrieked. He rushed across to us and thrust the dish at Laszio. "Look at that dirty mud! What did I tell you? By God, look! You owe me a hundred francs! A devil

28

of a son-in-law you are, and twice as old as I am anyhow, and ignorant of the very first essentials!"

Laszio quietly shrugged. "Did you warm the milk?"

"Me? Do I look like an egg-freezer?"

"Then perhaps the eggs were old."

"Louis!" Rossi whirled and pointed the spoon at Servan. "Do you hear that? He says you have old eggs!"

Servan chuckled. "But if you did it the way he said to, and it curdled, you have won a hundred francs. Where is the objection to that?"

"But everything wasted! Look: mud!" Rossi puffed. "These damn modern ideas! Vinegar is vinegar!"

Laszio said quietly, "I'll pay. To-morrow I'll show you how." He turned abruptly and went to the door to the large parlor and opened it, and the sound of the radio came through. Rossi trotted around the table with the dish of mud to show it to Servan and Berin. Vukcic stuffed his telegram in his pocket and went over to look at it. Lisette became aware of my presence and poked the plate at me and said something. I grinned at her and replied, "Jack Spratt could eat no fat, his wife could—"

"Archie!" Wolfe opened his eyes. "Miss Putti says that those wafers were made by the two hands of Mr. Keith, who brought the ingredients from India."

"Did you try them?"

"Yes."

"Are they any good?"

"No."

"Then will you kindly tell her that I never eat between meals?"

I wandered over to the parlor door and stood beside Phillip Laszio, looking at the three couples dancing—only it was apparent that he was only seeing one. Mamma and papa Mondor were panting but game, Ramsey Keith and the geisha were funny to look at but obviously not concerned with that aspect of the matter, and Dina Laszio and Vallenko apparently hadn't changed holds since my previous view. However, they soon did. Something was happening beside me. Laszio said nothing, and made no gesture that I saw, but he must have achieved some sort of communication, for the two stopped abruptly, and Dina murmured something to her partner and then alone crossed the floor to her husband. I sidestepped a couple of paces to give them room, but they weren't paying any attention to me.

She asked him, "Would you like to dance, dear?"

"You know I wouldn't. You weren't dancing."

"But what—" She laughed. "They call it dancing, don't they?"

"They may. But you weren't dancing." He smiled—that is, technically; it looked more like a smile to end smiles.

Vallenko came up. He stopped close to them, looked from his face to hers and back again, and all at once burst out laughing. "Ah, Laszio!" He slapped him on the back, not gently. "Ah, my friend!" He bowed to Dina. "Thank you, madame." He strode off.

She said to her husband, "Phillip dear, if you don't want me to dance with your colleagues you might have said so. I don't find it so great a pleasure—"

It didn't seem likely that they would need me to help out, so I went back out to the dining room and sat down. For half an hour I sat there and watched the zoo. Lawrence Coyne came in from the small parlor, rubbing his eyes and trying to comb his white whiskers with his fingers. He looked around and called "Lio!" in a roar that shook the windows, and his Chinese wife came trotting from the other room, got him in a chair and perched on his knee. Leon Blanc entered, immediately got into an argument with Berin and Rossi, and suddenly disappeared with them into the kitchen. It was nearly six o'clock when Constanza blew in. She had changed from her riding things. She looked around and offered a few greetings which nobody paid much attention to, then saw Vukcic and me and came over to us and asked where her father was. I told her, in the kitchen fighting about lemon juice. In the daylight the dark purple eyes were all and more than I had feared.

I observed, "I saw you and the horses a couple of hours ago. Will you have a glass of ginger ale?"

"No, thanks." She smiled as to an indulgent uncle. "It was very nice of you to tell father that Mr. Tolman is your friend."

"Don't mention it. I could see you were young and helpless, and thought I might as well lend a hand. Are things beginning to shape up?"

"Shape up?"

"It doesn't matter." I waved a hand. "As long as you're happy."

"Certainly I'm happy. I *love* America. I believe I'll have some ginger ale after all. No, don't move, I'll get it." She moved around the table toward a button.

I don't believe Vukcic, right next to me, heard any of it, because he had his eyes on his former wife as she sat with Laszio and Servan talking to Wolfe. I had noticed that tendency in him during lunch. I had also noticed that Leon Blanc unobtrusively avoided Laszio and had not once spoken to him who, according to Berin, had stolen Blanc's job at the Hotel Churchill; whereas Berin himself was inclined to find opportunities for glaring at Laszio at close quarters, but also without speaking. There was undoubtedly a little atmosphere around, what with Mamma Mondor's sniffs at Lisette Putti and a general air of comradely jealousy and arguments about lettuce and vinegar and the thumbs down clique on Laszio, and last but not least, the sultry mist that seemed to float around Dina Laszio. I have always had a belief that the swamp-woman—the kind who can move her eyelids slowly three times and you're stuck in a marsh and might as well give up—is never any better than a come-on for suckers; but I could see that if Dina Laszio once got you alone and she had her mind on her work and it was raining outdoors, it would take more than a sense of humor to laugh it off. She was way beyond the stage of spilling ginger ale on lawyers.

I watched the show and waited for Wolfe to display signs of motion. A little after six he made it to his feet, and I followed him onto the terrace and along the path to Upshur. Considering the terrible hardships of the train, he was navigating fine. In Suite 60 there had been a chambermaid around, for the bed was smoothed out again and the blanket folded up and put away. I went to my room, and a little later rejoined Wolfe in his. He was in a chair by the window which was almost big enough for him, leaning back with his eyes closed and a furrow in his brow, with his fingers meeting at the center of his paunch. It was a pathetic sight. No Fritz, no atlas to look at, no orchids to tend to, no bottle caps to count! I was sorry that the dinner was to be informal, since three or four of the masters were cooking it, because the job of getting into dinner clothes would have made him so mad that it would have taken his mind off of other things and really been a relief to him. As I stood and surveyed him he heaved a long deep shuddering sigh, and to keep the tears from coming to my eyes I spoke.

"I understand Berin is going to make saucisse minuit for lunch to-morrow. Huh?"

No score. I said, "How would you like to go back in an airplane? They have a landing field right here. Special service, on call, sixty bucks to New York, less than four hours."

Nothing doing. I said, "They had a train wreck over in Ohio last night. Freight. Over a hundred pigs killed."

He opened his eyes and started to sit up, but his hand slipped on the arm of the foreign chair and he slid back again. He declared, "You are dismissed from your job, to take effect upon our arrival at my house in New York. I *think* you are. It can be discussed after we get home."

That was more like it. I grinned at him. "That will suit me fine. I'm thinking of getting married anyhow. The little Berin girl. What do you think of her?"

"Pfui."

"Go on and phooey. I suppose you think living with you for ten years has destroyed all my sentiment. I suppose you think I am no longer subject—"

"Pfui!"

"Very well. But last night in the club car it came to me. I don't suppose you realize what a pippin she is, because you seem to be immune. And of course I haven't spoken to her yet, because I couldn't very well ask her to marry a—well, a detective. But I think if I can get into some other line of work and prove that I can make myself worthy of her—"

"Archie." He was sitting up now, and his tone was a menacing murmur. "You are lying. Look at me."

I gave him as good a gaze as I could manage, and I thought I had him. But then I saw his lids begin to droop, and I knew it was all off. So the best I could do was grin at him.

"Confound you!" But he sounded relieved at that. "Do you realize what marriage means? Ninety percent of men over thirty are married, and look at them! Do you realize that if you had a wife she would insist on cooking for you? Do you know that all women believe that the function of food begins when it reaches the stomach? Have you any idea that a woman can ever—what's that?"

The knocking on the outer door of the suite had sounded

twice, the first time faintly, and I had ignored it because I didn't want to interrupt him. Now I went out and through the inner hall and opened up. Whereupon I, who am seldom surprised, was close to astonished. There stood Dina Laszio.

Her eyes looked larger than ever, but not quite so sleepy. She asked in a low voice, "May I come in? I wish to see Mr. Wolfe."

I stood back, she went past, and I shut the door. I indicated Wolfe's room, "In there, please," and she preceded me. The only perceptible expression on Wolfe's face as he became aware of her was recognition.

He inclined his head. "I am honored, madam. Forgive me for not rising; I permit myself that discourtesy. That chair around, Archie?"

She was nervous. She looked around. "May I see you alone, Mr. Wolfe?"

"I'm afraid not. Mr. Goodwin is my confidential assistant."

"But I . . ." She stayed on her feet. "It is hard to tell even you . . ."

"Well, madam, if it is too hard . . ." Wolfe let it hang in the air.

She swallowed, looked at me again, and took a step toward him. "But it would be harder . . . I must tell someone. I have heard much of you, of course . . . in the old days, from Marko . . . and I must tell someone, and there is no one but you to tell. Somebody is trying to poison my husband."

"Indeed." Wolfe's eyes narrowed faintly. "Be seated. Please. It's easier to talk sitting down, don't you think, Mrs. Laszio?"

3

THE SWAMP-WOMAN lowered it into the chair I had placed. Needless to say, I leaned against the bedpost not as nonchalant as I looked. It sounded as if this might possibly be something that would help to pass the time, and justify my foresight in chucking my pistol and a couple of notebooks into my bag when I had packed.

She said, "Of course . . . I know you are an old friend of

Marko's. You probably think I wronged him when I . . . left him. But I count on your sense of justice . . . your humanity. . . ."

"Weak supports, madam." Wolfe was brusque. "Few of us have enough wisdom for justice, or enough leisure for humanity. Why do you mention Marko? Do you suggest that he is poisoning Mr. Laszio?"

"Oh, no!" Her hand fluttered from her lap and came to rest on the arm of her chair. "Only I am sorry if you are prejudiced against my husband and me, for I have decided that I must tell someone, and there is no one but you to tell. . . ."

"Have you informed your husband that he is being poisoned?"

She shook her head, with a little twist on her lips. "He informed me. To-day. You know, of course, that for luncheon several of them prepared dishes, and Phillip did the salad, and he had announced that he was going to make Meadowbrook dressing, which he originated. They all know that he mixes the sugar and lemon juice and sour cream an hour ahead of time, and that he always tastes in spoonfuls. He had the things ready, all together on a corner table in the kitchen, lemons, bowl of cream, sugar shaker. At noon he started to mix. From habit he shook sugar on to the palm of his hand and put his tongue to it, and it seemed gritty and weak. He shook some on to a pan of water, and little particles stayed on top, and when he stirred it some still stayed. He put sherry in a glass and stirred some of it into that, and only a small portion of it would dissolve. If he had mixed the dressing and tasted a spoonful or two, as he always does, it would have killed him. The sugar was mostly arsenic."

Wolfe grunted. "Or flour."

"My husband said arsenic. There was no taste of flour."

Wolfe shrugged. "Easily determined, with a little hydrochloric acid and a piece of copper wire. You do not appear to have the sugar shaker with you. Where is it?"

"I suppose, in the kitchen."

Wolfe's eyes opened wide. "Being used for our dinner, madam? You spoke of humanity—"

"No. Phillip emptied it down the sink and had it refilled by one of the Negroes. It was sugar, that time."

"Indeed." Wolfe settled, and his eyes were again half shut. "Remarkable. Though he was sure it was arsenic? He didn't turn it over to Servan? Or report it to anyone but you? Or preserve it as evidence? Remarkable."

34

"My husband is a remarkable man." A ray of the setting sun came through the window to her face, and she moved a little. "He told me that he didn't want to make things difficult for his friend, Louis Servan. He forbade me to mention it. He is a strong man and he is very contemptuous. That is his nature. He thinks he is too strong and competent and shrewd to be injured by anyone." She leaned forward and put out a hand, palm up. "I come to you, Mr. Wolfe! I am afraid!"

"What do you want me to do? Find out who put the arsenic in the sugar shaker?"

"Yes." Then she shook her head. "No. I suppose you couldn't, and even if you did, the arsenic is gone. I want to protect my husband."

"My dear madam." Wolfe grunted. "If anyone not a moron has determined to kill your husband, he will be killed. Nothing is simpler than to kill a man; the difficulties arise in attempting to avoid the consequences. I'm afraid I have nothing to suggest to you. It is doubly difficult to save a man's life against his will. Do you think you know who poisoned the sugar?"

"No. Surely there is something—"

"Does your husband think he knows?"

"No. Surely you can—"

"Marko? I can ask Marko if he did it?"

"No! Not Marko! You promised me you wouldn't mention—"

"I promised nothing of the sort. Nothing whatever. I am sorry, Mrs. Laszio, if I seem rude, but the fact is that I hate to be taken for an idiot. If you think your husband may be poisoned, what you need is a food taster, and that is not my profession. If you fear bodily violence for him, the best thing is a bodyguard, and I am not that either. Before he gets into an automobile, every bolt and nut and connection must be thoroughly tested. When he walks the street, windows and tops of buildings must be guarded, and passersby kept at a distance. Should he attend the theater—"

The swamp-woman got up. "You make a joke of it. I'm sorry."

"It was you who started the joke—"

But she wasn't staying for it. I moved to open the door, but she had the knob before I got to it, and since she felt that way about it I let her go on and do the outside one too. I saw that it was closed behind her, and then returned to Wolfe's room

35

and put on a fake frown for him which was wasted, because he had his eyes shut. I told his big round face:

"That's a fine way to treat a lady client who comes to you with a nice straight open-and-shut proposition like that. All we would have to do would be go down to the river where the sewer empties and swim around until we tasted arsenic—"

"Arsenic has no taste."

"Okay." I sat down. "Is she fixing up to poison him herself and preparing a line of negative presumptions in advance? Or is she on the level and just poking around trying to protect her man? Or is Laszio making up tales to show her how cute he is? You should have seen him looking at her when she was dancing with Vallenko. I suppose you've observed Vukcic lamping her with the expression of a moth in a cage surrounded by klieg lights. Or was someone really gump enough to endanger all our lives by putting arsenic in the sugar shaker? Incidentally, it'll be dinnertime in ten minutes, and if you intend to comb your hair and tuck your shirt in—did you know that you can have one of these greenjackets for a valet for an extra five bucks per diem? I swear to God I think I'll try it for half a day. I'd be a different person if I took proper care of myself."

I stopped to yawn. Insufficient sleep and outdoor sunshine had got me. Wolfe was silent. But presently he spoke:

"Archie. Have you heard of the arrangement for this evening?"

"No. Anything special?"

"Yes. It seems to have come about through a wager between Mr. Servan and Mr. Keith. After the digestion of dinner there is to be a test. The cook will roast squabs, and Mr. Laszio, who volunteered for the function, will make a quantity of Sauce Printemps. That sauce contains nine seasonings, besides salt: cayenne, celery, shallots, chives, chervil, tarragon, peppercorn, thyme and parsley. Nine dishes of it will be prepared, and each will lack one of the seasonings, a different one. The squabs and sauce dishes will be arrayed in the dining room, and Mr. Laszio will preside. The gathering will be in the parlor, and each will go to the dining room, singly to prevent discussion, taste the sauces on bits of squab, and record which dish lacks chives, which peppercorn, and so on. I believe Mr. Servan has wagered on an average of eighty percent correct."

"Well." I yawned again. "I can pick the one that lacks squab."

"You will not be included. Only the members of Les Quinze Maîtres and myself. It will be an instructive and interesting experiment. The chief difficulty will be with chives and shallots, but I believe I can distinguish. I shall drink wine with dinner, and of course no sweet. But the possibility occurred to me of a connection between this affair and Mrs. Laszio's strange report. Mr. Laszio is to make the sauce. You know I am not given to trepidation, but I came here to meet able men, not to see one or more of them murdered."

"You came here to learn how to make sausage. But forget it; I guess that's out. But how could there be a connection? It's Laszio that's going to get killed, isn't it? The tasters are safe. Maybe you'd better go last. If you get sick out here in the jungle I will have a nice time."

He shut his eyes. Soon he opened them again. "I don't like stories about arsenic in food. What time is it?"

Too darned lazy to reach in his pocket. I told him, and he sighed and began preparations for getting himself upright.

The dinner at Pocahontas Pavilion that evening was elegant as to provender, but a little confused in other respects. The soup, by Louis Servan, looked like any consommé, but it wasn't just any. He had spread himself, and it was nice to see his dignified old face get red with pleasure as they passed remarks to him. The fish, by Leon Blanc, was little six-inch brook trout, four to a customer, with a light brown sauce with capers in it, and a tang that didn't seem to come from lemon or any vinegar I had ever heard of. I couldn't place it, and Blanc just grinned at them when they demanded the combination, saying he hadn't named it yet. All of them, except Lisette Putti and me, ate the trout head and bones and all, even Constanza Berin, who was on my right. She watched me picking away and smiled at me and said I would never make a gourmet, and I told her not eating fishes' faces was a matter of sentiment with me on account of my pet goldfish. Watching her crunch those trout heads and bones with her pretty teeth, I was glad I had put the kibosh on my attack of leg-jealousy.

The entrée, by Pierre Mondor, was of such a nature that I imitated some of the others and had two helpings. It appeared to be a famous creation of his, well-known to the others, and Constanza told me that her father made it very well and that the main ingredients were beef marrow, cracker crumbs, white wine and chicken breast. In the middle of my second portion I caught Wolfe's eye across the table and winked at him, but he ignored me and hung on to solemn bliss. As far as he was concerned, we were in church, and Saint Peter was speaking. It was during the consumption of the entrée that Mondor and his plump wife, without any warning, burst into a screaming argument which ended with him bouncing up and racing for the kitchen, and her hot on his tail. I learned afterward that she had heard him ask Lisette Putti if she liked the entrée. She must have been abnormally moral for a Frenchwoman.

The roast was young duck à la Mr. Richards, by Marko Vukcic. This was one of Wolfe's favorites and I was well acquainted with the Fritz Brenner-Nero Wolfe version of it, and by the time it arrived I was so nearly filled that I was in no condition to judge, but the other men took a healthy gulp of Burgundy for a capital letter to start the new paragraph, and waded in as if they had been waiting for some such little snack to take the edge off their appetite. I noticed that the best the women could do was peck, particularly Lio, Lawrence Coyne's Chinese wife, and Dina Laszio. I also noticed that the greenjacket waiters were aware that they were looking on at a gastronomical World's Series, though they were trying not to show it. Before it was over those birds disposed of nine ducks. It looked to me as if Vukcic was overdoing it a little on the various brands of wine, and maybe that was why he was so quick on the trigger when Phillip Laszio began making remarks about duck stuffings which he regarded as superior to Mr. Richards' and proceeded from that to comments on the comparative discrimination of the clientele of the Hotel Churchill and Rusterman's Restaurant. I had come as Vukcic's guest, and anyway I liked him, and it was embarrassing to me when he hit Laszio square in the eye with a hunk of bread. The others seemed to resent it chiefly as an interruption, and Servan, next to Laszio, soothed him, and Vukcic glared at their remonstrances and drank more Burgundy, and a greenjacket retrieved the bread from the floor, and they went back to the duck.

The salad, by Domenico Rossi, was attended by something of an uproar. In the first place, Phillip Laszio left for the kitchen while it was being served and Rossi had feelings about that and continued to express them after Servan had explained that Laszio must attend to the preparation of the Sauce Printemps for the test that had been arranged. Rossi didn't stop his remarks about sons-in-law twice his age. Then he noticed that Pierre Mondor wasn't pretending to eat, and wanted to know if perchance he had discovered things crawling on the lettuce. Mondor replied, friendly but firm, that the juices necessary to impart a flavor to salads, especially vinegar, were notoriously bad companions for wine, and that he wished to finish his Burgundy.

Rossi said darkly, "There is no vinegar. I am not a barbarian."

"I have not tasted it. I smell salad juice, that is why I pushed it away."

"I tell you there is no vinegar! That salad is mostly by the good God, as He made things! Mustard sprouts, cress sprouts, lettuce! Onion juice with salt! Bread crusts rubbed with garlic! In Italy we eat it from bowls, with Chianti, and we thank God for it!"

Mondor shrugged. "In France we do not. France, as you well know, my dear Rossi, is supreme in these things. In what language—"

"Ha!" Rossi was on his hind legs. "Supreme because we taught you! Because in the sixteenth century you came and ate our food and copied us! Can you read? Do you know the history of gastronomy? Any history at all? Do you know that of all the good things in France, of which there are a certain number, the original is found in Italy? Do you know—"

I suppose that's how the war will start. On that occasion it petered out. They kept Mondor from firing up and got Rossi started on his own salad, and we had peace.

Coffee was served in the two parlors. Two, because Lawrence Coyne got stretched out on the divan in the small one again, and Keith and Leon Blanc sat by him and talked. I'm always more comfortable on my feet after a meal, and I wandered around. Back in the large parlor, Wolfe and Vukcic and Berin and Mondor were in a group in a corner, discussing the duck. Mamma Mondor came waddling in from the hall with a bag of knitting and got settled under a light. Lio Coyne was on a big chair with her feet tucked under her, listening to Vallenko tell her stories. Lisette Putti was filling Servan's coffee cup, and Rossi stood frowning at an Indian blanket thrown over a couch as if he suspected it was made in France.

I couldn't see Dina Laszio anywhere, and wondered idly whether she was off somewhere mixing poison or had merely gone to her room, which was in the left wing of Pocahontas, for some bicarbonate. Or maybe out in the kitchen helping her husband? I moseyed out there. In the dining room, as I went through, they were getting ready for the sauce test, with the chairs moved back to the walls, and the big screens in front of the serving tables, and a fresh cloth on the long table. I sidestepped a couple of greenjackets and proceeded. Dina wasn't in the kitchen. Half a dozen people in white aprons paid no attention to me, since in the past twelve hours they had got accustomed to the place being cluttered up with foreign matter. Laszio, also in an apron, was at the big range stirring and peering into a pan, with a shine at each elbow waiting for commands. The place smelled sort of unnecessary on account of what I still had in me, and I went out again and down the pantry hall and back to the parlor. Liqueurs were being passed, and I snared myself a stem of cognac and sought a seat and surveyed the scene.

It occurred to me that I hadn't noticed Constanza around. In a little while she came in, from the hall, ran her eyes over the room, and came and sat down beside me and crossed her knees flagrantly. I saw signs on her face, and leaned toward her to make sure.

"You've been crying."

She nodded. "Of course I have! There's a dance at the hotel, and Mr. Tolman asked me to go and my father won't let me! Even though we're in America! I've been in my room crying." She hitched her knee up a little. "Father doesn't like me to sit like this, that's why I'm doing it."

I grunted, "Leg-jealousy. Parental type."

"What?"

"Nothing. You might as well make yourself comfortable, he isn't looking at you. Can I get you some cognac?"

We whiled away a pleasant hour, punctuated by various movements and activities outside our little world. Dina Laszio came in from the hall, got herself a liqueur, stopped for a few words with Mamma Mondor, and then moved on to the little stool in front of the radio. She sipped the liqueur and monkeyed with the dials, but got nothing on it. In a minute or two Vukcic came striding across the room, pulled a chair up beside the stool, and sat down. Her smile at him, as he spoke to her, was very good, and I wondered if he was in any condition to see how good it was. Coyne and Keith and Blanc came in from the small parlor. Around ten o'clock we had a visitor—nothing less than Mr. Clay Ashley, the manager of Kanawha Spa. He was fifty, black-haired with no gray, polished inside and out; and had come to make a speech. He wanted us to know that Kanawha Spa felt itself deeply honored by this visit from the most distinguished living representatives of one of the greatest of the arts. He hoped we would enjoy and so forth. Servan indicated Nero Wolfe, the guest of honor, as the appropriate source of the reply, and for once Wolfe had to get up out of his chair without intending to go anywhere. He offered a few remarks, and thanks to Mr. Ashley, saying nothing about train rides and sausages, and Mr. Ashley went, after being presented to those he hadn't met.

It was then time for another little speech, this time by Louis Servan. He said everything was in readiness for the test and explained how it would be. On the dining table would be nine dishes of Sauce Printemps on warmers, each lacking one of the nine seasonings, also a server of squabs, and plates and other utensils. Each taster would slice his own bits of squab; it was not permitted to taste any sauce without squab. Water would be there to wash the palate. Only one taste from each dish was allowed. In front of each dish would be a number on a card, from 1 to 9. Each taster would be provided with a slip of paper on which the nine seasonings were listed, and after each seasoning he would write the number of the dish in which that was lacking. Laszio, who had prepared the sauce, would be in the dining room to preside. Those who had tasted were not to converse with those who had not tasted until all were finished. To avoid confusion the tasting would be done in this order—Servan read it from a slip:

> Mondor
> Coyne
> Keith
> Blanc
> Servan
> Berin
> Vukcic
> Vallenko
> Rossi
> Wolfe

41

Right away there was a little hitch. When the slips were passed out and it came to Leon Blanc, he shook his head. He told Servan apologetically but firmly, "No, Louis, I'm sorry. I have tried not to let my opinion of Phillip Laszio make discomfort for any of you, but under no circumstances will I eat anything prepared by him. He is... all of you know... but I'd better not say...."

He turned on his heel and beat it from the room, to the hall. The only thing that ruptured the silence was a long low growl from Jerome Berin, who had already accepted his slip.

Ramsey Keith said, "Too bad for him. Dear old Leon. We all know—but what the devil! Are you first, Pierre? I hope to God you miss all of 'em! Is everything ready in there, Louis?"

Mamma Mondor came trotting up to face her husband, holding her knitting against her tummy, and squeaked something at him in French. I asked Constanza what it was, and she said she told him if he made one mistake on such a simple thing there would be no forgiveness either by God or by her. Mondor patted her on the shoulder impatiently and reassuringly and trotted for the door to the dining room, closing it behind him. In ten minutes, maybe fifteen, the door opened again and he reappeared.

Keith, who had made the bet with Servan which had started it, approached Mondor and demanded, "Well?"

Mondor was frowning gravely. "We have been instructed not to discuss. I can say, I warned Laszio against an excess of salt and he ignored it. Even so, it will be utterly astounding if I have made a mistake."

Keith turned and roared across the room, "Lisette, my dearest niece! Give all of them cordials! Insist upon it! Seduce them!"

Servan, smiling, called to Coyne, "You next, Lawrence."

The old snowbank went. I could see it would be a long drawn out affair. Constanza had been called across to her father. I wondered what it would be like to dance with a swamp-woman, and went to where Dina Laszio still sat on the radio stool and Vukcic beside her, but got turned down. She gave me an indifferent glance from the long sleepy eyes and said she had a headache. That made me stubborn and I looked around for another partner, but it didn't look promising. Coyne's Chinese wife, Lio, wasn't there, though I hadn't noticed her leave the room. Lisette had taken Keith's command literally and was on a selling tour with a tray of

42

cordials. I didn't care to tackle Mamma Mondor for fear Pierre would get jealous. As for Constanza—well, I thought of all the children at home, and then I considered her, with her eyes close to me and my arm around her and that faint fragrance which made it seem absolutely necessary to get closer so you could smell it better, and I decided it wouldn't be fair to my friend Tolman. I cast another disapproving glance at Vukcic as he sat glued to the chair alongside Dina Laszio, and went over and copped the big chair where Lio Coyne had been.

I'm pretty sure I didn't go to sleep, because I was conscious of the murmur of the voices all the time, but there's no question that my eyes were closed for a spell, and I was so comfortable otherwise that it annoyed me that I couldn't keep from worrying about how those guys could swallow the squabs and sauces less than three hours after the flock of ducks had gone down. It was the blare of the radio starting that woke me—I mean made me open my eyes. Dina Laszio was on her feet, leaning over twisting the dial, and Vukcic was standing waiting for her. She straightened up and melted into him and off they went. In a minute Keith and Lisette Putti were also dancing, and then Louis Servan with Constanza. I looked around. Jerome Berin wasn't there, so apparently they had got down to him on the tasting list. I covered a yawn, and stretched without putting my arms out, and arose and moseyed over to the corner where Nero Wolfe was talking with Pierre Mondor and Lawrence Coyne. There was an extra chair, and I took it.

Pretty soon Berin entered from the dining room and crossed the room to our corner. I saw Servan, without interrupting his dancing, make a sign to Vukcic that he was next, and Vukcic nodded back but showed no inclination to break his clinch with Dina. Berin was scowling. Coyne asked him:

"How about it, Jerome? We've both been in. Number 3 is shallots. No?"

Mondor protested, "Mr. Wolfe hasn't tried it yet. He goes last."

Berin growled, "I don't remember the numbers. Louis has my slip. God above, it was an effort I tell you, with that dog of a Laszio standing there smirking at me." He shook himself. "I ignored him. I didn't speak to him."

They talked. I listened with only one ear, because of a play

I was enjoying out front. Servan had highballed Vukcic twice more to remind him it was his turn to taste, without any result. I could see Dina smile into Vukcic's face, and I noticed that Mamma Mondor was also seeing it and was losing interest in her knitting. Finally Servan parted from Constanza, bowed to her, and approached the other couple. He was too polite and dignified to grab, so he just got in their way and they had to stop. They untwined.

Servan said, "Please. It is best to keep the order of the list. If you don't mind."

Apparently Vukcic was no longer lit, and anyway he wouldn't have been rude to Servan. With a toss of his head he shook his hair-tangle back, and laughed. "But I think I won't do it. I think I shall join the revolt of Leon Blanc." He had to speak loud on account of the radio.

"My dear Vukcic!" Servan was mild. "We are civilized people, are we not? We are not children."

Vukcic shrugged. Then he turned to his dancing partner. "Shall I do it, Dina?" Her eyes were up to him, and her lips moved, but in too low a voice for me to catch it. He shrugged again, and turned and headed for the dining room door and opened it and went in, with her watching his back. She went back to the stool by the radio, and Servan resumed with Constanza. Pretty soon, at eleven-thirty, there was a program change and the radio began telling about chewing gum, and Dina switched it off.

She asked, "Shall I try another station?"

Apparently they had had enough, so she left it dead. In our corner, Wolfe was leaning back with his eyes shut and Coyne was telling Berin about San Francisco Bay, when his Chinese wife entered from the hall, looked around and saw us and trotted over, and stuck her right forefinger into Coyne's face and told him to kiss it because she had got it caught in a door and it hurt.

He kissed it. "But I thought you were outside looking at the night."

"I was. But the door caught me. Look! It hurts."

He kissed the finger again. "My poor little blossom!" More kisses. "My flower of Asia! Now we're talking, run away and let us alone."

She went off pouting.

Vukcic entered from the dining room, and came straight

44

across to Dina Laszio. Servan told Vallenko he was next. Vukcic turned to him:

"Here's my slip. I tasted each dish once. That's the rule, eh? Laszio isn't there."

Servan's brows went up. "Not there? Where is he?"

Vukcic shrugged. "I didn't look for him. Perhaps in the kitchen."

Servan called to Keith: "Ramsey! Phillip has left his post! Only Vallenko and Rossi and Mr. Wolfe are left. What about it?"

Keith said he would trust them if Servan would, and Vallenko went in. In due time he was back, and it was Rossi's turn. Rossi hadn't been in a scrap for over three hours, and I pricked my ears in expectation of hearing through the closed door some hot remarks about sons-in-law, in case Laszio had got back on the job, but there was so much jabber in the parlor that I wouldn't have heard it anyway. When Rossi returned he announced to the gathering that no one but a fool would put as much salt as that in Sauce Printemps, but no one paid any attention to him. Nero Wolfe, last but not least, pried himself loose from his chair and, as the guest of honor, was conducted to the door by Louis Servan. I was darned glad that at last I could see bedtime peeping over the horizon.

In ten minutes the door opened and Wolfe reappeared. He stood on the threshold and spoke:

"Mr. Servan! Since I am the last, would you mind if I try an experiment with Mr. Goodwin?"

Servan said no, and Wolfe beckoned to me. I was already on my feet, because I knew something was up. There are various kinds of experiments that Wolfe might try with me as the subject, but none of them would be gastronomical. I crossed the parlor and followed him into the dining room, and he shut the door. I looked at the table. There were the nine dishes, with numbered cards in front of them, and a big electric server, covered, and a pitcher of water and glasses, and plates and forks and miscellany.

I grinned at Wolfe. "Glad to help you out. Which one did you get stuck on?"

He moved around the table. "Come here." He went on, to the right, to the edge of the big Pocahontas screen standing there, and I followed him. Behind the screen he stopped, and pointed at the floor. "Look at that confounded mess."

45

I stepped back a step, absolutely surprised. I had discounted all the loose talk about killing on account of its being dagoes, and whatever I might have thought about the swamp-woman's little story, at least it hadn't prepared me for blood. But there was the blood, though there wasn't much of it, because the knife was still sticking in the left middle of Phillip Laszio's back, with only the hilt showing. He was on his face, with his legs straight out, so that you might have thought he was asleep if it hadn't been for the knife. I moved across and bent over and twisted the head enough to get a good look at one eye. Then I got up and looked at Wolfe.

He said bitterly, "A pleasant holiday! I tell you, Archie— but no matter. Is he dead?"

"Dead as a sausage."

"I see. Archie. We have never been guilty of obstructing justice. That's the legal term, let them have it. But this is not our affair. And at least for the present—what do you remember about our trip down here?"

"I think I remember we came on a train. That's about as far as I could go."

He nodded. "Call Mr. Servan."

4

AT THREE O'CLOCK in the morning I sat in the small parlor of Pocahontas Pavilion. Across a table from me sat my friend Barry Tolman, and standing back of him was a big-jawed squint-eyed ruffian in a blue serge suit, with a stiff white collar, red tie and pink shirt. His name and occupation had not been kept a secret: Sam Pettigrew, sheriff of Marlin County. There were a couple of nondescripts, one with a stenographer's notebook at the end of the table, and a West Virginia state cop was on a chair tilted against the wall. The door to the dining room stood open and there was still a faint smell of photographers' flashlight bombs, and a murmur of voices came through from sleuths doing fingerprints and similar chores.

The blue-eyed athlete was trying not to sound irritated: "I know all that, Ashley. You may be the manager of Kanawha

Spa, but I'm the prosecuting attorney of this county, and what do you want me to do, pretend he fell on the damn knife by accident? I resent your insinuation that I'm making a grab for the limelight—"

"All right, Barry. Forget it." Clay Ashley, standing beside me, slowly shook his head. "Of all the rotten breaks! I know you can't suppress it, of course. But for God's sake get it over with and get 'em out of here—all right, I know you will as soon as you can. Excuse me if I said things. . . . I'm going to try to get some sleep. Have them call me if I can do anything."

He beat it. Someone came from the dining room to ask Pettigrew a question, and Tolman shook himself and rubbed his bloodshot eyes with his fingers. Then he looked at me:

"I sent for you again, Mr. Goodwin, to ask if you have thought of anything to add to what you told me before."

I shook my head. "I gave you the crop."

"You haven't remembered anything at all that happened, in the parlor or anywhere else, any peculiar conduct, any significant conversation?"

I said no.

"Anything during the day, for instance?"

"Nope. Day or night."

"When Wolfe called you secretly into the dining room and showed you Laszio's body behind the screen, what did he say to you?"

"He didn't call me secretly. Everybody heard him."

"Well, he called you alone. Why?"

I lifted the shoulders and let them drop. "You'll have to ask him."

"What did he say?"

"I've already told you. He asked me to see if Laszio was dead, and I saw he was, and he asked me to call Servan."

"Was that all he said?"

"I think he remarked something about it being a pleasant holiday. Sometimes he's sarcastic."

"He seems also to be cold-blooded. Was there any special reason for his being cold-blooded about Laszio?"

I put my foot down a little harder on the brake. Wolfe would never forgive me if by some thoughtless but relevant remark I got this buzzard really down on us. I knew why Wolfe had bothered to get me in the dining room alone and inquire about my memory before broadcasting the news: it

47

had occurred to him that in a murder case a material witness may be required to furnish bond not to leave the state without permission, or to return to testify at the trial, and it was contrary to his idea of the good life to do either one. It wasn't easy to maintain outward respect for a guy who had been boob enough to fall for that ginger ale act in the club car, but while I had nothing at all against West Virginia I wasn't much more anxious to stay there or return there than Wolfe was.

I said, "Certainly not. He had never met Laszio before."

"Had anything happened during the day to make him—er, indifferent to Laszio's welfare?"

"Not that I know of."

"And had you or he knowledge of a previous attempt on Laszio's life?"

"You'll have to ask him. Me, no."

My friend Tolman forsook friendship for duty. He put an elbow on the table and pointed a finger at me and said in a nasty tone, "You're lying." I also noticed that the squint-eyed sheriff had a scowl on him not to be sneezed at, and the atmosphere of the whole room was unhealthy.

I put my brows up. "Me lying?"

"Yes, you. What did Mrs. Laszio tell you and Wolfe when she called at your suite yesterday afternoon?"

I hope I didn't gulp visibly. I know my brain gulped, but only once. No matter how he had found out, or how much, there was but one thing to do. I said, "She told us that her husband told her that he found arsenic in the sugar shaker and dumped it in the sink, and she wanted Wolfe to protect her husband. She also said that her husband had instructed her not to mention it to anyone."

"What else?"

"That's all."

"And you just told me that you had no knowledge of a previous attempt on Laszio's life. Didn't you?"

"I did."

"Well?" He stayed nasty.

I grinned at him. "Look, Mr. Tolman. I don't want to try to get smart with you, even if I knew how. But consider a few things. In the first place, without any offense—you're just a young fellow in your first term as a prosecutor—Nero Wolfe has solved more tough ones than you've even heard about. You know that, you know his reputation. Even if either of us

48

knew anything that would give you a trail, which we don't, it wouldn't pay you to waste time trying to squeeze juice out of us without our consent, because we're old hands. I'm not bragging, I'm just stating facts. For instance, about my knowing about an attempt to kill Laszio, I repeat I didn't. All I knew was that Mrs. Laszio told us that her husband told her that he found something in the sugar shaker besides sugar. How could he have been sure it was arsenic? Laszio wasn't poisoned, he was stabbed. In my experience—"

"I'm not interested in your experience." Still nasty. "I asked you if you remember anything that might have any significance regarding this murder. Do you?"

"I've told you what Mrs. Laszio told us—"

"So has she. Pass that for the moment. Anything else?"

"No."

"You're sure?"

"Yes."

Tolman told the state cop, "Bring Odell in."

It came to me. So that was it. A fine bunch of friends I had made since entering the dear old Panhandle State—which nickname I had learned from my pal Gershom Odell, house dick of Kanawha Spa. My brain was gulping again, and this time I wasn't sure whether it would get it down or not. The process was interrupted by the entry of my pal, ushered in by the cop. I turned a stare on him which he did not meet. He came and stood near me at the table, so close I could have smacked him one without getting up.

Tolman said, "Odell, what was it this man told you yesterday afternoon?"

The house dick didn't look at me. He sounded gruff. "He told me Phillip Laszio was going to be killed by somebody, and when I asked him who was going to do it he said they were going to take turns."

"What else?"

"That's all he said."

Tolman turned to me, but I beat the gun. I gave Odell a dig in the ribs that made him jump. "Oh, that's it!" I laughed. "I remember now, when we were out by the bridle path throwing stones, and you pointed out that ledge to me and told me—sure! Apparently you didn't tell Mr. Tolman *everything* we said, since he thinks—Did you tell him how I was talking about those dago and polack cooks, and how they're so jealous of each other they're apt to begin killing each other off any time, and how Laszio was the highest paid of the bunch, sixty thousand bucks a year, so they would be sure to pick on him first, and how they would take turns killing him first and then begin on the next one—and then I remember you began telling me about the ledge and how it happened you could leave the hotel at that time of day—" I turned to Tolman. "That's all that was, just a couple of guys talking to pass the time. You're welcome to any significance you can find in it. If I told you what Odell told me about that ledge—" I laughed and poked my pal in the ribs again.

Tolman was frowning, but not at me. "What about it, Odell? That's not the way you told it. What about it?"

I had to hand it to Odell for a good poker face, at that. He was the picture of a Supreme Court justice pretending that he had no personal interest in the matter. Still he didn't glance at me, but he looked Tolman quietly in the eye. "I guess my tongue kinda ran away with me. I guess it was about like he says, just shootin' off. But of course I remembered the name, Phillip Laszio, and any detective would jump at a chance to have a hot one on a murder. . . ."

The squint-eyed ruffian spoke, in a thin mild drawl that startled me. "You sound pretty inaccurate to me, Odell. Maybe you ought to do less guessin'?"

Tolman demanded, "Did he or did he not tell you Laszio was going to be killed?"

"Well . . . the way he just said it, yes. I mean about them all being jealous dagoes, and Laszio getting sixty thousand—I'm sure he said that. I guess that's all there was to it."

"What about it, Goodwin? Why did you pick on Laszio?"

I showed a palm. "I didn't pick on him. I happened to mention him because I knew he was the tops—in salary, anyhow. I had just read an article—want to see it?"

The sheriff drawled, "We're wastin' time. Get the hell out of here, Odell."

My pal, without favoring me with a glance, turned and made for the door. Tolman called to the cop:

"Bring Wolfe in."

I sat tight. Except for the little snags that had threatened to trip me up, I was enjoying myself. I was wondering what Inspector Cramer of the New York Homicide Squad would say if he could see Nero Wolfe letting himself be called in for a grilling by small town snoops at half-past three in the morning, because he didn't want to offend a prosecuting attorney! He hadn't been up as late as that since the night Clara Fox slept in his house in my pajamas. Then I thought I might as well offer what help I could, and got up and brought a big armchair from the other end of the room and put it in position near the table.

The cop returned, with my boss. Tolman asked the cop who was left out there, and the cop said, "That Vookshish or whatever it is, and Berin and his daughter. They tried to shoo her off to bed, but she wouldn't go. She keeps making passes to come in here."

Tolman was chewing his lip, and I kept one sardonic eye on him while I used the other one to watch Nero Wolfe getting himself into the chair I had placed. Finally Tolman said, "Send them to their rooms. We might as well knock off until morning. All right, Pettigrew?"

"Sure. Bank it up and sleep on it." He squinted at the cop. "Tell Plank to wait out there until we see what arrangements he's made. This is no time of night for anyone to be taking a walk."

The cop departed. Tolman rubbed his eyes, then, chewing at his lip again, leaned back and looked at Wolfe. Wolfe seemed placid enough, but I saw his forefinger tapping on the arm of his chair and knew what a fire was raging inside of him. He offered as a bit of information, "It's nearly four o'clock, Mr. Tolman."

"Thanks." Tolman sounded peevish. "We won't keep you long. I sent for you again because one or two things have come up." I observed that he and the sheriff both had me in the corner of their eyes, and I'd have sworn they were putting over a fast one and trying to catch me passing some kind of a sign to Wolfe. I let myself look sleepy, which wasn't hard.

Wolfe said, "More than one or two, I imagine. For instance, I suppose Mrs. Laszio has repeated to you the story she told me yesterday afternoon. Hasn't she?"

"What story was that?"

"Come now, Mr. Tolman." Wolfe stopped tapping with the finger and wiggled it at him. "Don't be circuitous with me. She was in here with you over half an hour, she must have told you that story. I figured she would. That was why I didn't mention it; it seemed preferable that you should get it fresh from her."

"What do you mean, you figured she would?"

51

"Only an assumption." Wolfe was mild and inoffensive. "After all, she is a participant in this tragedy, while I am merely a bystander—"

"Participant?" Tolman was frowning. "Do you mean she had a hand in it? You didn't say that before."

"Nor do I say it now. I merely mean, it was her husband who was murdered, and she seems to have had, if not premonition, at least apprehension. You know more about it than I do, since you have questioned her. She informed you, I presume, that her husband told her that at noon yesterday, in the kitchen of this place, he found arsenic in a sugar shaker which was intended for him; and that without her husband's knowledge or consent she came to ask my assistance in guarding him from injury and I refused it."

"Why did you refuse it?"

"Because of my incompetence for the task. As I told her, I am not a food taster or a body guard." Wolfe stirred a little; he was boiling. "May I offer advice, Mr. Tolman? Don't waste your energy on me. I haven't the faintest idea who killed Mr. Laszio, or why. It may be that you have heard of me; I don't know; if so, you have perhaps got the impression that when I am engaged on a case I am capable of sinuosities, though you wouldn't think it to look at me. But I am not engaged on this case, I haven't the slightest interest in it, I know nothing whatever about it, and you are as apt to receive pertinent information from the man in the moon as you are from me. My connection with it is threefold. First, I happened to be here; that is merely my personal misfortune. Second, I discovered Mr. Laszio's body; as I told you, I was curious as to whether he was childishly keeping secret surveillance over the table, and I looked behind the screen. Third, Mrs. Laszio told me someone was trying to poison her husband and asked me to prevent it; you have that fact; if there is a place for that piece in your puzzle, fit it in. You have, gentlemen, my sympathy and my best wishes."

Tolman, who after all wasn't much more than a kid, twisted his head to get a look at the sheriff, who was slowly scratching his cheek with his middle finger. Pettigrew looked back at him and finally turned to Wolfe:

"Look, mister, you've got us wrong I think. We're not aiming to make you any trouble or any inconvenience. We don't regard you as one of that bunch that if they knew anything they wouldn't tell us if they could help it. But you

52

say maybe we've heard of you. That's right. We've heard of you. After all, you was around with this bunch all day talking with 'em. You know? I don't know what Tolman here thinks, but it's my opinion it wouldn't hurt any to tell you what we've found out and get your slant on it. Since you say you've got no interest in it that might conflict. All right, Barry?"

Wolfe said, "You'd be wasting your time. I'm not a wizard. When I get results, I get them by hard work, and this isn't my case and I'm not working on it."

I covered a grin. Tolman put in, "The sooner this thing is cleaned up, the better for everybody. You realize that. If the sheriff—"

Wolfe said brusquely, "Very well. To-morrow."

"It's already to-morrow. God knows how late you'll sleep in the morning, but I won't. There's one thing in particular I want to ask you. You told me that the only one of these people you know at all well is Vukcic. Mrs. Laszio told me about her being married to Vukcic and getting divorced from him some years ago to marry Laszio. Could you tell me how Vukcic has been feeling about that?"

"No. Mrs. Laszio seems to have been quite informative."

"Well, it was her husband that got killed. Why? Have you got anything against her? That's the second dig you've taken at her."

"Certainly I have something against her. I don't like women asking me to protect their husbands. It is beneath the dignity of a man to rely, either for safety or salvation, on the interference of a woman. Pfui!"

Of course Wolfe wasn't in love. I hoped Tolman realized that. He said:

"I asked you that question, obviously, because Vukcic was one of the two who had the best opportunity to kill him. Most of them are apparently out of it, by your own testimony among others." He glanced at one of the papers on the table. "The ones who were in the parlor all the time, according to present information, are Mrs. Laszio, Mrs. Mondor, Lisette Putti and Goodwin. Servan says that when he went to the dining room to taste those sauces Laszio was there alive and nothing wrong, and at that time Mondor, Coyne and Keith had already been in, and it is agreed that none of them left the parlor again. They too are apparently out of it. The next two were Berin and Vukcic. Berin says that when he left the dining room Laszio was still there and still nothing wrong,

53

and Vukcic says that when he entered, some eight or ten minutes later on account of a delay, Laszio was gone and he saw nothing of him and noticed nothing wrong. The three who went last, Vallenko and Rossi and you, are also apparently out of it, but not as conclusively as the others, since it is quite possible that Laszio had merely stepped out to the terrace or gone to the toilet, and returned after Vukcic left the dining room. According to the cooks, he had not appeared in the kitchen, so he had not gone there."

Tolman glanced at the paper again. "That makes two probabilities, Berin and Vukcic, and three possibilities, Vallenko and Rossi and you. Besides that, there are three other possibilities. Someone could easily have entered the dining room from the terrace at any time; the glass doors were closed and the shades drawn, but they were not locked. And there were three people who could have done that: Leon Blanc, who refused to take part on account of animosity toward Laszio and was absent; Mrs. Coyne, who was outdoors alone for nearly an hour, including the interval between Berin's visit to the dining room and that of Vukcic; and Miss Berin. Blanc claims he went to his room and didn't leave it, and the hall attendants didn't see him go out, but there is a door to the little side terrace at the end of the left wing corridor which he could have used without observation. Mrs. Coyne says she was on the paths and lawns throughout her absence, was not on the dining room terrace, and re-entered by the main entrance and went straight to the parlor. As for Miss Berin, she returned to the parlor, from the room, before the tasting of the sauces began, and did not again leave; I mentioned her absence only to have the record complete."

I thought to myself, you cold-blooded hound! She was in her room crying for you, that was her absence, and you make it just part of a list!

"You were there, Mr. Wolfe. That covers it, doesn't it?"

Wolfe grunted. Tolman resumed, "As for motive, with some of them there was enough. With Vukcic, the fact that Laszio had taken his wife. And immediately preceding Vukcic's trip to the dining room he had been talking with Mrs. Laszio and gazing at her and dancing with her—"

Wolfe said sharply, "A woman told you that."

"By God," the sheriff drawled, "you seem to resent the few little things we have found out. I thought you said you weren't interested."

54

"Vukcic is my friend. I'm interested in him. I'm not interested in this murder, with which he had no connection."

"Maybe not." Tolman looked pleased, I suppose because he had got a rise out of Nero Wolfe. "Anyway, my talk with Mrs. Mondor was my first chance to make official use of my French. Next there is Berin. I got this not from Mrs. Mondor, but from him. He declares that Laszio should have been killed long before now, that he himself would have liked to do it, and that if he has any opportunity to protect the murderer he will do so."

Wolfe murmured, "Berin talks."

"I'll say he does. So does that little Frenchman Leon Blanc, but not the same style. He admits that he hated Laszio because he cheated him out of his job at the Hotel Churchill some years ago, but he says he wouldn't murder anybody for anything. He says that it does not even please him that Laszio is dead, because death doth not heal, it amputates. Those were his words. He's soft-spoken and he certainly doesn't seem aggressive enough to stab a man through the heart, but he's no fool and possibly he's smooth.

"There's the two probabilities and one possibility with motives. Of the four other possibilities, I guess you didn't do it. If Rossi or Vallenko had any feelings that might have gone as far as murder, I haven't learned it yet. As for Mrs. Coyne, she never saw Laszio before, and I can't discover that she has spoken to him once. So until further notice we have Berin and Vukcic and Blanc. Any of them could have done it, and I think one of them did. What do you think?"

Wolfe shook his head. "Thank heaven, it isn't my problem, and I don't have to think."

Pettigrew put in, in his mild drawl, "Do you suppose there's any chance you suspect your friend Vukcic did it and so you'd rather not think about it?"

"Chance? Certainly. Remote. If Vukcic did it, I hope with all my heart he left no rope for you to hang him by. And as for information regarding it, I have none, and if I had I wouldn't reveal it."

Tolman nodded. "That's frank, but not very helpful. I don't have to point out to you that if you're interested in your friend Vukcic and think he didn't do it, the quickest way to clear him is to find out who did. You were right there on the spot; you saw everyone and heard everything that was said. It seems to me that under those circumstances a man of your reputation and ability should find it possible to offer some help. If you don't it's bound to put more suspicion on your friend Vukcic, isn't it?"

"I don't know. Your suspicions are your affair; I can't regulate them. Confound it, it's four o'clock in the morning!" Wolfe sighed. Then he compressed his lips. He sat that way, and finally muttered, "Very well, I'll help for ten minutes. Tell me about the routine—the knife, fingerprints, anything found—"

"Nothing. There were two knives on the table for slicing the squab, and it was one of them. You saw for yourself there was not the slightest sign of a struggle. Nothing anywhere. No prints that seem to mean anything; those on the knife handle were all smudged. The levers on the door to the terrace are rough wrought iron. Men are still in there working it over, but that angle looks hopeless."

Wolfe grunted. "You've omitted possibilities. The cooks and waiters?"

"They've all been questioned by the sheriff, who knows how to deal with niggers. None of them went to the dining room, and they didn't see or hear anything. Laszio had told them he would ring if anything was wanted."

"Someone could have gone from the large parlor to the small one and from there entered the dining room and killed him. You should establish beyond doubt the presence of everyone in the large parlor, especially during the interim between Berin's leaving the dining room and Vukcic's entering it, which, as you say, was some eight or ten minutes."

"I have done so. Of course, I covered everybody pretty fast."

"Then cover them again. Another possibility: someone could have been concealed behind either of the screens and struck from there when the opportunity offered."

"Yeah? Who?"

"I'm sure I couldn't say." Wolfe frowned. "I may as well tell you, Mr. Tolman, I am extremely skeptical regarding your two chief suspects, Mr. Berin and Mr. Vukcic. That is putting it with restraint. As for Mr. Blanc, I am without an opinion; as you have pointed out, he could unquestionably have left his room, made an exit at the end of the left wing corridor, circled the building, entered by the dining room terrace, achieved his purpose, and returned the way he had come. In that case, might he not have been seen by Mrs. Coyne, who was outdoors at the time, looking at the night?"

Tolman shook his head. "She says not. She was at the front and the side both. She was no one but a nigger in uniform, and stopped him and asked him what the sound of a whippoorwill was. We've found him—one of the boys from the spring on his way to Mingo Pavilion."

"So. As for Berin and Vukcic, if I were you I would pigeonhole them for the present. Or at least—I offer a suggestion: get the slips, the tasting reports, from Mr. Servan—"

"I have them."

"Good. Compare them with the correct list, which you also got from Mr. Servan no doubt—"

"He didn't have it. It was in Laszio's pocket."

"Very well. Compare each list with it, and see how nearly each taster was correct."

Sheriff Pettigrew snorted. Tolman asked dryly, "You call that being helpful, do you?"

"I do. I am already—by the way!" Wolfe straightened a little. "If you have the correct list there—the one you took from Laszio's pocket—do you mind if I look at it a moment?"

Tolman, with his brows up, shuffled through the papers before him, extracted one, handed it to me, and I passed it to Wolfe. Wolfe looked at it with his forehead wrinkled, and exclaimed, "Good God!" He looked at it again, and turning to me, shaking the paper in his hand. "Archie. Coyne was right! Number 3 was shallots!"

Tolman asked sarcastically, "Comedy relief? Much obliged for *that* help."

I grinned at him. "Comedy hell, he won't sleep for a week, he guessed wrong."

Wolfe reproved me: "It was not a guess. It was a deliberate conclusion, and it was wrong." He handed me the paper. "Pardon me, Mr. Tolman, I've had a blow. Actually. I wouldn't expect you to appreciate it. As I was saying, I am already more than skeptical regarding Berin and Vukcic. I have known Mr. Vukcic all my life. I can conceive of his stabbing a man, under hypothetical conditions, but I am sure that if he did you wouldn't find the knife in the man's back. I don't know Mr. Berin well, but I saw him at close range and heard him speak less than a minute after he left the dining room last night, and I would stake something that he wasn't fresh from the commission of a cowardly murder. He had but a moment before sunk a knife in Mr. Laszio's back, and I detected no residue of that experience in his posture, his hands, his eyes, his voice? I don't believe it."

"And about comparing these lists—"

"I'm coming to that. I take it that Mr. Servan has described the nature of that test to you—each sauce lacking one or another of the seasonings. We were permitted but one taste from each dish—only one! Have you any conception of the delicacy and sensitivity required? It took the highest degree of concentration and receptivity of stimuli. To detect a single false note in one of the wood winds in a symphonic passage by full orchestra would be the same. So, compare those lists. If you find that Berin and Vukcic were substantially correct— say seven or eight out of nine—they are eliminated. Even six. No man about to kill another, or just having done so, could possibly control his nervous system sufficiently to perform such a feat. I assure you this is not comedy."

Tolman nodded. "All right, I'll compare them."

"It would be instructive to do so now."

"I'll attend to it. Any other suggestions?"

"No." Wolfe got his hands on the chair arms, pulled his feet back, braced, and arose. "The ten minutes are up." He did his little bow. "I offer you again, gentlemen, my sympathy and best wishes."

The sheriff said, "I understand you're sleepin' in Upshur. Of course you realize you're free to go anywhere you want to around the grounds here."

"Thank you, sir." Wolfe sounded bitter. "Come, Archie."

Not to crowd the path, I let him precede me among the greenery back to Upshur Pavilion. We didn't go through darkness, but through the twilight of dawn, and there were so many birds singing you couldn't help noticing it. In the main hall of the pavilion the lights were turned on, and a couple of state cops were sitting there. Wolfe passed them without a glance.

I went to his room with him to make sure that everything was jake. The bed had been turned down, and the colored rugs and things made it bright and pleasant, and the room was big and classy enough to make it worth at least half of the twenty bucks a day they charged for it, but Wolfe frowned around as if it had been a pigpen.

I inquired, "Can I help on the disrobing?"

"No."

"Shall I bring a pitcher of water from the bathroom?"

"I can walk. Goodnight."

"Goodnight, boss." I went.

His voice halted me at the door. "Archie. This Mr. Laszlo seems to have had unpleasant characteristics. Do you suppose there is any chance he deliberately made that list incorrect, to disconcert his colleagues—and me?"

"Huh-uh. Not the faintest. Professional ethics, you know. Of course I'm sorry you got so many wrong—"

"Two! Shallots and chives! Leave me! Get out!"

He sure was one happy detective that night.

5

AT TWO O'CLOCK the next day, Wednesday, I was feeling pretty screwy and dissatisfied with life, but in one way completely at home. Getting to bed too late, or having my sleep disturbed unduly, poisons my system, and I had had both to contend with. Having neglected to hang up a notice, a damn fool servant had got me to the door of our suite at nine o'clock to ask if we wanted baths drawn or any other little service, and I had told him to return at sundown. At ten-thirty the phone woke me; my friend Barry Tolman wanted to speak to Wolfe. I explained that Wolfe's first exposure to the light of day would have to be on his own initiative, and told the operator no more calls until further notice. In spite of that, an hour later the phone rang again and kept on ringing. It was Tolman, and he just had to speak to Wolfe. I told him absolutely nothing doing, without a search and seizure warrant, until Wolfe had announced himself as conscious. But that time I was roused enough to become aware of other necessities besides sleep, so I bathed and shaved and dressed and phoned Room Service for some breakfast, since I couldn't go and get it under the circumstances. I had finished the third cup of coffee when I heard Wolfe yelling for me. He was

59

certainly getting demoralized. At home in New York, I hadn't heard him yell more than three times in ten years.

He gave me his breakfast order, which I phoned, and then issued the instructions which made me feel at home. It was his intention to confine his social contacts for that afternoon exclusively to me. Business and professional contacts were out. The door was to be kept locked, and any caller, unless it should happen to be Marko Vukcic, was to be told that Wolfe was immersed in something, no matter what. Telephone calls were to be handled by me, since he knew nothing that I didn't know. (This jarred my aplomb, since it was the first time he had ever admitted it.) Should I feel the need of more fresh air than was obtainable through open windows, which was idiotic but probable, the DO NOT DISTURB card was to be hung on the door and the key kept in my pocket.

I phoned for whatever morning papers were available, and when they came passed a couple to Wolfe and made myself comfortable on a couch with the remainder. Those from New York and Pittsburgh and Washington, being early train editions, had no mention of the Laszio murder, but there were big headlines and a short piece in the Charleston *Journal*, which had only sixty miles to come.

But before the day was out Wolfe's arrangements for peaceful privacy got shot full of holes. The first and least important of the upsets came before he had finished with the newspapers when, around two o'clock, there were sounds at the outer door and I went and opened it a discreet twelve inches to find myself confronted by two gentlemen who did not look local and whom I had never seen before. One was shorter than me and somewhat older, dark-skinned, wiry and compact, in a neat gray herringbone with padded shoulders and cut-in waist; the other, medium both in age and size, wore his hairline well above his temples and had small gray eyes that looked as if nobody would ever have to irritate him again because he was already irritated for good. But he spoke and listened politely as he asked me if that was Mr. Nero Wolfe's suite and I informed him it was, and announced that he was Mr. Liggett and the padded specimen was Mr. Malfi, and he would like to see Wolfe. I explained that Wolfe was immersed, and he looked impatient and dug an envelope from his pocket and handed it to me. I apologized for shutting them in the hall before I did so, and returned to the pigpen.

"Two male strangers, vanilla and caramel. To see you."

Wolfe's eyes didn't leave his newspapers. "If either of them was Mr. Vukcic, I presume you would have recognized him."

"Not Vukcic, no, but you didn't prohibit letters, and he handed me one."

"Read it."

I took it from the envelope, saw that it was on engraved stationery, and wired it for sound:

New York
April 7, 1937

Dear Mr. Wolfe:

This will introduce my friend Mr. Raymond Liggett, manager and part owner of the Hotel Churchill. He wants to ask your advice or assistance, and has requested this note from me.

I hope you're enjoying yourself down there. Don't eat too much, and don't forget to come back to make life in New York pleasanter for us.

Yours

Burke Williamson

Wolfe grunted. "You said April 7th? That's today."

"Yeah, they must have flown. Formerly a figure of speech, now listed under common carriers. Do we let them in?"

"Confound it." Wolfe let the paper down. "Courtesy is one's own affair, but decency is a debt to life. You remember that Mr. Williamson was kind enough to let us use the grounds of his estate for the ambush and robbery of Miss Anna Fiore." He sighed. "Show them in."

I went and got them, pronounced names around, and placed chairs. Wolfe greeted them, made his customary statement regarding his tendency to stay seated, and then glanced a second time at the padded one.

"Did I catch your name, sir? Malfi? Perhaps, Albert Malfi?"

The wiry one's black eyes darted at him. "That's right. I don't know how you knew the Albert."

Wolfe nodded. "Formerly Alberto. I met Mr. Berin on the train coming down here, and he told me about you. He says you are an excellent entrée man, and it is always a pleasure to meet an artist and a sound workman."

Liggett put in, "Oh, you were with Berin on the train?"

61

"I was." Wolfe grimaced. "We shared that ordeal. Mr. Williamson says you wish to ask me something."

"Yes. Of course you know why we came. This—Laszio. It's terrible. You were right there, weren't you? You found the body."

"I did. You wasted no time, Mr. Liggett."

"I know damn well I didn't. I usually turn in late and get up late, but this morning Malfi had me on the telephone before eight o'clock. Reporters had been after me earlier, but of course didn't get through. The city editions had the story. I knew Williamson was a friend of yours, and sent to him for that note, and hired a plane from Newark. Malfi insisted on coming along, and I'm afraid one of your jobs will be to watch him as soon as they find out who did it." Liggett showed a thin smile. "He's a Corsican, and while Laszio wasn't any relation of his, he's got pretty devoted to him. Haven't you, Malfi?"

The padded one nodded emphatically. "I have. Phillip Laszio was a mean man and a great man. He was not mean to me." He spread both palms at Wolfe. "But of course Mr. Liggett is only joking. The world thinks all Corsicans stab people. That is a wrong idea and a bad one."

"But you wanted to ask me something, Mr. Liggett?" Wolfe sounded impatient. "You said one of my jobs. I have no jobs."

"I'm hoping you will have. First, to find out who killed Laszio. Judging from the account in the papers, it looks as if it will be too tough for a West Virginia sheriff. It seems likely that whoever did it was able to use finesse for other purposes than tasting the seasonings in Sauce Printemps. I can't say I was devoted to Laszio in the sense that Malfi here was, but after all he was the chef of my hotel, and I understand he had no family except his wife, and I thought—it's an obligation. It was a damned cowardly murder, a stab in the back. He ought to be caught, and I suspect it will take you to do it. That's what I came for. Knowing your—er, peculiarities, I took the precaution of getting that note from Williamson."

"It's too bad." Wolfe sighed. "I mean too bad you came. You could have telephoned from New York."

"I asked Williamson what he thought about that, and he said if I really wanted your services I'd better come and get them."

"Indeed. I don't know why Mr. Williamson should assume difficulties. My services are on the market. Of course, in this

62

particular instance they are unfortunately not available; that's why I say it's too bad you came."

"Why not available?"

"Because of the conditions."

"Conditions?" The irritation in Liggett's eyes became more intense. "I've made no conditions."

"Not you. Space. Geography. Should I undertake to discover Mr. Laszio's murderer, I would see it through. That might take a day, a week, with bad luck a fortnight. I intend to board a train for New York tomorrow night." Wolfe winced.

"Williamson warned me." Liggett compressed his lips. "But good Lord, man! It's your business! It's your—"

"I beg you, sir. Don't. I won't listen. If I offend by being curt, very well. Anyone has the privilege of offending who is willing to bear the odium. I will consider no engagement that might detain me in this parasitic outpost beyond to-morrow night. You said 'jobs.' Is there anything else you wish to discuss?"

"There was." Liggett looked as if he would prefer to continue the discussion with shrapnel or a machine gun. He sat and stared at Wolfe a while, then finally shrugged it off. He said, "The fact is, the main job is something quite different. The main thing I came down here for. Laszio is dead, and the way he died was terrible, and as a man I have, I hope, the proper feelings about it, but in addition to being a man I'm a business man, and the Hotel Churchill is left without a chef de cuisine. You know the Churchill's world-wide reputation, and it has to be maintained. I want to get Jerome Berin."

Wolfe's brows went up. "I don't blame you."

"Of course you don't. There are a few others as good as Berin, but they're out. Mondor wouldn't leave his Paris restaurant. Servan and Tassone are too old. I wouldn't mind having Leon Blanc back, but he is also too old. Vukcic is tied up at Rusterman's, and so on. I happen to know that Berin has received five offers from this country, two of them from New York, in the past two years, and has turned them all down. I'd like to have him. In fact, he's the only one that I consider both available and desirable. If I can't get him, Malfi can put a blue ribbon on his cap." He turned to his companion. "Is that in accord with our agreement, Albert? When you got that offer from Chicago a year ago, I told you that if you would stick, and the position of chef de cuisine at the

Churchill should become vacant, I would first try to get Berin, and if I couldn't, you could have it. Right?"

Malfi nodded. "That was the understanding."

Wolfe murmured, "This is all very interesting. But you were speaking of a job—"

"Yes. I want you to approach Berin for me. He's one of the best seven chefs in the world, but he's hard to handle. Last Saturday he deliberately spilled two plates of sausage in the middle of the carpet in my Resort Room. Williamson says you have remarkable ability as a negotiator, and you are the guest of honor here and Berin will listen to you with respect, and I believe unquestionably you can swing him. I would offer him forty thousand, but I tell you frankly I am willing to go to sixty, and your commission—"

Wolfe was showing him a palm. "Please, Mr. Liggett. It's no go. Absolutely out of the question."

"You mean you won't do it?"

"I mean I wouldn't undertake to persuade Mr. Berin to do anything whatever. I would as soon try to persuade a giraffe. I could elaborate—but I can't see that I owe you that."

"You won't even attempt it?"

"I will not. The truth is, you have come to me at the most inauspicious moment in the past twenty years, and with proposals much more likely to vex me than to interest me. I don't care a hang who your new chef will be, and while I always like to make money, that can wait until I am back in my office. There are others here better qualified to approach Mr. Berin for you than I am—Mr. Servan or Mr. Coyne, for instance, old friends of his."

"They're chefs themselves. I don't want that. You're the man to do it for me. . . ."

He was a persistent cuss, but it didn't get him anywhere. When he tried to insist Wolfe merely got curter, as he naturally would, and finally Liggett realized he was calling the wrong dog and gave it up. He popped up out of his chair, snapped at Malfi to come along, and without any ceremony showed Wolfe his back. Malfi trotted behind, and I followed them to the hall to see that the door was locked after them.

When I got back to the room, Wolfe was already behind his paper again. I felt muscle-bound and not inclined to settle down, so I said to him, "You know, Werowance, that's not a bad idea—"

A word he didn't know invariably got him. The paper went

down to the level of his nose. "What the devil is that? Did you make it up?"

"I did not. I got it from a piece in the Charleston *Journal*. Werowance is a term that was used for an Indian Chief in Virginia and Maryland. I'm going to call you Werowance instead of Boss as long as we're in this part of the country. As I was saying, Werowance, it might be a good idea to start an employment bureau for chefs and waiters, maybe later branch out into domestic help generally. You are aware, I suppose, that you have just turned down a darned good offer for a case. That Liggett has really got it in quantities. I suspect he may be half bright too; for instance, do you imagine he might have come to see you in order to let Alberto know indirectly that if he tried sticking something into Berin in order to make Berin ineligible for the Churchill job, it would have deplorable consequences? Which opens up a train of thought that might solve the unemployment question. If a job becomes vacant and you want it, first you kill all the other candidates and then—"

The paper was up again, so I knew I had made myself sufficiently obnoxious. I said, "I'm going out and wade in the brook, and maybe go to the hotel and ruin a few girls. See you later."

I got my hat, hung up the DO NOT DISTURB, and wandered out, noting that there was a greenjacket at the door of the main hall but no cop. Apparently vigilance was relaxed. I turned my nose to the hotel, just to see what there was to see, and it wasn't long before I regretted that, for if I hadn't gone to the hotel first I would have got to see the whole show that my friend Tolman was putting on, instead of arriving barely in time for the final curtain. As it was, I found various sights around the hotel entrance and lobby that served for mild diversion, including an intelligent-looking horse stepping on a fat dowager's foot so hard they had to carry her away, and it was around 3:30 when I decided to make an excursion to Pocahontas Pavilion and thank Vukcic, my host, for the good time I was having. In a secluded part of the path a guy with his necktie over his shoulder and needing a shave jumped out from behind a bush and grabbed my elbow, talking as he came: "Hey, you're Archie Goodwin, aren't you, Nero Wolfe's man? Listen, brother—"

I shook him off and told him, "Damn it, quit scaring people. I'll hold a press conference tomorrow morning in my study. I don't know a thing, and if I did and told you I'd get killed by my werowance. Do you know what a werowance is?"

He told me to go to hell and started looking for another bush.

The tableau at Pocahontas Pavilion was in two sections when I got there. The first section, not counting the pair of troopers standing outside the entrance, was in the main hall. The greenjacket who opened the door for me was looking popeyed in another direction as he pulled it open. The door to the large parlor was closed. Standing with her back against the right wall, with her arms folded tight against her and her chin up, and her dark purple eyes flashing at the guys who hemmed her in, was Constanza Berin. The hemmers were two state cops in uniform and a hefty bird in cits with a badge on his vest, and while they weren't actually touching her at the moment I entered, it looked as though they probably had been. She didn't appear to see me. A glance showed me that the door to the small parlor was open, and a voice was coming through. As I started for it one of the cops called a sharp command to me, but it seemed likely he was too occupied to interfere in person, so I ignored it and went on.

There were cops in the small parlor too, and the squint-eyed sheriff, and Tolman. Between two of the cops stood Jerome Berin, with handcuffs on his wrists. I was surprised that under the circumstances Berin wasn't breaking furniture or even skulls, but all he was doing was glaring and breathing. Tolman was telling him:

". . . . We appreciate that you're a foreign visitor and a stranger here, and we'll show you every consideration. In this country a man charged with murder can't get bail. Your friends will of course arrange for counsel for you. I have not only told you that anything you say may be used against you, I have advised you to say nothing until you have consulted with counsel.—Go on, boys. Take him by the back path to the sheriff's car."

But they didn't get started right then. Yells and other sounds came suddenly from the main hall, and Constanza Berin came through the door like a tornado with the cops behind. One in the parlor tried to grab her as she went by, but he might as well have tried to stop the great blizzard. I thought she was going right on over the table to get at Tolman, but she stopped there and turned with her eyes

66

blazing at the cops, and then wheeled to Tolman and yelled at him, "You fool! You pig of a fool! He's my father! Would he kill a man in the back?" She pounded the table with fists. "Let him go! Let him go, you fool!"

A cop made a pass at her arm. Berin growled and took a step, and the two held him. Tolman looked as if the one thing he could use to advantage would be a trap door. Constanza had jerked away from the cop, and Berin said something to her, low and quiet, in Italian. She walked to him, three steps, and he went to lift a hand and couldn't on account of the bracelets, and then stooped and kissed her on top of the head. She turned and stood still for ten seconds, giving Tolman a look which I couldn't see, but which probably made a trap door all the more desirable, and then turned again and walked out of the room.

Tolman couldn't speak. At least he didn't. Sheriff Pettigrew shook himself and said, "Come on, boys, I'll go along."

I shoved off without waiting for their exit. Constanza wasn't in the main hall. I halted there for an instant, thinking I might explore the large parlor in search of persons who might add to my information, and then decided that I had better first deposit what I had. So I went on out and hot-footed it back to Upshur.

Wolfe had finished with the papers and piled them neatly on the dresser, and was in the big chair, not quite big enough for him, with a book. He didn't look up as I went in, which meant that for the time being my existence was strictly my own affair. I adopted the suggestion and parked myself on the couch with a newspaper, which I opened up and looked at but didn't read. In about five minutes, after Wolfe had turned two pages, I said:

"By the way, it's a darned good thing you didn't take that job for Liggett. I mean the last one he offered. If you had, you would now be up a stump. As it stands now, you'd have a sweet time persuading Berin to be chef even for a soda fountain."

Neither he nor the book moved, but he did speak. "I presume Mr. Malfi has stabbed Mr. Berin. Good."

"No. He hasn't and he won't, because he can't get at him. Berin is wearing gyves on his way to jail. My friend Tolman has made a pinch. Justice has lit her torch."

"Pfui. If you must pester me with fairy tales, cultivate some imagination."

I said patiently, "Mr. Tolman has arrested Mr. Berin for the murder of Mr. Laszio and removed him to custody without bail. I saw it with these eyes."

The book went down. "Archie. If this is flummery—"

"No, sir. Straight."

"He has charged Berin?"

"Yes, sir."

"In the name of God, why? The man's a fool."

"That's what Miss Berin said. She said pig of a fool."

The book had remained suspended in the air; now it was lowered to rest on the expanse of thigh. In a few moments it was lifted again and opened for a page to get turned down, and was then deposited on a little stand beside the chair. Wolfe leaned back and shut his eyes and his fingers met at the front of his belly; and I saw his lips push out, then in again . . . then out, then in. . . . It startled me, and I wondered what all the excitement was about.

After a while he said without opening his eyes, "You understand, Archie, that I would hesitate to undertake anything which might conceivably delay our return to New York."

"It could be called hesitating. There're stronger words."

"Yes. On the other hand, I should be as great a fool as Mr. Tolman were I to ignore such an opportunity as this. It looks as if the only way to take advantage of it is to learn who killed Mr. Laszio. The question is, can we do it in thirty-one hours? Twenty-eight really, since at the dinner to-morrow evening I am to deliver my talk on American contributions to la haute cuisine. Can we do it in twenty-eight hours?"

"Sure we can." I waved a hand. "Gosh, with me to do the planning and you to handle the details—"

"Yes. Of course they may have abandoned the idea of that dinner, but I should think not, since only once in five years . . . well. The first step—"

"Excuse me." I had dropped the paper to the floor and straightened up, with a warm feeling that here was going to be a chance to get my circulation started. "Why not get in touch with Liggett and accept his offer? Since we're going to do it anyway, we might as well annex a fee along with it."

"No. If I engage with him and am not finished by to-morrow evening—no. Freedom is too precious collateral for any fee. We shall proceed. The first step is obvious. Bring Mr. Tolman here at once."

That was like him. Some day he would tell me to go get the Senate and the House of Representatives. I said, "Tolman's sore at you because you wouldn't come to the phone this morning. Also he thinks he has his man and is no longer interested. Also I don't believe—"

"Archie! You said you will do the planning. Please go for Mr. Tolman, and plan how to persuade him on the way."

I went for my hat.

6

I JOGGED smartly back along the path to Pocahontas, thinking I might catch Tolman before he got away, with my brain going faster than my feet trying to invent a swift one for him, but I was too late. The greenjacket at the door so advised me, saying that Tolman had got in his car on the driveway and headed west. I about-faced and broke into a gallop. If there had been a stop at the hotel, as seemed probable, I might head him off there. I was panting a little by the time I entered the lobby and began darting glances around through the palms and pillars and greenjackets, and customers in everything from riding togs to what resembled the last safeguard of Gypsy Rose Lee. I was about to advance to the desk to make an inquiry when I heard a grim voice at my elbow:

"Hello, cockroach."

I wheeled and narrowed my eyes at it. "Hello, rat. Not even rat. Something I don't know the name of, because it lives underground and eats the roots of weeds."

Gershom Odell shook his head. "Not me. Wrong number. What you said about Laszio getting croaked, I had already told the night clerk just as conversation, and of course they faced me with it after it happened, and what could I do? But your shooting off your face about throwing stones—didn't you have brains enough to know you would make the damn sheriff suspicious?"

"I haven't got any brains, I'm a detective. The sheriff's busy elsewhere anyhow." I waved a hand. "Forget it. I want to see Tolman. Is he around here?"

Odell nodded. "He's in the manager's office with Ashley.

Also a few other people, including a man from New York named Liggett. Which reminds me I want to see you. You think you're so damn smart I'd like to lay you flat and sit on you, but I'll have to let that go because I want you to do me a favor."

"Let it go anyway. Sit not lest you be sat on."

"Okay. What I wanted to ask you about, I'm fed up with the sticks. It's a good job here in a way, but in other ways it's pretty crummy. To-day when Raymond Liggett landed here in a plane, the first person he asked for was Nero Wolfe, and he hoofed it right over to Upshur without going to his room or even stopping to say hello to Ashley. So I figured Wolfe must stand pretty high with him, and it occurred to me that about the best berth in this country for a house detective is the Hotel Churchill." Odell's eyes gleamed. "Boy, would that be a spot for a good honest man like me! So while Liggett's here, if you could tell Wolfe about me and he could tell Liggett and arrange for me to meet him without the bunch here getting wise in case I don't land it. . . ."

I was thinking, sure as the devil we're turning into an employment agency. I hate to disappoint people, and therefore I kidded Odell along, without actually misrepresenting the condition of Wolfe's intimacy with Raymond Liggett, and keeping one eye on the closed door which was the entrance to the manager's office. I told him that I was glad to see that he wasn't satisfied to stay in a rut and had real ambition and so forth, and it was a very nice chat, but I knocked off abruptly when I saw the closed door open and my friend Barry Tolman emerge alone. Giving Odell a friendly clap on the shoulder with enough muscle in it to give him an idea how easy I would be to sit on, I left him and followed my prey among the pillars and palms, and at a likely spot near the main entrance pounced on him.

His blue eyes looked worried and his whole face untidy. He recognized me: "Oh. What do you want? I'm in a hurry."

I said, "So am I. I'm not going to apologize about Wolfe not coming to the phone this morning, because if you know anything about Nero Wolfe you know he's eccentric and try and change him. I happened to see you going by just now, and I met you on the train Monday night and liked your face because you looked like a straight-shooter, and a little while ago I saw you pinching Berin for murder—I suppose you didn't notice me, but I was there—and I went back to the suite and told Wolfe about it, and I think you ought to know what he did when I told him. He pinched his nose."

"Well?" Tolman was frowning. "As long as he didn't pinch mine—what about it?"

"Nothing, except that if you knew Wolfe as I do . . . I have never yet seen him pinch his nose except when he was sure that some fellow being was making a complete jackass of himself. Do as you please. You're young and so you've got most of your bad mistakes ahead of you yet. I just had a friendly impulse, seeing you go by, and I *think* I can persuade Wolfe to have a talk with you if you want to come over to the suite with me right now. Anyhow, I'm willing to try it." I moved back a step. "Suit yourself, since you're in a hurry. . . ."

He kept the frown on. But I was pleased to see that he didn't waste time in fiddle-faddle. He frowned into my frank eyes a few seconds, then said abruptly, "Come on," and headed for the exit. I trotted behind glowing like a boy scout.

When we got to Upshur I had to continue the play, but I didn't feel like leaving him loose in the public hall, so I took him to the suite and put him in my room and shut the door on him. Then I went across to Wolfe's room, shutting that door too, and sat down on the couch and grinned at the fat son-of-a-gun.

"Well?" he demanded. "Couldn't you find him?"

"Of course I could find him. I've got him." I thumbed to indicate where. "I had to come in first to try to persuade you to grant him an audience. It ought to take about five minutes. It's even possible he'll sneak into the foyer to listen at the door." I raised my voice. "What about justice? What about society? What about the right of every man? . . ."

Wolfe had to listen because there was no way out. I laid it on good and thick. When I thought enough time had elapsed I closed the valve, went to my room and gave Tolman the high sign with a look of triumph, and ushered him in. He looked so preoccupied with worry that for a second I thought he was going to miss the chair when he sat down.

He plunged into it. "I understand that you think I'm pulling a boner."

Wolfe shook his head. "Not my phrase, Mr. Tolman. I can't

71

very well have an intelligent opinion until I know the facts that moved you. Offhand, I fear you've been precipitate."

"I don't think so." Tolman had his chin stuck out. "I talked with people in Charleston on the phone, and they agreed with me. Not that I'm passing the buck; the responsibility is mine. Incidentally, I'm supposed to be in Charleston at six o'clock for a conference, and it's sixty miles. I'm not bull-headed about it; I'll turn Berin loose like that"—he snapped his fingers—"if I'm shown cause. If you've any information I haven't got I'd have been damned thankful to get it when I phoned you this morning, and I'd be thankful now. Not to mention the duty of a citizen..."

"I have no information that would prove Mr. Berin innocent." Wolfe's tone was mild. "It was Mr. Goodwin's ebullience that brought you here. I gave you my opinion last night. It might help if I knew what you based your decision on, short of what you value as secret. You understand I have no client. I am representing no one."

"I have no secrets. But I have enough to hold Berin and indict him and I think convict him. As for opportunity, you know about that. He has threatened Laszio's life indiscriminately, in the hearing of half a dozen people. I suppose he figured that it would be calculated that a murderer would not go around advertising it in advance, but I think he overplayed it. This morning I questioned everybody again, especially Berin and Vukcic, and I counted Vukcic out. I got various pieces of information. But I admit that the most convincing fact of all came through a suggestion from you. I compared those lists with the one we found in Laszio's pocket. No one except Berin got more than two wrong."

He got papers from his pocket and selected one. "The lists of five of them, among them Vukcic, agreed exactly with the correct list. Four of them, including you, made two mistakes each, and the same ones." He returned the papers to his pocket and leaned forward at Wolfe. "Berin had just two right! Seven wrong!"

In the silence Wolfe's eyes went nearly closed. At length he murmured, "Preposterous. Nonsense."

"Precisely!" Tolman nodded with emphasis. "It is incredible that in a test on which the other nine averaged over 90% correct, Berin should score 22%. It is absolutely conclusive of one of two things: either he was so upset by a murder he had just committed or was about to commit that he couldn't distinguish the tastes, or he was so busy with the murder that he didn't have time to taste at all, and merely filled out his list haphazard. I regard it as conclusive, and I think a jury will. And I want to say that I am mighty grateful to you for the suggestion you made. I freely admit it was damned clever and it was you who thought of it."

"Thank you. Did you inform Mr. Berin of this and request an explanation?"

"Yes. He professed amazement. He couldn't explain it."

"You said 'absolutely conclusive.' That's far too strong. There are other alternatives. Berin's list may be forged."

"It's the one he himself handed to Servan, and it bears his signature. It hadn't been out of Servan's possession when he gave the lists to me. Would you suspect Servan?"

"I suspect no one. The dishes or cards might have been tampered with."

"Not the cards. Berin says they were in consecutive order when he tasted, as they were throughout. As for the dishes, who did it, and who put them back in place again after Berin left?"

After another silence Wolfe murmured again, obstinately, "It remains preposterous."

"Sure it does." Tolman leaned forward, further than before. "Look here, Wolfe. I'm a prosecuting attorney and all that, and I've got a career to make and I know what it means to have a success in a sensational case like this, but you're wrong if you think it gave me any pleasure to make a quick grab for Berin as a victim. It didn't. I . . ." He stopped. He tried it again. "I . . . well, it didn't. For certain reasons, it was the hardest thing I've ever done in my life. But let me ask you a question. I want to make it a tight question. Granted these premises as proven facts: one, that Berin made seven mistakes on the list he filled out and signed; two, that when he tasted the dishes they and the cards were in the same condition and order as when the others did; three, that nothing can be discovered to cast doubt on those facts; four, that you have taken the oath of office as prosecuting attorney. Would you have Berin arrested for murder and try to convict him?"

"I would resign."

Tolman threw up both hands. "Why?"

"Because I saw Mr. Berin's face and heard him speak less than a minute after he left the dining room last night."

73

"Maybe you did, but I didn't. If our positions were reversed, would you accept my word and judgment as to the evidence of Berin's face and voice?"

"No."

"Or anyone's?"

"No."

"Have you any information that will explain, or help to explain, the seven errors on Berin's list?"

"No."

"Have you any information in addition to what you have given me that would tend to prove him innocent?"

"No."

"All right." Tolman sat back. He looked at me resentfully and accusingly, which struck me as unfair, and then let his eyes go back to Wolfe. His jaw was working, in a nervous side-to-side movement, and after awhile he seemed to become suddenly aware of that and clamped it tight. Then he loosened it again: "Candidly, I was hoping you would have. From what Goodwin said, I thought maybe you did. You said if you were in my place you'd resign. But what the devil good—"

I didn't get to hear the rest of it, on account of another rupture to Wolfe's plans for an afternoon of peaceful privacy. The knock on the outer door was loud and prolonged. I went to the foyer and opened up, half expecting to see the two visitors from New York again, in view of the recent developments, but instead it was a trio of a different nature: Louis Servan, Vukcic, and Constanza Berin.

Vukcic was brusque. "We want to see Mr. Wolfe."

I told them to come in. "If you wouldn't mind waiting in here?" I indicated my room. "He's engaged at the moment with Mr. Barry Tolman."

Constanza backed up and bumped the wall of the foyer. "Oh!" Her expression would have been justified if I had told her that I had my pockets full of toads and snakes and poisonous lizards. She made a dive for the knob of the outer door. Vukcic grabbed her arm and I said: "Now, hold it. Can Mr. Wolfe help it if an attractive young fellow insists on coming to cry on his shoulder? Here, this way, all of you—"

The door to Wolfe's room opened and Tolman appeared. It was a little dim in the foyer, and it took him a second to call the roll. When he saw her, he had called it a day. He stared at her and turned a muddy white, and his mouth

74

opened three times for words which got delayed en route. It didn't seem that she got any satisfaction out of the state he was in, for apparently she didn't see him; she looked at me and said that she supposed they could see Mr. Wolfe now, and Vukcic took her elbow, and Tolman sidestepped in a daze to let them by. I stayed behind to let Tolman out, which I did after he had exchanged a couple of words with Servan.

The new influx appeared neither to cheer Wolfe nor enrage him. He received Miss Berin without enthusiasm but with a little extra courtesy, and apologized to Vukcic and Servan for having stayed away all day from the gathering at Pocahontas Pavilion. Servan assured him politely that under the unhappy circumstances no apology was required, and Vukcic sat down and ran all his fingers through his dense tangle of hair and growled something about the rotten luck for the meeting of the fifteen masters. Wolfe inquired if the scheduled activities would be abandoned, and Servan shook his head. No, Servan said, they would continue with affairs although his heart was broken. He had for years been looking forward to the time when, as doyen of Les Quinze Maîtres, he would have the great honor of entertaining them as his guests; it was to have been the climax of his career, fittingly and sweetly in his old age; and what had happened was an incredible disaster. Nevertheless, they would proceed; he would that evening, as dean and host, deliver his paper on *Les Mystères du Goût*, on the preparation of which he had spent two years; at noon the next day they would elect new members—now, alas, four—to replace those deceased; and Thursday evening they would hear Mr. Wolfe's discourse on *Contributions Américaines à la Haute Cuisine*. What a calamity, what a destruction of friendly, confraternity!

Wolfe said, "But such melancholy, Mr. Servan, is the worst possible frame of mind for digestion. Since placidity is out of the question, wouldn't active hostility be better? Hostility for the person responsible?"

Servan's brows went up. "You mean for Berin?"

"Good heavens, no. I said the person responsible. I don't think Berin did it."

"Oh!" It was a cry from Constanza. From the way she jerked up in her chair, and the look she threw at Wolfe, I was expecting her to hop over and kiss him, or at least spill ginger ale on him, but she just sat and looked.

Vukcic growled, "They seem to think they have proof.

About those seven mistakes on his list of the sauces. How the devil could that be?"

"I have no idea. Why, Marko, do you think Berin did it?"

"No. I don't think." Vukcic ran his fingers through his hair again. "It's a hell of a thing. For awhile they suspected me; they thought because I had been dancing with Dina my blood was warm. It was warm!" He sounded defiant. "You wouldn't understand that, Nero. With a woman like that. She has a fire in her that warmed me once, and it could again, no doubt of that, if it came near and I felt it and let my head go I could throw myself in it." He shrugged, and suddenly got savage. "But to stab that dog in the back—I would not have done him that honor! Pull his nose well, is all one does with that sort of fellow!

"But look here, Nero." Vukcic tossed his head around. "I brought Miss Berin and Mr. Servan around to see you. I suggested it. If we had found that you thought Berin guilty, I don't know what could have been said, but luckily you don't. It has been discussed over there among most of us, and the majority have agreed to contribute to a purse for Berin's defense—since he is here in a country strange to him—and certainly I told them that the best way to defend him is to enlist you—"

"But please," Servan broke in earnestly. "Please, Mr. Wolfe, understand that we deplore the necessity we can't avoid—you are our guest, my guest, and I know it is unforgivable that under the circumstances we should dare to ask you—"

"But the fact is," Vukcic took it up, "that they were quite generous in their contributions to the purse, after I explained your habits in the matter of fees—"

Constanza had edged to the front of her chair and put in an oar: "The eleven thousand francs I promised, it will take awhile to get them because they're in the bank in Nice—"

"Confound it!" Wolfe had to make it almost a shout. He wiggled a finger at Servan. "Apparently, sir, Marko has informed you of my rapacity. He was correct; I need lots of money and ordinarily my clients get soaked. But he could have told you that I am also an incurable romantic. To me the relationship of host and guest is sacred. The guest is a jewel resting on the cushion of hospitality. The host is king, in his parlor and his kitchen, and should not condescend to a lesser rôle. So we won't discuss—"

76

"Damn all the words!" Vukcic gestured impatiently. "What do you mean, Nero, you won't do anything about Berin?"

"No. I mean we won't discuss purses and fees. Certainly I shall do something about Berin, I had already decided to before you came, but I won't take money from my hosts for it. And there is no time to lose, and I want to be alone here to consider the matter. But since you are here—" His eyes moved to Constanza. "Miss Berin. You seem to be convinced that your father didn't kill Mr. Laszio. Why?"

Her eyes widened at him. "Why . . . you're convinced too. You said so. My father wouldn't."

"Never mind about me. Speaking to the law, which is what we're dealing with, what evidence have you? Any?"

"Why . . . only . . . it's absurd! Anyone—"

"I see. You haven't any. Have you any notion, or any evidence, as to who did kill Laszio?"

"No! And I don't care! Only anyone would know—"

"Please, Miss Berin. I warn you, we have a difficult task and little time for it. I suggest that on leaving here you go to your room, compose your emotions, and in your mind thoroughly recapitulate—go back over—all you have seen and heard, everything, since your arrival at Kanawha Spa. Do it thoroughly. Write down anything that appears to have the faintest significance. Remember this is a job, and the only one you can perform that offers any chance of helping your father."

He moved his eyes again. "Mr. Servan. First, the same questions as Miss Berin. Proof of Berin's innocence, or surmise or evidence of another's guilt. Have you any?"

Servan slowly shook his head.

"That's too bad. I must warn you, sir, that it will probably develop that the only way of clearing Berin is to find where the guilt belongs and fasten it there. We can't clear everybody; after all, Laszio's dead. If you know of anything that would throw suspicion elsewhere, and withhold it, you can't pretend to be helping Berin."

The dean of the masters shook his head again. "I know of nothing that would implicate anybody."

"Very well. About Berin's list of the sauces. He handed it to you himself?"

"Yes, immediately on leaving the dining room."

"It bore his signature?"

77

"Yes. I looked at each one before putting it in my pocket, to be sure they could be identified."

"How sure are you that no one had a chance to change Berin's list after he handed it to you, before you gave it to Mr. Tolman?"

"Positive. Absolutely. The lists were in my inside breast pocket every moment. Of course, I showed them to no one."

Wolfe regarded him a little, sighed, and turned to Vukcic. "You, Marko. What do you know?"

"I don't know a damned thing."

"Did you ask Mrs. Laszio to dance with you?"

"I . . . what's that got to do with it?"

Wolfe eyed him and murmured, "Now, Marko. At the moment I haven't the faintest idea how I shall discover what must be discovered, and I must be permitted any question short of insult. Did you ask Mrs. Laszio to dance, or did she ask you?"

Vukcic wrinkled his forehead and sat. Finally he growled, "I think she suggested it. I might have if she didn't."

"Did you ask her to turn on the radio?"

"No."

"Then the radio and the dancing at that particular moment were her ideas?"

"Damn it." Vukcic was scowling at his old friend. "I swear I don't see, Nero—"

"Of course you don't. Neither do I. But sometimes it's astonishing how the end of a tangled knot gets buried. It is said that two sure ways to lose a friend are to lend him money and to question the purity of a woman's gesture to him. I wouldn't lose your friendship. It is quite likely that Mrs. Laszio found the desire to dance with you irresistible.—No, Marko, please; I mean no flippancy. And now, if you don't mind . . . Miss Berin? Mr. Servan? I must consider this business."

They got up. Servan tried, delicately, to mention the purse again, but Wolfe brushed it aside. Constanza went over and took Wolfe's hand and looked at him with an expression that may or may not have been pure but certainly had appeal in it. Vukcic hadn't quite erased his scowl, but joined the others in their thanks and seemed to mean it. I went to the foyer with them to open the door.

Returning, I sat and watched Wolfe consider. He was leaning back in his favorite position, though by no means as comfortably as in his own chair at home, with his eyes closed.

He might have been asleep but for the faint movement of his lips. I did a little considering on my own hook, but I admit mine was limited. It looked to me like Berin, but I was willing to let in either Vukcic or Blanc in case they insisted. As far as I could see, everyone else was absolutely out. Of course there was still the possibility that Laszio had been absent from the dining room only temporarily, during Vukcic's session with the dishes, and had later returned and Vallenko or Rossi had mistaken him for a pincushion before or after tasting, but I couldn't see any juice in that. I had been in the large parlor the entire evening, and I tried to remember whether I had at any time noticed anyone enter the small parlor—or rather, whether I would have been able to swear that no one had. I thought I would. After over half an hour of overworking my brain, it still looked to me like Berin, and I thought it just as well Wolfe had turned down two offers of a fee, since it didn't seem very probable he was going to earn one.

I saw Wolfe stir. He opened his mouth but not his eyes.

"Archie. Those two colored men on duty in the main foyer of Pocahontas Pavilion last evening. Find out where they are."

I went to the phone in my room, deciding that the quickest way was to get hold of my friend Odell and let him do it. In less than ten minutes I was back again with the report.

"They went on at Pocahontas again at six o'clock. The same two. It is now 6:07. Their names—"

"No, thanks. I don't need the names." Wolfe pulled himself up and looked at me. "We have an enemy who has sealed himself in. He fancies himself impregnable, and he well may be—no door, no gate, no window in his walls—or hers. Possibly hers. But there is one little crack, and we'll have to see if we can pry it open." He sighed. "Amazing what a wall that is; that one crack is all I see. If that fails us..." He shrugged. Then he said bitterly, "As you know, we are dressing for dinner this evening. I would like to get to the pavilion as quickly as possible. What the tongue has promised the body must submit to."

He began operations for leaving his chair.

7

IT WAS STILL twenty minutes short of seven o'clock when we got to Pocahontas. Wolfe had done pretty well with the black and white, considering that Fritz Brenner was nearly a thousand miles away, and I could have hired out as a window dummy.

Naturally I had some curiosity about Wolfe's interest in the greenjackets, but it didn't get satisfied. In the main hall, after we had been relieved of our hats, he motioned me on in to the parlor, and he stayed behind. I noted that Odell's information was correct; the two colored men were the same that had been on duty the evening before.

It was more than an hour until dinnertime, and there was no one in the large parlor except Mamma Mondor, knitting and sipping sherry, and Vallenko and Keith, with Lisette Putti between them, chewing the rag on a divan. I said hello and strolled over and tried to ask Mamma Mondor what was the French word for knitting, but she seemed dumb at signs and began to get excited, and it looked as it it might end in a fight, so I shoved off.

Wolfe entered from the hall, and I saw by the look in his eye that he hadn't lost the crack he had mentioned. He offered greetings around, made a couple of inquiries, and was informed that Louis Servan was in the kitchen overlooking the preparations for dinner. Then he came up to me and in a low tone outlined briefly an urgent errand. I thought he had a nerve to wait until I got my glad rags on to ask me to work up a sweat, particularly since no fee was involved, but I went for my hat without stopping to grumble.

I cut across the lawn to get to the main path and headed for the hotel. On the way I decided to use Odell again instead of trying to develop new contacts, and luckily I ran across him in the corridor by the elevators and without having to make inquiries. He looked at me pleased and expectant.

"Did you tell Wolfe? Has he seen Liggett?"

"Nope, not yet. Give us time, can't you? Don't you worry, old boy. Right now I need some things in a hurry. I need a good ink pad, preferably a new one, and fifty or sixty sheets of smooth white paper, preferably glazed, and a magnifying glass."

"Jumping Jesus." He stared at me. "Who you working for, J. Edgar Hoover?"

"No. It's all right, we're having a party. Maybe Liggett will be there. Step on it, huh?"

He told me to wait there and disappeared around the corner. In five minutes he was back, with all three items. As I took them he told me:

"I'll have to put the pad and paper on the bill. The glass is a personal loan, don't forget and skip with it."

I told him okay, thanked him, and beat it. On the way back I took the path which would carry me past Upshur, and I made a stop there and sought suite 60. I got a bottle of talcum powder from my bathroom and stuck it in my pocket, and my pen and a notebook, then found the copy of the *Journal of Criminology* I had brought along and thumbed through it to some plates illustrating new classifications of fingerprints. I cut one of the pages out of the magazine with my knife, rolled it up in the paper Odell had given me, and trotted out again and across to Pocahontas. All the time I was trying to guess at the nature of the crack Wolfe thought he was going to pry open with that array of materials.

I got no light on that point from Wolfe. He had apparently been busy, for though I hadn't been gone more than fifteen minutes I found him established in the biggest chair in the small parlor, alongside the same table behind which Tolman had been barricaded against the onslaught of Constanza Berin. Across the table from him, looking skeptical but resigned, was Sergei Vallenko.

Wolfe finished a sentence to Vallenko and then turned to me. "You have everything, Archie? Good. The pad and paper here on the table, please. I've explained to Mr. Servan that if I undertake this inquiry I shall have to ask a few questions of everyone and take fingerprint samples. He has sent Mr. Vallenko to us first. All ten prints, please."

That was a hot one. Nero Wolfe collecting fingerprints, especially after the cops had smeared all over the dining-room and it had been reopened to the public! I knew darned well it was phoney, but hadn't guessed his charade yet, so once again I had to follow his tail light without knowing the road. I got Vallenko's specimens, on two sheets, and labelled them, and Wolfe dismissed him with thanks.

I demanded, when we were alone, "What has this identification bureau—"

"Not now, Archie. Sprinkle powder on Mr. Vallenko's prints."

I stared at him. "In the name of God, why? You don't put powder—"

"It will look more professional and mysterious. Do it. Give me the page from the magazine.—Good. Satisfactory. We'll use only the upper half; cut it off and keep it in your pocket. Put the magnifying glass on the table—ah, Mme. Mondor? Asseyez-vous, s'il vous plaît."

She had her knitting along. He asked her some questions of which I never bothered him for a translation, and then turned her over to my department and I put her on record. I never felt sillier in my life than dusting that talcum powder on those fresh clear specimens. Our third customer was Lisette Putti, and she was followed by Keith, Blanc, Rossi, Mondor... Wolfe asked a few questions of all of them, but knowing his voice and manner as well as I did, it sounded to me as if his part of it was as phoney as mine. And it certainly didn't sound as if he was prying any crack open.

Then Lawrence Coyne's Chinese wife came in. She was dressed for dinner in red silk, with a sprig of mountain laurel in her black hair, and with her slim figure and little face and narrow eyes she looked like an ad for a Round the World cruise. At once I got a hint that it was her we were laying for, for Wolfe told me sharply to take my notebook, which he hadn't done for any of the others, but all he did was ask her the same line of questions and explain about the prints before I took them. However, there appeared to be more to come. As I gave her my handkerchief, already ruined, to wipe the tips of her fingers on, Wolfe settled back.

He murmured, "By the way, Mrs. Coyne, Mr. Tolman tells me that while you were outdoors last evening you saw no one but one of the attendants on one of the paths. You asked him about a bird you heard and he told you it was a whippoorwill. You had never heard a whippoorwill before?"

She had displayed no animation, and didn't now. "No, there aren't any in California."

"So I understand. I believe you went outdoors before the tasting of the sauces began, and returned to the parlor shortly after Mr. Vukcic entered the dining room. Isn't that right?"

"I went out before they began. I don't know who was in the dining room when I came back."

"I do. Mr. Vukcic." Wolfe's voice was so soft and unconcerned that I knew she was in for something. "Also, you told Mr. Tolman that you were outdoors all the time you were gone. Is that correct?"

She nodded. "Yes."

"When you left the parlor, after dinner, didn't you go to your room before you went outdoors?"

"No, it wasn't cold and I didn't need a wrap. . . ."

"All right. I'm just asking. While you were outdoors, though, perhaps you entered the left wing corridor by way of the little terrace and went to your room that way?"

"No." She sounded dull and calm. "I was outdoors all the time."

"You didn't go to your room at all?"

"No."

"Nor anywhere else?"

"Just outdoors. My husband will tell you, I like to go outdoors at night."

Wolfe grimaced. "And when you re-entered, you came straight through the main hall to the large parlor?"

"Yes, you were there. I saw you there with my husband."

"So you did. And now, Mrs. Coyne, I must admit you have me a little puzzled. Perhaps you can straighten it out. In view of what you have just told me, which agrees with your account to Mr. Tolman, what door was it that you hurt your finger in?"

She deadpanned him good. There wasn't a flicker. Maybe her eyes got a little narrower, but I couldn't see it. But she wasn't good enough to avoid stalling. After about ten seconds of the stony-facing she said, "Oh, you mean my finger." She glanced down at it and up again. "I asked my husband to kiss it."

Wolfe nodded. "I heard you. What door did you hurt it in?"

She was ready. "The big door at the entrance. You know how hard it is to push, and when it closed—"

He broke in sharply, "No, Mrs. Coyne, that won't do. The doorman and the hallman have been questioned and their statements taken. They remember your leaving and re-entering—in fact, they were questioned about it Tuesday night by Mr. Tolman. And they are both completely certain

83

that the doorman opened the door for you and closed it behind you, and there was no caught finger. Nor could it have been the door from the hall to the parlor, for I saw you come through that myself. What door was it?"

She was wearing the deadpan permanently. She said calmly, "The doorman is telling a lie because he was careless and let me get hurt."

"I don't think so."

"I know it. He is lying." Quickly and silently, she was on her feet. "I must tell my husband."

She was off, moving fast. Wolfe snapped, "Archie!" I skipped around and got in front of her, on her line to the door. She didn't try dodging, just stopped and looked up at my face. Wolfe said, "Come back and sit down. I can see that you are a person of decision, but so am I. Mr. Goodwin could hold you with one hand. You may scream and people will come, but they will go again and we'll be where we are now. Sit down, please."

She did so, and told him, "I have nothing to scream about. I merely wanted to tell my husband...."

"That the doorman lied. But he didn't. However, there's no need to torment you unnecessarily.—Archie, give me the photograph of those fingerprints on the dining room door."

I thought to myself, darn you, some day you're going to push the button for my wits when they're off on vacation, and then you'll learn to let me in on things ahead of time. But of course there was only one answer to this one. I reached in my pocket for the plate of reproductions I had cut from the magazine page, and handed it to him. Then, being on at last, I pushed across the specimens I had just taken from Lio Coyne's fingers. Wolfe took the magnifying glass and began to compare. He took his time, holding the two next to each other, looking closely through the glass back and forth, with satisfied nods at the proper intervals.

Finally he said, "Three quite similar. They would probably do. But the left index finger is absolutely identical and it's exceptionally clear. Here, Archie, see what you think."

I took the prints and the glass and put on a performance. The prints from the magazine happened to be from some blunt-fingered mechanic, and I don't believe I ever saw any two sets more unlike. I did a good job of it with the comparison, even counting out loud, and handed them back to Wolfe.

"Yes, sir." I was emphatic. "They're certainly the same. Anyone could see it."

Wolfe told Mrs. Coyne gently, almost tenderly, "You see, madam. I must explain. Of course everyone knows about fingerprints, but some of the newer methods of procuring them are not widely known. Mr. Goodwin here is an expert. He went over the doors from the dining room to the terrace—among other places—and brought out prints which the local police had been unable to discover, and made photographs of them. So as you see, modern methods of searching for evidence are sometimes fertile. They have given us conclusive proof that it was the door from the terrace to the dining room in which you caught your finger Tuesday evening. I had suspected it before, but there's no need to go into that. I am not asking you to explain anything. Your explanation, naturally, will have to be given to the police, after I have turned this evidence over to them, together with an account of your false statement that it was the main entrance door in which you caught your finger. And by the way, I should warn you to expect little courtesy from the police. After all, you didn't tell Mr. Tolman the truth, and they won't like that. It would have been more sensible if you had admitted frankly, when he asked about your excursion to see the night, that you had entered the dining room from the terrace."

She was as good at the wooden-face act as anyone I could remember. You would have sworn that if her mind was working at all it was on nothing more important than where she could have lost one of her chopsticks. At last she said, "I didn't enter the dining room."

Wolfe shrugged. "Tell the police that. After your lie to Mr. Tolman, and your lies to us here which are on record in Mr. Goodwin's notebook, and your attempt to accuse the doorman—and above all, these fingerprints."

She stretched a hand out. "Give them to me. I'd like to see them."

"The police may show them to you. If they choose. Forgive me, Mrs. Coyne, but this photograph is important evidence, and I'd like to be sure of turning it over to the authorities intact."

She stirred a little, but there was no change on her face. After another silence she said, "I did go into the left wing

85

corridor. By the little terrace. I went to my room and hurt my finger in the bathroom door. Then when Mr. Laszio was found murdered I was frightened and thought I wouldn't say I had been inside at all."

Wolfe nodded and murmured, "You might try that. Try it, by all means, if you think it's worth it. You realize, of course, that would leave your fingerprints on the dining room door to be explained. Anyhow you're in a pickle; you'll have to do the best you can." He turned abruptly to me and got snappy. "Archie, go to the booth in the foyer and phone the police at the hotel. Tell them to come at once."

I arose without excessive haste. I was prepared to stall with a little business with my notebook and pen, but it wasn't necessary. Her face showed signs of life. She blinked up at me and put out a hand at me, and then blinked at Wolfe, and extended both her cute little hands in his direction.

"Mr. Wolfe," she pleaded. "Please! I did no harm, I did nothing! Please not the police!"

"No harm, madam?" Wolfe was stern. "To the authorities investigating a murder you tell lies, and to me also, and you call that no harm? Archie, go on!"

"No!" She was on her feet. "I tell you I did nothing!"

"You entered the dining room within minutes, perhaps seconds, of the moment that Laszio was murdered. Did you kill him?"

"No! I did nothing! I didn't enter the dining room!"

"Your hand was on that door. What did you do?"

She stood with her eyes on him, and I stood with a foot poised, aching to call the cops I don't think. She ended the tableau by sitting down and telling Wolfe quietly, "I must tell you. Mustn't I?"

"Either me or the police."

"But if I tell you . . . you tell the police anyway."

"Perhaps. Perhaps not. It depends. In any event, you'll have to tell the truth sooner or later."

"I suppose so." Her hands were on the lap of her red dress with the fingers closely twined. "You see, I'm afraid. The police don't like the Chinese, and I am a Chinese woman, but that isn't it. I'm afraid of the man I saw in the dining room, because he must have killed Mr. Laszio. . . ."

Wolfe asked softly, "Who was it?"

"I don't know. But if I told about him, and he knew that I had seen him and had told . . . anyway, I am telling now. You

86

see, Mr. Wolfe, I was born in San Francisco and educated there, but I am Chinese, and we are never treated like Americans. Never. But anyway... what I told Mr. Tolman was the truth. I was outdoors all the time. I like outdoors at night. I was on the grass among the trees and shrubs, and I heard the whippoorwill, and I went across the driveway where the fountain is. Then I came back, to the side—not the left wing, the other side—and I could see dimly through the window curtains into the parlor, but I couldn't see into the dining room because the shades were drawn on the glass doors. I thought it would be amusing to watch the men tasting those dishes, which seemed very silly to me, so I went to the terrace to find a slit I could see through, but the shades were so tight there wasn't any. Then I heard a noise as if something had fallen over in the dining room. I couldn't hear just what it was like, because the sound of the radio was coming through the open window of the parlor. I stood there I don't know how long, but no other sound came, and I thought that if one of the men had got mad and threw the dishes on the floor that would be amusing, and I decided to open the door a crack and see, and I didn't think I'd be heard on account of the radio. So I opened it just a little. I didn't get it open enough even to see the table, because there was a man standing there by the corner of the screen, with his side turned to me. He had one finger pressed against his lips—you know, the way you do when you're hushing somebody. Then I saw who he was looking at. The door leading to the pantry hall was open, just a few inches, and the face of one of the Negroes was there, looking at the man by the screen. The man by the screen started to turn toward me, and I went to close the door in a hurry and my foot slipped, and I grabbed with my other hand to keep from falling, and the door shut on my finger. I thought it would be silly to get caught peeking in the dining room, so I ran back among the bushes and stood there a few minutes, and then I went to the main entrance—and you saw me enter the parlor."

Wolfe demanded, "Who was the man by the screen?"

She shook her head. "I don't know."

"Now, Mrs. Coyne. Don't start that again. You saw the man's face."

"I only saw the side of his face. Of course that was enough to tell he was a Negro."

Wolfe blinked. I blinked twice. Wolfe demanded, "A Negro? Do you mean one of the employees here?"

"Yes. In livery. Like the waiters."

"Was it one of the waiters at this pavilion?"

"No, I'm sure it wasn't. He was blacker than them and...I'm sure it wasn't. It wasn't anyone I could recognize."

"'Blacker than them and' what? What were you going to say?"

"That it wouldn't have been one of the waiters here because he came outdoors and went away. I told you I ran back among the bushes. I had only been there a few seconds when the dining room door opened and he came out and went around the path toward the rear. Of course I couldn't see very well from behind the bushes, but I supposed it was him."

"Could you see his livery?"

"Yes, a little, when he opened the door and had the light behind him. Then it was dark."

"Was he running?"

"No. Walking."

Wolfe frowned. "The one looking from the door to the pantry hall—was he in livery, or was it one of the cooks?"

"I don't know. The door was only open a crack, and I saw mostly his eyes. I couldn't recognize him either."

"Did you see Mr. Laszio?"

"No."

"No one else?"

"No. That's all I saw, just as I've told you. Everything. Then, later, when Mr. Servan told us that Mr. Laszio had been killed—then I knew what it was I had heard. I had heard Mr. Laszio fall, and I had seen the man that killed him. I knew that. I knew it must be that. But I was afraid to tell about it when they asked me questions about going outdoors...and anyway..." Her two little hands went up in a gesture to her bosom, and fell to her lap again. "Of course I was sorry when they arrested Mr. Berin, because I knew it was wrong. I was going to wait until I got back home, to San Francisco, and tell my husband about it, and if he said to I was going to write it all down and send it here."

"And in the meantime..." Wolfe shrugged. "Have you told anyone anything about it?"

"Nothing."

"Then don't." Wolfe sat up. "As a matter of fact, Mrs. Coyne, while you have acted selfishly, I confess you have acted wisely. But for the accident that you asked your husband to kiss your finger in my hearing, your secret was safe and therefore you were too. The murderer of Mr. Laszio probably knows that he was seen through that door, but not by whom, since you opened it only a few inches and outdoors was dark. Should he learn that it was you who saw him, even San Francisco might not be far enough away for you. It is in the highest degree advisable to do nothing that will permit him to learn it or cause him to suspect it. Tell no one. Should anyone show curiosity as to why you were kept so long in here while the other interviews were short, and ask you about it, tell him—or her—that you have a racial repugnance to having your fingerprints taken, and it required all my patience to overcome it. Similarly, I undertake that for the present the police will not question you, or even approach you, for that might arouse suspicion. And by the way—"

"You won't tell the police."

"I didn't say I wouldn't. You must trust my discretion. I was about to ask, has anyone questioned you particularly—except the police and me—regarding your visit to the night? Any of the guests here?"

"No."

"You're quite sure? Not even a casual question?"

"No, I don't remember . . ." Her brow was puckered above the narrow eyes. "Of course my husband—"

A tapping on the door interrupted her. Wolfe nodded at me and I went and opened it. It was Louis Servan. I let him in.

He advanced and told Wolfe apologetically, "I don't like to disturb you, but the dinner . . . it's five minutes past eight. . . ."

"Ah!" Wolfe made it to his feet in less than par. "I have been looking forward to this for six months. Thank you, Mrs. Coyne.—Archie, will you take Mrs. Coyne?—Could I have a few words with you, Mr. Servan? I'll make it as brief as possible?"

8

THE DINNER of the dean of The Fifteen Masters that evening, which by custom was given on the second day of their gathering once in every five years, was ample and elaborate as to fleshpots, but a little spotty as an occasion of festivity. The chatter during the hors d'oeuvres was nervous and jerky, and when Domenico Rossi made some loud remark in French three or four of them began to laugh and then suddenly stopped, and in the silence they all looked at one another.

To my surprise, Constanza Berin was there, but not adjoining me as on the evening before. She was on the other side, between Louis Servan, who was at the end, and a funny little duck with an uncontrolled mustache who was new to me. Leon Blanc, on my right, told me he was the French Ambassador. There were several other extra guests, among them my friend Odell's prospective employer, Raymond Liggett of the Hotel Churchill, Clay Ashley, the manager of Kanawha Spa, and Albert Malfi. Malfi's black eyes kept darting up and down the table, and on meeting the eyes of a master he delivered a flashing smile. Leon Blanc pointed a fork at him and told me, "See that fellow Malfi? He wants votes for to-morrow morning as one of Les Quinze Maîtres. Bah! He has no creation, no imagination! Berin trained him, that's all!" He waved the fork in contemptuous dismissal and then used it to scoop a mouthful of shad roe mousse.

The swamp-woman, now a swamp-widow, was absent, but everyone else—except Berin, of course—was there. Apparently Rossi hadn't been much impressed by the murder of his son-in-law; he was still ready for a scrap and full of personal and national comments. Mondor paid no attention to him. Vukcic was gloomy and ate like ten minutes for lunch. Ramsey Keith was close to pie-eyed, and about every five minutes he had a spell of giggles that might have been all right coming from his niece. During the entrée Leon Blanc told me, "That little Berin girl is a good one. You see her hold herself? Louis put her between him and the ambassador as a gesture to Berin. She justifies him; she represents her father bravely." Blanc sighed. "You heard what I told Mr. Wolfe in there when he questioned me. This was to be expected of Phillip Laszio, to let his sins catch up with him on this occasion. Infamy was in his blood. If he were alive I could kill him now—only I don't kill. I am a chef, but I couldn't be a butcher." He swallowed a mouthful of stewed rabbit and sighed again. "Look at Louis. This is a great affair for him, and this civet de lapin is in fact perfection, except for a slight excess of bouquet garni, possibly because the rabbits were young and tender flavored. Louis deserved gayety for this dinner and this salute to his cuisine, and look at us!" He went at the rabbit again.

The peak of the evening for me came with the serving of coffee and liqueurs, when Louis Servan arose to deliver his talk, which he had worked on for two years, on The Mysteries of Taste. I was warm and full inside, sipping a cognac which made me shut my eyes as it trickled into my throat—and I'm not a gourmet—so as not to leave any extra openings for the vapor to escape by, and I was prepared to be quietly entertained, maybe even instructed up to a point. Then he began: "Mesdames et messieurs, mes confrères des Quinze Maîtres: Il y a plus que cent ans un homme fameux, Brillat-Savarin le grand..." He went on from there. I was stuck. If I had known beforehand of the dean's intentions as to language I would have negotiated some sort of arrangement, but I couldn't simply get up and beat it. Anyway, the cognac bottle was two-thirds full, and the fundamental problem was to keep my eyes open, so I settled back to watch his gestures and mouth work. I guess it was a good talk. There were signs of appreciation throughout the hour and a half it lasted, nods and smiles and brows lifted, and applause here and there, and once in a while Rossi cried "Bravo!" and when Ramsey Keith got a fit of giggles Servan stopped and waited politely until Lisette Putti got him shushed. Once it got embarrassing, at least for me, when at the end of a sentence Servan was silent, and looked slowly around the table and couldn't go on, and two big tears left his eyes and rolled down his cheeks. There were murmurs, and Leon Blanc beside me blew his nose, and I cleared my throat a couple of times and reached for the cognac. When it was over they all left their places and gathered around him and shook hands, and a couple of them kissed him.

They drifted into the parlor in groups. I looked around for Constanza Berin, but apparently she had used up all her bravery for one evening, for she had disappeared. I turned to a hand on my arm and a voice:

"Pardon me, you are Mr. Goodwin? Mr. Rossi told me your name. I saw you... this afternoon with Mr. Wolfe...."

I acknowledged everything. It was Albert Malfi, the entrée man with no imagination. He made a remark or two about the dinner and Servan's speech and then went on, "I understand that Mr. Wolfe has changed his mind. He has been persuaded to investigate the . . . that is, the murder. I suppose that was because Mr. Berin was arrested?"

"No, I don't think so. It's just because he's a guest. A guest is a jewel resting on the cushion of hospitality."

"No doubt. Of course." The Corsican's eyes darted around and back to me. "There is something I think I should tell Mr. Wolfe."

"There he is." I nodded at where Wolfe was chinning with a trio of the masters. "Go tell him."

"But I don't like to interrupt him. He is the guest of honor of Les Quinze Maîtres." Malfi sounded awed. "I just thought I would ask you . . . perhaps I could see him in the morning? It may not be important. To-day we were talking with Mrs. Laszio—Mr. Liggett and I—and I was telling her about it—"

"Yeah?" I eyed him. "You a friend of Mrs. Laszio's?"

"Not a friend. A woman like her doesn't have friends, only slaves. I know her, of course. I was telling about this Zelota, and she and Mr. Liggett thought Mr. Wolfe should know. That was before Berin was arrested, when it was thought someone might have entered the dining room from the terrace—and killed Laszio. But if Mr. Wolfe is interested to clear Berin, certainly he should know." Malfi smiled at me. "You frown, Mr. Goodwin? You think if Berin is not cleared that would suit my ambition, and why am I so unselfish? I am not unselfish. It would be the greatest thing in my life if I could become chef de cuisine of the Hotel Churchill. But Jerome Berin saw my talent in the little inn at Ajaccio and took me into the world, and guided me with his genius, and I would not pay for my glory with his misfortune. Besides, I know him; he would not have killed Laszio that way, from behind. So I think I should tell Mr. Wolfe about Zelota. Mrs. Laszio and Mr. Liggett think the same. Mr. Liggett says it would do no good to tell the police, because they are satisfied with Berin."

I meditated on him. I was trying to remember where I had heard the name Zelota, and all at once it came to me. I said, "Uh-huh. You mean Zelota of Tarragona. Laszio stole something from him in 1920."

Malfi looked surprised. "You know of Zelota?"

"Oh, a little. A few things. What's he been up to? Or would you rather wait and tell Wolfe about it in the morning?"

"Not necessarily. Zelota is in New York."

"Well, he's got lots of company." I grinned. "Being in New

York is no crime. It's full of people who didn't kill Laszio. Now if he was in Kanawha Spa, that might be different."

"But maybe he is."

"He can't be in two places at once. Even a jury wouldn't believe that."

"But he might have come here. I don't know what you know about Zelota, but he hated Laszio more than—" Malfi shrugged. "He hated him bitterly. Berin often spoke to me about it. And about a month ago Zelota turned up in New York. He came and asked me for a job. I didn't give him one, because there is nothing left of him but a wreck, drink has ruined him, and because I remembered what Berin had told me about him and I thought perhaps he wanted a job at the Churchill only for a chance to get at Laszio. I heard later that Vukcic gave him a job on soup at Rusterman's, and he only lasted a week." He shrugged again. "That's all. I told Mrs. Laszio and Mr. Liggett about it, and they said I should tell Mr. Wolfe. I don't know anything more about Zelota."

"Well, much obliged. I'll tell Wolfe. Will you still be here in the morning?"

He said yes, and his eyes began to dart around again and he shoved off, apparently to electioneer. I strolled around a while, finding opportunities for a few morsels of harmless eavesdropping, and then I saw Wolfe's finger crooked at me and went to him. He announced that it was time to leave.

Which suited me. I was ready for the hay. I went to the hall and got our hats and waited with them, yawning, while Wolfe completed his good-nights. He joined me and we started out, but he stopped on the threshold and told me, "By the way, Archie. Give these men a dollar each. Appreciation for good memories."

I shelled out to the two greenjackets, from the expense roll.

In our own suite 60, over at Upshur, having switched on the lights and closed a window so the breeze wouldn't chill his delicate skin while undressing, I stood in the middle of his room and stretched and enjoyed a real yawn.

"It's a funny thing about me. If I once get to bed really late, like last night at four o'clock, I'm not really myself again until I catch up. I was afraid you were going to hang around over there and chew the rag. As it is, it's going on for midnight—"

I stopped because his actions looked suspicious. He wasn't

even unbuttoning his vest. Instead, he was getting himself arranged in the big chair in a manner which indicated that he expected to be there awhile. I demanded:

"Are you going to start your brain going at this time of night? Haven't you done enough for one evening?"

"Yes." He sounded grim. "But there is more to do. I arranged with Mr. Servan for the cooks and waiters of Pocahontas Pavilion to call on us soon as they have finished. They will be here in a quarter of an hour."

"Well for God's sake." I sat down. "Since when have we been on the night shift?"

"Since we found Mr. Laszio with a knife in him." He sounded grimmer. "We have but little time. Not enough perhaps, in view of Mrs. Coyne's story."

"And those blackbirds coming in a flock? At least a dozen."

"If by blackbirds you mean men with dark skin, yes."

"I mean Africans." I stood up again. "Listen, boss. You've lost your sense of direction, honest you have. Africans or blackbirds or whatever you like, they can't be handled this way. They don't intend to tell anything or they would have told that squint-eyed sheriff when he questioned them. Are you expecting me to use a carpetbeater on the whole bunch? The only thing is to get Tolman and the sheriff here first thing in the morning to hear Mrs. Coyne's tale, and let them go on from there."

Wolfe grunted. "They arrive at eight o'clock. They hear her story and they believe it or they don't—after all, she is Chinese. They question her at length, and even if they believe her they do not immediately release Berin, for her story doesn't explain the errors on his list. At noon they begin with the Negroes, singly. God knows what they do or how much time they take, but the chances are that Thursday midnight, when our train leaves for New York, they will not have finished with the Negroes, and they may have discovered nothing."

"They're more apt to than you are. I'm warning you, you'll see. These smokes can take it, they're used to it. Do you believe Mrs. Coyne's tale?"

"Certainly, it was obvious."

"Would you mind telling me how you knew she had hurt her finger in the dining room door?"

"I didn't. I knew she had told Tolman that she had gone directly outside, had stayed outside, and had returned direct-

94

ly to the parlor; and I knew that she had hurt her finger in a door. When she told me she had caught her finger in the main entrance door, which I knew to be untrue, I knew she was concealing something, and I proceeded to make use of the evidence we had prepared."

"*I* had prepared." I sat down. "Some day you'll try to bluff the trees out of their leaves. Would you mind telling me now what motive one of these smokes had for bumping off Laszio?"

"I suppose he was hired." Wolfe grimaced. "I don't like murderers, though I make my living through them. But I particularly dislike murderers who buy the death they seek. One who kills at least keeps the blood on his own hands. One who pays for killing—pfui! That is worse than repugnant, it is dishonorable. I presume the colored man was hired. Naturally, that's an annoying complication for us."

"Not so terrible." I waved a hand. "They'll be here pretty soon. I'll arrange them for you in a row. Then you'll give them a little talk on citizenship and the Ten Commandments, and explain how illegal it is to croak a guy for money even if you get paid in advance, and then you'll ask whoever stabbed Laszio to raise his hand and his hand will shoot up, and then all you'll have to do is ask who paid him and how much—"

"That will do, Archie." He sighed. "It's amazing how patiently and with what forbearance I have tolerated—but there they are. Let them in."

That was an instance when Wolfe himself jumped to an unwarranted conclusion, which was a crime he often accused me of. For when I made it through the foyer and opened the door to the hall, it wasn't Africans I found waiting there, but Dina Laszio. I stared at her a second, adjusting myself to the surprise. She put her long sleepy eyes on me and said:

"I'm sorry to disturb you so late, but—may I see Mr. Wolfe?"

I told her to wait and returned to the inner chamber.

"Not men with dark skin, but a woman. Mrs. Phillip Laszio wants to see you."

"What? Her?"

"Yes, sir. In a dark cloak and no hat."

Wolfe grimaced. "Confound that woman! Bring her in here."

I SAT AND WATCHED and listened and felt cynical. Wolfe rubbed his cheek with the tip of his forefinger, slowly and rhythmically, which meant he was irritated but attentive. Dina Laszio was on a chair facing him, with her cloak thrown back, her smooth neck showing above a plain black dress with no collar, her body at ease, her eyes dark in shadow.

Wolfe said, "No apology is needed, madam. Just tell me about it. I'm expecting callers and am pressed for time."

"It's about Marko," she said.

"Indeed. What about Marko?"

"You're so brusque." She smiled a little, and the smile clung to the corners of her mouth. "You should know that you can't expect a woman to be direct like that. We don't take the road, we wind around. You know that. Only I wonder how much you know about women like me."

"I couldn't say. Are you a special kind?"

She nodded. "I think I am. Yes, I know I am. Not because I want to be or try to be, but..." She made a little gesture. "It has made my life exciting, but not very comfortable. It will end...I don't know how it will end. Right now I am worried about Marko, because he thinks you suspect him of killing my husband."

Wolfe stopped rubbing his cheek. He told her, "Nonsense."

"No, it isn't. He thinks that."

"Why? Did you tell him so?"

"No. And I resent—" She stopped herself. She leaned forward, her head a little on one side, her lips not quite meeting, and looked at him. I watched her with pleasure. I suppose she was telling the truth when she said she didn't try to be a special kind of woman, but she didn't have to try. There was something in her—not only in her face, it came right out through her clothes—that gave you an instinctive impulse to start in that direction. I kept on being cynical, but it was easy to appreciate that there might be a time when cynicism wouldn't be enough.

She asked with a soft breath, "Mr. Wolfe, why do you

always jab at me? What have you got against me? Yesterday, when I told you what Phillip told me about the arsenic... and now when I tell you about Marko..."

She leaned back. "Marko told me once, long ago, that you don't like women."

Wolfe shook his head. "I can only say, nonsense again. I couldn't rise to that impudence. Not like women? They are astounding and successful animals. For reasons of convenience, I merely preserve an appearance of immunity which I developed some years ago under the pressure of necessity. I confess to a specific animus toward you. Marko Vukcic is my friend; you were his wife; and you deserted him. I don't like you."

"So long ago!" She fluttered a hand. Then she shrugged. "Anyway, I am here now in Marko's behalf."

"You mean he sent you?"

"No. But I came, for him. It is known, of course, that you have engaged to free Berin of the charge of killing my husband. How can you do that except by accusing Marko? Berin says Phillip was in the dining room, alive, when he left. Marko says Phillip was not there when he entered. So if not Berin, it must have been Marko. And then, you asked Marko to-day if he asked me to dance or suggested that I turn on the radio. There could be only one reason why you asked him that: because you suspected that he wanted the radio going so that no noise would be heard from the dining room when he... if anything happened in there."

"So Marko told you that I asked about the radio."

"Yes." She smiled faintly. "He thought I should know. You see, he has forgiven what you will not forgive—"

I missed the rest of that on account of a knock on the door. I went to the foyer, closing the door of Wolfe's room behind me, and opened up. The sight in the hall gave me a shock, even though I had been warned. It looked like half of Harlem. Four or five were greenjackets who a couple of hours back had been serving the dean's dinner to us, and the others, the cooks and helpers, were in their own clothes. The light brown middle-aged one in front with the bottom of one ear chopped off was the head waiter in charge at Pocahontas, and I felt friendly to him because it was he who had left the cognac bottle smack in front of me at the table. I told them to come on in and stepped aside not to get trampled, and directed them through to my room and followed them in.

"You'll have to wait in here, boys, Mr. Wolfe has a visitor. Sit on something. Sit on the bed, it's mine and it looks like I won't be using it anyway. If you go to sleep, snore a couple of good ones for me."

I left them there and went back to see how Wolfe was getting along with the woman he didn't like. Neither of them bothered with a glance at me as I sat down. She was saying:

"... but I know nothing about it beyond what I told you yesterday. Certainly I know there are other possibilities besides Berin and Marko. As you say, someone could have entered the dining room from the terrace. That's what you're thinking of, isn't it?"

"It's a possibility. But go back a little, Mrs. Laszio. Do you mean to say that Marko Vukcic told you of my asking him about the radio, and expressed the fear that I suspected him of having the radio turned on to give him an opportunity for killing your husband?"

"Well..." She hesitated. "Not exactly like that. Marko would not express a fear. But the way he told me about it—that was obviously in his mind. So I've come to you to find out if you do suspect him."

"You've come to defend him? Or to make sure that my clumsiness hasn't missed *that* inference from the timeliness of the radio?"

"Neither." She smiled at him. "You can't make me angry, Mr. Wolfe. Why, do you make other inferences? Many of them?"

Wolfe shook his head impatiently. "You can't do that, madam. Give it up. I mean your affected insouciance. I don't mind fencing when there's time for it, but it's midnight and there are men in that other room waiting to see me.—Please let me finish. Let me clear away some fog. I have admitted an animus toward you. I knew Marko Vukcic both before and after he married you. I saw the change in him. Then why was I not grateful when you suddenly selected a new field for your activities? Because you left débris behind you. It is not decent to induce the cocaine habit in a man, but it is monstrous to do so and then suddenly withdraw his supply of the drug. Nature plainly intends that a man should nourish a woman, and a woman a man, physically and spiritually, but there is no nourishment in you for anybody; the vapor that comes from you, from your eyes, your lips, your soft skin, your contours, your movements, is not beneficent but malignant. I'll grant you everything: you were alive, with your instincts and appetites, and you saw Marko and wanted him. You enveloped him with your miasma—you made that the only air he wanted to breathe—and then by caprice, without warning, you deprived him of it and left him gasping."

She didn't bat an eyelash. "But I told you I was a special kind—"

"Permit me. I haven't finished. I am seizing an opportunity to articulate a grudge. I was wrong to say caprice, it was cold calculation. You went to Laszio, a man twice your age, because it was a step up, not emotionally but materially. Probably you had also found that Marko had too much character for you. The devil only knows why you went no higher than Laszio, in so broad a field as New York, who after all—from your standpoint—was only a salaried chef; but of course you were young, in your twenties—how old are you now?"

She smiled at him.

He shrugged. "I suppose, too, it was a matter of intelligence. You can't have much. Essentially, in fact, you are a lunatic, if a lunatic is an individual dangerously maladjusted to the natural and healthy environment of its species—since the human equipment includes, for instance, a capacity for personal affection and a willingness to strangle selfish and predatory impulse with the rope of social decency. That's why I say you're a lunatic." He sat up and wiggled a finger at her. "Now look here. I haven't time for fencing. I do not suspect Marko of killing your husband, though I admit it is possible he did it. I have considered all the plausible inferences from the coincidence of the radio, am still considering them, and have reached no conclusion. What else do you want to know?"

"All that you said. . . ." Her hand fluttered and rested again on the arm of her chair. "Did Marko tell you all that about me?"

"Marko hasn't mentioned your name for five years. What else do you want to know?"

She stirred. I saw her breast go up and down, but there was no sound of the soft sigh. "It wouldn't do any good, since I'm a lunatic. But I thought I would ask you if Malfi had told you about Zelota."

"No. What about him? Who is he?"

I horned in. "He told me." Their eyes moved to me and I

went on, "I hadn't had a chance to report it. Malfi told me in the parlor after dinner that Laszio stole something a long time ago from a guy named Zelota, and Zelota had sworn to kill him, and about a month ago he showed up in New York and went to Malfi to ask for a job. Malfi wouldn't give him one, but Vukcic did, at Rusterman's, and Zelota only lasted a week and then disappeared. Malfi said he told Liggett and Mrs. Laszio about it and they thought he ought to tell you."

"Thanks.—Anything else, madam?"

She sat and looked at him. Her lids were so low that I couldn't see what her eyes were like, and I doubted if he could. Then without saying anything she pulled a hot one. She got up, taking her time, leaving her cloak there on the back of the chair, and stepped over to Wolfe and put her hand on his shoulder and patted it. He moved and twisted his big neck to look up at her, but she stepped away again with a smile at the corners of her mouth, and reached for the cloak. I hopped across to hold it for her, thinking I might as well get a pat too, but apparently she didn't believe in spoiling the help. She told Wolfe good-night, neither sweet nor sour, just good-night, and started off. I went to the foyer to let her out.

I returned and grinned down at Wolfe. "Well, how do you feel? Was she marking you for slaughter? Or putting a curse on you? Or is that how she starts the miasma going?" I peered at the shoulder she had patted. "About this Zelota business, I was going to tell you when she interrupted us. You noticed that Malfi said she told him to tell you about it. It seems that Malfi and Liggett were with her during the afternoon to offer consolation."

Wolfe nodded. "But, as you see, she is inconsolable. Bring those men in."

10

IT LOOKED hopeless to me. I would have made it at least ten to one that Wolfe's unlimited conceit was going to cost us most of a night's sleep with nothing to chalk up against it. It struck me as plain silly, and I might have gone so far as to say that his tackling that array of Africans in a body showed a dangerous maladjustment to the natural and healthy environment of a detective. Picture it: Lio Coyne had caught a glimpse of a greenjacket she couldn't recognize standing by the end of the screen with his finger on his lips, and another servant's face—chiefly his eyes, and she couldn't recognize him either— peeking through a crack in the door that led to the pantry hall and on to the kitchen. That was our crop of facts. And the servants had already told the sheriff that they had seen and heard nothing. Fat chance. There might have been a slim one if they had been taken singly, but in a bunch like that, not for my money.

The chair problem was solved by letting them sit on the floor. Fourteen altogether. Wolfe, using his man-to-man tone, apologized for that. Then he wanted to know their names, and made sure that he got everyone; that used up ten minutes. I was curious to see how he would start the ball rolling, but there were other preliminaries to attend to; he asked what they would like to drink. They mumbled that they didn't want anything, but he said nonsense, we would probably be there most of the night, which seemed to startle them and caused some murmuring. It ended by my being sent to the phone to order an assortment of beer, bourbon, ginger ale, charged water, glasses, lemons, mint and ice. An expenditure like that meant that Wolfe was in dead earnest. When I rejoined the gathering he was telling a plump little runt, not a greenjacket, with a ravine in his chin:

"I'm glad of this opportunity to express my admiration, Mr. Crabtree. Mr. Servan tells me that the shad roe mousse was handled entirely by you. Any chef would have been proud of it. I noticed that Mr. Mondor asked for more. In Europe they don't have shad roe."

The runt nodded solemnly, with reserve. They were all using plenty of reserve, not to mention constraint, suspicion and reticence. Most of them weren't looking at Wolfe or at much of anything else. He sat facing them, running his eyes over them. Finally he sighed and began:

"You know, gentlemen, I have had very little experience in dealing with black men. That may strike you as a tactless remark, but it really isn't. It is certainly true that you can't deal with all men alike. It is popularly supposed that in this part of the country whites adopt a well-defined attitude in dealing with the blacks, and blacks do the same in dealing with whites. That is no doubt true up to a point, but it is subject to enormous variation, as your own experience will show you. For instance, say you wish to ask a favor here at Kanawha Spa, and you approach either Mr. Ashley, the manager, or Mr. Servan. Ashley is bourgeois, irritable, conventional, and rather pompous, Servan is gentle, generous, sentimental, and an artist—and also Latin. Your approach to Mr. Ashley would be quite different from your approach to Mr. Servan.

"But even more fundamental than the individual differences are the racial and national and tribal differences. That's what I mean when I say I've had limited experience in dealing with black men. I mean black Americans. Many years ago I handled some affairs with dark-skinned people in Egypt and Arabia and Algiers, but of course that has nothing to do with you. You gentlemen are Americans, must more completely Americans than I am, for I wasn't born here. This is your native country. It was you and your brothers, black and white, who let me come here to live, and I hope you'll let me say, without getting maudlin, that I'm grateful to you for it."

Somebody mumbled something. Wolfe disregarded it and went on: "I asked Mr. Servan to have you come over here tonight because I want to ask you some questions and find out something. That's the only thing I'm interested in: the information I want to get. I'll be frank with you; if I thought I could get it by bullying you and threatening you, I wouldn't hesitate a moment. I wouldn't use physical violence even if I could, because one of my romantic ideas is that physical violence is beneath the dignity of a man, and that whatever you get by physical aggression costs more than it is worth. But I confess that if I thought threats or tricks would serve my purpose with you, I wouldn't hesitate to use them. I'm convinced they wouldn't, having meditated on this situation, and that's why I'm in a hole. I have been told by white Americans that the only way to get anything out of black Americans is by threats, tricks, or violence. In the first place, I doubt if it's true; and even if it is true generally I'm sure it isn't in this case. I know of no threats that would be effective, I can't think up a trick that would work, and I can't use violence."

Wolfe put his hands at them palms up. "I need the information. What are we going to do?"

Someone snickered, and others glanced at him—a tall skinny one squatting against the wall, with high cheekbones, dark brown. The runt whom Wolfe had complimented on the shad roe mousse glared around like a sergeant at talking in the ranks. The one that sat stillest was the one with the flattest nose, a young one, big and muscular, a greenjacket that I had noticed at the pavilion because he never opened his mouth to reply to anything. The headwaiter with the chopped-off ear said in a low silky tone:

"You just ask us and we tell you. That's what Mr. Servan said we was to do."

Wolfe nodded at him. "I admit that seems the obvious way, Mr. Moulton. And the simplest. But I fear we would find ourselves confronted by difficulties."

"Yes, sir. What is the nature of the difficulties?"

A gruff voice boomed: "You just ask us and we tell you anything." Wolfe aimed his eyes at the source of it:

"I hope you will. Would you permit a personal remark? That is a surprising voice to come from a man named Hyacinth Brown. No one would expect it. As for the difficulties—Archie, there's the refreshment. Perhaps some of you would help Mr. Goodwin?"

That took another ten minutes, or maybe more. Four or five of them came along, under the headwaiter's direction, and we carried the supplies in and got them arranged on a table against the wall. Wolfe was provided with beer. I had forgot to include milk in the order, so I made out with a bourbon highball. The muscular kid with the flat nose, whose name was Paul Whipple, took plain ginger ale, but all the rest accepted stimulation. Getting the drinks around, and back to their places on the floor, they loosened up a little for a few observations, but fell dead silent when Wolfe put down his empty glass and started off again:

"About the difficulties, perhaps the best way is to illustrate them. You know of course that what we are concerned with is the murder of Mr. Laszio. I am aware that you have told the sheriff that you know nothing about it, but I want some details from you, and besides, you may have recollected some incident which slipped your minds at the time you talked with the sheriff. I'll begin with you, Mr. Moulton. You were in the kitchen Tuesday evening?"

"Yes, sir. All evening. There was to be the oeufs au cheval served after they got through with those sauces."

"I know. We missed that. Did you help arrange the table with the sauces?"

"Yes, sir." The headwaiter was smooth and suave. "Three of us helped Mr. Laszio. I personally took in the sauces on the serving wagon. After everything was arranged he rang for me only once, to remove the ice from the water. Except for that, I was in the kitchen all the time. All of us were."

"In the kitchen, or the pantry hall?"

"The kitchen. There was nothing to go to the pantry for. Some of the cooks were working on the oeufs au cheval, and the boys were cleaning up, and some of us were eating what was left of the duck and other things. Mr. Servan told us we could."

"Indeed. That was superlative duck."

"Yes, sir. All of these gentlemen can cook like nobody's business. They sure can cook."

"They are the world's best. They are the greatest living masters of the subtlest and kindliest of the arts." Wolfe sighed, opened beer, poured, watched it foam to the top, and then demanded abruptly, "So you saw and heard nothing of the murder?"

"No, sir."

"The last you saw of Mr. Laszio was when you went in to take the ice from the water?"

"Yes, sir."

"I understand there were two knives for slicing the squabs. One of stainless steel with a silver handle, the other a kitchen carver. Were they both on the table when you took the ice from the water?"

The greenjacket hesitated only a second. "Yes, sir, I think they were. I glanced around the table to see that everything was all right, because I felt responsible, and I would have noticed if one of the knives had been gone. I even looked at the marks on the dishes—the sauces."

"You mean the numbered cards?"

"No, sir, you wouldn't, because the numbers were small, dishes with chalk so they wouldn't get mixed up in the kitchen or while I was taking them in."

"I didn't see them."

"No, sir, you wouldn't because the numbers were small, below the rim on the far side from you. When I put the dishes by the numbered cards I turned them so the chalk numbers were at the back, facing Mr. Laszio."

"And the chalk numbers were in the proper order when you took the ice from the water?"

"Yes, sir."

"Was someone tasting the sauces when you were in there?"

"Yes, sir, Mr. Keith."

"Mr. Laszio was there alive?"

"Yes, sir, he was plenty alive. He bawled me out for putting in too much ice. He said it froze the palate."

"So it does. Not to mention the stomach. When you were in there, I don't suppose you happened to look behind either of those screens."

"No, sir. We had shoved the screens back when we cleaned up after dinner."

"And after, you didn't enter the dining room again until after Mr. Laszio's body was discovered?"

"No, sir, I didn't."

"Nor look into the dining room?"

"No, sir."

"You're sure of that?"

"Sure I'm sure. I guess I'd remember my movements."

"I suppose you would." Wolfe frowned, fingered at this glass of beer, and raised it to his mouth and gulped. The headwaiter, self-possessed, took a sip of his highball, but I noticed that his eyes didn't leave Wolfe.

Wolfe put his glass down. "Thank you, Mr. Moulton." He put his eyes on the one on Moulton's left, a medium-sized one with gray showing in his kinky hair and wrinkles on his face. "Now Mr. Grant. You're a cook?"

"Yes, sir." His tone was husky and he cleared his throat and repeated, "Yes, sir. I work on fowl and game over at the hotel, but here I'm helping Crabby. All of us best ones, Mr. Servan sent us over here, to make an *impression*."

"Who is Crabby?"

"He means me." It was the plump runt with a ravine in his chin, the sergeant.

"Ah. Mr. Crabtree. Then you helped with the shad roe mousse."

Mr. Grant said, "Yes, sir. Crabby just super*vised*. I done the work."

"Indeed. My respects to you. On Tuesday evening, you were in the kitchen?"

"Yes, sir. I can make it short and sweet, mister. I was in the kitchen, I didn't leave the kitchen, and in the kitchen I remained. Maybe that covers it."

"It seems to. You didn't go to the dining room or the pantry hall?"

"No, sir. I just said about remaining in the kitchen."

"So you did. No offense, Mr. Grant. I merely want to make sure." Wolfe's eyes moved on. "Mr. Whipple. I know you, of course. You are an alert and efficient waiter. You anticipated my wants at dinner. You seem young to have developed such competence. How old are you?"

The muscular kid with the flat nose looked straight at Wolfe and said, "I'm twenty-one."

Moulton, the headwater, gave him an eye and told him, "Say sir." Then turned to Wolfe: "Paul's a college boy."

"I see. What college, Mr. Whipple?"

"Howard University. Sir."

Wolfe wiggled a finger. "If you feel rebellious about the sir, dispense with it. Enforced courtesy is worse than none. You are at college for culture?"

"I'm interested in anthropology."

"Indeed. I have met Franz Boas, and have his books autographed. You were, I remember, present on Tuesday evening. You waited on me at dinner."

"Yes, sir. I helped in the dining room after dinner, cleaning up and arranging for that demonstration with the sauces."

"Your tone suggests disapproval."

"Yes, sir. If you ask me. It's frivolous and childish for mature men to waste their time and talent, and other people's time—"

"Shut up, Paul." It was Moulton.

Wolfe said, "You're young, Mr. Whipple. Besides, each of us has his special set of values, and if you expect me to respect yours you must respect mine. Also I remind you that Paul Lawrence Dunbar said 'the best thing a 'possum ever does is fill an empty belly.'"

The college boy looked at him in surprise. "Do you know Dunbar?"

"Certainly. I am not a barbarian. But to return to Tuesday evening, after you finished helping in the dining room did you go to the kitchen?"

"Yes, sir."

"And left there—"

"Not at all. Not until we got word of what had happened."

"You were in the kitchen all the time?"

"Yes, sir."

"Thank you." Wolfe's eyes moved again. "Mr. Daggett..."

He went on, and got more of the same. I finished my highball and tilted my chair back against the wall and closed my eyes. The voices, the questions and answers, were just noises in my ears. I didn't get the idea, and it didn't sound to me as if there was any. Of course Wolfe's declaration that he wouldn't try any tricks because he didn't know any, was the same as a giraffe saying it couldn't reach up for a bite on account of its short neck. But it seemed to me that if he thought that monotonous ring around the rosie was a good trick, the sooner he got out of the mountain air of West Virginia and back to sea level, the better. On the questions and answers went; he didn't skimp anybody and he kept getting personal; he even discovered that Hyacinth Brown's wife had gone off and left him three pickaninnies to take care of. Once in awhile I opened my eyes to see how far around he had got, and then closed them again. My wrist watch said a quarter to two when I heard, through the open window, a rooster crowing away off.

I let my chair come down when I heard my name. "Archie. Beer please."

I was a little slow on the pickup and Moulton got to his feet and beat me to it. I sat down again. Wolfe invited the others to replenish, and a lot of them did. Then, after he had emptied a glass and wiped his lips, he settled back and ran his eyes over the gang, slowly around and back, until he had them all waiting for him.

He said in a new crisp tone: "Gentlemen, I said I would illustrate the difficulty I spoke of. It now confronts us. It was suggested that I ask for the information I want. I did so. You have all heard everything that was said. I wonder how many of you know that one of you told me a direct and deliberate lie."

Perfect silence. Wolfe let it gather for five seconds and then went on:

"Doubtless you share the common knowledge that on Tuesday evening some eight or ten minutes elapsed from the moment that Mr. Berin left the dining room until the moment that Mr. Vukcic entered it, and that Mr. Berin says that when he left Mr. Laszio was there alive, and Mr. Vukcic says that when he entered Mr. Laszio was not there at all. Of course Mr. Vukcic didn't look behind the screen. During that interval of eight or ten minutes someone opened the door from the terrace to the dining room and looked in, and saw two colored men. One, in livery, was standing beside the screen with his finger to his lips; the other had opened the door, a few inches, which led to the pantry hall, and was peering through, looking directly at the man by the screen. I have no idea who the man by the screen was. The one peering through the pantry hall door was one of you who are now sitting before me. That's the one who has lied to me."

Another silence. It was broken by a loud snicker, again from the tall skinny one who was still squatting against the wall. This time he followed it with a snort: "You tell 'em, boss!" Half a dozen black heads jerked at him and Crabtree said in disgust, "Boney, you damn drunken fool!" and then apologized to Wolfe, "He's a no good clown, that young man. Yes, sir. About what you say, we're all sorry you've got to feel that one of us told you a lie. You've got hold of some bad information."

"No. I must contradict you. My information is good."

Moulton inquired in his silky musical voice, "Might I ask who looked in the door and saw all that?"

"No. I've told you what was seen, and I know it was seen." Wolfe's eyes swept the faces. "Dismiss the idea, all of you, of impeaching my information. Those of you who have no knowledge of that scene in the dining room are out of this anyway; those who know of it know also that my information comes from an eye-witness. Otherwise how would I know, for instance, that the man by the screen had his finger to his lips? No, gentlemen, the situation is simple: I know that at least one of you lied, and he knows that I know it. I wonder if there isn't a chance of ending so simple a situation in a simple manner and have it done with? Let's try. Mr. Moulton, was it you who looked through that door—the door from the dining room to the pantry hall and saw the man by the screen with his finger to his lips?"

The headwaiter with the chopped-off ear slowly shook his head. "No, sir."

"Mr. Grant, was it you?"

"No, sir."

"Mr. Whipple, was it you?"

"No, sir."

He went on around, and piled up fourteen negatives out of

fourteen chances. Still batting a thousand. When he had completed that record he poured a glass of beer and sat and frowned at the foam. Nobody spoke and nobody moved. Finally, without drinking the beer, Wolfe leaned back and sighed patiently. He resumed in a murmur:

"I was afraid we would be here most of the night. I told you so. I also told you that I wasn't going to use threats, and I don't intend to. But by your unanimous denial you've turned a simple situation into a complicated one, and it has to be explained to you.

"First, let's say that you persist in the denial. In that case, the only thing I can do is inform the authorities and let them interview the person who looked into the dining room from the terrace. They will be convinced, as I am, of the correctness of the information, and they will start on you gentlemen with that knowledge in their possession. They will be certain that one of you saw the man by the screen. I don't pretend to know what they'll do to you, or how long you'll hold out, but that's what the situation will be, and I shall be out of it."

Wolfe sighed again, and surveyed the faces. "Now, whoever you are, let's say that you abandon your denial and tell me the truth, what will happen? Similarly, you will sooner or later have to deal with the local authorities, but under quite different circumstances. I am talking now to one of you—you know which one, I don't. It doesn't seem to me that any harm will be done if I tell Mr. Tolman and the sheriff that you and your colleagues came to see me at my request, and that you volunteered the information about what you saw in the dining room. There will be no reason why the person who first gave me the information should enter into it at all, if you tell the truth—though you may be sure that I am prepared to produce that person if necessary. Of course, they won't like it that you withheld so important a fact Tuesday night, but I think I can arrange beforehand that they'll be lenient about that. I shall make it a point to do so. None of the rest of you need be concerned in it at all.

"Now..." Wolfe looked around at them again "...here comes the hard part. Whoever you are, I can understand your denial and sympathize with it. You looked through the door—doubtless on account of a noise you had heard—and saw a man of your race standing by the screen, and some forty minutes later, when you learned what had happened, you knew that man had murdered Laszio. Or at the least, strongly suspected it. You not only knew that the murderer was a black man, you probably recognized him, since he wore the Kanawha Spa livery and was therefore a fellow employee, and he directly faced you as you looked through the door. And that presents another complication. If he is a man who is close to you and has a place in your heart, I presume you'll hold to your denial in spite of anything I may say and the sheriff may do. In that event your colleagues here will share a lot of discomfort with you, but that can't be helped.

"But if he is not personally close to you, if you have refused to expose him only because he is a fellow man—or more particularly because he is of your color—I'd like to make some remarks. First the fellow man. That's nonsense. It was realized centuries ago that it is impossible for a man to protect himself against murder, because it's extremely easy to kill a man, so it was agreed that men should protect each other. But if I help protect you, you must help protect me, whether you like me or not. If you don't do your part you're out of the agreement; you're an outlaw.

"But this murderer was a black man, and you're black too. I confess that makes it ticklish. The agreements of human society embrace not only protection against murder, but thousands of other things, and it is certainly true that in America—not to mention other continents—the whites have excluded the blacks from some of the benefits of those agreements. It is said that the exclusion has sometimes even extended to murder—that in parts of this country a white man may kill a black one, if not with impunity, at least with a good chance of escaping the penalty which the agreement imposes. That's bad. It's deplorable, and I don't blame black men for resenting it. But you are confronted with a fact, not a theory, and how do you propose to change it?

"I am talking to you who saw that man by the screen. If you shield him because he is dear to you, or for any valid personal reason, I have nothing to say, because I don't like futile talk, and you'll have to fight it out with the sheriff. But if you shield him because he is your color, there is a great deal to say. You are rendering your race a serious disservice. You are helping to perpetuate and aggravate the very exclusions which you justly resent. The ideal human agreement is one in which distinctions of race and color and religion are totally disregarded; anyone helping to preserve those distinctions is postponing that ideal; and you are certainly helping to

110

preserve them. If in a question of murder you permit your action to be influenced by the complexion of the man who committed it, no matter whether you yourself are white or pink or black—"

"You're wrong!"

It was a sharp explosion from the mouth of the muscular kid with the flat nose, the college boy. Some of them jumped, I was startled, and everybody looked at him.

Wolfe said, "I think I can justify my position, Mr. Whipple. If you'll let me complete—"

"I don't mean your position. You can have your logic. I mean your facts. One of them."

Wolfe lifted his brows. "Which one?"

"The complexion of the murderer." The college boy was looking him straight in the eye. "He wasn't a black man. I saw him. He was a white man."

11

RIGHT AWAY I got another shock. It was another explosion—this time something crashing to the floor. It took our attention away from the college boy, until we saw it was Boney, the tall skinny one by the wall, who had been lulled to sleep by Wolfe's oration, and, partly awakened by the electricity of Whipple's announcement, had jerked himself off balance and toppled over. He started to grumble and Crabtree glared him out of it. There was a general stir.

Wolfe asked softly, "You saw the man by the screen, Mr. Whipple?"

"Yes."

"When?"

"When he was standing by the screen. It was I who opened the door and looked through."

"Indeed. And you say he was white?"

"No." Whipple's gaze was steadfast at Wolfe; he hadn't turned at the sound of Boney's crash. "I didn't say he was white, I said he was a white man. When I saw him he was black, because he had blacked himself up."

"How do you know that?"

111

"Because I saw him. Do you think I can't tell burnt cork from the real thing? I'm a black man myself. But that wasn't all. As you said, he was holding his finger against his lips, and his hand was different. It wouldn't have taken a black man to see that. He had on tight black gloves."

"Why did you go to the pantry hall and look through the door?"

"I heard a noise in the dining room. Grant wanted some paprika for the oeufs au cheval, and the can was empty, and I went to the cupboard in the hall for a fresh can. That was how I happened to hear the noise. They were making a lot of racket in the kitchen and didn't hear it in there. I was up on the ladder steps looking for the paprika, and after I found it and got down I opened the door a crack to see what the noise had been."

"Did you enter the dining room?"

"No."

Wolfe slowly wiggled a finger. "May I suggest, Mr. Whipple, that the truth is usually good, and lies are sometimes excellent, but a mixture of the two is an abomination?"

"I'm telling the truth and nothing else."

"You didn't before. Since the murderer wasn't a colored man, why not?"

"Because I've learned not to mix up in the affairs of the superior race. If it had been a colored man I would have told. Colored men have got to stop disgracing their color and leave that to white men. You see how good your logic was."

"But my dear sir. That doesn't impugn my logic, it merely shows that you agree with me. We must discuss it some time. Then you withheld this fact because you considered it white men's business and none of yours, and you knew if you divulged it you'd be making trouble for yourself."

"Plenty of trouble. You're a northerner—"

"I'm a man, or try to be. You're studying me; you're an anthropologist. You expect to be a scientist. Give me a considered answer: how sure are you that it was a white man?"

Whipple considered. In a moment he said, "Not sure at all. Burnt cork would look like that on a light brown skin or even a rather dark one, and of course anyone can wear black gloves. But I'm sure about the burnt cork or something similar, and I'm sure about the gloves, and I don't see why a colored man should be painting the lily. Therefore I took it for granted he was a white man, but of course I'm not sure."

"It seems a safe deduction. What was he doing when you saw him?"

"Standing at the end of the screen, turning around. He must have seen me by accident; he couldn't have heard me. That door is noiseless, and I only opened it two or three inches, and there was quite a lot of sound from the radio in the parlor, though the door was closed."

"He was wearing the Kanawha Spa livery?"

"Yes."

"What about his hair?"

"He had a livery cap on. I couldn't see the back of his head."

"Describe him, height, weight. . . ."

"He was medium. I would guess five feet eight or nine, and a hundred and fifty-five or sixty. I didn't inspect him much. I saw at once that he was blacked up, and when he put his finger to his lips I thought he was one of the guests doing a stunt, probably a practical joke, and I supposed the noise I had heard was him jolting the screen or something. I let the door come shut and came away. As I did that, he was starting to turn."

"Toward the table?"

"I would say, toward the door to the terrace."

Wolfe pursed his lips. Then he opened them: "You thought it was a guest playing a joke. If you had tried to decide who it was, which guest would you have picked?"

"I don't know."

"Come, Mr. Whipple. I'm merely trying for general characteristics. Longheaded or round?"

"You asked me to name him. I couldn't name that man. I couldn't identify him. He was blacked up and his cap was pulled low. I think he had light-colored eyes. His face was neither round nor long, but medium. I only saw him one second."

"What about your feeling? Would you say that you had a feeling that you had ever seen him before?"

The college boy shook his head. "The only feeling I had was that I didn't want to interfere in a white man's joke. And afterwards, that I didn't want to interfere in a white man's murder."

The foam on Wolfe's glass of beer was all gone. Wolfe

113

picked it up, frowned at it, and carried it to his mouth and gulped five times, and set it down empty.

"Well." He put his eyes on Whipple again. "You must forgive me, sir, if I remind you that this story has been extracted from you against your will. I hope you haven't blacked it up—or whitewashed it. When you returned to the kitchen, did you tell anyone what you had seen?"

"No, sir."

"The unusual circumstances of a stranger in the dining room, in Kanawha Spa livery, blacked up with black gloves—you didn't think that worth mentioning?"

"No, sir."

"You damn fool, Paul." It was Crabtree, and he sounded irritated. "You think we ain't as much man as you are?" He turned to Wolfe. "This boy is awful conceited. He's got a good heart hid from people's eyesight, but his head's fixin' to bust. He's going to pack all the burden. No, sir. He came back to the kitchen and told us right off, just the same as he's told it here. We all heard it, passing it around. And for something more special about that, you might ask Moulton there."

The headwaiter with the chopped-off ear jerked around at him. "You talking, Crabby?"

The runt met his stare. "You heard me. Paul spilled it, didn't he? I didn't see anybody put you away on a shelf to save up for the Lord."

Moulton grunted. He stared at Crabtree some more seconds, then shrugged and turned to Wolfe and was again smooth and suave. "What he's referring to, I was about to tell you when Paul got through. I saw that man too."

"The man by the screen?"

"Yes, sir."

"How was that?"

"It was because I thought Paul was taking too long to find the paprika, and I went to the pantry hall after him. When I got there he was just turning away from the door, and he motioned to the dining room with his thumb and said somebody was in there. I didn't know what he meant; of course I knew Mr. Laszio was there, and I pushed the door a little to take a look. The man's back was toward me; he was walking toward the door to the terrace; so I couldn't see his face but I saw his black gloves, and of course I saw the livery he had on. I let the door come shut and asked Paul who it was, and he said he didn't know, he thought it was one of the guests blacked up. I sent Paul to the kitchen with the paprika, and opened the door another crack and looked through, but the man wasn't in sight, so I opened the door wider, thinking to ask Mr. Laszio if he wanted anything. He wasn't by the table. I went on through, and he wasn't anywhere. That looked funny, because I knew how the tasting was supposed to be done, but I can't say I was much surprised."

"Why not?"

"Well, sir . . . you'll allow me to say that these guests have acted very individual from the beginning."

"Yes, I'll allow that."

"Yes, sir. So I just supposed Mr. Laszio had gone to the parlor or somewhere."

"Did you look behind the screen?"

"No, sir. I didn't see any call for a posse."

"There was no one in the room?"

"No, sir. No one in sight."

"What did you do, return to the kitchen?"

"Yes, sir. I didn't figure—"

"You ain't shut yet." It was the plump little chef, warningly. "Mr. Wolfe here is a kindhearted man and he might as well get it and let him have it. We all remember it exactly like you told us about it."

"Oh, you do, Crabby?"

"We do you know."

Moulton shrugged and turned back to Wolfe. "What he's referring to, I was about to tell you. Before I went back to the kitchen I took a look at the table because I was responsible."

"The table with the sauces?"

"Yes, sir."

"Was one of the knives gone?"

"I don't know that. I think I would have noticed, but maybe I wouldn't, because I didn't lift the cover from the squabs, and one of them might have been under that. But I did notice something wrong. Somebody had monkeyed with the sauces. They were all changed around."

I let out a whistle before I thought. Wolfe sent me a sharp glance and then returned his eyes to Moulton and murmured, "Ah! How did you know?"

"I knew by the marks. The numbers chalked on the dishes. When I took them to the table, I put the dish with the chalk mark 1 in front of the card numbered 1, and the 2 in front of the 2, and so on. They weren't that way when I looked. They had been shifted around."

"How many of them?"

"All but two. Numbers 8 and 9 were all right, but the rest had all been moved."

"You can swear to that, Mr. Moulton?"

"I guess it looks like I'm going to have to swear to it."

"And can you?"

"I can, yes, sir."

"How would it be if at the same time you were asked to swear that, having noticed that the dishes had been moved, you replaced them in their proper positions?"

"Yes, sir. That's what I did. I suppose that's what will get me fired. It was none of my business to be correcting things, I knew it wasn't. But if Mr. Servan will listen to me, it was him I did it for. I didn't want him to lose his bet. I knew he had bet with Mr. Keith that the tasters would be eighty percent correct, and when I saw the dishes had been shifted I thought someone was framing him, so I shifted them back. Then I got out of there in a hurry."

"I don't suppose you remember just how they had been changed—where, for instance, number 1 had been moved to?"

"No, sir. I couldn't say that."

"No matter." Wolfe sighed. "I thank you, Mr. Moulton, and you, Mr. Whipple. It is late. I'm afraid we won't get much sleep, for we'll have to deal with Mr. Tolman and the sheriff as early as possible. I suppose you live on the grounds here?"

They told him yes.

"Good. I'll be sending for you. I don't think you'll lose your job, Mr. Moulton. I remember my commitment regarding beforehand arrangements with the authorities and I'll live up to it. I thank all of you gentlemen for your patience. I suppose your hats are in Mr. Goodwin's room?"

They helped me get the bottles and glasses cleared out and stacked in the foyer, and with that expert assistance it didn't take long. The college boy didn't help us because he hung back for a word with Wolfe. The hats and caps finally got distributed, and I opened the foyer door and they filed out. Hyacinth Brown had Boney by the arm, and Boney was still muttering when I shut the door.

In Wolfe's room the light of dawn was at the window, even through the thick shrubbery just outside. It was my second

dawn in a row, and I was beginning to feel that I might as
well join the Milkmen's Union and be done with it. My eyes
felt as if someone had painted household cement on my lids
and let it dry. Wolfe had his open, and was still in his chair.

I said, "Congratulations. All you need is wings to be an
owl. Shall I leave a call for twelve noon? That would leave
you eight hours till dinnertime, and you'd still be ahead of
schedule."

He made a face. "Where have they got Mr. Berin in jail?"

"I suppose at Quinby, the county seat."

"How far away is it?"

"Oh, around twenty miles."

"Does Mr. Tolman live there?"

"I don't know. His office must be there, since he's the
prosecuting attorney."

"Please find out, and get him on the phone. We want him
and the sheriff here at eight o'clock. Tell him—no. When you
get him, let me talk to him."

"Now?"

"Now."

I spread out my hands. "It's 4:30 a.m. Let the man—"

"Archie. Please. You tried to instruct me how to handle
colored men. Will you try it with white men too?"

I went for the phone.

12

PETTIGREW, the squint-eyed sheriff, shook his head and drawled,
"Thank you just the same. I got stuck in the mud and had to
flounder around and I'd get that chair all dirty. I'm a pretty
good stander anyhow."

My friend Barry Tolman didn't look any too neat himself,
but he wasn't muddy and so he hadn't hesitated about taking
a seat. It was 8:10 Thursday morning. I felt like the last nickel
in a crap game, because like a darned fool I had undraped
myself a little after five o'clock and got under the covers,
leaving a call for 7:30, and hauling myself out again after only
two hours had put me off key for good. Wolfe was having
breakfast in the big chair, with a folding table pulled up to

117

him, in a yellow dressing gown, with his face shaved and his hair combed. He possessed five yellow dressing gowns and we had brought along the light woolen one with brown lapels and a brown girdle. He had on a necktie, too.

Tolman said, "As I told you on the phone, I'm supposed to be in court at 9:30. If necessary my assistant can get a postponement, but I'd like to make it if possible. Can't you rush it?"

Wolfe was sipping at his cocoa for erosion on the bite of roll he had taken. When that was disposed of he said, "It depends a good deal on you, sir. It was impossible for me to go to Quinby, as I said, for reasons that will appear. I'll do all I can to hurry it. I haven't been to bed—"

"You said you have information—"

"I have. But the circumstances require a preamble. I take it that you arrested Mr. Berin only because you were convinced he was guilty. You don't especially fancy him as a victim. If strong doubt were cast on his guilt—"

"Certainly." Tolman was impatient. "I told you—"

"So you did. Now let's suppose something. Suppose that a lawyer has been retained to represent Mr. Berin, and I have been engaged to discover evidence in Berin's defense. Suppose further that I have discovered such evidence, of a weight that would lead inevitably to his acquittal when you put him on trial, and it is felt that it would be imprudent to disclose that evidence to you, the enemy, for the present. Suppose you demand that I produce that evidence now. It's true, isn't it, that you couldn't legally enforce that demand? That such evidence is our property until the time we see fit to make use of it—provided you don't discover it independently for yourselves?"

Tolman was frowning. "That's true, of course. But damn it, I've told you that if the evidence against Berin can be explained—"

"I know. I offer, here and now, an explanation that will clear him; but I offer it on conditions."

"What are they?"

Wolfe sipped cocoa and wiped his lips. "They're not onerous. First, that if the explanation casts strong doubt on Berin's guilt, he is to be released immediately."

"Who will decide how strong the doubt is?"

"You."

"All right, I agree. The court is sitting and it can be done in five minutes."

"Good. Second, you are to tell Mr. Berin that I discovered the evidence which set him free, I am solely responsible for it, and God only knows what would have happened to him if I hadn't done it."

Tolman, still frowning, opened his mouth, but the sheriff put in, "Now wait, Barry. Hold your horses." He squinted down at Wolfe. "If you've really got this evidence it must be around somewhere. I suppose we're pretty slow out here in West Virginia—"

"Mr. Pettigrew. Please. I'm not talking about the public credit, I'm not interested in it. Tell the newspaper men whatever you want to. But Mr. Berin is to know, unequivocally, that I did it, and Mr. Tolman is to tell him so."

Tolman asked, "Well, Sam?"

The sheriff shrugged. "I don't give a damn."

"All right," Tolman told Wolfe. "I agree to that."

"Good." Wolfe set the cocoa cup down. "Third, it is understood that I am leaving for New York at 12:40 to-night and under no circumstances—short of a suspicion that I killed Mr. Laszio myself or was an accomplice—am I to be detained."

Pettigrew said good-humoredly, "You go to hell."

"No, not hell." Wolfe sighed. "New York."

Tolman protested, "But what if this evidence makes you a material and essential witness?"

"It doesn't, you must take my word for that. I'm preparing to take yours for several things. I give you my word that within thirty minutes you'll know everything of significance that I know regarding that business in the dining room. I want it agreed that I won't be kept here beyond my train time merely because it is felt I might prove useful. Anyway, I assure you that under those circumstances I wouldn't be useful at all; I would be an insufferable nuisance. Well, sir?"

Tolman hesitated, and finally nodded. "Qualified as you put it, I agree."

If there is a way a canary bird sighs when you let it out of a cage, Wolfe sighed like that. "Now, sir. The fourth and last condition is a little vaguer than the others, but I think it can be defined. The evidence that I am going to give you was brought to me by two men. I led up to its disclosure by methods which seemed likely to be effective, and they were so. You will resent it that these gentlemen didn't give you

119

these facts when they had an opportunity, and I can't help that. I can't estop your feelings, but I can ask you to restrain them, and I have promised to do so. I want your assurance that the gentlemen will not be bullied, badgered or abused, nor be deprived of their freedom, nor in any way persecuted. This is predicated on the assumption that they are merely witnesses and have no share whatever in the guilt of the murder."

The sheriff said, "Hell, mister, we don't abuse people."

"Bullied, badgered, abused, deprived of freedom, persecuted, all excluded. Of course you'll question them as much as you please."

Tolman shook his head. "They'll be material witnesses. They might leave the state. In fact, they will. You're going to, to-night."

"You can put them under bond to remain."

"Until the trial."

Wolfe wiggled a finger. "Not Mr. Berin's trial."

"I don't mean Berin. If this evidence is as good as you say it is. But you can be damn sure there's going to *be* a trial."

"I sincerely hope so." Wolfe was breaking off a piece of roll and buttering it. "What about it, sir? Since you want to get to court. I'm not asking much; merely a decent restraint with my witnesses. Otherwise you'll have to try to dig them out for yourself, and in the meantime the longer you hold Mr. Berin the more foolish you'll look in the end."

"Very well." The blue-eyed athlete nodded. "I agree."

"To the condition as I have stated it?"

"Yes."

"Then the preamble is finished.—Archie, bring them in."

I smothered a yawn as I lifted myself up and went to my room to get them. They had been in there overlooking progress while I had dressed—Wolfe having had a telephone plugged in in his own chamber, and done his own assembling for the morning meeting, during my nap. They had reported in livery. Paul Whipple looked wide awake and defiant, and Moulton, the headwaiter, sleepy and nervous. I told them the stage was set, and let them precede me.

Wolfe told me to push chairs around, and Moulton jumped to help me. Tolman was staring. Pettigrew exclaimed, "Well I'll be damned! It's a couple of niggers! Hey, you, take that chair!" He turned to Wolfe with a grievance: "Now listen, I questioned all those boys, and by God if they—"

120

Wolfe snapped, "These are my witnesses. Mr. Tolman wants to get to court. I said you'd resent it, didn't I? Go ahead, but keep it to yourself." He turned to the college boy. "Mr. Whipple, I think we'll have your story first. Tell these gentlemen what you told me last night."

Pettigrew had stepped forward with a mean eye. "We don't mister niggers here in West Virginia, and we don't need anybody coming down here to tell us—"

"Shut up, Sam!" Tolman was snappy too. "We're wasting time.—Your name's Whipple? What do you do?"

"Yes, sir." The boy spoke evenly. "I'm a waiter. Mr. Servan put me on duty at Pocahontas Pavilion Tuesday noon."

"What have you got to say?"

The upshot of it was that Tolman couldn't have got to court on time, for it was after nine-thirty when he left Kanawha Spa. It took only a quarter of an hour to get all the details of the two stories, but they went on from there, or rather, back and around. Tolman did a pretty good job of questioning, but Pettigrew was too mad to be of much account. He kept making observations about how educated Whipple thought he was, and how he knew what kind of lessons it was that Whipple really needed. Tolman kept pushing the sheriff off and doing some real cross-examining, and twice or thrice I saw Wolfe, who was finishing his breakfast at leisure, give a little nod as an acknowledgment of Tolman's neat job. Whipple kept himself even-toned right through, but I could see him holding himself in when the sheriff made observations about his education and the kind of lessons he needed. Moulton started off jerky and nervous, but he smoothed off as he went along, and his only job was to stick to his facts in reply to Tolman's questions, since Pettigrew was concentrating on Whipple.

Finally Tolman's string petered out. He raised his brows at Wolfe, glanced at the sheriff, and looked back again at Moulton with a considering frown.

Pettigrew demanded, "Where did you boys leave your caps? We'll have to take you down to Quinby with us."

Wolfe was crisp right away. "Oh, no. Remember the agreement. They stay here on their jobs. I've spoken with Mr. Servan about that."

"I don't give a damn if you've spoken with Ashley himself. They go to jail till they get bond."

Wolfe's eyes moved. "Mr. Tolman?"

"Well... it was agreed they could be put under bond."

121

"But that was when you supposed that they were persons who were likely to leave your jurisdiction. These men have jobs here; why should they leave? Mr. Moulton has a wife and children. Mr. Whipple is a university man." He looked at the sheriff. "Your assumption that you know how to deal with colored men and I don't is impertinent nonsense. Tuesday night, as an officer of the law engaged in the investigation of a crime, at which you are supposed to be expert, you questioned these men and failed to learn anything. You didn't even have your suspicions aroused. Last night I had a talk with them and uncovered vital information regarding that crime. Surely you have enough intelligence to see how utterly discredited you are. Do you want your whole confounded county to know about it? Pfui!" He turned to the two greenjackets. "You men get out of here and go to your stations and get to work. You understand, of course, that Mr. Tolman will need your evidence and you will hold yourselves subject to his proper demands. If he requires bond, any lawyer can arrange it. Well, go on!"

Paul Whipple was already on his way to the door. Moulton hesitated only an instant, glancing at Tolman, and then followed. I got up and moseyed out to see that the outside door was shut behind them.

When I got back Pettigrew was in the middle of some remarks, using whatever words happened to come handy, regarding the tribal customs and personal habits of aborigines. Tolman was back on his shoulders with his hands thrust in his pockets, surveying Wolfe, and Wolfe was daintily collecting crumbs and depositing them on the fruit plate. Neither was paying any attention to the sheriff, and eventually he fizzed out.

Wolfe looked up. "Well, sir?"

Tolman nodded. "Yep, I guess you win. It looks like they're telling the truth. They can make up fancy ones when they feel like it, but this doesn't sound like their kind." His blue eyes narrowed a little. "Of course, there's something else to consider. I understand you've been appealed to, to get Berin clear, and also I've heard that you were offered a good commission to get Berin for the job that Laszio had. I learned that from Clay Ashley, who had it from his friend Liggett of the Hotel Churchill. Naturally that raises the question as to how far you yourself might go in discovering evidence that would free Berin."

"You put it delicately." The corners of Wolfe's lips went up a little. "You mean manufacturing evidence. I assure you I'm not that stupid or that desperate, to bribe strangers to tell intricate lies. Besides, I would have had to bribe not two men, but fourteen. Those stories were uncovered in this room last night, in the presence of all the cooks and waiters on duty at Pocahontas Pavilion. You may question them all. No, sir; those stories are bona fide." He upturned a palm. "But you know that; you put them to a good test. And now—since you were anxious to return to Quinby in time for your appearance in court—"

"Yeah, I know." Tolman didn't move. "This is a sweet mess now, this murder. If those niggers are telling it straight, and I guess they are, do you realize what it means? Among other things, it means that all of that bunch are out of it, except that fellow Blanc who says he was in his room. And he's a stranger here, and how the devil could he have got hold of a Kanawha Spa uniform? If you eliminate him, all you've got left is the wide world."

Wolfe murmured, "Yes, it's a pretty problem. Thank goodness it isn't mine. But as to our agreement—I've performed my part, haven't I? Have I cast strong doubt on Mr. Berin's guilt?"

The sheriff snorted. Tolman said shortly, "Yes. The fact that those sauce dishes were shifted around—certainly. But damn it, who shifted them?"

"I couldn't say. Perhaps the murderer, or possibly Mr. Laszio himself, to make a fool of Berin." Wolfe shrugged. "Quite a job for you. You will set Berin free this morning?"

"What else can I do? I can't hold him now."

"Good. Then if you don't mind . . . since you're in a hurry, and I haven't been to bed . . ."

"Yeah." Tolman stayed put. He sat with his hands still in his pockets, his legs stretched out, the toes of his shoes making little circles in the air. "A hell of a mess," he declared after a silence. "Except for Blanc, there's nowhere to begin. That nigger's description might be almost anyone. Of course, it's possible that it was a nigger that did it and used black gloves and burnt cork to throw us off, but what nigger around here could have any reason for wanting to kill Laszio?" He was silent again. Finally he abruptly sat up. "Look here. I'm not sorry you got Berin out of it, whether you made it into a mess or not. And I'll meet the conditions I agreed to, including no

123

interference with your leaving here tonight. But since you're turning over evidence, what else have you got? I admit you're good and you've made a monkey out of me on this Berin business—not to mention the sheriff here. Maybe you can come across with some more of the same. What more have you found out?"

"Nothing whatever."

"Have you any idea who it was the niggers saw in the dining room?"

"None."

"Do you think that Frenchman did it? Blanc?"

"I don't know. I doubt it."

"The Chinese woman who was outdoors—do you think she was mixed up in it?"

"No."

"Do you think the radio being turned on at that particular time had anything to do with it?"

"Certainly. It drowned the noise of Laszio's fall—and his outcry, if he made one."

"But was it turned on purposely—for that?"

"I don't know."

Tolman frowned. "When I had Berin, or thought I had, I decided that the radio was a coincidence, or a circumstance that he took advantage of. Now that's open again." He leaned forward at Wolfe. "I want you to do something for me. I don't pass for a fool, but I admit I'm a little shy on experience, and you're not only an old hand, you're recognized as one of the best there is. I'm not too proud to yell for help if I need it. It looks like the next step is a good session with Blanc, and I'd like to have you in on it. Better still, handle it yourself and let me sit and listen. Will you do that?"

"No, sir."

Tolman was taken aback. "You won't?"

"No. I won't even discuss it. Confound it, I came down here for a holiday!" Wolfe made a face. "Monday night, on the train, I got no sleep. Tuesday night it was you who kept me up until four o'clock. Last night my engagement to clear Mr. Berin prevented my going to bed at all. This evening I am supposed to deliver an important address to a group of eminent men, on their own subject. I need the refreshment of sleep, and there is my bed. As for your interview with Mr. Blanc, I remind you that you agreed to free Mr. Berin immediately upon presentation of my evidence."

124

He looked and sounded very final. The sheriff started to growl something, but I was called away by a knock on the door. I went to the foyer, telling myself that if it was anyone who was likely to postpone the refreshment of sleep any longer, I would lay him out with a healthy sock on the button and just leave him there.

Which might have done for Vukcic, big as he was, but I wouldn't strike a woman merely because I was sleepy, and he was accompanied by Constanza Berin. I flung the door the rest of the way and she crossed the threshold. Vukcic began a verbal request, but she wasn't bothering with amenities, she was going right ahead.

I reached for her and missed her. "Hey, wait a minute! We have company. Your friend Barry Tolman is in there."

She wheeled on me. "Who?"

"You heard me. Tolman."

She wheeled again and opened the door to Wolfe's room and breezed on through. Vukcic looked at me and shrugged, and followed her, and I went along, thinking that if I needed a broom and dustpan I could get them later.

Tolman had jumped to his feet at sight of her. For two seconds he was white, then a nice pink, and then he started for her:

"Miss Berin! Thank God—"

An icy blast hit him and stopped him in his tracks with his mouth open. It wasn't vocal; her look didn't need any accompaniment. With him frozen, she turned a different look, practically as devastating, on Nero Wolfe:

"And you said you would help us! You said you would make them free my father!" Nothing but a superworm could deserve such scorn as that. "And it was you who suggested that about his list—about the sauces! I suppose you thought no one would know—"

"My dear Miss Berin—"

"Now everybody knows! It was you who brought the evidence against him! *That* evidence! And you pretending to Mr. Servan and Mr. Vukcic and me—"

I got Wolfe's look and saw his lips moving at me, though I couldn't hear him. I stepped across and gripped her arm and turned her. "Listen, give somebody a chance—"

She was pulling, but I held on. Wolfe said sharply, "She's hysterical. Take her out of here."

125

I felt her arm relax, and turned her loose, and she moved to face Wolfe again.

She told him quietly, "I'm not hysterical."

"Of course you are. All women are. Their moments of calm are merely recuperative periods between outbursts. I want to tell you something. Will you listen?"

She stood and looked at him.

He nodded. "Thank you. I make this explanation because I don't want unfriendliness from your father. I made the suggestion that the lists be compared with the correct list, not dreaming that it would result in implicating your father—in fact, thinking that it would help to clear him. Unfortunately it happened differently, and it became necessary to undo the mischief I had unwittingly caused. The only way to do that was to discover other evidence which would establish his innocence. I have done so. Your father will be released within an hour."

Constanza stared at him, and went nearly as white as Tolman had on seeing her, and then her blood came back as his had done. She stammered, "But—but—I don't believe it. I've just been over to that place—and they wouldn't even let me see him—"

"You won't have to go again. He will rejoin you here this morning. I undertook with you and Mr. Servan and Mr. Vukcic to clear your father of this ridiculous charge, and I have done that. The evidence has been give to Mr. Tolman. Don't you understand what I'm saying?"

Apparently she was beginning to, and it was causing drastic internal adjustments. Her eyes were drawing together, diagonal creases were appearing from the corners of her nose to the corners of her mouth, her cheeks were slowly puffing up, and her chin began to move. She was going to cry, and it looked as if it might be a good one. For half a minute, evidently, she thought she was going to be able to stave it off; then all of a sudden she realized that she wasn't. She turned and ran for the door. She got it open and disappeared. That galvanized Tolman. Without stopping for farewells he jumped for the door she had left open—and he was gone too.

Vukcic and I looked at each other. Wolfe sighed.

The sheriff made a move. "Admitting you're smart," he drawled at Wolfe, "and all that, if I was Barry Tolman you wouldn't take the midnight or any other train out of here until certain details had been attended to."

Wolfe nodded and murmured, "Good day, sir."

126

He went, and banged the foyer door so hard behind him that I jumped. I sat down and observed, "My nerves are like fishing worms on hooks." Vukcic sat down too.

Wolfe looked at him and inquired, "Well, Marko? I suppose we might as well say good morning. Is that what you came for?"

"No." Vukcic ran his fingers through his hair. "It fell to me, more or less, to stand by Berin's daughter, and when she wanted to drive to Quinby—that's the town where the jail is—it was up to me to take her. Then they wouldn't let her see him. If I had known you had already found evidence to clear him . . ." He shook himself. "By the way, what's the evidence? If it isn't a secret."

"I don't know whether it's a secret or not. It doesn't belong to me any more; I've handed it over to the authorities, and I suppose they should be permitted to decide about divulging it. I can tell you one thing that's no secret: I didn't get to bed last night."

"Not at all?"

"No."

Vukcic grunted. "You don't look done up." He ran his fingers through his hair again. "Listen, Nero. I'd like to ask you something. Dina came to see you last night. Didn't she?"

"Yes."

"What did she have to say? That is, if it's proper to tell me."

"You can judge of the propriety. She told me that she is a special kind of woman and that she thought that you thought that I suspected you of killing Laszio." Wolfe grimaced. "And she patted me on the shoulder."

Vukcic said angrily, "She's a damned fool."

"I suppose so. But a very dangerous fool. Of course, a hole in the ice offers peril only to those who go skating. This is none of my business, Marko, but you brought it up."

"I know I did. What the devil made her think that I thought you suspected me of murdering Laszio?"

"Didn't you tell her so?"

"No. Did she say I did?"

Wolfe shook his head. "She wasn't on the road, she was winding around. She did say, however, that you told her of my questions about the radio and the dancing."

Vukcic nodded gloomily, and was silent. At length he shook himself. "Yes, I had a talk with her. Two talks. There's no

127

doubt about her being dangerous. She gets ... you must realize that she was my wife for five years. Again yesterday I had her close to me, I had her in my arms. It isn't her tricks, I'm on to all her tricks, it's the mere fact of what she is. You wouldn't see that, Nero, or feel it, it wouldn't have any effect on you, because you've put yourself behind a barricade. As you say, a hole in the ice is dangerous only to those who go skating. But damn it, what does life consist of if you're afraid to take—"

"Marko!" Wolfe sounded peevish. "I've often told you that's your worst habit. When you argue with yourself, do it inside your head; don't pretend it's me you're persuading and shout platitudes at me. You know very well what life consists of, it consists of the humanities, and among them is a decent and intelligent control of the appetites which we share with dogs. A man doesn't wolf a carcass or howl on a hillside from dark to dawn; he eats well-cooked food, when he can get it, in judicious quantities; and he suits his ardor to his wise convenience."

Vukcic was standing up. He frowned and growled down at his old friend: "So I'm howling, am I?"

"You are and you know it."

"Well. I'm sorry. I'm damned sorry."

He turned on his heel and strode from the room.

I got up and went to the window to retrieve a curtain that had been whipped out by the draft from the opened door. In the thick shrubbery just outside a bird was singing, and I startled it. Then I went and planted myself in front of Wolfe. He had his eyes closed, and as I gazed at him his massive form went up with the leverage of a deep sigh, and down again.

I yawned and said, "Anyhow, thank the Lord they all made a quick exit. It's moving along for ten o'clock, and you need sleep, not to mention me."

He opened his eyes. "Archie. I have affection for Marko Vukcic. I hunted dragonflies with him in the mountains. Do you realize that that fool is going to let that fool make a fool of him again?"

I yawned. "Listen to you. If I did a sentence like that you'd send me from the room. You're in bad shape. I tell you, we both need sleep. Did you mean it when you told Tolman that as far as this murder is concerned you're not playing any more?"

"Certainly. Mr. Berin is cleared. We are no longer interested. We leave here to-night."

"Okay. Then for God's sake let's go to bed."

He closed his eyes and sighed again. It appeared that he wanted to sit and worry about Vukcic a while, and I couldn't help him any with that, so I turned and started out, intending not only to display the DO NOT DISTURB but also to leave positive instructions with the greenjacket, in the main hall. But just as I had my hand on the knob his voice stopped me.

"Archie. You've had more sleep than I have. I was about to say, we haven't gone over that speech since we got here. I intended to rehearse it at least twice. Do you know which bag it's in? Get it, please."

If we had been in New York I would have quit the job.

13

AT TEN O'CLOCK I sat on a chair by the open window and yawned, with my eyes on the typescript, my own handiwork. We had worked through it to page 9.

Wolfe, facing me, was sitting up in bed with four cushions at his back, displaying half an acre of yellow silk pajamas. On the bedstand beside him were two empty beer bottles and an empty glass. He appeared to be frowning intently at my socks as he went on:

"... but the indescribable flavor of the finest of Georgia hams, the quality which places them, in my opinion, definitely above the best to be found in Europe, is not due to the post mortem treatment of the flesh at all. Expert knowledge and tender care in the curing are indeed essential, but they are to be found in Czestochowa and Westphalia more frequently even than in Georgia. Poles and Westphalians have the pigs, the scholarship and the skill; what they do not have is peanuts."

He stopped to blow his nose. I shifted position. He resumed: "A pig whose diet is fifty to seventy percent peanuts grows a ham of incredibly sweet and delicate succulence which, well-cured, well-kept and well-cooked, will take precedence over any other ham the world affords. I offer this as an illustration of one of the sources of the American contributions I am discussing, and as another proof that American offerings to the roll of honor of fine food are by no means confined to those items which were found here already ripe on the tree, with nothing required but the plucking. Red Indians were eating turkeys and potatoes before white men came, but they were not eating peanut-fed pigs. Those unforgettable hams are not gifts of nature; they are the product of the inventor's enterprise, the experimenter's persistence, and the connoisseur's discrimination. Similar results have been achieved by the feeding of blueberries to young chickens, beginning usually—"

"Hold it. Not chickens, poultry."

"Chickens are poultry."

"You told me to stop you."

"But not to argue with me."

"You started the argument, I didn't."

He showed me a palm. "Let's go on . . . beginning usually at the age of one week. The flavor of a four months old cockerel, trained to eat large quantities of blueberries from infancy, and cooked with mushrooms, tarragon and white wine—or, if you would add another American touch, made into a chicken and corn pudding, with onion, parsley and eggs—is not only distinctive, it is unique; and it is assuredly haute cuisine. This is even a better illustration of my thesis than the ham, for Europeans could not have fed peanuts to pigs, since they had no peanuts. But they did have chickens—chickens, Archie?"

"Poultry."

"No matter. They did have chickens and blueberries, and for centuries no one thought of having the one assimilate the other and bless us with the result. Another demonstration of the inventiveness—"

. "Hey, wait! You left out a whole paragraph. 'You will say perhaps—'"

"Very well. Do you think you might sit still? You keep that chair creaking. You will say, perhaps, that all this does not belong in a discussion of cookery, but on consideration I believe you will agree that it does. Vatel had his own farm, and gave his personal attention to its husbandry. Escoffier refused fowl from a certain district, however plump and well-grown, on account of minerals in the drinking water available for them there. Brillat-Savarin paid many tributes . . ."

I was on my feet. Seated, I had twitches in my arms and legs and I couldn't sit still. With my eye on the script, I moved across to the table and got hold of the carafe and poured myself a glass of water and drank it. Wolfe went on, droning it out. I decided not to sit down again, and stood in the middle of the floor, flexing and unflexing the muscles of my legs to make the twitching stop.

I don't know what it was that alarmed me. I couldn't have seen anything, because my eyes were on the script, and the open window was at my left, at least a dozen feet away, at right angles to my line of vision. I don't think I heard anything. But something made me jerk my head around, and even then all I saw was a movement in the shrubbery outside the window, and I have no idea what made me throw the script. But I threw it, straight at the window. At the same moment a gun went off, good and loud. Simultaneously smoke and the smell of powder came in at the window, the script fluttered and dropped to the floor, and I heard Wolfe's voice behind me:

"Look here, Archie."

I looked and saw the blood running down the side of his face. For a second I stood dead in my tracks. I wanted to jump through the window and catch the son of a—the sharp-shooter, and give him personal treatment. And Wolfe wasn't dead, he was still sitting up. But the blood looked plenteous. I jumped to the side of the bed.

He had his lips compressed tight, but he opened them to demand, "Where is it? Is it my skull?" He shuddered. "Brains?"

"Hell no." I was looking, and was so relieved my voice cracked. "Where would brains come from? Take your hand away and hold still. Wait till I get a towel." I raced to the bathroom and back, and wrapped one towel around his neck and sopped with the other one. "I don't think it touched the cheekbone at all, it just went through skin and meat. Do you feel faint?"

"No. Bring me my shaving mirror."

"You wait till I—"

"Bring the mirror!"

"For God's sake. Hold that towel there." I hopped to the bathroom again for the mirror and handed it to him, and then went to the phone. A girl's voice said good morning sweetly.

"Yeah. Swell morning. Has this joint got a doctor? . . . No,

131

wait, I don't want to speak to him, send him over here right away, a man's been shot in Suite 60, Upshur Pavilion.... I said shot, and step on it, and send the doctor, and that Odell the house detective, and a state cop if there's one around loose, and a bottle of brandy. Got it?... Good for you, you're a wonder."

I went back to Wolfe, and whenever I want to treat myself to a laugh all I have to do is remember how he looked on that occasion. With one hand he was keeping the towel from unwinding from his neck, and with the other he was holding up the mirror, into which he was glaring with unutterable indignation and disgust. I saw he was holding his lips tight so blood wouldn't get in his mouth, and went and got some of his handkerchiefs and did some more sopping.

He moved his left shoulder up and down a little. "Some blood ran down my neck." He moved his jaw up and down, and from side to side. "I don't feel anything when I do that." He put the mirror down on the bed. "Can't you stop the confounded bleeding? Look out, don't press so hard! What's that there on the floor?"

"It's your speech. I think there's a bullet hole through it, but it's all right. You've got to get stretched out and turned over on your side. —Now damn it, don't argue—here, wait till I get rid of these cushions...."

I got him horizontal, with his head raised on a couple of pillows, and went to the bathroom for a towel soaked in cold water and came back and poulticed him. He had his eyes shut. I had just got back to him with another cold towel when there was a loud knock on the door.

The doctor, a bald-headed little squirt with spectacles, had a bag in his hand and a nurse with him. As I was ushering them in somebody else came trotting down the hall, and I let him in too when I saw it was Clay Ashley, the Kanawha Spa manager. He was sputtering at me, "Who did it how did it happen where is he who is it..." I told him to save it up and followed the doctor and nurse inside.

The bald-headed doc was no slouch, at that. The nurse pulled up a chair for the bag and opened it, and I shoved a table over by the bed, while the doc bent over Wolfe without asking me anything. Wolfe started to turn over but was commanded to lie still.

Wolfe protested, "Confound it, I have to see your face!"

"What for? To see if I'm compos mentis? I'm all right. Hold still."

Clay Ashley's voice sounded at my elbow. "What the devil is it? You say he was shot? What happened?"

The doctor spoke without turning, with authority: "Quiet in here, until I see what we've got."

There was another loud knock on the door. I went out to it, and Ashley followed me. It was my friend Odell and a pair of state cops, and behind them the greenjacket from the main hall. Ashley told the greenjacket:

"Get out of here, and keep your mouth shut."

I just wanted to tell you, sir, I heard a shot, and two of the guests want to know—"

"Tell them you know nothing about it. Tell them it was a backfire. Understand?"

"Yes, sir."

I took the quartette to my room. I ignored Ashley, because I had heard Wolfe say he was bourgeois, and spoke to the cops:

"Nero Wolfe was sitting up in bed, rehearsing a speech he is to deliver tonight, and I was standing four yards from the open window looking at the script to prompt him. Something outside caught my attention, I don't know whether a sound or a movement, and I looked at the window and all I consciously saw was a branch of the shrubbery moving, and I threw the script at the window. At the same time a gun went off, outside, and Wolfe called to me, and I saw his cheek was bleeding and went to him and took a look. Then I phoned the hotel, and got busy mopping blood until the doctor came, which was just before you did."

One of the cops had a notebook out. "What's your name?"

"Archie Goodwin."

He wrote it down. "Did you see anyone in the shrubbery?"

"No. If you'll permit a suggestion, it's been less than ten minutes since the shot was fired. I've told you all I know. If you let the questions wait and get busy out there, you might pick up a hot trail."

"I want to see Wolfe."

"To ask him if I shot him? Well, I didn't. I even know who did, it was the man that stabbed Laszio in Pocahontas Pavilion Tuesday night. I don't know his name, but it was that guy. Would you like to grab that murderer, you two? Get out there on the trail before it cools off."

"How do you know it was the one that killed Laszio?"

"Because Wolfe started digging too close to his hole and he didn't like it. There's plenty of people that would like to see Nero Wolfe dead, but not in this neighborhood."

"Is Wolfe conscious?"

"Certainly. That way, through the foyer."

"Come on, Bill."

They tramped ahead, and Ashley and I followed, with Odell behind us. In Wolfe's room the nurse had the table half covered with bandages and things, and an electric sterilizer had been plugged into an outlet. Wolfe, on his right side, had his back to us, and the doctor was bending over him with busy fingers.

"What about it, Doc?"

"Who—" The doctor's head twisted at us. "Oh, it's you fellows. Only a flesh wound in the upper cheek. I'll have to sew it."

Wolfe's voice demanded, "Who is that?"

"Quit talking. State police."

"Archie? Where are you, Archie?"

"Right here, boss." I stepped up. "The cops want to know if I shot you."

"They would. Idiots. Get them out of here. Get everybody out but you and the doctor. I'm in no condition for company."

The cop spoke up. "We want to ask you, Mr. Wolfe—"

"I have nothing to tell you, except that somebody shot at me through the window. Hasn't Mr. Goodwin told you that? Do you think *you* can catch him? Try it."

Clay Ashley said indignantly, "That's no attitude to take, Wolfe. All this damned mess comes from my permitting a gathering of people who are not of my clientele. Far from it. It seems to me—"

"I know who that is." Wolfe's head started to move, and the doctor held it firm. "That's Mr. Ashley. His clientele! Pfui! Put him out too. Put them all out. Do you hear me, Archie?"

The doctor said decisively, "That's enough. When he talks it starts bleeding."

I told the cops, "Come on, shove off. He's far enough away now so that you're in no danger." To Ashley: "You too. Give your clientele my love. Scat."

Odell had stayed over by the door and so was the first one out. Ashley and the cops were close behind. I followed them, on through the foyer, and into the public hall. There I stopped one of the cops and kept him by fastening onto a corner of his tunic, and his brother, seeing him stay, stayed with him while Ashley and Odell went on ahead. Ashley was tramping along in a fury and Odell was trotting in the rear.

"Listen," I told the cop. "You didn't like my first suggestion to get jumping, I'll try another. This individual that stabbed Laszio and took a shot at Wolfe seems to be pretty active. He might even take it into his head to try some more target practice on the same range. It's a nice April day and Wolfe wouldn't want the windows closed and the curtains drawn, and damned if I'm going to sit in there all day and watch the shrubbery. We came into your state alive, and we'd like to go out the same way at 12:40 to-night. How would it be if you stationed a guard where he could keep an eye on those windows and the shrubbery from behind? There's a nice seat not far away, by the brook."

"Much obliged." He sounded sarcastic. "Maybe you'd like to have the colonel come down from Charleston so you can give him instructions."

I waved a hand. "I'm upset. I've had no sleep and my boss got shot and darned near had his brains spilled. I'm surprised I've been as polite as I have. It *would* be nice to know that those windows are being watched. Will you do it?"

"Yes. I'll phone in a report and get a couple of men." He eyed me. "You didn't see any more than you told me. Huh?"

I told him no, and he turned and took his brother with him.

In Wolfe's room the ministrations were proceeding. I stood at the foot of the bed and watched for a few minutes, then, turning, my eye fell on the script still lying on the floor, and I picked it up and examined it. Sure enough, the bullet had gone right through it, and had torn loose one of the metal fasteners which had held the sheets together. I smoothed it out and tossed it on the bureau and resumed my post at the foot of the bed.

The doctor was a little slow but he was good and thorough. He had started the sewing, and Wolfe, who lay with his eyes closed, informed me in a murmur that he had declined the offer of a local anesthetic. His hand on the coverlet was clenched into a fist, and each time the needle went through the flesh he grunted. After a few stitches he asked, "Does my grunting hamper you?" The doctor told him no, and then the grunts got louder. When the sewing was done and the bandaging started, the doctor told me, as he worked, that the wound was superficial but would be somewhat painful and the patient should have rest and freedom from disturbance. He was dressing it so that it needn't be touched again until we got to New York. The patient insisted that he intended to deliver a speech that evening and wouldn't be persuaded out of it, and in case such excessive muscular action started a hemorrhage the doctor must be called. It was desirable for the patient to stay in bed until dinnertime.

He finished. The nurse helped him gather up paraphernalia and débris, including bloody towels. She offered to help Wolfe change the soiled pajama top for a fresh one, but he refused. I got out the expense roll, but the doctor said it would be put on the bill, and then walked around to the other side of the bed to get a front view of Wolfe's face and give him some parting admonitions.

I accompanied them as far as the main hall to tell the greenjacket there that no visitors of any description would be desired in Suite 60. Back in Wolfe's room, the patient was still lying on his right side with his eyes closed.

I went to the phone. "Hello, operator? Listen. The doctor says Mr. Wolfe must have rest and quiet. Will you please announce to the switchboard that this phone is not to ring? I don't care who—"

"Archie! Cancel that."

I told the mouthpiece, "Wait a minute.—Yes, sir?"

Wolfe hadn't moved, but he spoke again. "Cancel that order about the phone."

"But you—"

"Cancel it."

I told the operator to return to the status quo ante, and hung up, and approached the patient. "Excuse me. I wouldn't butt in on your personal affairs for anything. If you want that phone bell jangling—"

"I don't want it." He opened his eyes. "But we can't do anything if we're incommunicado. Did you say the bullet went through my speech? Let me see it, please."

His tone was such that I got the script from the bureau and handed it to him without demur. Frowning, he fingered it, and as he saw the extent of the damage the frown deepened. He handed it back. "I suppose you can decipher it. What did you throw it for?"

"Because I had it in my hand. If it hadn't deflected the bullet you might have got it for good—or it might have

136

missed you entirely, I admit that. Depending on how good a shot he is."

"I suppose so. That man's a dolt. I had washed my hands of it. He stood an excellent chance of avoiding exposure, and now he's done for. We'll get him."

"Oh. We will."

"Certainly. I have plenty of forbearance, God knows, but I'm not a complacent target for firearms. While I was being bandaged I considered probabilities, and we have little time to act. Hand me that mirror. I suppose I'm a spectacle."

"You're pretty well decorated." I passed the mirror to him, and he studied his reflection with his lips compressed. "About getting this bird, I'm for it, but from the way you look and what the doctor said—"

"It can't be helped. Close the windows and draw the shades."

"It'll be gloomy. I told the cop to put a guard outside—"

"Do as I say, please. I don't trust guards. Besides, I would be constantly glancing at the window, and I don't want my mental processes interrupted. —No, clear to the bottom, there'll be plenty of light. That's better. The others too. —Good. Now bring me underwear, a clean shirt, the dressing gown from the closet . . ."

"You've got to stay in bed."

"Nonsense. There's more blood in the head lying down than sitting up. If people come here I can't very well make myself presentable, with the gibbosity of this confounded bandage, but at least I needn't give offense to decency. Get the underwear."

I collected garments while he manipulated his mass, first to a sitting position on the edge of the bed, and then onto his feet, using grunts for punctuation. He frowned in distaste at the bloody pajama top when he got it off, and I brought towels, wet and dry. As the operations progressed he instructed me as to details of the program:

"All we can do is try our luck on the possibilities until we find a fact that will allow only one interpretation. I detest alternatives, and at present that is all we have. Do you know how to black a man up with burnt cork? —Well, you can try. Get some corks—I suppose we can use matches—and get a Kanawha Spa livery, medium size, including cap. But first of all, New York on the telephone. —No, not those socks, black ones, I may not feel like changing again before dinner. We'll have to find time to finish that speech. —I presume you know the numbers of Saul Panzer and Inspector Cramer. But if we should get our fact from there, it would be undesirable to run the risk of that blackguard learning we had asked for it. We must prevent that..."

14

MY FRIEND ODELL stood beside a lobby pillar with an enormous leaf of a palm spread over his head, looking at me with a doubtful glint in his eye that I didn't deserve.

I said, "Nor am I trying to negotiate a hot date, nor am I engaged in snooping. I've told you straight, I merely want to make sure that a private phone call is private. It's not suspicion, it's just precaution. As for your having to consult the manager, what the hell kind of a house dick are you if you haven't even got the run of your own corral? You come along and stay with me, and if I start anything you don't like you can throw stones at me. Which reminds me, this Kanawha Spa seems to be pretty hard on guests. If you don't get hit with a rock you get plugged with a bullet. Huh?"

Without erasing the doubt, he made to move. "Okay. The next time I tell a man a joke it'll be the one about Pat and Mike. Come on, Rollo."

He led me through the lobby, down past the elevators, and along a ways to a narrow side corridor. It had doors with frosted glass panels, and he opened one on the right side and motioned me in. It was a small room, and all its furniture consisted of a switchboard running its entire length, perhaps fifteen feet, six maidens in a row with their backs to us, and the straight-backed chairs which the maidens inhabited. Odell went to the one at the end and conversed a moment, and then thumbed me over to the third in the line. From the back her neck looked a little scrawny, but when she turned to us she had smooth white skin and promising blue eyes. Odell said something to her, and she nodded, and I told her:

"I've just thought up a new way to make a phone call. Mr.

Wolfe in Suite 60, Upshur Pavilion, wants to put in a call to New York and I'm going to stay and watch you do it."

"Suite 60? That's the man that was shot."

"Yep."

"And it was you that told me I'm a wonder."

"Yep. In a way I came to check up. If you'll just get—"

"Excuse me." She turned and talked and listened, and monkeyed with some plugs. When she was through I said:

"Get New York, Liberty 2-3306, and put it on Suite 60."

She grinned. "Personally conducted phone calls, huh?"

"Right. I haven't had so much fun in ages."

She got busy. I became aware of activity at my elbow, and saw that Odell had got out a notebook and pencil and was writing something down. I craned the neck for a glimpse of his scrawl, and then told him pleasantly, "I like a man that knows his job the way you do. To save you the trouble of listening for the next one, it's going to be Spring 7-3100. New York Police Headquarters."

"Much obliged. What's he doing, yelling for help because he got a little scratch on the face?"

I made a fitting reply with my mind elsewhere, because I was watching operations. The board was an old style, and it was easy to tell if she was listening in. Her hands were all over the place, pushing and dropping plugs, and it was only five minutes or so before I heard her say, "Mr. Wolfe? Ready with New York. Go ahead, please." She flashed me a grin. "Who was I supposed to tell about it? Mr. Odell here?"

I grinned back. "Don't you bother your little head about it. Be good, dear child—"

"And let who will wear diamonds. I know. Have you heard the one—excuse me."

Odell stayed with me till the end. He had a long wait, for Wolfe's talk with Saul Panzer lasted a good quarter of an hour, and the second one, with Inspector Cramer—provided he got Cramer—almost as long. When it was finished and the plugs had been pulled, I thought it was only sociable to ask the maiden whether she preferred oblong diamonds or round ones, and she replied that she would much rather have a copy of the Bible because most of hers were getting worn out, she read them so much. I made a feint to pat her on the head and she ducked and Odell plucked me by the sleeve.

I left him in the lobby with thanks and an assurance that I hadn't forgotten his aspirations to the Hotel Churchill, regarding which Mr. Wolfe would sound out Mr. Liggett at the first opportunity.

A minute later I had an opportunity myself, but was too busy to take advantage of it. Going away from the main entrance in the direction of my next errand took me past the mounting block, and there was a bunch of horses around, some mounted and some not, with greenjacket grooms. I like the look of horses at a distance of ten feet or more, and I slowed down as I went by. It was there I saw Liggett, with the right clothes on which I suppose he had borrowed, dismounting from a big bay. Another reason I slowed down was because I thought I might see another guest get stepped on, but it didn't happen so. Not that I have anything against guests as guests; it's only my natural feeling about people who pay twenty bucks a day for a room to sleep in, and they always look either too damn sleek or as if they had been born with a bellyache. I know if I was a horse . . .

But I had errands. Wolfe had already been alone in that room for over half an hour, and although I had left strict orders with the greenjacket to admit no one to Suite 60 under any pretext, and the door was locked, I didn't care much for the setup. So I got along to Pocahontas Pavilion in quick time. I met Lisette Putti and Vallenko, with tennis rackets, near the entrance, and Mamma Mondor was on the veranda knitting. On the driveway a state cop and a plug-ugly in cits sat in a car smoking cigarettes. Inside both parlors were empty, but there was plenty going on in the kitchen—cooks and helpers, greenjackets, masters, darting around looking concentrated. Apparently another free-for-all lunch was in preparation, not to mention the dinner for that evening, which was to illustrate the subject of Wolfe's speech by consisting of dishes that had originated in America. That, of course, was to be concocted under the direction of Louis Servan, and he was there in white cap and apron, moving around feeling, looking, smelling, tasting, and instructing. I allowed myself a grin at the sight of Albert Malfi the Corsican fruit slicer, also capped and aproned, trotting at Servan's heels, before I went across to accost the dean, just missing a collision with Domenico Rossi as he bounced away from a range.

Servan's dignified old face clouded over when he saw me. "Ah, Mr. Goodwin! I've just heard of that terrible . . . to Mr. Wolfe. Mr. Ashley phoned from the hotel. That a guest of mine—our guest of honor—terrible! I'll call on him as soon as I can manage to leave here. It's not serious? He can be with us?"

I reassured him, and two or three others trotted up, and I accepted their sympathy for my boss and told them it would be just as well not to pay any calls for a few hours. Then I told Servan I hated to interrupt a busy man but needed a few words with him, and he went with me to the small parlor. After some conversation he called in Moulton, the headwaiter with a piece out of his ear, and gave him instructions.

When Moulton had departed Servan hesitated before he said, "I wanted to see Mr. Wolfe anyway. Mr. Ashley tells me that he got a startling story from two of my waiters. I can understand their reluctance... but I can't have... my friend Laszio murdered here in my own dining room...." He passed his hand wearily across his forehead. "This should have been such a happiness.... I'm over seventy years old, Mr. Goodwin, and this is the worst thing that has ever happened to me...and I must get back to the kitchen...Crabtree's a good man, but he's flighty and I don't trust him with all that commotion in there...."

"Forget it." I patted his arm. "I mean forget the murder. Let Nero Wolfe do the worrying, I always do. Did you elect your four new members this morning?"

"Yes. Why?"

"I was just curious about Malfi. Did he get in?"

"Malfi? In Les Quinze Maîtres? Good heavens, no!"

"Okay. I was just curious. You go on back to the kitchen and enjoy yourself. I'll give Wolfe your message about lunch."

He nodded and pattered away. I had then been gone from Upshur more than an hour, and I hotfooted it back by the shortest path.

Going in after the outdoor sunshine, Wolfe's room seemed somber, but the maid had been in and the bed was made and everything tidy. He had the big chair turned to face the windows, and sat there with his speech in his hand, frowning at the last page. I had sung out from the foyer to let him know all was well, and now approached to take a look at the bandage. It seemed in order, and there was no sign of any fresh bleeding.

I reported: "Everything's set. Servan turned the details over to Moulton. They all send their best regards and wish you were along. Servan's going to send a couple of trays of

141

lunch over to us. It's a grand day outdoors, too bad you're cooped up like this. Our client has taken advantage of it by going horseback riding."

"We have no client."

"I was referring to Mr. Liggett. I still think that since he offered to pay for a job of detective work you might as well give him that pleasure. Not to mention hiring Berin for him. Did you get Saul and Cramer?"

"Weren't you at the switchboard?"

"Yes, but I didn't know who you got."

"I got them. That alternative is being cared for." He sighed. "This thing hurts. What are they cooking for lunch?"

"Lord, I don't know. Five or six of them are messing around. Certainly it hurts, and you won't collect a damn cent for it." I sat down and rested my head against the back of the chair because I was tired of holding it up. "Not only that, it seems to have made you more contrary even than usual, it and the loss of sleep. I know you sneer at what you call routine, but I've seen you get results from it now and then, and no matter how much of a genius you are it wouldn't do any harm to find out what various people were doing at a quarter past ten this morning. For instance, if you found that Leon Blanc was in the kitchen making soup, he couldn't very well have been out there in the shrubbery shooting at you. I'm just explaining how it's done."

"Thank you."

"Thank me, and go on being contrary, huh?"

"I'm not contrary, merely intelligent. I've often told you, a search for negative evidence is a desperate last resort when no positive evidence can be found. Collecting and checking alibis is dreary and usually futile drudgery. No. Get your positive evidence, and if you find it confronted by an alibi, and if your evidence is any good, break the alibi. Anyhow, I'm not interested in the man who shot me. The man I want is the one who stabbed Laszio."

I stared. "What's this, a riddle? You yourself said it was the same one."

"Certainly. But since it was his murdering Laszio that led to his shooting me, obviously it's the murder we must prove. Unless we can prove he killed Laszio, how can we give him a motive for trying to kill me? And if you can't demonstrate a motive, what the devil does it matter where he was at a quarter past ten? The only thing that will do us any good is direct evidence that he committed the murder."

"Oh, well." I waved a hand, feebly. "If that's all. Naturally you've got *that*."

"I have. It is being tested."

"I'll call. What evidence and who?"

He started to shake his head, and winced and stopped. "It is being tested. I don't pretend that the evidence is conclusive, far from it. We must await the test. It is so little conclusive that I have arranged for this performance with Mr. Blanc because we are pressed for time and no alternative can be ignored. And after all it is quite possible—though I shouldn't think he would have a gun— There's someone at the door."

The performance with Blanc was elaborate but a complete wash-out. Its only advantage was that it kept me occupied and awake until lunch time. I wasn't surprised at the result, and I don't think Wolfe was either; he was just being thorough and not neglecting anything.

The first arrivals were Moulton and Paul Whipple, and they had the props with them. I took them into Wolfe for an explanation of the project, and then deposited them in my room and shut the door on them. A few minutes later Leon Blanc came.

The chef and the gastronome had quite a chat. Blanc was of course distressed at Wolfe's injury and said so at length. Then they got on to the business. Blanc had come, he said, at Servan's request, and would answer any questions Mr. Wolfe might care to ask. That was an order for anybody, but Blanc filled it pretty well, including the pointed and insistent queries regarding the extent of his acquaintanceship with Mrs. Laszio. Blanc stuck to it that he had known her rather well when she had been Mrs. Vukcic and he had been chef de cuisine at the Churchill, but that in the past five years, since he had gone to Boston, he had seen her only two or three times, and they had never been at all intimate. Then Wolfe got onto Tuesday night and the period Blanc had spent in his room at Pocahontas Pavilion, while the others were tasting Sauce Printemps and someone was stabbing Laszio. I heard most of it from a distance because I was in the bathroom, with the door open a crack, experimenting with the burnt cork on the back of my hand. Servan had sent an alcohol burner and enough corks for a minstrel show.

143

Blanc balked a little when Wolfe got to the suggestion of the masquerade test, but not very strenuously, and I opened the bathroom door and invited him in. We had a picnic. With him stripped to his underwear, I first rubbed in a layer of cold cream and then started with the cork. I suppose I didn't do it like an expert, since I wasn't one, but by gosh I got him black. The ears and the edge of the hair were a problem, and he claimed I got some in his eye, but it was only because he blinked too hard. Then he put on the suit of livery, including the cap, and it wasn't a bad job at all, except that Moulton hadn't been able to dig up any black gloves, and we had to use dark brown ones.

I took him in to Wolfe for approval, and telephoned Pocahontas Pavilion and got Mrs. Coyne and told her we were ready.

In five minutes she was there. I stepped into the corridor to give her a brief explanation of the program, explaining that she wasn't to open her mouth if she wanted to help Wolfe keep her out of it, and then, admitting her to the foyer and leaving her there, I went back in to pose Blanc. He had got pretty well irritated before I had finished with him in the bathroom, but now Wolfe had him all soothed down again. I stood him over beyond the foot of the bed, at what looked like the right distance, pulled his cap lower, had him put his finger to his lips, and told him to hold it. Then I went to the door to the foyer and opened it six inches.

After ten seconds I told Blanc that would do for that pose and went to the foyer and took Lio Coyne out to the corridor again.

"Well?"

She shook her head. "No. It wasn't that man."

"How do you know it wasn't?"

"His ears are too big. It wasn't him."

"Could you swear to that in a court?"

"But you..." Her eyes got narrow. "You said I wouldn't..."

"All right, you won't. But how sure are you?"

"I'm very sure. This man is more slender, too."

"Okay. Much obliged. Mr. Wolfe may want to speak to you later on."

The others said the same thing. I posed Blanc twice more, once facing the door for Paul Whipple, and the second time with his back to it for Moulton. Whipple said he would be willing to swear that the man he had seen by the screen in the dining room was not the one he had seen in Wolfe's room, and Moulton said he couldn't swear to it because he had only seen the man's back, but he thought it wasn't the same man. I sent them back to Pocahontas.

Then I had to help Blanc clean up. Getting it off was twice as hard as putting it on, and I don't know if he ever did get his ears clean again. Considering that he wasn't a murderer at all, he was pretty nice about it. What with Wolfe's blood and Blanc's burnt cork, I certainly raised cain with Kanawha Spa towels that day.

Blanc stood and told Wolfe: "I have submitted to all this because Louis Servan requested it. I know murderers are supposed to be punished. If I were one, I would expect to be. This is a frightful experience for all of us, Mr. Wolfe, frightful. I didn't kill Phillip Laszio, but if it were possible for me to bring him to life again by lifting a finger, do you know what I'd do? I would do this." He thrust both hands into his pockets as far as they would go, and kept them there.

He turned to go, but his departure was postponed a few minutes longer, by a new arrival. The change in program had of course made it necessary to tell the greenjacket in the hall that the embargo on visitors was lifted, and now came the first of a string that kept knocking at the door intermittently all afternoon.

This one was my friend Barry Tolman.

"How's Mr. Wolfe?"

"Battered and belligerent. Go on in."

He entered, opened his mouth at Wolfe, and then saw who was standing there.

"Oh. You here, Mr. Blanc?"

"Yes. At Mr. Servan's request—"

Wolfe put in, "We've been doing an experiment. I don't believe you'll need to waste time with Mr. Blanc. What about it, Archie? Did Mr. Blanc kill Laszio?"

I shook my head. "No, sir. Three outs and the side's retired."

Tolman looked at me, at Wolfe, at Blanc. "Is that so. Anyhow, I may want to see you later. You'll be at Pocahontas?"

Blanc told him yes, not very amiably, expressed a hope that Wolfe would feel better by dinnertime, and went. When I got back from escorting him to the door, Tolman had sat down and had his head cocked on one side for a look at Wolfe's bandage, and Wolfe was saying:

"Not to me, no, sir. The doctor called it superficial. But I assure you it is highly dangerous to the man who did it. And look here." He displayed the mangled script of the speech. "The bullet did that before it struck me. Mr. Goodwin saved my life by tossing my speech at the window. So he says. I am willing to grant it. Where is Mr. Berin?"

"Here. At Pocahontas with . . . with his daughter. I brought him myself, just now. They phoned me at Quinby about your being shot. Do you think it was the one that stabbed Laszio who did it?"

"Who else?"

"But why was he after you? You were through with it."

"He didn't know that." Wolfe stirred in his chair, winced, and added bitterly, "I'm not through with it now."

"That suits me. I don't say I'm glad you got shot . . . and you started on Blanc? What made you decide it wasn't him?"

Wolfe started to explain, but another interruption took me away. This time it was the lunch trays, and Louis Servan had certainly put on the dog. There were three enormous trays and three waiters, and a fourth greenjacket as an outrider for opening doors and clearing traffic. I was hungry, and the smells that came from under the covered services made me more so. The outrider, who was Moulton himself, after a bow and an announcement to Wolfe, unfolded serving stands for the trays and advanced to the table with a cloth in his hand.

Wolfe told Tolman, "Excuse me, please." With a healthy grunt he lifted himself from his chair and made his way across to the serving stands. Moulton joined him and hovered deferentially. Wolfe lifted one of the covers, bent his head and gazed, and sniffed. Then he looked at Moulton. "Piroshki?"

"Yes, sir. By Mr. Vallenko."

"Yes. I know." He lifted other covers, bent and smelled, with careful nods to himself. He straightened up again. "Artichokes barigoule?"

"I think, sir, he called them drigante. Mr. Mondor. Something like that."

"No matter. Leave it all here, please. We'll serve ourselves, if you don't mind."

"But Mr. Servan told me—"

"I prefer it that way. Leave it here on the trays."

"I'll leave a man—"

"No. Please. I'm having a conversation. Out, all of you."

They went. It appeared that if I was going to get anything

146

to eat I'd have to work for it, so I called on the muscles for another effort. As Wolfe returned to his chair I asked, "How do we do it? Boardinghouse style à la scoop shovel?"

He waited until he got deposited before he answered. Then he sighed first. "No. Telephone the hotel for a luncheon menu."

I stared at him. "Maybe you're delirious?"

"Archie." He sounded savage. "You may guess the humor I'm in. That piroshki is by Vallenko, and the artichokes are by Mondor. But how the devil do I know who was in that kitchen or what happened there? These trays were intended for us, and probably everyone knew it. For me. I am still hoping to go home to-night. Phone the hotel, and get those trays out of here so I can't smell them. Put them in your room and leave them there."

Tolman said, "But my God, man...if you really think...we can have that stuff analyzed...."

"I don't want to analyze it, I want to eat it. And I can't. I'm not going to. There probably is nothing at all wrong with it, and look at me, terrorized, intimidated by that blackguard! What good would it do to analyze it? I tell you, sir—Archie?"

It was the door again. The smell from those covered dishes had me in almost as bad a state as Wolfe, and I was hoping it might be a food inspector from the Board of Health to certify them unadulterated, but it was only the greenjacket from the hall. He had a telegram addressed to Nero Wolfe.

I went back in with it, tore the envelope open, and handed it to him.

He pulled it out and read it.

He murmured, "Indeed." At the sound of the new tone in his voice I gave him a sharp glance. He handed the telegram back to me, unfolded. "Read it to Mr. Tolman."

I did so:

NERO WOLFE KANAWHA SPA W VA
NOT MENTIONED ANY PAPER STOP CRAMER
COOPERATING STOP PROCEEDING STOP WILL
PHONE FROM DESTINATION

PANZER

Wolfe said softly, "That's better. Much better. We might almost eat that piroshki now, but there's a chance...no. Phone the hotel, Archie. And Mr. Tolman, I believe there will be an opportunity for you also to cooperate...."

15

JEROME BERIN shook both his fists so that his chair trembled under him. "God above! Such a dirty dog! Such a—" He stopped himself abruptly and demanded, "You say it was not Blanc? Not Vukcic? Not my old friend Zelota?"

Wolfe murmured, "None of them, I think."

"Then I repeat, a dirty dog!" Berin leaned forward and tapped Wolfe on the knee. "I tell you frankly, it did not take a dog to kill Laszio. Anyone might have done that, anyone at all, merely as an incident in the disposal of garbage. En passant. True, it is bad to stab a man in the back, but when one is in a hurry the niceties must sometimes be overlooked. No, only for killing Laszio, even in that manner, I would not say a dog. But to shoot at you through a window—you, the guest of honor of Les Quinze Maîtres! Only because you had interested yourself in the cause of justice! Because you had undertaken to establish my innocence! Because you had the good sense to know that I could not possibly have made seven mistakes of those nine sauces! And let me tell you... will you credit it when I tell you what they gave me to eat in that place... in that jail in that place?"

He went on to tell, and it sounded awful. He had come, with his daughter, to express his appreciation of Wolfe's efforts in his behalf. It was nearly four o'clock, and there was sunlight in the room, for Tolman had arranged for a double guard on the windows, the other side of the shrubbery, and the shades were up and the windows open. The lunch from the hotel may not have been piroshki by Vallenko, but it had been adequate for my purposes, and Wolfe had been able to get it down in spite of the difficulty he had chewing. I had completely abandoned the idea of a little nap; there wasn't a chance. Tolman had stayed nearly until the end of lunch, and after that was finished Rossi and Mondor and Coyne had dropped in to offer commiseration for Wolfe's wound, and they had been followed by others. Even Louis Servan had made it for a few minutes, though I didn't understand how he had been able to get away from the kitchen. Also, around

148

three o'clock, there had been a phone call from New York, which Wolfe took himself. His end of it consisted mostly of grunts, and all I knew about it when he got through was that he had been talking with Inspector Cramer. But I knew he hadn't got any bad news, for afterwards he sat and rubbed the side of his nose and looked self-satisfied.

Constanza Berin sat for twenty minutes on the edge of her chair trying to get a word in, and when her father called an intermission to get his pipe lit she finally succeeded.

"Mr. Wolfe, I...I was terrible this morning."

He moved his eyes at her. "You were indeed, Miss Berin. I have often noticed that the more beautiful a woman is, especially a young one, the more liable she is to permit herself unreasonable fits. It's something that you acknowledge. Tell me, when you feel it coming on like that, is there nothing you can do to stop it? Have you ever tried?"

She laughed at him. "But it isn't fits. I don't have fits. I was scared and mad because they had put my father in jail for murder, and I knew he hadn't done it, and they seemed to think they had proof against him, and then I was told that it was you who had found the proof.... How was I going to be reasonable about that? And in a strange country I had never been in before.... America is an awful country."

"There are those who would disagree with you."

"I suppose so.... I suppose it isn't so much the country... maybe it's the people who live here.... Oh, excuse me, I don't mean you, or Mr. Goodwin...I'm sure you are very amiable, and of course Mr. Goodwin is, with a wife and so many children...."

"Indeed." Wolfe shot me a withering glance. "How are the children, Archie? Well, I hope?"

"Fine, thanks." I waved a hand. "Doggone the little shavers, I sure do miss 'em, away from home like this. I can hardly wait to get back."

Berin took his pipe from his mouth to nod at me. "The little ones are nice. Now my daughter here..." He shrugged. "She is nice, naturally, but God above, she drives me mad!" He leaned to tap Wolfe's knee with the stem of the pipe. "Speaking of getting back. Is it true what I am told, that these dogs can keep us here on and on until they permit us to go? Merely because that Laszio got a knife in his back? My daughter and I were to leave to-night, for New York, and then to Canada. I am out of jail but I am not free. Is that it?"

149

"I'm afraid that's it. Were you intending to take the midnight train to New York?"

"I was. And now they tell me no one leaves this place until they learn who killed that dog! If we wait on that for that imbecile Tolman, and that other one, that one who squints..." He replaced his pipe and puffed until he had clouds.

"But we needn't wait on them." Wolfe sighed. "Thank God. I think, sir, it would be wise to have your bags packed, and if you have reservations on that train, keep them. Fortunately you did not have to wait for Mr. Tolman to discover the truth about those sauces. If you had..."

"I might not have left at all. I know that. I might have got this." Berin used the edge of his hand for a cleaver to slice off his head. "Certainly I would still be in that jail, and within three days I would have starved. We Catalans can take death when it comes, but God above, a man that can swallow that food is not a man, he is not even a beast! I know what I owe you, and I called for blessings on you with every bite of my lunch. I discussed it with Servan. I told him how greatly I am indebted to you, and that I do no man the honor of remaining in debt to him. I told Servan I must pay you... he is our host here, and a man of delicacy. He said you would not take pay. He said it had been offered, and you had scorned it. I understand and respect your feeling, since you are our guest of honor—"

Another knock on the door made me leave Wolfe simmering in the juice of the stew he had made. I had always known that some day he would talk too much for his own good, and as I went to the foyer I was wearing a grin—I admit malicious—and reflecting on how it probably felt at the moment to be a jewel on the cushion of hospitality.

The new arrival was only Vukcic, but he served as well as another bullet through the window would have done to make a break in the conversation and take it away from vulgar things like payments for services rendered. Vukcic was in a mood. He acted embarrassed, gloomy, nervous and abstracted. A few minutes after he arrived the Berins left, and then he stood in front of Wolfe with his arms folded, frowning down, and told him that in spite of Wolfe's impertinence that morning on the subject of howling on a hillside, it was a duty of old friendship to call personally to offer sympathy and regrets for an injury suffered....

Wolfe snapped, "I was shot over six hours ago. I might have died by now."

"Oh, come, Nero. Surely not. They said it was only your cheek, and I can see for myself—"

"I lost a quart of blood.—Archie! Did you say a quart?"

I hadn't said anything, but I'm always loyal. "Yes, sir. At least that. Closer to two. Of course I couldn't stop to measure it, but it came out like a river, like Niagara Falls, like—"

"That will do. Thank you."

Vukcic still stood frowning down. His tangle of hair was tumbling for his eyes, but he didn't unfold his arms to comb it back with his fingers. He growled, "I'm sorry. It was a close call. If he had killed you..." A pause. "Look here, Nero. Who was it?"

"I don't know. Not with certainty—yet."

"Are you finding out?"

"Yes."

"Was it the murderer of Laszio?"

"Yes—Confound it, I like to move my head when I talk, and I can't." Wolfe put the tips of his fingers gingerly to the bandage, felt it, and let his hand drop again. "I'll tell you something, Marko. This mist that has arisen between your eyes and mine—we can't ignore it and it is futile to discuss it. All I can say is, it will shortly be dispelled."

"The devil it will. How?"

"By the course of history. By Atropos, and me as her agent. At any rate, I am counting on that. In the meantime, there is nothing we can say to each other. You are drugged again— there, I didn't mean to say that. You see we can't talk. I would offend you, and you would bore me insufferably. Au revoir, Marko."

"Good God, I don't deny I'm drugged."

"I know it. You know what you're doing, and you do it anyway. Thank you for coming."

Vukcic did then unfold his arms to comb his hair. He ran his fingers through it three times, slowly, and then without saying anything turned and walked out.

Wolfe sat a long while with his eyes closed. Then he sighed deeply and asked me to take the script of the speech for a final rehearsal.

The only interruptions that time were some phone calls, from Tolman and Clay Ashley and Louis Servan. It was six o'clock before we had another caller, and when I opened the

151

door and saw it was Raymond Liggett of the Hotel Churchill, I put on a welcoming grin because right away I smelled a fee, and among all the other irritations I was being subjected to was my dislike of seeing Wolfe exercising his brain, blowing money on long distance calls and drinks for fourteen dark-skinned men, losing two nights' sleep, and getting shot, with maybe a permanent scar, all for nothing relating to the bank account. As a side issue, there was also the question of a job for my friend Odell. Not that I owed him anything, but in the detective business around New York you never know in which spot it may become desirable to be greeted by a friendly face. To have the house dick of the Churchill, or even one of his staff, a protégé of mine, might come in handy any time.

Sure enough, it appeared that a fee was in prospect. The first thing Liggett said, after he had got seated and expressed the proper sentiments regarding Wolfe's facial casualty, was that one of the objects of his call was to ask if Wolfe would be willing to reconsider the matter of approaching Berin about the job of chef de cuisine at the Hotel Churchill.

Wolfe murmured, "I'm surprised that you still want him—a man who has been accused of murder. The publicity?"

Liggett dismissed that with a gesture. "Why not? People don't eat publicity, they eat food. And you know what Berin's prestige is. Frankly, I'm more interested in his prestige than in his food. I have an excellent kitchen staff, from top to bottom."

"People do eat prestige then." Wolfe gently patted his tummy. "I don't believe I'd care for it."

Liggett smiled his thin smile. His gray eyes looked about as irritated as they had Wednesday morning, not less, and they couldn't more. He shrugged. "Well, they seem to like it. About Berin. I know that yesterday morning you said you wouldn't do it, but you also said you wouldn't investigate Laszio's murder, and I understand you've reconsidered that. Ashley tells me you've done something quite remarkable, I didn't gather just what."

Wolfe inclined his head an eighth of an inch. "Thank you."

"That's what Ashley said. Besides, it was what you discovered, whatever that was, that caused Berin's release. Berin knows that, and therefore you are in a particularly advantageous position to make a suggestion to him—or even a request. I explained to you yesterday why I'm especially anxious to get him. I can add to that, confidentially—"

"I don't want confidences, Mr. Liggett."

Liggett impatiently brushed that aside. "It's not much of a secret. A competitor has been after Berin for two years. Branting of the Alexander. I happen to know that Berin has an appointment with Branting in New York to-morrow afternoon. That's the main reason I rushed down here. I have to get at him before he sees Branting."

"And soon after your arrival he was taken to jail. That was unfortunate. But he's out now, and is this minute probably at Pocahontas Pavilion. He left here two hours ago. Why the deuce don't you go and see him?"

"I told you yesterday. Because I don't think I can swing him." Liggett leaned forward. "Look here. The situation as it stands now is ideal. You got him out of jail, and he's impulsive and emotional, and he's feeling grateful to you. You can do it in one talk with him. One trouble is that I don't know what Branting has offered him, or is going to offer him, but whatever it is, I'll top it. I told you yesterday that I'd like to have him for forty thousand but would go to sixty if I had to. Now the time's short and I think I might even make it seventy. You can offer him fifty at the start—"

"I haven't agreed to offer him anything."

"But I'm telling you. You can offer him fifty thousand dollars a year. That's a lot more than he's getting at San Remo, but he may have a percentage there. Anyway, New York is something else. And if you land him I'll pay you ten thousand dollars cash."

Wolfe lifted his brows. "You want him, don't you?"

"I've got to have him. My directors have discussed this—after all, Laszio was getting along in years—and I must get him. Of course I don't own the Churchill, though I have a good block of stock. You still have time to start the ball rolling before dinner. I wanted to see you earlier this afternoon, when they brought Berin back, but on account of your accident..."

"Not an accident. Chance is without intention." Wolfe touched his bandage. "This was intended—or rather, worse."

"That's true. Of course. Will you see Berin now?"

"No."

"To-night?"

"No."

Liggett jerked up. "But damn it, are you crazy? A chance to make ten thousand dollars"—he snapped his fingers—"just like that! Why not?"

"It's not my business, hiring chefs. I'm a detective. I stick to my profession."

"I'm not asking you to make a business of it. All it means probably, under the circumstances, is one good talk with him. You can tell him he will be executive chef, with complete control and no interference from the hotel administration, and nothing to report but results. Our cost distribution is handled—"

Wolfe was wiggling a finger. "Mr. Liggett. Please. This is a waste of time. I shall not approach Mr. Berin on behalf of the Hotel Churchill."

Silence. I covered a yawn. I was surprised that Liggett wasn't bouncing up with exasperation, since his tendencies seemed to run in that direction, but all he did was sit still, not a muscle moving, and look at Wolfe. Wolfe, likewise motionless, returned the gaze with half-shut eyes.

The silence lasted all of a minute. Finally Liggett said, in a level tone with no exasperation at all, "I'll give you twenty thousand cash to get Berin for me."

"It doesn't tempt me, Mr. Liggett."

"I'll . . . I'll make it thirty thousand. I can give it to you in currency to-morrow morning."

Wolfe stirred a little, without unfocusing his eyes. "No. It wouldn't be worth it to you. Mr. Berin is a master chef, but not the only one alive. See here. This childish pretense is ridiculous. You were ill-advised to come to me like this. You are probably a man of some natural sense, and with only your own interests to consult, and left to your own counsel and devices, I am sure you would never have done such a thing. You were sent here, Mr. Liggett. I know that. It was a mistake that might have been expected, considering who did it. Pfui! You might, I suppose, go back and report your failure, but if you are moved to consult further it would be vastly better to consult only yourself."

"I don't know what you're talking about. I'm making you a straight proposal."

Wolfe shrugged. "If I am incoherent, that ends communication. Report failure, then, to yourself."

"I'm not reporting failure to anyone." Liggett's eyes were hard and so was his tone. "I came to you only because it

154

seemed practical. To save annoyance. I can do—whatever I want done—without you."

"Then by all means do it."

"But I would still like to save annoyance. I'll pay you fifty thousand dollars."

Wolfe slowly, barely perceptibly, shook his head. "You'll have to report failure, Mr. Liggett. If it is true, as the cynic said, that every man has his price, you couldn't hand me mine in currency."

The phone rang. When a man turns cold and still I like to keep my eye on him in case, so I sidled around beyond Liggett's chair without turning my back on him. The first voice I heard in the receiver sounded like the blue-eyed belle, and she said she had a New York call. Then I heard gruff tones demanding Nero Wolfe, and was informed that Inspector Cramer wanted him. I turned:

"For you, sir. Mr. Purdy."

With a grunt, he labored to lift it from the chair. He stood and looked down at our caller:

"This is a confidential affair, Mr. Liggett. And since our business is concluded . . . if you don't mind? . . ."

Liggett took it as it was given. Without a word, without either haste or hesitation, he arose and departed. I strolled behind him to the foyer, and when he was out and the door closed I turned the key.

Wolfe's conversation with Cramer lasted more than ten minutes, and this time, as I sat and listened, I got something out of it besides grunts, but not enough to make a good picture. It seemed to me that he had distrusted my powers of dissimulation as far as was necessary, so when he hung up I was all set to put in a requisition for light and lucidity, but he had barely got back in his chair when the phone rang again. This time she told me it was a call from Charleston, and after some clicking and crackling I heard a voice in my ears that was as familiar as the Ventura Skin Preserver theme song.

"Hello, Mr. Wolfe?"

"No, you little shrimp, this is the Supreme Court speaking."

"Oh, Archie! How goes it?"

"Marvelous. Having a fine rest. Hold it, here's Mr. Wolfe." I handed him the receiver. "Saul Panzer from Charleston."

That was another ten minute talk, and it afforded me a few more hints and scraps of the alternative that Wolfe had apparently settled on, though it still seemed fairly incredible

155

in spots. When it was finished Wolfe ambled back to his seat again, leaned back with careful caution, and got his fingers joined at the dome of his rotunda.

He demanded, "What time is it?"

I glanced at my wrist. "Quarter to seven."

He grunted. "Only a little over an hour till dinner. Don't let me forget to have that speech in my pocket when we go over there. Can you remember a few things without putting them down?"

"Sure. Any quantity."

"They are all important. First I must talk with Mr. Tolman; I suppose he is at the hotel as arranged. Then I must telephone Mr. Servan; that may be difficult; I believe it is not customary to have guests the last evening. In this case the tradition must be violated. While I am telephoning you will lay out everything we shall need, pack the bags, and arrange for their delivery at the train. We may be pressed for time around midnight. Also send to the hotel for our bill, and pay it. Did I hear you say you have your pistol along?—Good. I trust it won't be needed, but carry it. And confound it, send for a barber, I can't shave myself. Then get Mr. Tolman, and start on the bags. I'll discuss the evening program while we're dressing. . . ."

16

THE TRADITION was violated, and I overheard a few grumbles about it, in the big parlor before the door to the dining room was thrown open and Louis Servan appeared on the threshold to invite us in. Chiefly, though, as they sipped sherry or vermouth in scattered groups, the grumbles were on another subject: the decree that had been issued that none of them was to leave the jurisdiction of West Virginia until permission had been given by the authorities. Domenico Rossi orated about it, making it plenty loud enough to be heard by Barry Tolman, who stood by the radio looking worried but handsome; Ramsey Keith bellowed his opinion of the outrage; while Jerome Berin said God above, it was barbarous, but they would be fools to let it interfere with digestion. Albert

Malfi, looking a little subdued but with darts still in his eyes, seemed to have decided that courting Mamma Mondor was a sensible first step in his campaign for election in 1942; Raymond Liggett sat on the couch conversing quietly with Marko Vukcic. My friend Tolman got it right in the neck, or rather he didn't get it at all, when Constanza Berin came in and he went up to her looking determined, and spoke. She failed to see or hear him so completely that for a second I thought he wasn't there at all, I had just imagined it.

A couple of minutes before we started for the dining room Dina Laszio entered. The noise died down. Rossi, her father, hurried over to her, and not far behind him was Vukcic; then several others went up to pay their respects to the widow. She resembled a grieving widow about as much as I resemble a whirling dervish, but of course it can't be expected that every time a woman packs for a little trip with her husband she will take weeds along in case he happens to get bumped off. And I couldn't very well disapprove of her showing up at the feast, since I knew that Nero Wolfe had requested Servan to see her personally and insist on it.

At the table I was next to Constanza again, which was tolerable. Wolfe was at Servan's right. Vukcic was on the other side of Dina Laszio, down a ways. Liggett and Malfi were directly across from me, next to each other. Berin was across from Wolfe, on Servan's left, which seemed to me quite an honor for a guy just out of jail, and next to him was Clay Ashley, not making much of a success of attempts to appear affable. The others were here and there, with the meager supply of ladies spotted at intervals. On each plate when we sat down was an engraved menu:

LES QUINZE MAITRES
Kanawha Spa, West Virginia,
Thursday, April 8th, 1937.

AMERICAN DINNER

Oysters Baked in the Shell

Terrapin Maryland   Beaten Biscuits

Pan Broiled Young Turkey

Rice Croquettes with Quince Jelly

Lima Beans in Cream   Sally Lunn

Avocado Todhunter

Pineapple Sherbet   Sponge Cake

Wisconsin Dairy Cheese   Black Coffee

As the waiters, supervised by Moulton, smoothly brought and took, Louis Servan surveyed the scene with solemn and anxious dignity. The first course should have helped to allay the anxiety, for the oysters were so plump and savory, not to mention aromatic, that it seemed likely they had been hand-fed on peanuts and blueberries. They were served with ceremony and a dash of pomp. As the waiters finished distributing the enormous tins, each holding a dozen oysters, they stood back in a line against one of the screens—the one which forty-eight hours previously had concealed the body of Phillip Laszio—and the door to the pantry hall opened to admit a brown-skinned cook in immaculate white cap and apron. He came forward a few paces, looking embarrassed enough to back right out again, but Servan stood up and beckoned to him and then turned to the table and announced to the gathering, "I wish to present to you Mr. Hyacinth Brown, the fish chef of Kanawha Spa. The baked oysters we are about to eat is his. You will judge whether it is worthy of the honor of being served to Les Quinze Maîtres. Mr. Brown wishes me to tell you that he appreciates that honor.—Isn't that so, Brown?"

"Yes, sir. You said it."

There was a ripple of applause. Brown looked more embarrassed than ever, bowed, and turned and went. The masters lifted forks and waded in, and the rest of us followed suit. There were grunts and murmurs of appreciation. Rossi called something across the length of the table. Pierre Mondor stated with quiet authority, "Superb. Extreme oven?" Servan nodded gravely, and the forks played on.

With the terrapin the performance was repeated, this time the introduction being accorded to Crabtree; and when the course was finished there was a near riot of enthusiasm and it was demanded that Crabtree reappear. Most of them got up to shake his hand, and he wasn't embarrassed at all, though he was certainly pleased. Two of them came in with the turkey. One was Grant, with wrinkled face and gray kinky hair, and the other was a tall black one that I didn't know, since he hadn't been at the party Wednesday night. I never tasted better turkey, but the other servings had been gener-ous and my capacity limited me to one portion. Those guys eating were like a woman packing a trunk—it's not a question of capacity but of how much she has to put in. Not to mention the claret they washed it down with. They were getting merrier as they went along, and even old Servan was sending happy smiles around.

Unquestionably it was first class fodder. I went slow on the wine. My head was fuzzy anyhow, and if I was going to be called on to save Wolfe's life again I might need what wits I had left.

There was nothing strained about the atmosphere, it was just a nice party with everyone well filled and the smell of good coffee and brandy in front of us, when finally, a little after ten o'clock, Wolfe arose to start his speech. He looked more like the plaintiff in a suit for damages than an after-dinner speaker, and he was certainly aware of it, but it didn't seem to bother him. We all got our chairs moved around to face him more comfortably and got settled into silence. He began in an easy informal tone:

"Mr. Servan, Ladies, Masters, Fellow Guests. I feel a little silly. Under different circumstances it might be both instructive and amusing for you, at least some of you, to listen to a discussion of American contributions to la haute cuisine, and it might be desirable to use what persuasiveness I can command to convince you that those contributions are neither negligible nor meager. But when I accepted an invitation to offer you such a discussion, which greatly pleased and flattered me, I didn't realize how unnecessary it would be at the moment scheduled for its delivery. It is delightful to talk about food, but infinitely more delightful to eat it; and we have eaten. A man once declared to me that one of the keenest pleasures in life was to close his eyes and dream of beautiful women, and when I suggested that it would be still more agreeable to open his eyes and look at them, he said not at all, for the ones he dreamed about were *all* beautiful, far more beautiful than any his eye ever encountered. Similarly it might be argued that if I am eloquent the food I talk to you about may be better than the food you have eaten; but even that specious excuse is denied me. I can describe, and pay tribute to, some superlative American dishes, but I can't surpass the oysters and terrapin and turkey which were so recently there"—he indicated the table—"and are now here." With a gentle palm he delicately patted the appropriate spot.

They applauded. Mondor cried, "Bien dit!" Servan beamed.

Properly speaking, he hadn't started the speech yet, for that wasn't in it. Now he started. For the first ten minutes or so I was uneasy. There was nothing in the world I would enjoy more than watching Nero Wolfe wallowing in discomfiture, but not in the presence of outsiders. When that happy time came, which it never had yet, I wanted it to be a special command performance for Archie Goodwin and no one else around. And I was uneasy because it seemed quite possible that the hardships on the train and loss of sleep and getting shot at might have upset him so that he would forget the darned speech, but after the first ten minutes I saw there was nothing to worry about. He was sailing along. I took another sip of brandy and relaxed.

By the time he was half through I began to worry about something else. I glanced at my wrist. It was getting late. Charleston was only sixty miles away, and Tolman had said it was a good road and could easily be made in an hour and a half. Knowing how complicated the program was, it was my opinion that there wasn't much chance of getting away that night anyhow, but it would have ruined the setup entirely if anything had happened to Saul. So my second big relief came when the greenjacket from the hall entered softly from the parlor, as he had been instructed, and gave me the high sign. I sidled out of my chair with as little disturbance as possible and tiptoed out.

There in the small parlor sat a little guy with a big nose, in need of a shave, with an old brown cap hanging on his knee. He stood up and stuck out his hand and I took it with a grin.

"Hello, darling, I never would have thought that the time would come when you would look handsome to me. Turn around, how do you look behind?"

Saul Panzer demanded, "How's Mr. Wolfe?"

"Swell. He's in there making a speech I taught him."

"You sure he's all right?"

"Why not? Oh, you mean his casualty." I waved a hand. "A mere nothing. He thinks he's a hero. I wish to God they'd shoot me next time so he'd stop bragging. Have you got anything?"

Saul nodded. "I've got everything."

"Is there anything you need to explain to Wolfe before he springs it?"

"I don't think so. I've got everything he asked for. The whole Charleston police force jumped into it."

"Yeah, I know. My friend Mr. Tolman arranged that. I've

160

got another friend named Odell that throws stones at people—remind me to tell you about it sometime. This is a jolly place. Then you wait here till you're called. I'd better go back in. Have you had anything to eat?"

He said his inside was attended to, and I left him. Back in the dining room again, I resumed my seat beside Constanza, and when Wolfe paused at the end of a paragraph, I took my handkerchief from my breast pocket, passed it across my lips, and put it back again. He gave me a fleeting glance to acknowledge the signal. he had reached the part about the introduction of filé powder to the New Orleans market by the Choctaw Indians on Bayou Lacombe, so I knew he had got to page 14. It looked as though he was putting it over in good style. Even Domenico Rossi looked absorbed, in spite of the fact that in one place Wolfe specifically stated that in the three most important centers of American contributions to fine cooking—Louisiana, South Carolina, and New England—there had been no Italian influence whatever.

He reached the end. Even though I knew his program, and knew the time was short, I had supposed he would at least pause there, and perhaps give Louis Servan a chance to make a few remarks of appreciation, but he didn't even stop long enough for them to realize that the speech was finished. He looked around—a brief glance at the rectangle of faces—and went right on:

"I hope I won't bore you if I continue, but on another subject. I count on your forbearance, for what I have to say is as much in your interest as in my own. I have finished my remarks on cooking. Now I'm going to talk to you about murder. The murder of Phillip Laszio."

There were stirs and murmurs. Lisette Putti squeaked. Louis Servan put up a hand:

"If you please. I would like to say, Mr. Wolfe does this by arrangement. It is distressing to end thus the dinner of Les Quinze Maîtres but it appears...unavoidable. We do not even...however, there is no help..."

Ramsey Keith, glancing at Tolman, Malfi, Liggett, Ashley, growled inhospitably, "So that's the reason these people—"

"Yes, that's the reason." Wolfe was brisk. "I beg you, all of you, don't blame me for intruding a painful subject into an occasion of festivity. The intruder was the man who killed Laszio, and thereby worked disaster on a joyous gathering, cast the gloom of suspicion over a group of eminent men, and ruined my holiday as well as yours. So not only do I have a special reason for rancor for that man"—he put the tip of a finger to his bandage—"but we all have a general one. Besides, before dinner I heard several of you complaining of the fact that you will all be detained here until the authorities release you. But you know that's a natural consequence of the misfortune that overtook you. The authorities can't be expected to let you disperse to the four corners of the earth as long as they have reason to suspect that one of you is a murderer. That's why I say I count on your forbearance. You can't leave here until the guilty man is discovered. So that's what I intend to do here and now. I'm going to expose the murderer, and demonstrate his guilt, before we leave this room."

Lisette Putti squeaked again, and then covered her mouth with her palm. There were no murmurs. A few glanced around, but most of them kept their eyes on Wolfe.

He went on, "First I think I'd better tell you what was done here—in this room—Tuesday evening, and then we can proceed to the question of who did it. There was nothing untoward until Mondor, Coyne, Keith and Servan had all been here and tasted the sauces. The instant Servan left, Laszio reached across the table and changed the position of the dishes, all but two. Doubtless he would have shifted those also if the door had not begun to open for the entrance of Berin. It was a childish and malicious trick intended to discredit Berin, and possibly Vukcic too. It may be that Laszio intended to replace the dishes when Berin left, but he didn't, because he was killed before he got a chance to.

"While Berin was in here the radio in the parlor was turned on. That was a prearranged signal for a man who was waiting for it out in the shrubbery. He was close enough to the parlor window—"

"Wait a minute!" The cry wasn't loud, nor explosive; it was quite composed. But everyone was startled into turning to Dina Laszio, who had uttered it. There was as little turmoil in her manner as in her voice, though maybe her eyes were a little longer and sleepier even than usual. They were directed at Wolfe: "Do we interrupt you when you tell lies?"

"I think not, madam—granting your premise. If each of my statements is met with a challenge we'll never get anywhere. Why don't you wait till I'm through? By that time, if I have lied, you can bankrupt me with a suit for slander."

162

"I turned on the radio. Everyone knows that. You said it was a prearranged signal. . . ."

"So I did. I beg you, let's don't turn this into a squabble. I'm discussing murder and making serious charges. Let me finish, let me expose myself, then rebut me if you can; and either I shall be discredited and disgraced, or someone here will be . . . do you hang in West Virginia, Mr. Tolman?"

Tolman, his eyes riveted on Wolfe's face, nodded.

"Then someone will die at the end of a rope.—As I was saying, the man concealed in the shrubbery out there"—he pointed to the door leading to the terrace—"was close enough to the open parlor window so that when the radio warned him he could observe the return of Berin to the parlor. Instantly he proceeded to the terrace and entered this room by that door. Laszio, here alone by the table, was surprised at the entrance of a liveried servant—for the man wore Kanawha Spa livery and had a black face. The man approached the table and made himself known, for Laszio knew him well. 'See,' the man said with a smile, 'don't you know me, I am Mr. White'—we may call him that for the present, for he was in fact a white man—'I am Mr. White, masquerading, ha ha, and we'll play a joke on these fellows. It will be quite amusing, ha ha, Laszio old chap. You go behind that screen and I'll stay here by the table . . .'

"I confess that no one except Laszio heard those words, or any others. The words actually spoken may have been quite different, but whatever they were, the upshot was that Laszio went behind the screen, and Mr. White, having procured a knife from the table, followed him there and stabbed him to the heart, from behind. It was certainly done with finesse and dispatch, since there was no struggle and no outcry loud enough to be heard in the pantry hall. Mr. White left the knife where he had put it, seeing that it had done its work, and emerged from behind the screen. As he did so a glance showed him that the door to the pantry hall—that door—was open a few inches and a man, a colored man, was peering at him through the crack. Either he had already decided what to do in case of such an emergency, or he showed great presence of mind, for he merely stood still at the end of the screen, looking straight at the eyes peering at him, and placed his finger to his lips. A simple and superb gesture. He may or may not have known—probably he didn't—that at the same moment the door leading to the terrace, behind him,

163

had also opened, and a woman was looking through at him. But his masquerade worked both ways. The colored man knew he was a fake, a white man blacked up, took him for one of the guests playing a joke, and so was not moved to inquire or interfere. The woman supposed he was a servant and let it go at that. Before he left this room Mr. White was seen by still another man—the headwaiter, Moulton here—but by the time Moulton looked through the door Mr. White was on his way out and his back was turned, so Moulton didn't see his face.—We might as well record names as we go along. The man who first peered through the door was Paul Whipple, one of our waiters here—who, by the way, is studying anthropology at Howard University. The one who saw Mr. White going out was Moulton. The woman who looked through the terrace door was Mrs. Lawrence Coyne."

Coyne jerked around to look, startled, at his wife. She put up her chin at Wolfe. "But . . . you promised me . . ."

"I promised you nothing. I'm sorry, Mrs. Coyne, but it's much better not to leave out anything I don't think—"

Coyne sputtered indignantly. "I've heard nothing—nothing—"

"Please." Wolfe put up a nand. "I assure you, sir, you and your wife have no cause for worry. Indeed, we should all be grateful to her. If she hadn't hurt her finger in the door, and asked you to kiss it in my hearing, it's quite probable that Mr. Berin would have got the noose instead of the man who earned it. But I needn't go into that.

"That's what happened here Tuesday night. I'll clear up a point now about the radio. It might be thought of, since it was turned on, as a prearranged signal, while Berin was in here tasting the sauces, that it was timed at that moment so as to throw suspicion on Berin, but not so. There was probably no intention to have suspicion aimed at any specific person, but if there was, that person was Marko Vukcic. The arrangement was that the radio should be turned on a few minutes prior to the visit of Vukcic to the dining room, no matter who was tasting the sauces at that moment. It was chance that made it Berin, and chance also that Laszio had shifted the sauces around to trick Berin. And the chance trap for Berin was actually sprung, innocently, by Moulton, who came to the table and changed the dishes back again before Vukcic entered. I haven't told you about that. But the point I am making is that the radio signal was given a few minutes prior to the scheduled entrance of Vukcic to the dining room, because Vukcic was the one man here whom Mrs. Laszio could confidently expect to detain in the parlor, delaying his visit to the dining room, and giving Mr. White the necessary time alone with Laszio to accomplish his purpose. As we all know, she insured the delay by putting herself into Vukcic's arms for dancing, and staying there."

"Lies! You know it's lies—"

"Dina! Shut up!"

It was Domenico Rossi, glaring at his daughter. Vukcic, with his jaw set, was gazing at her. Others sent glances at her and looked away again.

"But he tells lies—"

"I say shut up!" Rossi was much quieter, and more impressive, than when he was picking a scrap. "If he tells lies, let him tell all of them."

"Thank you, sir." Wolfe inclined his head half an inch. "I think now we had better decide who Mr. White is. You will notice that the fearful risks he took in this room Tuesday night were more apparent than real. Up to the moment he sank the knife into Laszio's back he was taking no risk at all; he was merely an innocent masquerader. And if afterwards he was seen—well, he *was* seen, and what if he was, since he was blacked up? The persons who saw him here Tuesday night have all seen him since, with the blacking and livery gone, and none has suspected him. He depended for safety on his certainty that he would never be suspected at all. He had several bases for that certainty, but the chief one was that on Tuesday evening he wasn't in Kanawha Spa; he was in New York."

Berin burst out, "God above! If he wasn't here—"

"I mean he wasn't supposed to be here. It is always assumed that a man is where probability places him, unless suspicion is aroused that he is somewhere else, and Mr. White figured that such a suspicion was an impossibility. But he was too confident and too careless. He permitted his own tongue to create the suspicion in a conversation with me.

"As you all know, I've had wide experience in affairs of this kind. It's my business. I told Mr. Tolman Tuesday night that I was sure Berin hadn't done it, but I withheld my best reason for that assurance, because it wasn't my case and I don't like to involve people where I have no concern. That reason was this, I was convinced that Mrs. Laszio had signaled to the murderer by turning on the radio. Other details connected with that might be attributed to chance, but it would take great credulity to believe that her hanging onto Vukcic in that dance, delaying his trip to the dining room while her husband was being killed, was also coincidence. Especially when, as I did, one saw her doing it. She made a bad mistake there. Ordinary intelligence might have caused her to reflect that I was present and that therefore more subtlety was called for.

"When Berin was arrested I did become interested, as you know, but when I had got him released I was again unconcerned with the affair. Whereupon another idiotic mistake was made, almost unbelievable. Mr. White thought I was discovering too much, and without even taking the trouble to learn that I had withdrawn, he sneaked through the shrubbery outside my window and shot me. I think I know how he approached Upshur Pavilion. My assistant, Mr. Goodwin, an hour or so later, saw him dismounting from a horse at the hotel. The bridle path runs within fifty yards of the rear of Upshur. He could easily have left the path, tied his horse, advanced through the shrubbery to my window, and after the shot got back to the horse again and off on the path without being seen. At all events, he made that mistake, and by it, instead of removing me, he encountered me. My concern revived.

"I assumed, as I say, that the murderer was in league with Mrs. Laszio. I dismissed the idea that it was solely her project and he had been hired by her, for that would have rendered the masquerade meaningless; besides, it was hard to believe that a hired murderer, a stranger to Laszio, could have entered this room, got a knife from the table, enticed Laszio behind the screen, and killed him, without an outcry or any struggle. And just as yesterday, when Berin was arrested and I undertook to find evidence to free him, I had one slender thread to start with, Mrs. Coyne's appeal to her husband to kiss her finger because she had caught it in a door, so to-day, when I undertook to catch the murderer, I had another thread just as slender. It was this. Yesterday about two o'clock Mr. Malfi and Mr. Liggett arrived at Kanawha Spa after a nonstop airplane flight from New York. They came directly to my room at Upshur Pavilion before talking with anyone but servants, and had a conversation with me. During the conversation Liggett said—I think this is verbatim: 'It seems likely that whoever did it was able to use finesse for other purposes than tasting the seasonings in Sauce Printemps.' Do you remember that, sir?"

"For God's sake." Liggett snorted. "You damn fool, are you trying to drag me into it?"

"I'm afraid I am. You may enter your action for slander along with Mrs. Laszio. Do you remember saying that?"

"No. Neither do you."

Wolfe shrugged. "It's unimportant now. It was vital in its function as my thread.—Anyway, it seemed suitable for inquiry. It seemed unlikely that such a detail as the name of the sauce we were tasting had been included in the first brief reports of the murder wired to New York. I telephoned there, to an employee of mine, and to Inspector Cramer of the police. My requests to Mr. Cramer were somewhat inclusive: for instance, I asked him to check on all passengers of airplanes, scheduled or specially chartered, from all airports, leaving New York Tuesday, which had stopped no matter where in this part of the country in time for a passenger to have arrived at Kanawha Spa by nine o'clock Tuesday evening. I made it nine o'clock because when we went to the parlor after dinner Tuesday Mrs. Laszio immediately disappeared and was not seen again for an hour; and if there was anything to my theory at all it seemed likely that that absence was for a rendezvous with her collaborator. I also asked Mr. Cramer to investigate Mrs. Laszio's life in New York—her friends and associates—now, madam. Please. You'll get a chance.—For suspicion was at that point by no means confined to Liggett. There was even one of you here not entirely clear; and I want to express publicly to Mr. Blanc my thanks for his tolerance and good nature in assisting with the experiment which eliminated him. No doubt he thought it ridiculous.

"At one o'clock this afternoon I received a telegram telling me that Sauce Printemps had not been mentioned in the account in any New York paper Tuesday morning. Since Liggett had left in the airplane before ten o'clock, had come non-stop, and had talked with no one before seeing me, how had he known it was Sauce Printemps? Probably he *had* talked with someone. He had talked with Mrs. Laszio around nine-thirty Tuesday evening, somewhere in the grounds around this building, making the arrangements which resulted in Laszio's murder."

I wasn't any too well pleased, because I couldn't see

Liggett's hands; he was across from me and the table hid them. Nor his eyes either, because they were on Wolfe. All I could see was the corner of his thin smile on the side of his mouth that was toward me, and the cord on the side of his neck as he held his jaw clamped. From where he sat he couldn't see Dina Laszio, but I could, and she had her lower lip caught by her teeth. And at that, that was the only outward sign that she wasn't quite as nonchalant as she had been when she patted Wolfe's shoulder.

Wolfe went on, "At three o'clock I had a phone call from Inspector Cramer. Among other things, he told me that Saul Panzer, my employee, had left on an airplane for Charleston in accordance with my instructions. Then—I might as well mention this—around six o'clock another silly mistake was made. To do Mr. Liggett justice, I doubt if it was his own idea; I suspect it was Mrs. Laszio who thought of it and persuaded him to try it. He came to my room and offered me fifty thousand dollars cash to ask Mr. Berin to take the job of chef de cuisine at the Hotel Churchill."

Lisette Putti squeaked again. Jerome Berin exploded, "That robbers' den! That stinking hole! Me? Rather would I fry eggs on my finger nails—"

"Just so. I declined the offer. Liggett was foolish to make it, for I am not too self-confident to welcome the encouragement of confession from the enemy, and his offer of the preposterous sum was of course confession of guilt. He will deny that; he will probably even deny he made the offer; no matter. I received other and more important encouragement: another phone call from Inspector Cramer. Time is short, and I won't bore you with all the details, but among them was the information that he had uncovered rumors of a mutual interest, going back two years, between Liggett and Mrs. Laszio. Also he had checked another point I had inquired about. Coming here on the train Monday night, Mr. Berin had told me of a visit he had made last Saturday to the Resort Room of the Hotel Churchill, where the waiters were dressed in the liveries of famous resorts, among them that of Kanawha Spa. Inspector Cramer's men had discovered that about a year ago Mr. Liggett had had a duplicate of the Kanawha Spa livery made for himself and had worn it at a fancy dress ball. No doubt it was that fact that he already owned that livery which suggested the technique he adopted for his project. So as you see, I was getting a good sketch for my picture:

Liggett had known of the Sauce Printemps before he had any right to; he was on terms with Mrs. Laszio; and he had a Kanawha Spa livery in his wardrobe. There were other items, as for instance he had left the hotel Tuesday noon, ostensibly to play golf, but had not appeared at either of the clubs where he habitually plays; but we shall have to do some skipping. Mr. Tolman can collect these things after Liggett is arrested. Now we'd better get on to Saul Panzer—I haven't mentioned that he telephoned me from Charleston immediately after the call from Inspector Cramer.—Will you bring him, please, from the small parlor?"

Moulton trotted out.

Liggett said in an even tone, "The cleverest lie you've told is about my trying to bribe you. And the most dangerous lie, because there's some truth in it. I did go to your room to ask you to approach Berin for me. And I suppose your man is primed to back up the lie that I offered fifty thousand—"

"Please, Mr. Liggett." Wolfe put up a palm at him. "I wouldn't talk extempore if I were you. You'd better think it over carefully before you—ah, hello, Saul! It's good to see you."

"Yes, sir. Same to you." Saul Panzer came and stood beside my chair. He had on his old gray suit with the pants never pressed, and the old brown cap in his hand. After one look at Wolfe his sharp eyes darted around the rectangle of faces, and I knew that each of those phizzes had in that moment been registered in a portrait gallery where it would stay forever in place.

Wolfe said, "Speak to Mr. Liggett."

"Yes, sir." Saul's eyes fastened on the target instantly. "How do you do, Mr. Liggett."

Liggett didn't turn. "Bah. It's a damned farce."

Wolfe shrugged. "We haven't much time, Saul. Confine yourself to the essentials. Did Mr. Liggett play golf Tuesday afternoon?"

"No, sir." Saul was husky and he cleared his throat. "On Tuesday at 1:55 p.m. he boarded a plane of Interstate Airways at the Newark Airport. I was on the same plane to-day, with the same hostess, and showed her Liggett's picture. He left the plane at Charleston when it stopped there at 6:18—and so did I, to-day. About half past six he appeared at Little's Garage on Marlin Street and hired a car, a 1936 Studebaker, leaving a deposit of $200 in twenty-dollar bills. I drove the same car here this evening; it's out in front now. I inquired at a few places on the way, but I couldn't find where he stopped on the way back to wash the black off his face—I had to hurry because you told me to get here before eleven o'clock. He showed up again at Little's Garage about a quarter after one Tuesday night and had to pay ten dollars for a fender he had dented. He walked away from the garage and on Laurel Street took a taxi, license C3428, driver Al Bissell, to the Charleston airport. There he took the night express of Interstate Airways, which landed him at Newark at 5:34 Wednesday morning. From there I don't know, but he went to New York, because he was in his apartment a few minutes before eight, when a telephone call was put through to him from Albert Malfi. At half past eight he phoned Newark to charter a plane to take him and Malfi to Kanawha Spa, and at 9:52—"

"That's enough, Saul. By then his movements were overt. You say you drove here this evening in the same car that Liggett hired Tuesday?"

"Yes, sir."

"Well. That's rubbing it in. And you had pictures of Liggett with you to show all those people—the hostess, the garage man, the taxi driver—"

"Yes, sir. He was white when he left the garage."

"No doubt he stopped for alterations on the way. It isn't as difficult as you might think; we blacked a man in my room this afternoon. Cleaning it off is harder. I don't suppose remnants of it were noticed by the man at the garage or the taxi driver?"

"No, sir. I tried that."

"Yes. You would. Of course they wouldn't examine his ears. You didn't mention luggage."

"He had a medium sized suitcase, dark tan cowhide, with brass fastenings and no straps."

"At all appearances?"

"Yes, sir. Coming and going both."

"Good. Satisfactory. I think that will do. Take that chair over by the wall."

Wolfe surveyed the faces, and though he had kept their attention with his speech on cookery, he was keeping it better now. You could have heard a pin swishing through the air before it lit. He said, "Now we're getting somewhere. You understand why I said that such details as Liggett's mention of Sauce Printemps are no longer of much importance. It is obvious that he treated so fatal a crime as murder with incredible levity, but we should remember two things: first, that he supposed that his absence from Kanawha Spa would never be questioned, and second, he was actually not sentient. He was drugged. He had drunk of the cup which Mrs. Laszio had filled for him. As far as Liggett is concerned, we seem to be done; there appears to be nothing left but for Mr. Tolman to arrest him, prepare the case, try him, and convict him. Have you any remarks on that, Mr. Liggett? I wouldn't advise any."

"I'm not saying anything." Liggett's voice was as good as ever. "Except that if Tolman swallows this and acts on it the way you've framed it, he'll be damn near as sorry as you're going to be." Liggett's chin went up a little. "I know you, Wolfe. I've heard about you. God knows why you've picked on me for this, but I'm going to know before I get through with you."

Wolfe gravely inclined his head. "Your only possible attitude. Of course. But I'm through with you, sir. I turn you over. Your biggest mistake was shooting at me when I had become merely a bystander. Look here." He reached in his pocket and pulled out the script and unfolded it. "That's where your bullet went, right through my speech, before it struck me.—Mr. Tolman, do you have women on murder juries in your state?"

"No. Men only."

"Indeed." Wolfe directed his gaze at Mrs. Laszio; he hadn't looked at her since beginning on Liggett. "That's a piece of luck for you, madam. It'll be a job to persuade twelve men to pronounce your doom." Back to Tolman: "Are you prepared to charge Liggett with the murder of Laszio?"

Tolman's voice was clear: "I am."

"Well, sir? You didn't hesitate with Mr. Berin."

Tolman got up. He had only four paces to walk. He put his hand on Liggett's shoulder and said in a loud tone, "I arrest you, Raymond Liggett. A formal charge of murder will be laid to-morrow morning." He turned and spoke sharply to Moulton: "The sheriff is out front. Tell him to come in."

Liggett twisted his head around to get Tolman's eye. "This will ruin you, young man."

Wolfe, stopping Moulton with a gesture, appealed to Tolman, "Let the sheriff wait a little. If you don't mind? I don't like him." He put his eyes at Mrs. Laszio again. "Besides, mad-

171

am, we still have you to consider. As far as Liggett is concerned, well . . . you see . . ." He moved a hand to indicate Tolman standing at Liggett's shoulder. "Now about you. You're not arrested yet. Have you got anything to say?"

The swamp-woman looked sick. I suppose she was good enough at make-up so that ordinarily only an expert would have noticed the extent of it, but it wasn't calculated to handle emergencies like this. Her face was spotty. Her lower lip didn't match the upper, on account of having been chewed on. Her shoulders were humped up and her chest pulled in. She said in a thin tone, not her rich swampy voice at all, "I didn't . . . only . . . only what I said, it's lies. Lies!"

"Do you mean what I've said about Liggett is lies? And what Saul Panzer has said? I warn you, madam, things that can be proven are not lies. You say lies. What?"

"It's all lies . . . about me."

"And about Liggett?"

"I . . . I don't know."

"Indeed. But about you. You did turn on the radio. Didn't you?"

She nodded without speaking. Wolfe snapped. "Didn't you?"

"Yes."

"And whether by accident or design, you did detain Vukcic and dance with him while your husband was being murdered?"

"Yes."

"And Tuesday evening after dinner you were absent from the gathering here nearly an hour?"

"Yes."

"And since your husband is dead . . . if it were not for the unfortunate circumstance that Liggett will soon be dead too, you would expect to marry him, wouldn't you?"

"I . . ." Her mouth twisted. "No! You can't say . . . no!"

"Please, Mrs. Laszio. Keep your nerve. You need it." Wolfe's tone suddenly got gentle. "I don't want to bully you. I am perfectly aware that as regards you the facts permit of two vastly different constructions. One something like this: You and Mr. Liggett wanted each other—at least he wanted you, and you wanted his name and position and wealth. But your husband was the sort of man who hangs on to his possessions, and that made it difficult. The time finally arrived when the desire was so great, and the obstacle so stubborn, that you and Liggett decided on a desperate course. It appeared that

172

the meeting of Les Quinze Maîtres offered a good opportunity for the removal of your husband, for there would be three persons present who hated him—plenty of targets for suspicion. So Liggett came to Charleston by airplane and on here by car, and met you somewhere outside, as previously arranged, at half past nine Tuesday evening. It was only then that the arrangements were perfected in detail, for Liggett could not previously have known about the wager between Servan and Keith and the test of Sauce Printemps that was being prepared to decide it. Liggett posted himself in the shrubbery. You returned to the parlor, and turned on the radio at the proper time, and delayed Vukcic by dancing with him in order to give Liggett the opportunity to enter the dining room and kill your husband. Confound it, madam, don't stare at me like that! As I say, that is one possible interpretation of your actions."

"But it's wrong. It's lies! I didn't—"

"Permit me. Don't deny too much. I confess there may be lies in it, for there's another possible construction. But understand this, and consider it well." Wolfe aimed a finger at her, and pointed his tone. "It is going to be proven that Liggett came here, and was told by someone about the test of the sauces, and that he knew precisely the moment when he could safely enter this room to kill Laszio without danger of interruption; that he *knew* that Vukcic would not enter to disturb him before the deed was done. Otherwise his proceeding as he did was senseless. That's why I say don't deny too much. If you try to maintain that you didn't meet Liggett outdoors, that you made no arrangement with him, that your turning on the radio when you did was coincidence, that your keeping Vukcic from the dining room during those fatal minutes was also coincidence—then I fear for you. Even a jury of twelve men, and even looking at you on the stand—I'm afraid they wouldn't swallow it. I believe, to put it brutally, I believe you would be convicted of murder.

"But I haven't said you're a murderer." Wolfe's tone was almost soothing. "Since the crime was committed you have unquestionably, at least by silence, tried to shield Liggett, but a woman's heart being what it is . . ." He shrugged. "No jury would convict you for that. And no jury would convict you at all, you wouldn't even be in jeopardy, if it could be shown that the arrangement you entered into with Liggett Tuesday evening, when you met him outdoors there, was on

173

your part an innocent one. Merely as a hypothesis, let's say, for example, that you understood that Liggett was engaged in nothing more harmful than a practical joke. No matter what; I couldn't guess at the details even as a hypothesis, for I'm not a practical joker. But the joke required that he have a few minutes alone with Laszio before the entrance of Vukcic. That of course would explain everything—your turning on the radio, your detaining Vukcic—everything you did, without involving you in guilt. You understand, Mrs. Laszio, I'm not suggesting this as a retreat for you. I am only saying that while you can't deny what happened, you may possibly have an explanation for it that will save you. In that case, it would be quixotic to try to save Liggett too. You can't do it. And if there is such an explanation, I wouldn't wait too long . . . until it's too late. . . ."

It was too much for Liggett. Slowly his head turned, irresistibly as if gripped in enormous pliers, square around, until he faced Dina Laszio. She didn't look at him. She was chewing at her lip again, and her eyes were on Wolfe, fixed and fascinated. You could almost see her chewing her brain too. That lasted a full half a minute, and then by God she smiled. It was a funny one, but it was a smile; and then I saw that her eyes had shifted to Liggett and the smile was supposed to be one of polite apology. She said in a low tone but without anything shaky in it, "I'm sorry, Ray. Oh, I'm sorry, but . . ."

She faltered. Liggett's eyes were boring at her.

She moved her gaze to Wolfe and said firmly, "You're right. Of course you're right and I can't help it. When I met him outdoors after dinner as we had arranged—"

"Dina! Dina, for God's sake—"

Tolman, the blue-eyed athlete, jerked Liggett back in his chair. The swamp-woman was going on:

"He had told me what he was going to do, and I believed him, I thought it was a joke. Then afterwards he told me that Phillip had attacked him, had struck at him—"

Wolfe said sharply, "You know what you're doing, madam. You're helping to send a man to his death."

"I know. I can't help it! How can I go on lying for him? He killed my husband. When I met him out there and he told me what he had planned—"

"You tricky bastard!" Liggett broke training completely. He jerked from Tolman's grasp, plunged across Mondor's legs,

174

knocked Blanc and his chair to the floor, trying to get at Wolfe. I was on my way, but by the time I got there Berin had stopped him, with both arms around him, and Liggett was kicking and yelling like a lunatic.

Dina Laszio, of course, had stopped trying to talk, with all the noise and confusion. She sat quietly looking on with her long sleepy eyes.

17

JEROME BERIN said positively, "She'll stick to it. She'll do whatever will push danger farthest from her, and that will be it."

The train was sailing like a gull across New Jersey on a sunny Friday morning, somewhere east of Philadelphia. In sixty minutes we would be tunneling under the Hudson. I was propped against the wall of the pullman bedroom again, Constanza was on the chair, and Wolfe and Berin were on the window seats with beer between them. Wolfe looked pretty seedy, since of course he wouldn't have tried to shave on the train even if there had been no bandage, but he knew that in an hour the thing would stop moving and the dawn of hope was on his face.

Berin asked, "Don't you think so?"

Wolfe shrugged. "I don't know and I don't care. The point was to nail Liggett down by establishing his presence at Kanawha Spa on Tuesday evening, and Mrs. Laszio was the only one who could do that for us. As you say, she is undoubtedly just as guilty as Liggett, maybe more, depending on your standard. I rather think Mr. Tolman will try her for murder. He took her last night as a material witness, and he may keep her that way to clinch his case against Liggett—or he may charge her as an accomplice. I doubt if it matters much. Whatever he does, he won't convict her. She's a special kind of woman, she told me so herself. Even if Liggett is bitter enough against her to confess everything in order to involve her in his doom, to persuade any dozen men that the best thing to do with that woman is to kill her would be quite a feat. I question whether Mr. Tolman is up to it."

175

Berin, filling his pipe, frowned at it. Wolfe upped his beer glass with one hand as he clung to the arm of the seat with the other.

Constanza smiled at me. "I try not to hear them. Talking about killing people." She shivered delicately.

I grunted. "You seem to be doing a lot of smiling. Under the circumstances."

She lifted brows above the dark purple eyes. "What circumstances?"

I just waved a hand. Berin had got his pipe lit and was talking again. "Well, it turned my stomach. Poor Rossi, did you notice him? Poor devil. When Dina Rossi was a little girl and I had her many times on this knee, and she was quiet and very sly but a nice girl. Of course, all murderers were once little children, which seems astonishing." He puffed until the little room was nicely filled with smoke. "By the way, did you know that Vukcic made this train?"

"No."

Berin nodded. "He came leaping on at the last minute, I saw him, like a lion with fleas after him. I haven't seen him around this morning, though I've been back and forth. No doubt your man told you that I stopped here at your room around eight o'clock."

Wolfe grimaced. "I wasn't dressed."

"So he told me. So I came back. I wasn't comfortable. I never am comfortable when I'm in debt, and I've got to find out what I owe you and pay it. There at Kanawha Spa you were a guest and didn't want to talk about it, but now you can. You got me out of a bad hole and maybe you even saved my life, and you did it at the request of my daughter for your professional help. That makes it a debt and I want to pay it, only I understand your fees are pretty steep. How much do you charge for a day's work?"

"How much do you?"

"What?" Berin stared. "God above. I don't work by the day. I am an artist, not a potato peeler."

"Neither am I." Wolfe wiggled a finger. "Look here, sir. Let's admit it as a postulate that I saved your life. If I did, I am willing to let it go as a gesture of amity and goodwill and take no payment for it. Will you accept that gesture?"

"No. I'm in debt to you. My daughter appealed to you. It is not to be expected that I, Jerome Berin, would accept such a favor."

176

"Well . . ." Wolfe sighed. "If you won't take it in friendship, you won't. In that case, the only thing I can do is render you a bill. That's simple. If any valuation at all is to be placed on the professional services I rendered it must be a high one, for the services were exceptional. So . . . since you insist on paying . . . you owe me the recipe for saucisse minuit."

"What!" Berin glared at him. "Pah! Ridiculous!"

"How ridiculous? You ask what you owe. I tell you."

Berin sputtered. "Outrageous, damn it!" He waved his pipe until sparks and ashes flew. "That recipe is priceless! And you ask it. . . . God above, I've refused half a million francs! And you have the impudence, the insolence—"

"If you please." Wolfe snapped. "Let's don't row about it. You put a price on your recipe. That's your privilege. I put a price on my services. That's mine. You have refused half a million francs. If you were to send me a check for half a million dollars I would tear it up—or for any sum whatever. I saved your life or I rescued you from a minor annoyance, call it what you please. You ask me what you owe me, and I tell you, you owe me that recipe, and I will accept nothing else. You pay it or you don't, suit yourself. It would be an indescribable pleasure to be able to eat saucisse minuit at my own table—at least twice a month, I should think—but it would be quite a satisfaction, of another sort, to be able to remind myself—much oftener than twice a month—that Jerome Berin owes me a debt which he refuses to pay."

"Bah!" Berin snorted. "Trickery!"

"Not at all. I attempt no coercion. I won't sue you. I'll merely regret that I employed my talents, lost a lot of sleep, and allowed myself to get shot at, without either acquiring credit for a friendly and generous act, or receiving the payment due me. I suppose I should remind you that I offered a guarantee to disclose the recipe to no one. The sausage will be prepared only in my house and served only at my table. I would like to reserve the right to serve it to guests—and of course to Mr. Goodwin, who lives with me and eats what I eat."

Berin, staring at him, muttered, "Your cook."

"He won't know it. I spend quite a little time in the kitchen myself."

Berin continued to stare, in silence. Finally he growled, "It can't be written down. It never has been."

"I won't write it down. I have a facility for memorizing."

Berin got his pipe to his mouth without looking at it, and puffed. Then he stared some more. At length he heaved a shuddering sigh and looked around at Constanza and me. He said gruffly, "I can't tell it with these people in here."

"One of them is your daughter."

"Damn it, I know my daughter when I see her. They'll have to get out."

I got up and put up my brows at Constanza. "Well?" The train lurched and Wolfe grabbed for the other arm of the seat. It would have been a shame to get wrecked then.

Constanza arose, reached down to pat her father on the head, and passed through the door as I held it open.

I supposed that was the fitting end to our holiday, since Wolfe was getting that recipe, but there was one more unexpected diversion to come. Since there was still an hour to go I invited Constanza to the club car for a drink, and she swayed and staggered behind me through three cars to that destination. There were only eight or ten customers in the club car, mostly hid behind morning papers, and plenty of seats. She specified ginger ale, which reminded me of old times, and I ordered a highball to celebrate Wolfe's collection of his fee. We had only taken a couple of sips when I became aware that a fellow passenger across the aisle had arisen, put down his paper, walked up to us, and was standing in front of Constanza, looking down at her.

He said, "You can't do this to me, you *can't*! I don't deserve it and you can't do it." He sounded urgent. "You ought to see—you ought to realize—"

Constanza said to me, chattering prettily, "I didn't suppose my father would *ever* tell that recipe to *any*one. Once in San Remo I heard him tell an Englishman, some very important person—"

The intruder moved enough inches to be standing between us, and rudely interrupted her: "Hello, Goodwin. I want to ask you—"

"Hello, Tolman." I grinned up at him. "What's the idea? You with two brand new prisoners in your jail, and here you are running around—"

"I had to get to New York. For evidence. It was too important.... Look here. I want to ask you if Miss Berin has any right to treat me like this. Your unbiased opinion. She won't speak to me. She won't look at me. Didn't I have to do what I did? Was there anything else I could do?"

178

"Certainly. You could have resigned. But then of course you'd have been out of a job, and God knows when you'd have been able to marry. It was really a problem, I see that. But I wouldn't worry. Only a little while ago I wondered why Miss Berin was doing so much smiling, there didn't seem to be any special reason for it, but now I understand. She was smiling because she knew you were on the train."

"Mr. Goodwin! That isn't true!"

"But if she won't even speak to me—"

I waved a hand. "She'll speak to you all right. You just don't know how to go about it. Her own method is as good a one as I've seen recently. Watch me now, and next time you can do it yourself."

I tipped my highball glass and spilled about a jigger on her skirt where it was round over her knee.

She ejaculated and jerked. Tolman ejaculated and bent over and reached for his handkerchief. I arose and reassured them, "It's rite all kight, it doodn't stain." Then I went over and picked up his morning paper and sat down where he had been.

Champagne for One

Introduction

I first met Rex Stout sometime in the early 1950s when our daughters were classmates at Oakwood School, a Quaker boarding school in upstate New York. My husband, Lennie Hayton, and I became fast family friends with the Stouts. Rex was a kind of big, bearded Hoosier patriarch, and Pola, his beautiful *Mitteleuropean*-accented wife, was a celebrated weaver and textile designer. We were amused by the fact that Lennie, like Rex, had a beard. I remember much good conversation on the subjects of children, politics, and the artistic scene. And I remember a visit to their wonderful 1930s-modern Connecticut hilltop house—full of Pola's rugs and Rex's orchids. I remember walking into a place with literally thousands of orchids. I was thrilled, of course—it was just like Nero Wolfe's plant rooms. I was as much a fan as a friend. I enjoyed the Stouts as a family, but I had been a fan of Rex's for years before we met.

In a peripatetic "showbiz" life on the road—particularly in the 1950s, when I went from country to country, not just city to city—Nero Wolfe was a sort of solace. I was a fanatic reader traveling from hotel to hotel and dressing room to dressing room. I read between shows and I read in the wee hours of the morning, when showbiz kept me too keyed up to sleep. I loved mysteries. Mysteries satisfied every level of excitement and enjoyment. Nero Wolfe, however, was special. I read Nero Wolfe whenever I was homesick—buying the books at Harrods in London, and in English-language bookshops all over Europe.

It wasn't the crime element as much as the lifestyle that so attracted me to the books. It was Nero's house, and Archie's New York, that really spoke to me. First of all, Nero lived in a New York brownstone. I was born in a Brooklyn brownstone that was my happiest childhood home, my only sense of roots. I could picture the house so clearly. And I could understand how Nero, despite his bulk, would never want to leave it. As an astrological Cancerian, I appreciated Nero's nesting instinct. I especially liked how he felt about food. It was not about eating: it was more an appreciation of food as an art form. I loved reading descriptions of Fritz the chef's meals. Next to mysteries and historical biographies, I loved reading cookbooks—maybe a reaction to a life of hotels and restaurants. I enjoyed everything about Nero: his fatness, his orchids, his Sunday-afternoon reading, his brains.

And, of course, there was Archie Goodwin, Nero's legman. Archie had superior wit, a deadpan style, and a deceptively "unrequited" love life. Archie had depth—and he had New York. It was the New York that I missed whenever I was somewhere else. Archie knew the city streets and avenues: brownstones in the West Thirties, bars and grills on Eighth Avenue, coffee shops on Lexington, the Village. He took the

Introduction

subway and buses and taxis; he read the Sunday *New York Times*. I could picture it all. It satisfied all sorts of homesickness. When I reread Nero Wolfe now, I can see that old beloved New York, and I still miss it. And I can read about Nero's home life and remember my own.

—Lena Horne

Chapter 1

If it hadn't been raining and blowing that raw Tuesday morning in March I would have been out, walking to the bank to deposit a couple of checks, when Austin Byne phoned me, and he might have tried somebody else. But more likely not. He would probably have rung again later, so I can't blame all this on the weather. As it was, I was there in the office, oiling the typewriter and the two Marley .38's, for which we had permits, from the same can of oil, when the phone rang and I lifted it and spoke.

"Nero Wolfe's office, Archie Goodwin speaking."

"Hello there. This is Byne. Dinky Byne."

There it is in print for you, but it wasn't for me, and I didn't get it. It sounded more like a dying bull-frog than a man.

"Clear your throat," I suggested, "or sneeze or something, and try again."

"That wouldn't help. My tubes are all clogged. Tubes. Clogged. Understand? Dinky Byne—B-y-n-e."

"Oh, hallo. I won't ask how you are, hearing how you sound. My sympathy."

"I need it. I need more than sympathy, too." It

was coming through slightly better. "I need help. Will you do me a hell of a favor?"

I made a face. "I might. If I can do it sitting down and it doesn't cost me any teeth."

"It won't cost you a thing. You know my Aunt Louise. Mrs. Robert Robilotti."

"Only professionally. Mr. Wolfe did a job for her once, recovered some jewelry. That is, she hired him and I did the job—and she didn't like me. She resented a remark I made."

"That won't matter. She forgets remarks. I suppose you know about the dinner party she gives every year on the birthday date of my Uncle Albert, now resting in peace perhaps?"

"Sure. Who doesn't?"

"Well, that's it. Today. Seven o'clock. And I'm to be one of the chevaliers, and listen to me, and I've got some fever. I can't go. She'll be sore as the devil if she has to scout around for a fill-in, and when I phone her I want to tell her she won't have to, that I've already got one. Mr. Archie Goodwin. You're a better chevalier than me any day. She knows you, and she has forgotten the remark you made, and anyhow she has resented a hundred remarks I've made, and you'll know exactly how to treat the lady guests. Black tie, seven o'clock, and you know the address. After I phone her, of course she'll ring you to confirm it. And you can do it sitting down, and I'll guarantee nothing will be served that will break your teeth. She has a good cook. My God, I didn't think I could talk so long. How about it, Archie?"

"I'm chewing on it," I told him. "You waited long enough."

"Yeah, I know, but I kept thinking I might be able

to make it, until I pried my eyes open this morning. I'll do the same for you some day."

"You can't. I haven't got a billionaire aunt. I doubt if she has forgotten the remark I made because it was fairly sharp. What if she vetoes me? You'd have to ring me again to call it off, and then ring someone else, and you shouldn't talk that much, and besides, my feelings would be hurt."

I was merely stalling, partly because I wanted to hear him talk some more. It sounded to me as if his croak had flaws in it. Clogged tubes have no effect on your esses, as in "seven" and "sitting," but he was trying to produce one, and he turned "long" into "lawd" when it should have been more like "lawg." So I was suspecting that the croak was a phony. If I hadn't had my full share of ego I might also have been curious as to why he had picked on me, since we were not chums, but of course that was no problem. If your ego is in good shape you will pretend you're surprised if a National Chairman calls to tell you his party wants to nominate you for President of the United States, but you're not *really* surprised.

I only stalled him long enough to be satisfied that the croak was a fake before I agreed to take it on. The fact was that the idea appealed to me. It would be a new experience and should increase my knowledge of human nature. It might also be a little ticklish, and even dismal, but it would be interesting to see how they handled it. Not to mention how I would handle it myself. So I told him I would stand by for a call from his Aunt Louise.

It came in less than half an hour. I had finished the oiling job and was putting the guns in their drawer in my desk when the phone rang. A voice I recognized said she was Mrs. Robilotti's secretary and Mrs. Robilotti wished to speak with me, and I said, "Is it jewelry again, Miss Fromm?" and she said, "She will tell you what it is, Mr. Goodwin."

Then another voice, also recognized. "Mr. Goodwin?"

"Speaking."

"My nephew Austin Byne says he phoned you."

"I guess he did."

"You *guess* he did?"

"The voice said it was Byne, but it could have been a seal trying to bark."

"He has laryngitis. He told you so. Apparently you haven't changed any. He says that he asked you to take his place at dinner at my home this evening, and you said you would if I invited you. Is that correct?"

I admitted it.

"He says that you are acquainted with the nature and significance of the affair."

"Of course I am. So are fifty million other people— or more."

"I know. I regret the publicity it has received in the past, but I refuse to abandon it. I owe it to my dear first husband's memory. I am inviting you, Mr. Goodwin."

"Okay. I accept the invitation as a favor to your nephew. Thank you."

"Very well." A pause. "Of course it is not usual, on inviting a dinner guest, to caution him about his conduct, but for this occasion some care is required. You appreciate that?"

"Certainly."

"Tact and discretion are necessary."

"I'll bring mine along," I assured her.

"And of course refinement."

"I'll borrow some." I decided she needed a little comfort. "Don't worry, Mrs. Robilotti, I understand the set-up and you can count on me clear through to the coffee and even after. Relax. I am fully briefed. Tact, discretion, refinement, black tie, seven o'clock."

"Then I'll expect you. Please hold the wire. My secretary will give you the names of those who will be present. It will simplify the introductions if you know them in advance."

Miss Fromm got on again. "Mr. Goodwin?"

"Still here."

"You should have paper and pencil."

"I always have. Shoot."

"Stop me if I go too fast. There will be twelve at table. Mr. and Mrs. Robilotti. Miss Celia Grantham and Mr. Cecil Grantham. They are Mrs. Robilotti's son and daughter by her first husband."

"Yeah, I know."

"Miss Helen Yarmis. Miss Ethel Varr. Miss Faith Usher. Am I going too fast?"

I told her no.

"Miss Rose Tuttle. Mr. Paul Schuster. Mr. Beverly Kent. Mr. Edwin Laidlaw. Yourself. That makes twelve. Miss Varr will be on your right and Miss Tuttle will be on your left."

I thanked her and hung up. Now that I was booked, I wasn't so sure I liked it. It would be interesting, but it might also be a strain on the nerves. However, I was booked, and I rang Byne at the number he had given me and told him he could stay home and gargle. Then I went to Wolfe's desk and wrote on his calendar Mrs. Robilotti's name and phone number. He wants to know where to reach me when I'm out,

even when we have nothing important on, in case
someone yells for help and will pay for it. Then I went
to the hall, turned left, and pushed through the swinging door to the kitchen. Fritz was at the big table,
spreading anchovy butter on shad roes.

"Cross me off for dinner," I told him. "I'm doing
my good deed for the year and getting it over with."

He stopped spreading to look at me. "That's too
bad. Veal birds in casserole. You know, with mushrooms and white wine."

"I'll miss it. But there may be something edible
where I'm going."

"Perhaps a client?"

He was not being nosy. Fritz Brenner does not
pry into other people's private affairs, not even mine.
But he has a legitimate interest in the welfare of that
establishment, of the people who live in that old
brownstone on West Thirty-fifth Street, and he
merely wanted to know if my dinner engagement was
likely to promote it. It took a lot of cash. I had to be
paid. He had to be paid. Theodore Horstmann, who
spent all his days and sometimes part of his nights
with the ten thousand orchids up in the plant rooms,
had to be paid. We all had to be fed, and with the kind
of grub that Wolfe preferred and provided and Fritz
prepared. Not only did the orchids have to be fed, but
only that week Wolfe had bought a Coelogyne from
Burma for eight hundred bucks, and that was just
routine. And so on and on and on, and the only source
of current income was people with problems who
were able and willing to pay a detective to handle
them. Fritz knew we had no case going at the moment, and he was only asking if my dinner date might
lead to one.

I shook my head. "Nope, not a client." I got on a stool. "A former client, Mrs. Robert Robilotti—someone swiped a million dollars' worth of rings and bracelets from her a couple of years ago and we got them back—and I need some advice. You may not be as great an expert on women as you are on food, but you have had your dealings, as I well know, and I would appreciate some suggestions on how to act this evening."

He snorted. "Act with women? You? Ha! With your thousand triumphs! Advice from me? Archie, that is upside down!"

"Thanks for the plug, but these women are special." With a fingertip I wiped up a speck of anchovy butter that had dropped on the table and licked it off. "Here's the problem. This Mrs. Robilotti's first husband was Albert Grantham, who spent the last ten years of his life doing things with part of the three or four hundred million dollars he had inherited—things to improve the world, including the people in it. I assume you will admit that a girl who has a baby but no husband needs improving."

Fritz pursed his lips. "First I would have to see the girl and the baby. They might be charming."

"It's not a question of charm, or at least it wasn't with Grantham. His dealing with the problem of unmarried mothers wasn't one of his really big operations, but he took a personal interest in it. He would rarely let his name be attached to any of his projects, but he did with that one. The place he built for it up in Dutchess County was called Grantham House and still is. What's that you're putting in?"

"Marjoram. I'm trying it."

"Don't tell him and see if he spots it. When the

improved mothers were graduated from Grantham
House they were financed until they got jobs or husbands, and even then they were not forgotten. One
way of keeping in touch was started by Grantham
himself a few years before he died. Each year on his
birthday he had his wife invite four of them to dinner
at his home on Fifth Avenue, and also invite, for their
dinner partners, four young men. Since his death, five
years ago, his wife has kept it up. She says she owes it
to his memory—though she is now married to a specimen named Robert Robilotti who has never been in
the improving business. Today is Grantham's birthday, and that's where I'm going for dinner. I am one
of the four young men."

"No!" Fritz said.

"Why no?"

"You, Archie?"

"Why not me?"

"It will ruin everything. They will all be back at
Grantham House in less than a year."

"No," I said sternly. "I appreciate the compliment,
but this is a serious matter and I need advice. Consider: these girls are mothers, but they are improved
mothers. They are supposed to be trying to get a toe-
hold on life. Say they are. Inviting them to dinner at
that goddam palace, with four young men from the
circle that woman moves in as table partners, whom
they have never seen before and don't expect ever to
see again, is one hell of a note. Okay, I can't help that;
I can't improve Grantham, since he's dead, and I
would hate to undertake to improve Mrs. Robilotti,
dead or alive, but I have my personal problem: how do
I act? I would welcome suggestions."

Fritz cocked his head. "Why do you go?"

"Because a man I know asked me to. That's another question, why he picked me, but skip it. I guess I agreed to go because I thought it would be fun to watch, but now I realize it may be pretty damn grim. However, I'm stuck, and what's my program? I can try to make it gay, or clown it, or get one of them talking about the baby, or get lit and the hell with it, or shall I stand up and make a speech about famous mothers like Venus and Mrs. Shakespeare and that Roman woman who had twins?"

"Not that. No."

"Then what?"

"I don't know. Anyway, you are just talking."

"All right, you talk a while."

He aimed a knife at me. "I know you so well, Archie. As well as you know me, maybe. This is just talk and I enjoy it. You need no suggestions. Program?" He slashed at it with the knife. "Ha! You will go there and look at them and see, and act as you feel. You always do. If it is too painful you will leave. If one of the girls is enchanting and the men surround her, you will get her aside and tomorrow you will take her to lunch. If you are bored you will eat too much, no matter what the food is like. If you are offended— There's the elevator!" He looked at the clock. "My God, it's eleven! The larding!" He headed for the refrigerator.

I didn't jump. Wolfe likes to find me in the office when he comes down, and if I'm not there it stirs his blood a little, which is good for him, so I waited until the elevator door opened and his footsteps came down the hall and on in. I have never understood why he doesn't make more noise walking. You would think that his feet, which are no bigger than mine, would make quite a business of getting along under his seventh of a ton, but they don't. It might be someone half his weight. I gave him enough time to cross to his desk and get himself settled in his custom-built over-size chair, and then went. As I entered he grunted a good morning at me and I returned it. Our good morn-ings usually come then, since Fritz takes his breakfast to his room on a tray, and he spends the two hours from nine to eleven, every day including Sunday, up in the plant rooms with Theodore and the orchids.

When I was at my desk I announced, "I didn't de-posit the checks that came yesterday on account of the weather. It may let up before three."

He was glancing through the mail I had put on his desk. "Get Dr. Vollmer," he commanded.

The idea of that was that if I let a little thing like a cold gusty March rain keep me from getting checks to the bank I must be sick. So I coughed. Then I sneezed. "Nothing doing," I said firmly. "He might put me to bed, and in all this bustle and hustle that wouldn't do. It would be too much for you."

He shot me a glance, nodded to show that he was on but was dropping it, and reached for his desk cal-endar. That always came second, after the glance at the mail.

"What is this phone number?" he demanded. "Mrs. Robilotti? That woman?"

"Yes, sir. The one who didn't want to pay you twenty grand but did."

"What does she want now?"

"Me. That's where you can get me this evening from seven o'clock on."

"Mr. Hewitt is coming this evening to bring a Den-drobium and look at the Renanthera. You said you would be here."

"I know, I expected to, but this is an emergency. She phoned me this morning."

"I didn't know she was cultivating you, or you her."

"We're not. I haven't seen her or heard her since she paid that bill. This is special. You may remember that when she hired you and we were discussing her, I mentioned a piece about her I had read in a magazine, about the dinner party she throws every year on her first husband's birthday. With four girls and four men as guests? The girls are unmarried mothers who are being rehabil—"

"I remember, yes. Buffoonery. A burlesque of hospitality. Do you mean you are abetting it?"

"I wouldn't say abetting it. A man I know named Austin Byne phoned and asked me to fill in for him because he's in bed with a cold and can't go. Anyhow, it will give me a fresh outlook. It will harden my nerves. It will broaden my mind."

His eyes had narrowed. "Archie."

"Yes, sir."

"Do I ever intrude in your private affairs?"

"Yes, sir. Frequently. But you think you don't, so go right ahead."

"I am not intruding. If it is your whim to lend yourself to that outlandish performance, very well. I merely suggest that you demean yourself. Those creatures are summoned there for an obvious purpose. It is hoped that they, or at least one of them, will meet a man who will be moved to pursue the acquaintance and who will end by legitimating, if not the infant already in being, the future produce of the womb. Therefore your attendance there will be an imposture, and you know it. I begin to doubt if you will ever let a woman plant her foot on your neck, but if you do she will have qualities that would make it impossible for her to share the fate of those forlorn creatures. You will be perpetrating a fraud."

I was shaking my head. "No, sir. You've got it wrong. I let you finish just to hear it. If that were the purpose, giving the girls a chance to meet prospects, I would say hooray for Mrs. Robilotti, and I wouldn't go. But that's the hell of it, that's not it at all. The men are from her own social circle, the kind that wear black ties six nights a week, and there's not a chance. The idea is that it will buck the girls up, be good for their morale, to spend an evening with the cream and get a taste of caviar and sit on a chair made by Congreve. Of course—"

"Congreve didn't make chairs."

"I know he didn't, but I needed a name and that one popped in. Of course that's a lot of hooey, but I won't be perpetrating a fraud. And don't be too sure I won't meet my doom. It's a scientific fact that some girls are more beautiful, more spiritual, more fascinating, after they have had a baby. Also it would be an advantage to have the family already started."

"Pfui. Then you're going."

"Yes, sir. I've told Fritz I won't be here for dinner." I left my chair. "I have to see to something. If you want to answer letters before lunch I'll be down in a couple of minutes."

I had remembered that Saturday evening at the Flamingo someone had spilled something on the sleeve of my dinner jacket, and I had used cleaner on it when I got home, and hadn't examined it since. Mounting the two flights to my room, I took a look and found it was okay.

Chapter 2

I was well acquainted with the insides of the Grantham mansion, now inhabited by Robilottis, on Fifth Avenue in the Eighties, having been over every inch of it, including the servants' quarters, at the time of the jewelry hunt; and, in the taxi on my way uptown, preparing my mind for the scene of action, I had supposed that the pre-dinner gathering would be on the second floor in what was called the music room. But no. For the mothers, the works.

Hackett, admitting me, did fine. Formerly his manner with me as a hired detective had been absolutely perfect; now that I was an invited guest in uniform he made the switch without batting an eye. I suppose a man working up to butler could be taught all the ins and outs of handling the hat-and-coat problem with different grades of people, but it's so darned tricky that probably it has to be born in him. The way he told me good evening, compared with the way he had formerly greeted me, was a lesson in fine points.

I decided to upset him. When he had my hat and coat I inquired with my nose up, "How's it go, Mr. Hackett?"

It didn't faze him. That man had nerves of iron. He merely said, "Very well, thank you, Mr. Goodwin. Mrs. Robilotti is in the drawing room."

"You win, Hackett. Congratulations." I crossed the reception hall, which took ten paces, and passed through the arch.

The drawing room had a twenty-foot ceiling and could dance fifty couples easily, with an alcove for the orchestra as big as my bedroom. The three crystal chandeliers that had been installed by Albert Grantham's mother were still there, and so were thirty-seven chairs—I had counted them one day—of all shapes and sizes, not made by Congreve, I admit, but not made in Grand Rapids either. Of all the rooms I had seen, and I had seen a lot, that was about the last one I would pick as the place for a quartet of unwed mothers to meet a bunch of strangers and relax. Entering and casting a glance around, I took a walk—it amounted to that—across to where Mrs. Robilotti was standing with a group near a portable bar. As I approached she turned to me and offered a hand.

"Mr. Goodwin. So nice to see you."

She didn't handle the switch as perfectly as Hackett had, but it was good enough. After all, I had been imposed on her. Her pale gray eyes, which were set in so far that her brows had sharp angles, didn't light up with welcome, but it was a question whether they ever had lit up for anyone or anything. The angles were not confined to the brows. Whoever had designed her had preferred angles to curves and missed no opportunities, and the passing years, now adding up to close to sixty, had made no alterations. At least they were covered below the chin, since her dress, pale gray like her eyes, had sleeves above the elbows and reached up to the base of her corrugated neck. During the jewelry business I had twice seen her exposed for the evening, and it had been no treat. The only jewelry tonight was a string of pearls and a couple of rings.

I was introduced around and was served a champagne cocktail. The first sip of the cocktail told me something was wrong, and I worked closer to the bar to find out what. Cecil Grantham, the son of the first husband, who was mixing, was committing worse than murder. I saw him. Holding a glass behind and below the bar top, he put in a half-lump of sugar, a drop or two of bitters, and a twist of lemon peel, filled it half full of soda water, set it on the bar, and filled it nearly to the top from a bottle of Cordon Rouge. Killing good champagne with junk like sugar and bitters and lemon peel is of course a common crime, but the soda water was adding horror to homicide. The motive was pure, reducing the voltage to protect the guests of honor, but faced with temptation and given my choice of self-control or soda water in champagne, I set my jaw. I was going to keep an eye on Cecil to see if he did to himself as he was doing to others, but another guest arrived and I had to go to be introduced. He made up the dozen.

By the time our hostess led the way through the arch and up the broad marble stairs to the dining-room on the floor above, I had them sorted out, with names fitted to faces. Of course I had previously met Robilotti and the twins, Cecil and Celia. Paul Schuster was the one with the thin nose and quick dark eyes. Beverly Kent was the one with the long narrow face and big ears. Edwin Laidlaw was the little guy who hadn't combed his hair, or if he had, it refused to oblige.

I had had a sort of an idea that with the girls the best way would be as an older brother who liked sisters and liked to kid them, of course with tact and refinement, and their reactions had been fairly satisfactory. Helen Yarmis, tall and slender, a little too slender, with big brown eyes and a wide curved mouth that would have been a real asset if she had kept the corners up, was on her dignity and apparently had some. Ethel Varr was the one I would have picked for my doom if I had been shopping. She was not a head-turner, but she carried her own head with an air, and she had one of those faces that you keep looking back at because it changes as it moves and catches different angles of light and shade.

I would have picked Faith Usher, not for my doom, but for my sister, because she looked as if she needed a brother more than the others. Actually she was the prettiest one of the bunch, with a dainty little face and greenish flecks in her eyes, and her figure, also dainty, was a very nice job, but she was doing her best to cancel her advantages by letting her shoulders sag and keeping her face muscles so tight she would soon have wrinkles. The right kind of brother could have done wonders with her, but I had no chance to get started during the meal because she was across the table from me, with Beverly Kent on her left and Cecil Grantham on her right.

At my left was Rose Tuttle, who showed no signs of needing a brother at all. She had blue eyes in a round face, a pony tail, and enough curves to make a contribution to Mrs. Robilotti and still be well supplied; and she had been born cheerful and it would take more than an accidental baby to smother it. In fact, as I soon learned, it would take more than two of them. With an oyster balanced on her fork, she turned her face to me and asked, "Goodwin? That's your name?"

"Right. Archie Goodwin."

"I was wondering," she said, "because that woman told me I would sit between Mr. Edwin Laidlaw and Mr. Austin Byne, but now your name's Goodwin. The other day I was telling a friend of mine about coming here, this party, and she said there ought to be unmarried fathers here too, and you seem to have changed your name—are you an unmarried father?"

Remember the tact, I warned myself. "I'm half of it," I told her. "I'm unmarried. But not, as far as I know, a father. Mr. Byne has a cold and couldn't come and asked me to fill in for him. His bad luck and my good luck."

She ate the oyster, and another one—she ate cheerfully too—and turned again. "I was telling this friend of mine that if all society men are like the ones that were here the other time, we weren't missing anything, but I guess they're not. Anyway, you're not. I noticed the way you made Helen laugh—Helen Yarmis. I don't think I ever did see her laugh before. I'm going to tell my friend about you if you don't mind."

"Not at all." Time out for an oyster. "But I don't want to mix you up. I'm not society. I'm a working man."

"Oh!" She nodded. "That explains it. What kind of work?"

Remember the discretion, I warned myself. Miss Tuttle should not be led to suspect that Mrs. Robilotti had got a detective there to keep an eye on the guests of honor. "You might," I said, "call it trouble-shooting. I work for a man named Nero Wolfe. You may have heard of him."

"I think I have." The oysters gone, she put her fork down. "I'm pretty sure . . . Oh, I remember, that murder, that woman, Susan somebody. He's a detective."

"That's right. I work for him. But I—"

"You too. You're a detective!"

"I am when I'm working, but not this evening. Now I'm playing. I'm just enjoying myself—and I am, too. I was wondering what you meant—"

Hackett and two female assistants were removing the oyster service, but it wasn't that that stopped me. The interruption was from Robert Robilotti, across the table, between Celia Grantham and Helen Yarmis, who was demanding the general ear; and as other voices gave way, Mrs. Robilotti raised hers. "Must you, Robbie? That flea again?"

He smiled at her. From what I had seen of him during the jewelry hunt I had not cottoned to him, smiling or not. I'll try to be fair to him, and I know there is no law against a man having plucked eyebrows and a thin mustache and long polished nails, and my suspicion that he wore a girdle was merely a suspicion, and if he had married Mrs. Albert Grantham for her money I freely admit that no man marries without a reason and with her it would have been next to impossible to think up another one, and I concede that he may have had hidden virtues which I had missed. One thing for sure, if my name were Robert and I had married a woman fifteen years older than me for a certain reason and she was composed entirely of angles, I would not let her call me Robbie.

I'll say this for him: he didn't let her gag him. What he wanted all ears for was the story about the advertising agency executive who did a research job on the flea, and by gum he stuck to it. I had heard it told better by Saul Panzer, but he got the point in, with only fair audience response. The three society men laughed with tact, discretion, and refinement. Helen Yarmis let the corners of her mouth come up. The Grantham twins exchanged a glance of sympathy. Faith Usher caught Ethel Varr's eye across the table, shook her head, just barely moving it, and dropped her eyes. Then Edwin Laidlaw chipped in with a story about an author who wrote a book in invisible ink, and Beverly Kent followed with one about an army general who forgot which side he was on. We were all one big happy family—well, fairly happy—by the time the squabs were served. Then I had a problem. At Wolfe's table we tackle squabs with our fingers, which is of course the only practical way, but I didn't want to wreck the party. Then Rose Tuttle got her fork on to hers with one hand, and with the other grabbed a leg and yanked, which settled it.

Miss Tuttle had said something that I wanted to go into, tactfully, but she was talking with Edwin Laidlaw, on her left, and I gave Ethel Varr, on my right, a look. Her face was by no means out of surprises. In profile, close up, it was again different, and when it turned and we were eye to eye, once more it was new.

"I hope," I said, "you won't mind a personal remark."

"I'll try not to," she said. "I can't promise until I hear it."

"I'll take a chance. In case you have caught me staring at you I want to explain why."

"I don't know." She was smiling. "Maybe you'd better not. Maybe it would let me down. Maybe I'd rather think you stared just because you wanted to."

"You can think that too. If I hadn't wanted to I wouldn't have stared. But the idea is, I was trying to catch you looking the same way twice. If you turn your head only a little one way or the other it's a different face. I know there are people with faces that do that, but I've never seen one that changes as much as yours. Hasn't anyone ever mentioned it to you?"

She parted her lips, closed them, and turned right away from me. All I could do was turn back to my plate, and I did so, but in a moment she was facing me again. "You know," she said, "I'm only nineteen years old."

"I was nineteen once," I assured her. "Some ways I liked it, and some ways it was terrible."

"Yes, it is," she agreed. "I haven't learned how to take things yet, but I suppose I will. I was silly—just because you said that. I should have just told you yes, someone did mention that to me once. About my face. More than once."

So I had put my foot in it. How the hell are you going to be tactful when you don't know what is out of bounds and what isn't? Merely having a face that changes isn't going to get a girl a baby. I flopped around. "Well," I said, "I know it was a personal remark, and I only wanted to explain why I had stared at you. I wouldn't have brought it up if I had known there was anything touchy about it. I think you ought to get even. I'm touchy about horses because once I caught my foot in the stirrup when I was getting off, so you might try that. Ask me something about horses and *my* face will change."

"I suppose you ride in Central Park. Was it in the park?"

"No, it was out West one summer. Go ahead. You're getting warm."

We stayed on horses until Paul Schuster, on her right, horned in. I couldn't blame him, since he had Mrs. Robilotti on his other side. But Edwin Laidlaw still had Rose Tuttle, and it wasn't until the dessert came, cherry pudding topped with whipped cream, that I had a chance to ask her about the remark she had made.

"Something you said," I told her. "Maybe I didn't hear it right."

She swallowed pudding. "Maybe I didn't say it right. I often don't." She leaned to me and lowered her voice. "Is this Mr. Laidlaw a friend of yours?"

I shook my head. "Never saw him before."

"You haven't missed anything. He publishes books. To look at me, would you think I was dying to know how many books were published last year in America and England and a lot of other countries?"

"No, I wouldn't. I would think you could make out all right without it."

"I always have. What was it I said wrong?"

"I didn't say you said it wrong. I understood you to say something about the society men that were here the other time, and I wasn't sure I got it. I didn't know whether you meant another party like this one."

She nodded. "Yes, that's what I meant. Three years ago. She throws one every year, you know."

"Yes, I know."

"This is my second one. This friend of mine I mentioned, she says the only reason I had another baby
was to get invited here for some more champagne,
but believe me, if I liked champagne so much I could
get it a lot quicker and oftener than that, and anyway,
I didn't have the faintest idea I would be invited
again. How old do you think I am?"

I studied her. "Oh—twenty-one."

She was pleased. "Of course you took off five years
to be polite, so you guessed it exactly. I'm twenty-six.
So it isn't true that having babies makes a girl look
older. Of course, if you had a lot of them, eight or ten,
but by that time you would *be* older. I just don't believe I would look younger if I hadn't had two babies.
Do you?"

I was on a spot. I had accepted the invitation with
my eyes and ears open. I had told my hostess that I
was acquainted with the nature and significance of the
affair and she could count on me. I had on my shoulders the responsibility of the moral and social position
of the community, some of it anyhow, and here this
cheerful unmarried mother was resting the whole
problem on the single question, had it aged her any?
If I merely said no, it hadn't, which would have been
both true and tactful, it would imply that I agreed
that the one objection to her career was a phony. To
say no and then proceed to list other objections that
were not phonies would have been fine if I had been
ordained, but I hadn't, and anyway she had certainly
heard of them and hadn't been impressed. I worked it
out in three seconds, on the basis that while it was
none of my business if she kept on having babies, I

absolutely wasn't going to encourage her. So I lied to her.

"Yes," I said.

"What?" She was indignant. "You do?"

I was firm. "I do. You admitted that I took you for twenty-six and deducted five years to be polite. If you had had only one baby I might have taken you for twenty-three, and if you had had none I might have taken you for twenty. I can't prove it, but I might. We'd better get on with the pudding. Some of them have finished."

She turned to it, cheerfully.

Apparently the guests of honor had been briefed on procedure, for when Hackett, on signal, pulled back Mrs. Robilotti's chair as she arose, and we chevaliers did likewise for our partners, they joined the hostess as she headed for the door. When they were out we sat down again.

Cecil Grantham blew a breath, a noisy gust, and said, "The last two hours are the hardest."

Robilotti said, "Brandy, Hackett."

Hackett stopped pouring coffee to look at him. "The cabinet is locked, sir."

"I know it is, but you have a key."

"No, sir, Mrs. Robilotti has it."

It seemed to me that that called for an embarrassed silence, but Cecil Grantham laughed and said, "Get a hatchet."

Hackett poured coffee.

Beverly Kent, the one with a long narrow face and big ears, cleared his throat. "A little deprivation will be good for us, Mr. Robilotti. After all, we understood the protocol when we accepted the invitation."

"Not protocol," Paul Schuster objected. "That's

not what protocol means. I'm surprised at you, Bev. You'll never be an ambassador if you don't know what protocol is."

"I never will anyway," Kent declared. "I'm thirty years old, eight years out of college, and what am I? An errand boy in the Mission to the United Nations. So I'm a diplomat? But I ought to know what protocol is better than a promising young corporation lawyer. What do you know about it?"

"Not much." Schuster was sipping coffee. "Not much *about* it, but I know what it is, and you used it wrong. And you're wrong about me being a promising young corporation lawyer. Lawyers never promise anything. That's about as far as I've got, but I'm a year younger than you, so there's hope."

"Hope for who?" Cecil Grantham demanded. "You or the corporations?"

"About that word 'protocol,'" Edwin Laidlaw said, "I can settle that for you. Now that I'm a publisher I'm the last word on words. It comes from two Greek words, *prōtos*, meaning 'first,' and *kolla*, meaning 'glue.' Now why glue? Because in ancient Greece a *prōtokollon* was the first leaf, containing an account of the manuscript, glued to a roll of papyrus. Today a protocol may be any one of various kinds of documents—an original draft of something, or an account of some proceeding, or a record of an agreement. That seems to support you, Paul, but Bev has a point, because a protocol can also be a set of rules of etiquette. So you're both right. This affair this evening does require a special etiquette."

"I'm for Paul," Cecil Grantham declared. "Locking up the booze doesn't come under etiquette. It comes under tyranny."

Kent turned to me. "What about you, Goodwin? I understand you're a detective, so maybe you can detect the answer."

I put my coffee cup down. "I'm a little hazy," I said, "as to what you're after. If you just want to decide whether you used the word 'protocol' right, the best plan would be to get the dictionary. There's one upstairs in the library. But if what you want is brandy, and the cabinet is locked, the best plan would be for one of us to go to a liquor store. There's one at the corner of Eighty-second and Madison. We could toss up."

"The practical man," Laidlaw said. "The man of action."

"You notice," Cecil told them, "that he knows where the dictionary is and where the liquor store is. Detectives know everything." He turned to me. "By the way, speaking of detectives, are you here professionally?"

Not caring much for his tone, I raised my brows. "If I were, what would I say?"

"Why—I suppose you'd say you weren't."

"And if I weren't what would I say?"

Robert Robilotti let out a snort. "*Touché*, Cece. Try another one." He pronounced it "Seese." Cecil's mother called him "Sessel," and his sister called him "Sesse."

Cecil ignored his father-in-law. "I was just asking," he told me. "I shouldn't ask?"

"Sure, why not? I was just answering." I moved my head right and left. "Since the question has been asked, it may be in all your minds. If I were here professionally I would let it stand on my answer to Grantham, but since I'm not, you might as well know it. Austin Byne phoned this morning and asked me to take his place. If any of you are bothered enough you can check with him."

"I think," Robilotti said, "that it is none of our business. I know it is none of my business."

"Nor mine," Schuster agreed.

"Oh, forget it," Cecil snapped. "What the hell, I was just curious. Shall we join the mothers?"

Robilotti darted a glance at him, not friendly. After all, who was the host? "I was about to ask," he said, "if anyone wants more coffee. No?" He left his chair. "We will join them in the music room and escort them downstairs and it is understood that each of us will dance first with his dinner partner. If you please, gentlemen?"

I got up and shook my pants legs down.

Chapter 3

I'll be darned if there wasn't a live band in the alcove—piano, sax, two violins, clarinet, and traps. A record player and speaker might have been expected, but for the mothers, spare no expense. Of course, in the matter of expense, the fee for the band was about balanced by the saving on liquids—the soda water in the cocktails, the pink stuff passing for wine at the dinner table, and the brandy ban—so it wasn't too extravagant. The one all-out splurge on liquids came after we had been dancing an hour or so, when Hackett appeared at the bar and began opening champagne, Cordon Rouge, and poured it straight, no dilution or adulteration. With only an hour to go, apparently Mrs. Robilotti had decided to take a calculated risk.

As a dancing partner Rose Tuttle was not a bargain. She was equipped for it physically and she had some idea of rhythm, that wasn't it; it was her basic attitude. She danced cheerfully, and of course that was no good. You can't dance cheerfully. Dancing is too important. It can be wild or solemn or gay or lewd or art for art's sake, but it can't be cheerful. For one thing, if you're cheerful you talk too much. Helen Yarmis was better, or would have been if she hadn't been too *damn* solemn. We would work into the rhythm together and get going fine, when all of a sudden she would stiffen up and was just a dummy making motions. She was a good size for me, too, with the top of her head level with my nose, and the closer you get to her wide, curved mouth the better you liked it—when the corners were up.

Robilotti took her for the next one, and a look around showed me that all the guests of honor were taken, and Celia Grantham was heading for me. I stayed put and let her come, and she stopped at arm's length and tilted her head back.

"Well?" she said.

The tact, I figured, was for the mothers, and there was no point in wasting it on the daughter. So I said, "But is it any better?"

"No," she said, "and it never will be. But how are you going to avoid dancing with me?"

"Easy. Say my feet hurt, and take my shoes off."

She nodded. "You would, wouldn't you?"

"I could."

"You really would. Just let me suffer. Will I never be in your arms again? Must I carry my heartache to the grave?"

But I am probably giving a false impression, though I am reporting accurately. I had seen the girl—I say "girl" in spite of the fact that she was perhaps a couple of years older than Rose Tuttle, who was twice a mother—I had seen her just four times. Three of them had been in that house during the jewelry hunt, and on the third occasion, when I had been alone with her briefly, the conversation had somehow

resulted in our making a date to dine and dance at the
Flamingo, and we had kept it. It had not turned out
well. She was a good dancer, very good, but she was
also a good drinker, and along toward midnight she
had raised an issue with another lady, and had developed it to a point where we got tossed out. In the next
few months she had phoned me off and on, say twenty
times, to suggest a rerun, and I had been too busy.
For me the Flamingo has the best band in town and I
didn't want to get the cold stare for good. As for her
persisting, I would like to think that, once she had
tasted me, no other flavor would do, but I'm afraid she
was just too pigheaded to drop it. I had supposed that
she had long since forgotten all about it but here she
was again.

"It's not your heart," I said. "It's your head.
You're too loyal to yourself. We're having a clash of
wills, that's all. Besides, I have a hunch that if I took
you in my arms and started off with you, after one or
two turns you would break loose and take a swing at
me and make remarks, and that would spoil the party.
I see the look in your eye."

"The look in my eye is passion. If you don't know
passion when you see it you ought to get around
more. Have you got a Bible?"

"No, I forgot to bring it. There's one in the library." From my inside breast pocket I produced my
notebook, which is always with me. "Will this do?"

"Fine. Hold it flat." I did so and she put her palm
on it. "I swear on my honor that if you dance with me
I will be your kitten for better or for worse and will
do nothing that will make you wish you hadn't."

Anyway, Mrs. Robilotti, who was dancing with
Paul Schuster, was looking at us. Returning the note-

book to my pocket, I closed with her daughter, and in three minutes had decided that every allowance should be made for a girl who could dance like that.

The band had stopped for breath, and I had taken Celia to a chair, and was considering whether it would be tactful to have another round with her, when Rose Tuttle approached, unaccompanied, and was at my elbow. Celia spoke to her, woman to woman.

"If you're after Mr. Goodwin I don't blame you. He's the only one here that can dance."

"I'm not after him to dance," Rose said. "Anyway I wouldn't have the nerve because I'm no good at it. I just want to tell him something."

"Go ahead," I told her.

"It's private."

Celia laughed. "That's the way to do it." She stood up. "That would have taken me at least a hundred words, and you do it in two." She moved off toward the bar, where Hackett had appeared and was opening champagne.

"Sit down," I told Rose.

"Oh, it won't take long." She stood. "It's just something I thought you ought to know because you're a detective. I know Mrs. Robilotti wouldn't want any trouble, and I was going to tell her, but I thought it might be better to tell you."

"I'm not here as a detective, Miss Tuttle. As I told you. I'm just here to enjoy myself."

"I know that; but you *are* a detective, and you can tell Mrs. Robilotti if you think you ought to. I don't want to tell her because I know how she is, but if something awful happened and I hadn't told anybody I would think maybe I was to blame."

"Why should something awful happen?"

She had a hand on my arm. "I don't say it should, but it might. Faith Usher still carries that poison around, and she has it with her. It's in her bag. But of course you don't know about it."

"No, I don't. What poison?"

"Her private poison. She told us girls at Grantham House it was cyanide, and she showed it to some of us, in a little bottle. She always had it, in a little pocket she made in her skirt, and she made pockets in her dresses. She said she hadn't made up her mind to kill herself, but she might, and if she did she wanted to have that poison. Some of the girls thought she was just putting on, and one or two of them used to kid her, but I never did. I thought she might really do it, and if she did and I had kidded her I would be to blame. Now she's away from there and she's got a job, and I thought maybe she had got over it, but upstairs a while ago Helen Yarmis was with her in the powder room, and Helen saw the bottle in her bag and asked her if the poison was still in it, and she said yes."

She stopped. "And?" I asked.

"And what?" she asked.

"Is that all?"

"I think it's enough. If you knew Faith like I do. Here in this grand house, and the butler, and the men dressed up, and that powder room, and the champagne—this is where she might do it if she ever does." All of a sudden she was cheerful again. "So would I," she declared. "I would drop the poison in my champagne and get up on a chair with it and hold it high, and call out 'Here goes to all our woes'—that's what one of the girls used to say when she drank a Coke— and drink it down, and throw the glass away and get off the chair, and start to sink down to the floor, and the men would rush to catch me—how long would it take me to die?"

"A couple of minutes, or even less if you put enough in." Her hand was still on my arm and I patted it. "Okay, you've told me. I'd forget it if I were you. Did you ever see the bottle?"

"Yes, she showed it to me."

"Did you smell the stuff in it?"

"No, she didn't open it. It had a screw top."

"Was it glass? Could you see the stuff?"

"No, I think it was some kind of plastic."

"You say Helen Yarmis saw it in her bag. What kind of a bag?"

"Black leather." She turned for a look around. "It's there on a chair. I don't want to point—"

"You've already pointed with your eyes. I see it. Just forget it. I'll see that nothing awful happens. Will you dance?"

She would, and we joined the merry whirl, and when the band paused we went to the bar for champagne. Next I took Faith Usher.

Since Faith Usher had been making her play for a year or more, and the stuff in the plastic bottle might be aspirin or salted peanuts, and even if it were cyanide I didn't agree with Rose Tuttle's notion of the ideal spot for suicide, the chance of anything happening was about one in ten million, but even so, I had had a responsibility wished on me, and I kept an eye both on the bag and on Faith Usher. That was simple when I was dancing with her, since I could forget the bag.

As I said, I would have picked her for my sister because she looked as if she needed a brother, but her being the prettiest one of the bunch may have been a factor. She had perked up some too, with her face muscles relaxed, and, in spite of the fact that she got off the beat now and then, it was a pleasure to dance with her. Also now and then, when she liked something I did, there would be a flash in her eyes with the greenish flecks, and when we finished I wasn't so sure that it was a brother she needed. Maybe cousin would be better.

However, it appeared that she had ideas of her own, if not about brothers and cousins, at least about dancing partners. We were standing at a window when Edwin Laidlaw, the publisher, came up and bowed to her and spoke.

"Will you dance with me, Miss Usher?"

"No," she said.

"I would be honored."

"No."

Naturally I wondered why. He had only a couple of inches on her in height, and perhaps she liked them taller—me, for instance. Or perhaps it was because he hadn't combed his hair, or if he had it didn't look it. If it was more personal, if he had said something that offended her, it hadn't been at the table, since they hadn't been close enough, but of course it could have been before or after. Laidlaw turned and went, and as the band opened up I was opening my mouth to suggest that we try an encore, when Cecil Grantham came and got her. He was about my height and every hair on his head was in place, so that could have been it. I went and got Ethel Varr and said nothing whatever about her face changing. As we danced I tried not to keep twisting my head around, but I had to maintain surveillance on Faith Usher and her bag, which was still on the chair.

When something awful did happen I hadn't the
slightest idea that it was coming. I like to think that I
can count on myself for hunches, and often I can, but
not that time, and what makes it worse is that I was
keeping an eye on Faith Usher as I stood talking with
Ethel Varr. If she was about to die, and if I am any
damn good at hunches, I might at least have felt myself breathing a little faster, but not even that. I saw
her escorted to a chair by Cecil Grantham, fifteen feet
away from the chair the bag was on, and saw her sit,
and saw him go and return in a couple of minutes with
champagne and hand her hers, and saw him raise his
glass and say something. I had been keeping her in
the corner of my eye, not to be rude to Ethel Varr,
but at that point I had both eyes straight at Faith
Usher. Not that I am claiming a hunch; it was simply
that Rose Tuttle's idea of poison in champagne was
fresh in my mind and I was reacting to it. So I had
both eyes on Faith Usher when she took a gulp and
went stiff, and shook all over, and jerked halfway to
her feet, and made a noise that was part scream and
part moan, and went down. Going down, she teetered
on the edge of the chair for a second and then would
have been on the floor if Cecil hadn't grabbed her.

When I got there he was trying to hold her up. I
said to let her down, took her shoulders, and called
out to get a doctor. As I eased her to the floor she
went into convulsion, her head jerking and her legs
thrashing, and when Cecil tried to catch her ankles I
told him that was no good and asked if someone was
getting a doctor, and someone behind me said yes. I
was on my knees, trying to keep her from banging her
head on the floor, but managed a glance up and
around, and saw that Robilotti and Kent and the band

leader were keeping the crowd back. Pretty soon the convulsions eased up, and then stopped. She had been breathing fast in heavy gasps, and when they slowed down and weakened, and I felt her neck getting stiff, I knew the paralysis was starting, and no doctor would make it in time to help.

Cecil was yapping at me, and there were other voices, and I lifted my head to snap, "Will everybody please shut up? There's nothing I can do or anyone else." I saw Rose Tuttle. "Rose, go and guard that bag. Don't touch it. Stick there and don't take your eyes off it." Rose moved.

Mrs. Robilotti took a step toward me and spoke. "You are in my house, Mr. Goodwin. These people are my guests. What's the matter with her?"

Having smelled the breath of her gasps, I could have been specific, but that could wait until she was dead, not long, so I skipped it and asked, "Who's getting a doctor?"

"Celia's phoning," someone said.

Staying on my knees, I turned back to her. A glance at my wristwatch showed me five past eleven. She had been on the floor six minutes. There was foam on her mouth, her eyes were glassy, and her neck was rigid. I stayed put for two minutes, looking at her, ignoring the audience participation, then reached for her hand and pressed hard on the nail of the middle finger. When I removed my fingers the nail stayed white; in thirty seconds there was no sign of returning pink.

I stood up and addressed Robilotti. "Do I phone the police or do you?"

"The police?" He had trouble getting it out.

"Yes. She's dead. I'd rather stick here, but you must phone at once."

"No," Mrs. Robilotti said. "We have sent for a doctor. I give the orders here. I'll phone the police myself when I decide it is necessary."

I was sore. Of course that was bad; it's always a mistake to get sore in a tough situation, especially at yourself; but I couldn't help it. Not more than half an hour ago I had told Rose to leave it to me, I would see that nothing awful happened, and look. I glanced around. Not a single face, male or female, looked promising. The husband and the son, the two guests of honor, the butler, the three chevaliers—none of them was going to walk over Mrs. Robilotti. Celia wasn't there. Rose was guarding the bag. Then I saw the band leader, a guy with broad shoulders and a square jaw, standing at the entrance to the alcove with his back to it, surveying the tableau calmly, and called to him.

"My name's Goodwin. What's yours?"

"Johnson."

"Do you want to stay here all night, Mr. Johnson?"

"No."

"Neither do I. I think this woman was murdered, and if the police do too you know what that means, so the sooner they get here the better. I'm a licensed private detective and I ought to stay with the body. There's a phone on a stand in the reception hall. The number is Spring seven-three-one-hundred."

"Right." He headed for the arch. When Mrs. Robilotti commanded him to halt and moved to head him off he just side-stepped her and went on, not bothering to argue, and she called to her men, "Robbie! Cecil! Stop him!"

When they failed to react she wheeled to me. "Leave my house!"

"I would love to," I told her. "If I did, the cops would soon bring me back. Nobody is going to leave your house for a while."

Robilotti was there, taking her arm. "It's no use, Louise. It's horrible, but it's no use. Come and sit down." He looked at me. "Why do you think she was murdered? Why do you say that?"

Paul Schuster, the promising young lawyer, spoke up. "I was going to ask that, Goodwin. She had a bottle of poison in her bag."

"How do you know she did?"

"One of the guests told me. Miss Varr."

"One of them told me too. That's why I asked Miss Tuttle to guard the bag. I still think she was murdered, but I'll save my reason for the police. You people might—"

Celia Grantham came running in, calling, "How is she?" and came on, stopping beside me, looking down at Faith Usher. "My God," she whispered, and seized my arm and demanded, "Why don't you *do* something?" She looked down again, her mouth hanging open, and I put my hands on her shoulders and turned her around. "Thanks," she said. "My God, she was so pretty. Is she dead?"

"Yes. Did you get a doctor?"

"Yes, he's coming. I couldn't get ours. I got— What good is a doctor if she's dead?"

"Nobody is dead until a doctor says so. It's a law." Some of the others were jabbering, and I turned and raised my voice. "You people might as well rest your legs and there are plenty of chairs, but stay away from the one the bag is on. If you want to leave the room I can't stop you, but I advise you not to. The police might misunderstand it, and you'd only have more questions to answer." A buzzer sounded and Hackett was going, but I stopped him. "No, Hackett, you'd better stay, you're one of us now. Mr. Johnson will let them in."

He was doing so. There was no sound of the door opening because doors on mansions do not make noises, but there were voices in the reception hall, and everybody turned to face the arch. In they came, a pair, two precinct men in uniform. They marched in and stopped, and one of them asked, "Mr. Robert Robilotti?"

"I'm Robert Robilotti," he said.

"This your house? We got—"

"No," Mrs. Robilotti said. "It's my house."

Chapter 4

Wwhen I mounted the seven steps of the stoop of the old brownstone at twelve minutes after seven Wednesday morning and let myself in, I was so pooped that I was going to drop my topcoat and hat on the hall bench, but breeding told, and I put the coat on a hanger and the hat on a shelf and went to the kitchen.

Fritz, at the refrigerator, turned and actually left the refrigerator door open to stare at me.

"Behold!" he said. He had told me once that he had got that out of his French-English dictionary, many years ago, as a translation of *voilà*.

"I want," I said, "a quart of orange juice, a pound of sausage, six eggs, twenty griddle cakes, and a gallon of coffee."

"No doughnuts with honey?"

"Yes. I forgot to mention them." I dropped on to the chair I occupy at breakfast, groaning. "Speaking of honey, if you want to make a friend who will never fail you, you might employ the eggs in a hedgehog omelet, with plenty— No. It would take too long. Just fry 'em."

"I never fry eggs." He was stirring a bowl of batter. "You have had a night?"

"I have. A murder with all the trimmings."

"Ah! Terrible! A client, then?"

I do not pretend to understand Fritz's attitude toward murder. He deplores it. To him the idea of one human being killing another is insupportable; he has told me so, and he meant it. But he never has the slightest interest in the details, not even who the victim was, or the murderer, and if I try to tell him about any of the fine points it just bores him. Beyond the bare fact that again a human being has done something insupportable, the only question he wants answered is whether we have a client.

"No client," I told him.

"There may be one, if you were there. Have you had nothing to eat?"

"No. Three hours ago they offered to get me a sandwich at the District Attorney's office, but my stomach said no. It preferred to wait for something that would stay down." He handed me a glass of orange juice. "Many, many thanks. That sausage smells marvelous."

He didn't like to talk or listen when he was actually cooking, even something as simple as broiling sausage, so I picked up the *Times*, there on my table as usual, and gave it a look. A murder has to be more than run-of-the-mill to make the front page of the *Times*, but this one certainly qualified, having occurred at the famous unmarried-mothers party at the home of Mrs. Robert Robilotti, and it was there, with a three-column lead on the bottom half of the page, carried over to page 23. But the account didn't amount to much, since it had happened so late, and there were no pictures, not even of me. That settled, I propped the paper on the reading rack and tackled a sausage and griddle cake.

I was arranging two poached eggs on the fourth cake when the house phone buzzed, and I reached for it and said good morning and had Wolfe's voice.

"So you're here. When did you get home?"

"Half an hour ago. I'm eating breakfast. I suppose it was on the seven-thirty newscast."

"Yes. I just heard it. As you know, I dislike the word 'newscast.' Must you use it?"

"Correction. Make it the seven-thirty radio news broadcast. I don't feel like arguing, and my cake is getting cold."

"You will come up when you have finished."

I said I would. When I had cradled the phone Fritz asked if he was in humor, and I said I didn't know and didn't give a damn. I was still sore at myself.

I took my time with the meal, treating myself to three cups of coffee instead of the usual two, and was taking the last swallow when Fritz returned from taking up the breakfast tray. I put the cup down, got up, had a stretch and a yawn, went to the hall, mounted the flight of stairs in no hurry, turned left, tapped on a door, and was told to come in.

Entering, I blinked. The morning sun was streaking in and glancing off the vast expanse of Wolfe's yellow pajamas. He was seated at a table by a window, barefooted, working on a bowl of fresh figs with cream. When I was listing the cash requirements of the establishment I might have mentioned that fresh figs in March, by air from Chile, are not hay.

He gave me a look. "You are disheveled," he stated.

"Yes, sir. Also disgruntled. Also disslumbered. Did the broadcast say she was murdered?"

"No. That she died of poison and the police are investigating. Your name was not mentioned. Are you involved?"

"Up to my chin. I had been told by a friend of hers that she had a bottle of cyanide in her bag, and I was keeping an eye on her. We were together in the drawing room, dancing, all twelve of us, not counting the butler and the band, when a man brought her a glass of champagne, and she took a gulp, and in eight minutes she was dead. It was cyanide, that's established, and the way it works it had to be in the champagne, but she didn't put it there. I was watching her, and I'm the one that says she didn't. Most of the others, maybe all of them, would like to have it that she did. Mrs. Robilotti would like to choke me, and some of the others would be glad to lend a hand. A suicide at her party would be bad enough, but a homicide is murder. So I'm involved."

He swallowed a bite of fig. "You are indeed. I suppose you considered whether it would be well to reserve your conclusion."

I appreciated that—his not questioning my eyesight or my faculty of attention. It was a real tribute, and the way I felt, I needed one. I said, "Sure I considered it. But I had to include that I had been told she had cyanide in her bag, since the girl who told me would certainly include it, and Cramer and Stebbins and Rowcliff would know damn well that in that case I would have had my eyes open, so I had no choice. I couldn't tell them yes, I was watching her and the bag, and yes, I was looking at her when Grantham took her the champagne and she drank it, and yes, she might have put something in the champagne before she drank when I was absolutely certain she hadn't."

"No," he agreed. He had finished the figs and taken one of the ramekins of shirred eggs with sausage from the warmer. "Then you're in for it. I take it that we expect no profitable engagement."

"We do not. God knows, not from Mrs. Robilotti."

"Very well." He put a muffin in the toaster. "You may remember my remarks yesterday."

"I do. You said I would demean myself. You did not say I would get involved in an unprofitable homicide. I'll deposit the checks this morning."

He said I should go to bed, and I said if I did it would take a guided missile to get me up again.

After a shower and shave and tooth brush, and clean shirt and socks, and a walk to the bank and back, I began to think I might last the day out. I had three reasons for making the trip to the bank: first, people die, and if the signer of a check dies before the check reaches his bank the bank won't pay it; second, I wanted air; and third, I had been told at the District Attorney's office to keep myself constantly available, and I wanted to uphold my constitutional freedom of movement. However, the issue wasn't raised, for when I returned Fritz told me that the only phone call had been from Lon Cohen of the *Gazette*.

Lon has done us various favors over the years, and besides, I like him, so I gave him a ring. What he wanted was an eye-witness story of the last hours of Faith Usher, and I told him I'd think it over and let him know. His offer was five hundred bucks, which would have been not for Nero Wolfe but for me, since my presence at the party had been strictly personal, and of course he pressed—journalists always press—

but I stalled him. The bait was attractive, five C's and my picture in the paper, but I would have to include the climax, and if I reported that exactly as it happened, letting the world know that I was the one obstacle to calling it suicide, I would have everybody on my neck from the District Attorney to the butler. I was regretfully deciding that I would have to pass when the phone rang, and I answered it and had Celia Grantham's voice. She wanted to know if I was alone. I told her yes but I wouldn't be in six minutes, when Wolfe would descend from the plant rooms.

"It won't take that long." Her voice was croaky, but not necessarily from drink. Like all the rest of them, including me, she had done a lot of talking in the past twelve hours. "Not if you'll answer a question. Will you?"

"Ask it."

"Something you said last night when I wasn't there—when I was phoning for a doctor. My mother says that you said you thought Faith Usher was murdered. Did you?"

"Yes."

"Why did you say it? That's the question."

"Because I thought it."

"Please don't be smart, Archie. Why did you think it?"

"Because I had to. I was forced to by circumstances. If you think I'm dodging, I am. I would like to oblige a girl who dances as well as you do, but I'm not going to answer your question—not now. I'm sorry, but nothing doing."

"Do you still think she was murdered?"

"Yes."

"But *why?*"

I don't hang up on people. I thought I might have to that time, but she finally gave up, just as Wolfe's elevator jolted to a stop at the bottom. He entered, crossed to his chair behind his desk, got his bulk arranged in it to his satisfaction, glanced through the mail, looked at his calendar, and leaned back to read a three-page letter from an orchid-hunter in New Guinea. He was on the third page when the doorbell rang. I got up and stepped to the hall, saw, through the one-way glass panel of the front door, a burly frame and a round red face, and went and opened the door.

"Good Lord," I said, "don't you ever sleep?"

"Not much," he said, crossing the sill.

I got the collar of his coat as he shed it. "This is an honor, since you must be calling on me. Why not invite me down—Cramer!"

He had headed for the office. My calling him "Cramer" instead of "Inspector" was so unexpected that he stopped and about-faced. "Why," I demanded, "don't you ever learn? You know damn well he hates to have anyone march in on him, even you, or especially you, and you only make it harder. Isn't it me you want?"

"Yes, but I want him to hear it."

"That's obvious, or you would have sent for me instead of coming. If you will kindly—"

Wolfe's bellow came out to us. "Confound it, come in here!"

Cramer wheeled and went, and I followed. Wolfe's only greeting was a scowl. "I cannot," he said coldly, "read my mail in an uproar."

Cramer took his usual seat, the red leather chair

near the end of Wolfe's desk. "I came," he said, "to see Goodwin, but I—"

"I heard you in the hall. You would enlighten me? That's why you want me present?"

Cramer took a breath. "The day I try to enlighten you they can send me to the loony house. It's just that I know Goodwin is your man and I want you to understand the situation. I thought the best way would be to discuss it with him with you present. Is that sensible?"

"It may be. I'll know when I hear the discussion."

Cramer aimed his sharp gray eyes at me. "I don't intend to go all over it again, Goodwin. I've questioned you twice myself, and I've read your statement. I'm only after one point, the big point. To begin with, I'll tell you something that is not to be repeated. There is not a thing, not a word, in what any of the others have said that rules out suicide. Not a single damn thing. And there's a lot that makes suicide plausible, even probable. I'm saying that if it wasn't for you suicide would be a reasonable assumption, and it seems likely, I only say likely, that that would be the final verdict. You see what that means."

I nodded. "Yeah. I'm the fly in the soup. I don't like it any better than you do. Flies don't like being swamped in soup, especially when it's hot."

He got a cigar from a pocket, rolled it in his palms, put it between his teeth, which were white and even, and removed it. "I'll start at the beginning," he said. "Your being there when it happened. I know what you say, and it's in your statement—the phone call from Austin Byne and the one from Mrs. Robilotti. Of course that happened. When you say anything that can be checked it will always check. But did you or

Wolfe help it to happen? Knowing Wolfe, and knowing you, I have got to consider the possibility that you wanted to be there, or Wolfe wanted you to, and you made arrangements. Did you?"

I was yawning and had to finish it. "I beg your pardon. I could just say no, but let's cover it. How and why I was there is fully explained in my statement. Nothing related to it was omitted. Mr. Wolfe thought I shouldn't go because I would demean myself."

"None of the people who were there was or is Wolfe's client?"

"Mrs. Robilotti was a couple of years ago. The job was finished in nine days. Except for that, no."

His eyes went to Wolfe. "You confirm that?"

"Yes. This is gratuitous, Mr. Cramer."

"With you and Goodwin it's hard to tell what is and what isn't." He came back to me. "I'm going to tell you how it stands up to now. First, it was cyanide. That's settled. Second, it was in the champagne. It was in what spilled on the floor when she dropped the glass, and anyway it acts so fast it must have been. Third, a two-ounce plastic bottle in her bag was half full of lumps of sodium cyanide. The laboratory calls them amorphous fragments; I call them lumps. Fourth, she had shown that bottle to various people and told them she wanted to kill herself; she had been doing that for more than a year."

He shifted in the chair. He always sat so as to have Wolfe head-on, but now he was at me. "Since the bag was on a chair fifteen feet away from her, and the bottle was in it, she couldn't have taken a lump from it when Grantham brought her the champagne, or just before, but she could have taken it any time during the preceding hour or so and had it concealed in her handkerchief. Testing the handkerchief for traces is out because she dropped it and it fell in the spilled champagne—or rather, it's not out but it's no help. So that's the set-up for suicide. Do you see holes in it?"

I killed a yawn. "Certainly not. It's perfect. I don't say she mightn't have committed suicide, I only say she didn't. As you know, I have good eyes, and she was only twenty feet from me. When she took the champagne from Grantham with her right hand her left hand was on her lap, and she didn't lift it. She took the glass by the stem, and when Grantham raised his glass and said something she raised hers a little higher than her mouth and then lowered it and drank. Are you by any chance hiding an ace? Does Grantham say that when he handed her the glass she dropped something in it before she took hold of it?"

"No. He only says she might have put something in it before she drank; he doesn't know."

"Well, I do. She didn't."

"Yeah. You signed your statement." He pointed the cigar at me.

"Look, Goodwin. You admit there are no holes in the set-up for suicide; how about the set-up for murder? The bag was there on the chair in full view. Did someone walk over and pick it up and open it and take out the bottle and unscrew the cap and shake out a lump and screw the cap back on and put the bottle back in the bag and drop it on the chair and walk away? That must have taken nerve."

"Nuts. You're stacking the deck. All someone had to do was get the bag—of course I started watching it—and take it to a room that could be locked on the inside—there was one handy—and get a lump and conceal it in his or her handkerchief—thank you for suggesting the handkerchief—and return the bag to the chair. That would take care, but no great nerve, since if he had any reason to think he had been seen taking the bag or returning it he wouldn't use the lump. He might or might not have a chance to use it, anyway." A yawn got me.

He pointed the cigar again. "And that's the next point, the chance to use it. The two glasses of champagne that Grantham took were poured by the butler, Hackett; he did all the pouring. One of them had been sitting on the bar for four or five minutes, and Hackett poured the other one just before Grantham came. Who was there, at the bar, during those four or five minutes? We haven't got that completely straight yet, but apparently everybody was, or nearly everybody. You were. By your statement, and Ethel Varr agrees, you and she went there and took two glasses of champagne of the five or six that were there waiting, and then moved off and stood talking, and soon after—you say three minutes—you saw Grantham bring the two glasses to Faith Usher. So you were there. So you might have dropped cyanide in one of the glasses? No. Even granting that you are capable of poisoning somebody's champagne, you would certainly make sure that the right one got it. You wouldn't just drop it in one of the glasses on the bar and walk away, and that applies to all the others, except Edwin Laidlaw, Helen Yarmis, and Mr. and Mrs. Robilotti. They hadn't walked away. They were there at the bar when Grantham came and got the two glasses. But he took *two* glasses. If one of those four people saw him coming and dropped the cyanide in one of the glasses, you've got to assume that he or she didn't give a damn whether Grantham got it or Faith Usher got it, which is too much for me. But not for you?" He clamped his teeth on the cigar. He never lit one.

"As you tell it," I conceded, "I wouldn't buy it. But I have two comments. The first one is that there is one person who did know which glass Faith Usher would get. He handed it to her."

"Oh? You put it on Grantham?"

"I don't put it on anybody. I merely say that you omitted a detail."

"Not an important one. If Grantham dropped the poison in at the bar before he picked up the glasses, there were five people right there, and that *did* take nerve. If he dropped it in while he was crossing to Faith Usher it was quite a trick, with a glass in each hand. If he dropped it in after he handed her the glass you would have seen him. What's your second comment?"

"That I have not implied, in my sessions with you and the others, that I have the slightest notion who did it, or why. What you have just told me was mostly news to me. My attention was divided between my companion, Ethel Varr, and the bag, and Faith Usher. I didn't know who was at the bar when Grantham came and got the champagne, or who had been there since Hackett poured the glasses that Grantham took. And I still have no notion who did it, or why or how. I only know that Faith Usher put nothing whatever in the champagne before she drank it, and therefore if it was poison in the champagne that killed her she did not commit suicide. That's the one thing I know."

"And you won't discuss it."

"I won't? What are we doing?"

"I mean you won't discuss the possibility that you're wrong."

"That, no. You wouldn't expect me to discuss the possibility that I'm wrong in thinking you're Inspector Cramer, you're Willie Mays."

He regarded me a long moment with narrowed eyes, then moved to his normal position in the red leather chair, confronting Wolfe. "I'm going to tell you," he said, "exactly what I think."

Wolfe grunted. "You often have."

"I know I have, but I hoped it wouldn't come to this. I hoped Goodwin had realized that it wouldn't do. I think I know what happened. Rose Tuttle told him that Faith Usher had a bottle of cyanide in her bag, and that she was afraid she might use it right there, and Goodwin told her to forget it, that he would see that nothing happened, and from then on he kept surveillance on both Faith Usher and the bag. That is admitted."

"It is stated."

"Okay, stated. When he sees her drink champagne and collapse and die, and smells the cyanide, what would his reaction be? You know him and so do I. You know how much he likes himself. He would be hit where it hurts. He would hate it. So, without stopping to consider, he tells them that he thinks she was murdered. When the police come, he knows that what he said will be reported, so he repeats it to them, and then he's committed, and when Sergeant Stebbins and I arrive he repeats it to us. But to us he has to give a reason, so he has one, and a damn good one, and as long as there was a decent possibility that she *was* murdered we gave it full weight. But now— You heard me explain how it is. I was hoping that when he heard me and realized the situation he would see that his best course is to say that maybe he has been a little too positive. That he can't absolutely swear that she didn't put something in the champagne. He has had time to think it over, and he is too intelligent not to see that. That's what I think. I hope you will agree."

"It's not a question of agreement, it's a question of fact." Wolfe turned to me. "Archie?"

"No, sir. Nobody likes me better than I do, but I'm not that far gone."

"You maintain your position?"

"Yes. He contradicts himself. First he says I acted like a double-breasted sap and then he says I'm intelligent. He can't have his suicide and eat me too. I stand pat."

Wolfe lifted his shoulders an eighth of an inch, lowered them, and turned to Cramer. "I'm afraid you're wasting your time, Mr. Cramer. And mine."

I was yawning.

Cramer's red face was getting redder, a sure sign that he had reached the limit of something and was about to cut loose, but a miracle happened: he put on the brake in time. It's a pleasure to see self-control win a tussle. He moved his eyes to me.

"I'm not taking this as final, Goodwin. Think it over. Of course, we're going on with the investigation. If we find anything at all that points to homicide we'll follow it up. You know that. But it's only fair to warn you. If our final definite opinion is that it was suicide, and we say so, and you give your friend Lon Cohen of the *Gazette* a statement for publication saying that you know it was murder, you'll regret it. That, or anything like it. Why in hell it had to be that *you* were there, God only knows. Such a statement from you, as an eye-witness—"

The doorbell rang. I arose, asked Cramer politely to excuse me, stepped to the hall, and through the one-way glass saw a recent social acquaintance, though it took me a second to recognize him because his forty-dollar fedora covered the uncombed hair. I went and opened the door, confronted him, said, "Ssshhh," patted my lips with a forefinger, backed up, and beckoned him in. He hesitated, looking slightly startled, then crossed the threshold. I shut the door and, without stopping to relieve him of his hat and coat, opened the door to the front room, which is on the same side of the hall as the office, motioned him in, followed him, and shut the door.

"It's all right here," I told him. "Soundproofed, doors and all."

"All right for what?" Edwin Laidlaw asked.

"For privacy. Unless you came to see Inspector Cramer of Homicide?"

"I don't know what you're talking about. I came to see you."

"I thought you might have, and I also thought you might prefer not to collide with Cramer. He's in the office chatting with Mr. Wolfe, and is about ready to go, so I shunted you in here."

"I'm glad you did. I've seen all I want of policemen for a while." He glanced around. "Can we talk here?"

"Yes, but I must go and see Cramer off. I'll be back soon. Have a chair."

I went to the door to the hall and opened it, and there was Cramer heading for the front. He didn't even look at me, let alone speak. I thought if he could be rude I could too, so I let him get his own hat and coat and let himself out. When the door had closed behind him I went to the office and crossed to Wolfe's desk. He spoke.

"I will make one remark, Archie. To bedevil Mr. Cramer for a purpose is one thing; to do so merely for pastime is another."

"Yes, sir. I wouldn't dream of it. You're asking me if my position with you, privately, is the same as it was with him. The answer is yes."

"Very well. Then he's in a pickle."

"That's too bad. Someone else is too, apparently. Yesterday when I was invited to the party and given the names of the male guests, I wanted to know who they were and phoned Lon Cohen. One of them, Edwin Laidlaw, is a fairly important citizen for a man his age. He used to be pretty loose around town, but three years ago his father died and he inherited ten million dollars, and recently he bought a controlling interest in the Malvin Press, book publishers, and apparently he intends to settle down and—"

"Is this of interest?"

"It may be. He's in the front room. He came to see me, and since my only contact with him was last night it *could* be of interest. I can talk with him there, but I thought I should tell you because you might possibly want to sit in—or stand in. At the hole. In case I need a witness."

"Pfui."

"Yeah, I know. I don't want to shove, but we haven't had a case for two weeks."

He was scowling at me. It wasn't so much that he would have to leave his chair and walk to the hall and on to the alcove, and stand at the hole—after all, that amount of exercise would be good for his appetite—as it was that the very best that could come of it, getting a client, would also be the worst, since he would have to work. He heaved a sigh, not letting it interfere with the scowl, muttered, "Confound it," put his palms on the desk rim to push his chair back, and got up and went.

The hole was in the wall, at eye level, eight feet to the right of Wolfe's desk. On the office side it was covered by a picture of a pretty waterfall. On the other side, in a wing of the hall across from the kitchen, it was covered by nothing, and you could not only see through but also hear through. I had once stood there for four solid hours, waiting for someone to appear from the front room to snitch something from my desk. I allowed Wolfe a minute to get himself posted and then went and opened the door to the front room and spoke.

"In here, Laidlaw. It's more comfortable." I moved one of the yellow chairs around to face my desk.

Chapter 5

Laidlaw sat and looked at me. Three seconds. Six seconds. Evidently he needed priming, so I obliged.

"I thought it was a nice party up to a point, didn't you? Even with the protocol."

"I can't remember that far back." He leaned forward. His hair was still perfectly uncombed. "Look, Goodwin. I want to ask you a straight question, and I hope you'll answer it. I don't see why you shouldn't."

"I may not either. What?"

"About what you said last night, that you thought that girl was murdered. You said it not only to us, but to the police and the District Attorney. I can tell you confidentially that I have a friend, it doesn't matter who or where, who has given me a little information. I understand that they would be about ready to call it suicide and close the investigation if it weren't for you, so your reason for thinking it was murder must be a pretty good one. That's my question. What is it?"

"Your friend didn't tell you that?"

"No. Either he wouldn't, or he couldn't because he doesn't know. He says he doesn't know."

I crossed my legs. "Well, I can't very well say that. So I'll say that I have told only the police and the D.A.'s office and Mr. Wolfe, and for the present that's enough."

"You won't tell me?"

"At the moment, no. Rules of etiquette."

"Don't you think the people who are involved just because they were there—don't you think they have a right to know?"

"Yes, I do. I think they have a right to demand that the police tell them exactly why they are going ahead with a homicide investigation when everything seems to point to suicide. But they have no right to demand that *I* tell them."

"I see." He considered that. "But the police refuse to tell us."

"Yeah, I know. I've had experiences with them. I've just had one with Inspector Cramer."

He regarded me. Four seconds. "You're in the detective business, Goodwin. People hire you to get information for them, and they pay for it. That's all I want, information, an answer to my question. I'll give you five thousand dollars for it. I have it in my pocket in cash. Of course, I would expect a definitive answer."

"You would deserve one, for five grand." I was finding that meeting his eyes halfway, not letting them come on through me, took a little effort. "Five grand in cash would suit me fine, since the salary Mr. Wolfe pays me is far from extravagant. But I'll have to say no even if you double it. This is how it is. When the police make up their minds about it one way or the other, that I'm right or I'm wrong, no matter which, I'll feel free to tell you or anybody else. But if I go spreading it around before then they will say I am interfering with an official investigation, and they will interfere with me. If I lost my license as a private detective your five grand wouldn't last long."

"Ten would last longer."

"Not much."

"I own a publishing business. I'd give you a job."

"You'd soon fire me. I'm not a very good speller."

His eyes were certainly straight and steady. "Will you tell me this? How good is your reason for thinking it was murder? Is it good enough to keep them on it the whole way, in spite of the influence of a woman in Mrs. Robilotti's position?"

I nodded. "Yes, I'll answer that. It was good enough to bring Inspector Cramer here when he hadn't had much sleep. In my opinion it is good enough to keep them from crossing it off as suicide until they have dug as deep as they can go."

"I see." He rubbed his palms together. Then he rubbed them on the chair arms. He had transferred his gaze to a spot on the rug, which was a relief. It was a full minute before he came back to me. "You say you have told only the police, the District Attorney, and Nero Wolfe. I want to have a talk with Wolfe."

I raised my brows. "I don't know."

"You don't know what?"

"Whether . . ." I let it trail, screwing my lips. "He doesn't like to mix in when I'm involved personally. Also he's pretty busy. But I'll see." I arose. "With him you never can tell." I moved.

As I turned left in the hall Wolfe appeared at the corner of the wing. He stood there until I had passed and pushed the swing door, and then followed me into the kitchen. When the door had swung shut I spoke.

"I must apologize for that crack about salary. I forgot you were listening."

He grunted. "Your memory is excellent and you shouldn't disparage it. What does that man want of me?"

I covered a yawn. "Search me. If I had had some sleep I might risk a guess, but it's all I can do to get enough oxygen for my lungs so my brain's doing without. Maybe he wants to publish your autobiography. Or maybe he wants you to make a monkey of me by proving it was suicide."

"I won't see him. You have supplied a reason: that you are involved personally."

"Yes, sir. I am also involved personally in the income of your detective business. So is Fritz. So is the guy who wrote you that letter from New Guinea, or he'd like to be."

He growled, as a lion might growl when it realizes it must leave its cosy lair to scout around for a meal. I admit that for him a better comparison would be an elephant, but elephants don't growl. Fritz, at the table shucking clams, started humming a tune, very low, probably pleased at the prospect of a client. Wolfe glared at him, reached for a clam, popped it into his mouth, and chewed. When I pushed the door open and held it, he waited until the clam was down before passing through.

He doesn't like to shake hands with strangers, and when we entered the office and I pronounced names he merely gave Laidlaw a nod en route to his desk. Before I went to mine I asked Laidlaw to move to the red leather chair so I wouldn't have him in profile as he faced Wolfe. As I sat, Laidlaw was saying that he supposed Goodwin had told Wolfe who he was, and Wolfe was saying yes, he had.

Laidlaw's straight, steady eyes were now at Wolfe instead of me. "I want," he said, "to engage you professionally. Do you prefer the retainer in cash, or a check?"

Wolfe shook his head. "Neither, until I accept the engagement. What do you want done?"

"I want you to get some information for me. You know what happened at Mrs. Robilotti's house last evening. You know that a girl named Faith Usher was poisoned and died. You know of the circumstances indicating that she committed suicide. Don't you?"

Wolfe said yes.

"Do you know that the authorities have not accepted it as a fact that she killed herself? That they are continuing with the investigation on the assumption that she might have been murdered?"

Wolfe said yes.

"Then it's obvious that they must have knowledge of some circumstance other than the ones I know about—or that any of us know about. They must have some reason for not accepting the fact that it was suicide. I don't know what that reason is, and they won't tell me, and as one of the people involved—involved simply because I was there—I have a legitimate right to know. That's the information I want you to get for me. I'll give you a retainer now, and your bill can be any amount you think is fair, and I'll pay it."

I was not yawning. I must say I admired his gall. Though he didn't know that Wolfe had been at the hole, he must have assumed that I had reported the offer he had made, and here he was looking Wolfe straight in the eye, engaging him professionally, and telling him he could name his figure, no matter what, whereas with me ten grand had been his limit. The gall of the guy! I had to admire him.

The corners of Wolfe's mouth were up. "Indeed," he said. Laidlaw took a breath, but it came out merely as used air, not as words.

"Mr. Goodwin has told me," Wolfe said, "of the proposal you made to him. I am at a loss whether to respect your doggedness and applaud your dexterity or to deplore your naïveté. In any case I must decline the engagement. I already have the information you're after, but I got it from Mr. Goodwin in confidence and may not disclose it. I'm sorry, sir."

Laidlaw took another breath. "I'm not as dogged as you are," he declared. "Both of you. In the name of God, what's so top secret about it? What are you afraid of?"

Wolfe shook his head. "Not afraid, Mr. Laidlaw, merely discreet. When a matter in which we have an interest and a commitment requires us to nettle the police we are not at all reluctant. In this affair Mr. Goodwin is involved solely because he happened to be there, just as you are, and I am not involved at all. It is not a question of fear or of animus. I am merely detached. I will not, for instance, tell the police of the offers you have made Mr. Goodwin and me because it would stimulate their curiosity about you, and since I assume you have made the offers in good faith I am not disposed to do you an ill turn."

"But you're turning me down."

"Yes. Flatly. In the circumstances I have no choice. Mr. Goodwin can speak for himself."

Laidlaw's head turned to me and I had the eyes

again. I wouldn't have put it past him to renew his offer, with an amendment that he would now leave the figure up to me, but if he had that in mind he abandoned it when he saw my steadfast countenance. When, after regarding me for eight seconds, he left his chair, I thought he was leaving the field and Wolfe wouldn't have to go to work after all, but no. He only wanted to mull, and preferred to have his face to himself. He asked, "May I have a minute?" and, when Wolfe said yes, he turned his back and moseyed across the rug toward the far wall, where the big globe stood in front of bookshelves; and, for double the time he had asked for, at least that, he stood revolving the globe. Finally he about-faced and returned to the red leather chair, not moseying.

"I must speak with you privately," he told Wolfe.

"You are," Wolfe said shortly. "If you mean alone, no. If a confidence weren't as safe with Mr. Goodwin as with me he wouldn't be here. His ears are mine, and mine are his."

"This isn't only a confidence. I'm going to tell you something that no one on earth knows about but me. I'm going to risk telling you because I have to, but I'm not going to double the risk."

"You will not be doubling it." Wolfe was patient. "If Mr. Goodwin left us I would give him a signal to listen to us on a contraption in another room, so he might as well stay."

"You don't make it any easier, Wolfe."

"I don't pretend to make things easier. I only make them manageable—when I can."

Laidlaw looked as if he needed to mull some more, but he got it decided without going to consult the globe again. "You'll have all you can do to manage this," he declared. "I couldn't go to my lawyer with it, or anyhow I wouldn't, and even if I had it would have been too much for him. I thought I couldn't go to anybody, and then I thought of you. You have the reputation of a wizard, and God knows I need one. First I wanted to know why Goodwin thinks it was murder, but evidently you're not going—by the way—"

He took a pen from a pocket and a checkbook from another, put the book on the little table at his elbow, and wrote. He yanked the check off, glanced it over, got up to put it on Wolfe's desk, and returned to the chair.

"If twenty thousand isn't enough," he said, "for a retainer and advances for expenses, say so. You haven't accepted the job, I know, but I'm camping here until you do. You spoke of managing things. I want you to manage that if they go on with their investigation it doesn't go deep enough to uncover and make public a certain event in my life. I also want you to manage that I don't get arrested and put on trial for murder."

Wolfe grunted. "I could give no guarantee against either contingency."

"I don't expect you to. I don't expect you to pass miracles, either. And two things I want to make plain: first, if Faith Usher was murdered I didn't kill her and don't know who did; and second, my own conviction is that she committed suicide. I don't know what Goodwin's reason is for thinking she was murdered, but whatever it is, I'm convinced that he's wrong."

Wolfe grunted again. "Then why come to me in a dither? If you're convinced it was suicide. Since they are human the police do frequently fumble, but usually they arrive at the truth. Finally."

"That's the trouble. Finally. This time, before they arrive, they might run across the event I spoke of, and if they do, they might charge me with murder. Not they might, they would."

"Indeed. It must have been an extraordinary event. If that is what you intend to confide in me, I make two remarks: that you are not yet my client, and that even if you were, disclosures to a private detective by a client are not a privileged communication. It's an impasse, Mr. Laidlaw. I can't decide whether to accept your job until I know what the event was; but I will add that if I do accept it I will go far to protect the interest of a client."

"I'm desperate, Wolfe," Laidlaw said. He pushed his hair back, but it needed more than a push. "I admit it. I'm desperate. You'll accept the job because there's no reason why you shouldn't. What I'm going to tell you is known to no one on earth but me, I'm pretty sure of that, but not absolutely sure, and that's the devil of it."

He pushed at his hair again. "I'm not proud of this, what I'm telling you. I'm thirty-one years old. In August, nineteen fifty-six, a year and a half ago, I went into Cordoni's on Madison Avenue to buy some flowers, and the girl who waited on me was attractive, and that evening I drove her to a place in the country for dinner. Her name was Faith Usher. Her vacation was to start in ten days, and by the time it started I had persuaded her to spend it in Canada with me. I didn't use my own name; I'm almost certain she never knew what it was. She only had a week, and when we got back she went back to work at Cordoni's, and I went to Europe and was gone two months. When I returned I had no idea of resuming any relations with her, but I had no reason to avoid her, and I stopped in at Cordoni's one day. She was there, but she would barely speak to me. She asked me, if I came to Cordoni's again, to get someone else to wait on me."

"I suggest," Wolfe put in, "that you confine this to the essentials."

"I am. I want you to know just how it was. I don't like to feel that I owe anyone anything, especially a woman, and I phoned her twice to get her to meet me and have a talk, but she wouldn't. So I dropped it. I also stopped buying flowers at Cordoni's, but some months later, one rainy day in April, I went there because it was convenient, and she wasn't there. I didn't ask about her. I include these details because you ought to know what the chances are that the police are going to dig this up."

"First the essentials," Wolfe muttered.

"All right, but you ought to know how I found out that she was at Grantham House. Grantham House is an institution started by—"

"I know what it is."

"Then I don't have to explain it. A few days after I had noticed that she wasn't at Cordoni's a friend of mine told me—his name is Austin Byne, and he is Mrs. Robilotti's nephew—he told me that he had been at Grantham House the day before on an errand for Mrs. Robilotti and had seen a girl there that he recognized. He said I might recognize her too—the girl with the little oval face and green eyes who used to work at Cordoni's. I told him I doubted it, that I didn't remember her. But I—"

"Was Mr. Byne's tone or manner suggestive?"

"No. I didn't think—I'm sure it wasn't. But I wondered. Naturally. It had been eight months since the trip to Canada, and I did not believe that she had been promiscuous. I decided that I must see her and talk with her. I prefer to think that my chief reason was my feeling of obligation, but I don't deny that I also wanted to know if she had found out who I was, and if so whether she had told anyone or was going to. In arranging to see her I took every possible precaution. Shall I tell you exactly how I managed it?"

"Later, perhaps."

"All right, I saw her. She said that she had agreed to meet me only because she wanted to tell me that she never wanted to see me or hear from me again. She said she didn't hate me—I don't think she was capable of hate—but that I meant only one thing to her, a mistake that she would never forgive herself for, and that she only wanted to blot me out. Those were her words: 'blot you out.' She said her baby would be given for adoption and would never know who its parents were. I had money with me, a lot of it, but she wouldn't take a cent. I didn't raise the question whether there could be any doubt that I was the father. You wouldn't either, if it had been you, with her, the way she was."

He stopped and set his jaw. After a moment he released it. "That was when I decided to quit playing around. I made an anonymous contribution to Grantham House. I never saw her again until last night. I didn't kill her. I am convinced she killed herself, and I hope to God my being there, seeing me again, wasn't what made her do it."

He stopped again. Then he went on, "I didn't kill her, but you can see where I'll be if the police go on investigating and dig this up somehow—though I don't know how. They would have me. I was standing

at the bar when Cecil Grantham came and got the
champagne and took it to her. Even if I wasn't convicted of murder, even if I was never put on trial, this
would all come out and that would be nearly as bad.
And evidently, if it weren't for Goodwin, for what he
has told them, they would almost certainly call it suicide and close it. Can you wonder that I want to know
what he told them? At any price?"

"No," Wolfe conceded. "Accepting your account as
candid, no. But you have shifted your ground. You
wanted to hire me to tell you what Mr. Goodwin has
told the police, though you didn't put it that way, and
I declined. What do you want to hire me to do now?"

"To manage this for me. You said you manage
things. To manage that this is not dug up, that my
connection with Faith Usher does not become known,
that I am not suspected of killing her."

"You're already suspected. You were there."

"That's nonsense. You're quibbling. I wouldn't be
suspected if it weren't for Goodwin. Nobody would
be."

I permitted myself an inside grin. "Quibble" was
one of Wolfe's pet words. Dozens of people, sitting in
the red leather chair, had been told by him that they
were quibbling, and now he was getting it back, and
he didn't like it.

He said testily, "But you *are* suspected, and you'd
be a ninny to hire me to prevent something that has
already happened. You have admitted you're desperate, and desperate men can't think straight, so I
should make allowances, and I do. That the police will
not discover your connection with Faith Usher is a
forlorn hope. Surely she knew your real name.

Weren't you known at Cordoni's? Didn't you have a charge account?"

"No. I have charge accounts, of course, but not at any florist's. I always paid cash for flowers—in those days. Now it doesn't matter, but then it was more— uh—it was wiser. I don't think she ever knew my name, and even if she did I'm almost certain she never told anyone about me—about the trip to Canada."

Wolfe was skeptical. "Even so," he grumbled. "You appeared with her in public places. On the street. You took her to dinner. If the police persist it's highly probable that they'll turn it up; at that sort of thing they're extremely proficient. The only way to ward that off with any assurance would be to arrange that they do not persist, and that rests with Mr. Goodwin." His head turned. "Archie. Has anything that Mr. Laidlaw said persuaded you that you might have been mistaken?"

"No," I said. "Now that we can name the figure I admit it's a temptation, but I'm committed. No."

"Committed to *what*?" Laidlaw demanded.

"To my statement that Faith Usher didn't kill herself."

"Why? For God's sake, *why*?"

Wolfe took over. "No, sir. That is still reserved, even if I accept your retainer. If I do, I'll proceed on the hypothesis that your account of your relations with Faith Usher is bona fide, but only as a hypothesis. Over the years I have found many hypotheses untenable. It is quite possible that you did kill Faith Usher and your coming to me is a step in some devious and crafty stratagem. Then—"

"I didn't."

"Very well. That's an item of the hypothesis. Then

the situation is this: since Mr. Goodwin is unyielding, and since if the police persist they will surely bare your secret and then harass you, I can do your job only (a) by proving that Faith Usher committed suicide and Mr. Goodwin is wrong, or (b) by identifying and exposing the murderer. That would be a laborious and expensive undertaking, and I'll ask you to sign a memorandum stating that, no matter who the murderer is, if I expose him you'll pay my bill."

Laidlaw didn't hesitate. "I'll sign it."

"With, as I said, no guarantee."

"As I said, I don't expect any."

"Then that's understood." Wolfe reached to pick up the check. "Archie. You may deposit this as a retainer and advance for expenses."

I got up and took it and dropped it in a drawer of my desk.

"I want to ask a question," Laidlaw said. He was looking at me. "Evidently you didn't tell the police what happened when I asked Faith Usher to dance with me, and she refused. If you had told them they would certainly have asked me about it. Why didn't you?"

I sat down. "That's about the only thing I left out. For a reason. From the beginning they were on my neck about my thinking it was murder, and if I had told them about her refusing to dance with you they would have thought I was also trying to pick the murderer, and they already had certain feelings about me on account of former collisions. And if you denied it when they asked you about it, they might think I was playing hopscotch. I could always remember it and report it later, if developments called for it."

Wolfe was frowning. "You didn't report this to me."

"No, sir. Why should I? You weren't interested."

"I am now. But now, conveniently, her refusal is already explained." He turned to the client. "Did you know Miss Usher would be there before you went?"

"No," Laidlaw said. "If I had I wouldn't have gone."

"Did she know you would be there?"

"I don't know, but I doubt it. I think that goes for her too; if she had she wouldn't have gone."

"Then it was a remarkable coincidence. In a world that operates largely at random, coincidences are to be expected, but any one of them must always be mistrusted. Had you attended any of those affairs previously? Those annual dinners?"

"No. It was on account of Faith Usher that I accepted the invitation. Not to see her—as I said, I wouldn't have gone if I had known she would be there —just some feeling about what had happened. I suppose a psychiatrist would call it a feeling of guilt."

"Who invited you?"

"Mrs. Robilotti."

"Were you a frequent guest at her house?"

"Not frequent, no, just occasional. I have known Cecil, her son, since prep school, but we have never been close. Her nephew, Austin Byne, was in my class at Harvard. What are you doing, investigating me?"

Wolfe didn't reply. He glanced up at the wall clock: ten minutes past one. He took in a couple of bushels of air through his nose, and let it out through his mouth. He looked at the client, not with enthusiasm.

"This will take hours, Mr. Laidlaw. Just to get started with you—what you know about those people—since I must proceed, tentatively, on the hypothesis that Mr. Goodwin is right and Miss Usher was murdered, and you didn't kill her, and therefore one of the others did. Eleven of them, if we include the butler—no, ten, since I shall arbitrarily eliminate Mr. Goodwin. Confound it, an army! It's time for lunch, and I invite you to join us, and then we'll resume. Clams hashed with eggs, parsley, green peppers, chives, fresh mushrooms, and sherry. Mr. Goodwin drinks milk. I drink beer. Would you prefer white wine?"

Laidlaw said yes, he would, and Wolfe got up and headed for the kitchen.

Chapter 6

At a quarter past five that afternoon, when Laidlaw left, I had thirty-two pages of shorthand, my private brand, in my book. Of course, Wolfe had gone up to the plant rooms at four o'clock so for the last hour and a quarter I had been the emcee. When Wolfe came down to the office at six I had typed four pages from my notes and was banging away on the fifth.

Most of it was a waste of time and paper, but there were items that might come in handy. To begin with, there was nothing whatever on the three unmarried mothers who were still alive. Laidlaw had never seen or heard of Helen Yarmis or Ethel Varr or Rose Tuttle before the party. Another blank was Hackett. All I had got on him was that he was a good butler, which I already knew, and that he had been there for years, since before Grantham had died.

Mrs. Robilotti. Laidlaw didn't care much for her. He didn't put it that way, but it was obvious. He called her a vulgarian. Her first husband, Albert Grantham, had had genuine philanthropic impulses and knew what to do with them, but she was a phony.

She wasn't actually continuing to support his philan-
thropies; they had been provided for in his will; she
spent a lot of time on them, attending board meetings
and so on, only to preserve her standing with her betters. "Betters," for Laidlaw, evidently didn't mean
people with more money, which I thought was a
broad-minded attitude for a man with ten million of
his own.

Robert Robilotti. Laidlaw cared for him even less,
and said so. Mrs. Albert Grantham, widow, had acquired him in Italy and brought him back with her
luggage. That alone showed she was a vulgarian, but
here, it seemed to me, things got confused, because
Robilotti was not a vulgarian. He was polished, civilized, and well informed. In all this I'm merely quoting
Laidlaw. Of course, he was also a parasite. When I
asked if he looked elsewhere for the female refresh-
ments that were in short supply at home, Laidlaw
said there were rumors, but there were always rumors.

Celia Grantham. Here I had got a surprise—nothing startling, but enough to make me lift a brow.
Laidlaw had asked her to marry him six months ago
and she had refused. "I tell you that," he said, "so you
will know that I can't be very objective about her.
Perhaps I was lucky. That was when I was getting a
hold on myself after what had happened with Faith
Usher, and perhaps I was just looking for help. Celia
could help a man all right if she wanted to. She has
character, but she hasn't decided what to do with it.
The reason she gave for refusing to marry me was
that I didn't dance well enough." It was while we
were on Celia that I learned that Laidlaw had an old-
fashioned streak. When I asked him what about her

relations with men and got a vague answer, and made
it more specific by asking if he thought she was a
virgin, he said of course, since he had asked her to
marry him. An old fogy at thirty-one.

Cecil Grantham. On him it struck me that Laidlaw
was being diplomatic, and I thought I guessed why.
Cecil was three years younger than Laidlaw, and I
gathered that his interests and activities were along
the same lines as Laidlaw's had been three years ago
before the event with Faith Usher had pushed his
nose in—with qualifications, one being that whereas
Laidlaw's pile had been left to him with no strings
attached, Cecil's was in a trust controlled by his
mother and he had to watch his budget. He had been
heard to remark that he would like to do something to
earn some money but couldn't find any spare time for
it. Each year he spent three summer months on a
ranch in Montana.

Paul Schuster. He was a prodigy. He had worked
his way through college and law school, and when he
had graduated with high honors a clerkship had been
offered him by a justice of the United States Supreme
Court, but he had preferred to go to work for a Wall
Street firm with five names at the top, and a dozen at
the side, of its letterhead. Probably a hundred and
twenty bucks a week. Even more probably, at fifty he
would be raking in half a million a year. Laidlaw knew
him only fairly well and could furnish no information
about the nature and extent of his intimacies with
either sex. The owner of one of the five names at the
top of the letterhead, now venerable, had been Albert
Grantham's lawyer, and that was probably the connection that had got Schuster at Mrs. Robilotti's dinner table.

Beverly Kent. Of the Rhode Island Kents, if that means anything to you. It didn't to me. His family was still hanging on to three thousand acres and a couple of miles of a river named Usquepaugh. He too had been in Laidlaw's class at Harvard, and had followed a family tradition when he chose the diplomatic service for a career. In Laidlaw's opinion it wasn't likely that he had ever been guilty of an indiscretion, let alone an outrage, with a female.

Edwin Laidlaw. A reformed man, a repentant sinner, and a recovered soul. He said he had more appropriate clichés handy, but I told him those would do. When he had inherited his father's stack, three years ago, he had gone on as before, horsing around, and had caught up with himself only after the Faith Usher affair. He had not, to the best of his knowledge, ever made any other woman a mother, married or unmarried. It had taken more than half of his assets to buy the Malvin Press, and for four months he had been spending ten hours a day at his office, five days a week, not to mention evenings and weekends. He thought he would be on to the publishing business in five years.

As for Faith Usher, his thinking that she had not been promiscuous, and his not raising the question, at his last meeting with her, whether there was any doubt about his being the father of the baby she was carrying, had been based entirely on the impression he had got of her. He knew nothing whatever about her family or background. He hadn't even known where she lived; she had refused to tell him. She had given him a phone number and he had called her at it, but he didn't remember what it was, and he had made a little private ceremony of destroying his phone-

number book when he had reformed. When I said that
on a week's vacation trip there is time for a lot of talk,
he said they had done plenty of talking, but she had
shied away from anything about her. His guess was
that she had probably graduated from high school.

We had spent a solid hour with him on the party
before Wolfe went up to the plant rooms. Wolfe took
him through every minute of it, trying to get some
faint glimmer of a hint. Laidlaw was sure that neither
he nor Faith Usher had said or done anything that
could have made anyone suspect they had ever met
before, except her refusing to dance with him, and no
one had heard that but me. He had asked her to dance
because he thought it would be noticed if he didn't.

Of course the main point was when Cecil Grantham came to the bar to get the champagne. Laidlaw
had been standing there with Helen Yarmis, with
whom he had just been dancing, and Mr. and Mrs.
Robilotti. As he and Helen Yarmis approached the
bar, Beverly Kent and Celia Grantham were moving
away, and Mr. and Mrs. Robilotti were there, and of
course Hackett. Laidlaw thought he and Helen
Yarmis had been there more than a minute, but not
more than two, when Cecil Grantham came; that was
what he had told the police. He couldn't say whether,
when he had taken two glasses of champagne for
Helen Yarmis and himself, there had been other
glasses on the bar with champagne in them; he simply
hadn't noticed. The police had got him to try to recall
the picture, but he couldn't. All he was sure of was
that he hadn't poisoned any champagne, but he was
almost as sure that Helen Yarmis hadn't either. She
had been right at his elbow.

There was more, a lot more, but that's enough for

here. You can see why I said that most of it was a
waste of time and paper. I might mention that Wolfe
had dictated the memorandum, and I had typed it,
and Laidlaw had signed it. Also, as instructed by
Wolfe, as soon as Laidlaw had gone I phoned Saul
Panzer, Fred Durkin, and Orrie Cather, and asked
them to drop in at nine o'clock.

At six, on the dot as always, Wolfe entered and
crossed to his desk. I collated the originals of the four
finished pages, took them to him, and went back to
the typewriter. I was rolling out the fifth page when
he spoke.

"Archie."

I twisted my neck. "Yes, sir?"

"Your attention, please."

I swiveled. "Yes, sir."

"You will agree that this is a devil of a problem,
with monstrous difficulties in a disagreeable context."

"Yes, sir."

"I have asked you three times regarding your con-
tention that Miss Usher did not commit suicide. The
first time it was merely civil curiosity. The second
time, in the presence of Mr. Cramer, it was merely
rhetorical, to give you an opportunity to voice your
resolution. The third time, in the presence of Mr.
Laidlaw, it was merely by the way, since I knew you
wouldn't pull back with him here. Now I ask you
again. You know how it stands. If I undertake this job,
on the assumption that she was murdered, an assumption based solely on your testimony, you know what it
will entail in time, energy, wit, and vexation. The expense will be on Mr. Laidlaw, but the rest will be on
me. I don't care to risk, in addition, the chance that I
am burrowing in an empty hole. So I ask you again."

I nodded. "I knew this would come. Naturally. I stand pat. I can make a speech if you want one."

"No. You have already explained your ground. I will only remind you that the circumstances as described by Mr. Cramer indicate that it would have been impossible for anyone to poison that glass of champagne with any assurance that it would get to Miss Usher."

"I heard him."

"Yes. There is the same objection to supposing that it was intended for any other particular person, and its getting to Miss Usher was a mishap."

"Right."

"There is also the fact that she was the most likely target, since the poison was in her bag, making it highly probable that the conclusion would be that she had killed herself. But for you, that would be the conclusion. Therefore it was almost certainly intended for her."

"Right."

"But, for the reasons given by Mr. Cramer, it couldn't possibly have been intended for her."

I grinned at him. "What the hell," I said. "I know it's a lulu. I admit I wouldn't know where to start, but I'm not supposed to. That's your part. Speaking of starting, Saul and Fred and Orrie will be here at nine o'clock."

He made a face. He had to cook up chores for them, nine o'clock was less than three hours away, for one of the hours he would be dining, and he would not work his brain at the table.

"I have," he growled, "only this moment committed myself, after consulting you. Mr. Laidlaw's check could have been returned." He flattened his palms on the chair arms. "Then I'm in for it, and so are you. You will go tomorrow morning to that institution, Grantham House, and learn about Faith Usher. How she got there, when she came and when she left, what happened to her infant—everything. Cover it."

"I will if I can get in. I mention as a fact, not an objection, that that place has certainly had a lot of visitors today. At least a dozen assorted journalists, not to mention cops. Have you any suggestions?"

"Yes. You told me yesterday morning that a man you know named Austin Byne had phoned to ask you to take his place at that gathering. Today Mr. Laidlaw said that a man named Austin Byne, Mrs. Robilotti's nephew, had once gone to Grantham House on an errand for his aunt. I suppose the same man?"

"You suppose." I crossed my legs. "It wouldn't hurt you any, and would be good for my morale, if you let me take a trick now and then. Austin Byne had already occurred to me, and I asked for suggestions only to be polite. I already know what your powers of observation and memory are and you didn't have to demonstrate them by remembering that I had mentioned his name on the fly and— Why the snort?"

"At the notion that your morale needs any encouragement. Do you know where to reach Mr. Byne?"

I said I did and, before resuming at the typewriter, dialed his number. No answer. During the next hour and a half I interrupted my typing four times to dial the number, and still no answer. By then it was dinnertime. For himself, Wolfe will permit nothing and no one to interfere with the course of a meal, and, since we dine together in the dining room, my leaving the table is a sort of interference and he doesn't like it, but that time I had to. Three times during dinner I went to the office to dial Byne's number, with no luck, and I tried again when, having finished the baked pears, we transferred to the office and Fritz brought coffee. I accept a "no answer" verdict only after counting thirteen rings, and had got nine when the doorbell rang and Fritz announced Saul Panzer. The other two came a minute later.

That trio, the three that Wolfe always called on when we needed more eyes and ears and legs, were as good as you could get in the metropolitan area. In fact, Saul Panzer, a little guy with a big nose who never wore a hat, compromising on a cap when the weather was rough, was better. With an office and a staff he could have cleaned up, but that wouldn't have left him enough time for playing the piano or playing pinochle or keeping up with his reading, so he preferred to freelance at seventy bucks a day. Fred Durkin, bulky and bald-headed, had his weak points, but he was worth at least half as much as Saul, which was his price, if you gave him the right kind of errands. If Orrie Cather had been as smart as he was brave and handsome he would have been hiring people instead of being hired, and Wolfe would have had to find someone else, which wouldn't have been easy because good operatives are scarce.

They were on yellow chairs in a row facing Wolfe's desk. We hadn't seen any of them for two months, and civilities had been exchanged, including handshakes. They are three of the nine or ten people to whom Wolfe willingly offers a hand. Saul and Orrie had accepted offers of coffee; Fred had preferred beer.

Wolfe sipped coffee, put his cup down, and surveyed them. "I have undertaken," he said, "to find an explanation for something that can't possibly be explained."

Fred Durkin frowned, concentrating. He had decided long ago that there was a clue in every word Wolfe uttered, and he wasn't going to miss one if he could help it. Orrie Cather smiled to show that he recognized a gag when he heard it, and finally appreciated it. Saul Panzer said, "Then the job is to invent one."

Wolfe nodded. "It may come to that, Saul. Either that or abandon it. Usually, as you know, I merely give you specific assignments, but in this case you will have to be told the situation and the background. We are dealing with the death of a woman named Faith Usher who drank poisoned champagne at the home of Mrs. Robert Robilotti. I suppose you have heard of it."

They all had.

Wolfe drank coffee. "But you should know all that I know, except the identity of my client. Yesterday morning Archie got a phone call from a man he knows, by name Austin Byne, the nephew of Mrs. Robilotti. He asked Archie . . ."

Seeing that I could be spared for a while, and thinking it was time for another try at Byne, I got up, circled around the trio, went to the kitchen, and dialed the number on the extension there. After five rings I was thinking I was going to draw a blank again, but then I had a voice saying hallo.

"Byne?" I asked. "Dinky Byne?"

"Who is this?"

"Archie Goodwin."

"Oh, hallo there. I've been thinking you might call.

To give me hell for getting you into a mess. I don't blame you. Go on and say it."

"I could all right, but I've got another idea. You said you'd return the favor someday, and tomorrow is the day. I want to run up to Grantham House and have a talk with someone there, preferably the woman in charge, and they're probably having too many visitors and won't let me in. So I thought you might say a word for me—on the phone, or write a letter I can take, or maybe even go along. How about it?"

Silence. Then: "What makes you think a word from me would help?"

"You're Mrs. Robilotti's nephew. And I heard somebody say, I forget who, that she has sent you there on errands."

Another silence. "What are you after? What do you want to talk about?"

"I'm just curious about something. Some questions the cops have asked me because I was there last night, the mess you got me into, have made me curious."

"What questions?"

"That's a long story. Also complicated. Just say I'm nosy by nature, that's why I'm in the detective business. Maybe I'm trying to scare up a client. Anyway, I'm not asking you to attend a death by poisoning, as you did me, though you didn't know it. I just want you to make a phone call."

"I can't, Archie."

"No? Why not?"

"Because I'm not in a position to. It wouldn't be— It might look as if— I mean I just can't do it."

"Okay, forget it. I'll have to feed some other curiosity—I've got plenty. For instance, my curiosity about why you asked me to fill in for you because you had such a cold you could hardly talk when you didn't have a cold—at least not the kind you tried to fake. I haven't told the cops about that, your faking the cold, so I guess I'd better do that and ask them to ask you why. I'm curious."

"You're crazy. I did have a cold. I wasn't faking."

"Nuts. Take care of yourself. I'll be seeing you, or the cops will."

Silence, a short one. "Don't hang up, Archie."

"Why not? Make an offer."

"I want to talk this over. I want to see you, but I don't want to leave here because I'm expecting a phone call. Maybe you could come here?"

"Where is here?"

"My apartment. Eighty-seven Bowdoin Street, in the Village. It's two blocks south—"

"I know where it is. I'll be there in twenty minutes. Take some aspirin."

When I had hung up, Fritz, who was at the sink, turned to say, "As I thought, Archie. I knew there would be a client, since you were there."

I told him I'd have to think that over to decide how to take it, and went to the office to tell the conference it would have to manage without me for a while.

Chapter 7

There's no telling what 87 Bowdoin Street had been like a few years back—or rather, there is, if you know the neighborhood—but someone had spent some dough on it, and it wasn't at all bad when you got inside. The tile floor was a nice dark green, the walls were a lighter green but the same tone, and the frame of the entrance for the do-it-yourself elevator was outlined with a plain wide strip of dull aluminum. Having been instructed over the intercom in the vestibule, I entered the elevator and pushed the button marked 5.

When I emerged on the fifth floor Byne was there to greet me and ushered me in. After taking my hat and coat he motioned me through a doorway, and I found myself in a room that I would have been perfectly willing to move to when the day came that Wolfe fired me or I quit, with perhaps a few minor changes. The rugs and chairs were the kind I like, and the lights were okay, and there was no fireplace. I hate fireplaces. When Byne had got me in a chair and asked if I would like a drink, and I had declined with thanks, he stood facing me. He was tall and lanky and loose-jointed, with not much covering for his face bones except skin.

"That was a hell of a mess I got you into," he said. "I'm damn sorry."

"Don't mention it," I told him. "I admit I wondered a little why you picked me. If you want some free advice, free but good, next time you want to cook up a reason for skipping something, don't overdo it. If you make it a cold, not that kind of a cold, just a plain everyday virus."

He turned a chair around and sat. "Apparently you've convinced yourself that was a fake."

"Sure I have, but my convincing myself doesn't prove anything. The proof would have to be got, and of course it could be if it mattered enough—items like people you saw or talked to Monday evening, or phoned to yesterday or they phoned you, and whoever keeps this place so nice and clean, if she was here yesterday—things like that. That would be for the cops. If I needed any proof personally, I got it when as soon as I mentioned that the cold was a fake you had to see me right away. So why don't we just file that?"

"You said you haven't told the cops."

"Right. It was merely a conclusion I had formed."

"Have you told anyone else? My aunt?"

"No. Certainly not her. I was doing you a favor, wasn't I?"

"Yes, and I appreciate it. You know that, Archie, I appreciate it."

"Good. We all like to be appreciated. I would appreciate knowing what it is you want to talk over."

"Well." He clasped his hands behind his head, showing how casual it was, just a pair of pals chatting free and easy. "To tell the truth, I'm in a mess too. Or I will be if you'd like to see me squirm. Would you like to see me squirm?"

"I might if you're a good squirmer. How do I go about it?"

"All you have to do is spill it about my faking a cold. No matter who you spill it to it will get to my aunt, and there I am." He unclasped his hands and leaned forward. "Here's how it was. I've gone to those damn annual dinners on my uncle's birthday the last three years and I was fed up, and when my aunt asked me again I tried to beg off, but she insisted, and there are reasons why I couldn't refuse. But Monday night I played poker all night, and yesterday morning I was fuzzy and couldn't face it. The question was who to tap. For that affair it can't be just anybody. The first two candidates I picked were out of town, and the next three all had dates. Then I thought of you. I knew you could handle yourself in any situation, and you had met my aunt. So I called you, and you were big-hearted enough to say yes."

He sat back. "That's how it was. Then this morning comes the news of what happened. I said I was sorry I got you into it, and I am, I'm damned sorry, but frankly, I'm damned glad I wasn't there. It certainly wasn't a pleasant experience, and I'm just selfish enough to be glad I missed it. You'll understand that."

"Sure. Congratulations. I didn't enjoy it much myself."

"I'll bet you didn't. So that's what I wanted, to explain how it was, so you'd see it wouldn't help matters any for anyone to know about my faking a cold. It certainly wouldn't help me, because it would get to my aunt sooner or later, and you know how she'd be about a thing like that. She'd be sore as hell."

I nodded. "I don't doubt it. Then it's an ideal situation. You want something from me, and I want something from you. Perfect. We'll swap. I don't broadcast about the phony cold, and you get me an audience at Grantham House. What's that woman's name? Irving?"

"Irwin. Blanche Irwin." He scratched the side of his neck with a forefinger. "You want to swap, huh?"

"I do. What could be fairer?"

"It's fair enough," he conceded. "But I told you on the phone I'm not in a position to do that."

"Yeah, but then I was asking a favor. Now I'm making a deal."

His neck itched again. "I might stretch a point. I might, if I knew what you want with her. What's the idea?"

"Greed. Desire for dough. I've been offered five hundred dollars for an eye-witness story on last night, and I want to decorate it with some background. Don't tell Mrs. Irwin that, though. She's probably down on journalists by now. Just tell her I'm your friend and a good loyal citizen and have only been in jail five times."

He laughed. "That'll do it all right. Wait till you see her." He sobered. "So that's it. It's a funny world, Archie. A girl gets herself in a fix she sees only one way out of, to kill herself, and you're there to see her do it just because I had had all I wanted of those affairs, and here you're going to collect five hundred dollars just because you were there. It's a funny world. So I didn't do you such a bad turn after all."

I had to admit that was one way of looking at it.

He said he felt like saluting the funny world with a drink, and wouldn't I join him, and I said I'd be glad to. When he had gone and brought the requirements, a scotch and water for me and bourbon on the rocks for him, and we had performed the salute, he got at the phone and made a person-to-person call to Mrs. Irwin at Grantham House. Apparently there was nothing at all wrong with his position; he merely told her he would appreciate it if she would see a friend of his, and that was all there was to it. She said morning would be better than afternoon. After he hung up we discussed the funny world while finishing the drinks, and when I left one more step had been taken toward the brotherhood of man.

Back home, the conference was over, the trio had gone, and Wolfe was at his desk with his current book, one he had said I must read, *World Peace Through World Law*, by Grenville Clark and Louis B. Sohn. He finished a paragraph, lowered it, and told me to enter expense advances to Saul and Fred and Orrie, two hundred dollars each. I went to the safe for the book and made the entries, returned the book, locked the safe, and asked him if I needed to know anything about their assignments. He said that could wait, meaning that he wanted to get on with his reading, and asked about mine. I told him it was all set, that he wouldn't see me in the morning because I would be leaving for Grantham House before nine.

"I now call Austin Byne 'Dinky,'" I told him. "I suppose because he's an inch over six feet, but I didn't ask. I should report that he balked and I had to apply a little pressure. When he phoned yesterday he tried to sound as if his tubes were clogged, but he boggled it. He had no cold. He now says that he had been to

three of those affairs and had had enough, and he rang
me only after he had tried five others and they
weren't available. So we made a deal. He gets me in at
Grantham House, and I won't tell his aunt on him. He
seems to feel that his aunt might bite."

Wolfe grunted. "Nothing is as pitiable as a man
afraid of a woman. Is he guileless?"

"I would reserve it. He is not a dope. He might be
capable of knowing that someone was going to kill
Faith Usher so that it would pass for suicide, and he
wanted somebody there alert and brainy and obser-
vant to spot it, so he got me, and he is now counting
on me, with your help, to nail him. Or her. Or he may
be on the level and merely pitiable."

"You and he have not been familiar?"

"No, sir. Just acquaintances. I have only seen him
at parties."

"Then his selecting you is suggestive *per se.*"

"Certainly. That's why I took the trouble to go to
see him. To observe. There were other ways of getting to Mrs. Irwin of Grantham House."

"But you have formed no conclusion."

"No, sir. Question mark."

"Very well. Pfui. Afraid of a woman." He lifted his
book, and I went to the kitchen for a glass of milk.

At eight-twenty the next morning, Thursday, I
was steering the 1957 Heron sedan up the Forty-sixth
Street ramp to the West Side Highway. Buying the
sedan, the year before, had started an argument that
wasn't finished yet. Wolfe pays for the cars, but I do
the driving, and I wanted one I could U-turn when
the occasion arose, and that clashed with Wolfe's notion that anyone in a moving vehicle was in constant
deadly peril, and that the peril was in inverse ratio to

the size of the vehicle. In a forty-ton truck he might actually have been able to relax. So we got the Heron, and I must say that I had nothing against it but its size.

I soon had proof of what I had been hearing and reading, that the forty-eight-hour rain in New York had been snow a little to the north. At Hawthorne Circle it was already there at the roadside, and the farther I rolled on the Taconic State Parkway the more there was of it. The sun was on it now, glancing off the slopes of the drifts and banks, and it was very pleasant, fighting the hardships of an old-fashioned winter by sailing along on the concrete at fifty-eight m.p.h. with ridges of white four and five feet high only a step from the hubcaps. When I finally left the parkway and took a secondary road through the hills, the hardships closed in on me some for a few miles, and when I turned in at an entrance between two stone pillars, with "Grantham House" on one of them, and headed up a curving driveway climbing a hill, only a single narrow lane had been cleared, and as I rounded a sharp curve the hubcaps scraped the ridge.

Coming out of another curve, I braked and stopped. I was blocked, though not by snow. There were nine or ten of them standing there facing me, pink-faced and bright-eyed in the sunshine, in an assortment of jackets and coats, no hats, some with gloves and some without. They would have been taken anywhere for a bunch of high school girls except for one thing: they were all too bulky around the middle. They stood and grinned at me, white teeth flashing.

I cranked the window down and stuck my head out. "Good morning. What do you suggest?"

One in front, with so much brown hair that only the middle of her face showed, called out, "What paper are you from?"

"No paper. I'm sorry if I ought to be. I'm just an errand boy. Can you get by?"

Another one, a blonde, had advanced to the fender. "The trouble is," she said, "that you're right in the center. If you edge over we can squeeze past." She turned and commanded, "Back up and give him room."

They obeyed. When they were far enough away I eased the car forward and to the right until the fender grazed the snowbank, and stopped. They said that was fine and started down the alley single file. As they passed the front fender they turned sidewise, every darned one, which seemed to me to be faulty tactics, since their spread fore and aft was more than from side to side. Also they should have had their backs to the car so their fronts would be against the soft snow, but no, they all faced me. A couple of them made friendly remarks as they went by, and one with a sharp little chin and dancing dark eyes reached in and pulled my nose. I stuck my head out to see that they were all clear, waved good-bye, and pressed gently on the gas.

Grantham House, which had once been somebody's mansion, sprawled over about an acre, surrounded by evergreen trees loaded with snow and other trees still in their winter skeletons. A space had been cleared with enough room to turn around, barely, and I left the car there, followed a path across a terrace to a door, opened it, entered, crossed the vestibule, and was in a hall about the size of Mrs. Robilotti's drawing room. A man who would never see eighty again came hobbling over, squeaking at me, "What's your name?"

I told him. He said Mrs. Irwin was expecting me, and led me into a smaller room where a woman was sitting at a desk. As I entered she spoke, with a snap. "I hope to goodness you didn't run over my girls."

"Absolutely not," I assured her. "I stopped to let them by."

"Thank you." She motioned to a chair. "Sit down. The snow has tried to smother us, but they have to get air and exercise. Are you a newspaperman?"

I told her no and was going to elaborate, but she had the floor. "Mr. Byne said your name is Archie Goodwin and you're a friend of his. According to the newspaper there was an Archie Goodwin at that party at Mrs. Robilotti's. Was that you?"

I was at a disadvantage. With her smooth hair, partly gray, her compact little figure, and her quick brown eyes wide apart, she reminded me of Miss Clark, my high school geometry teacher out in Ohio, and Miss Clark had always had my number. I had waited until I saw her to decide just what line to take. First I had to decide whether to say it was me or it was I.

"Yes," I said, "that was me. It also said in the paper that I work for a private detective named Nero Wolfe."

"I know it did. Are you here as a detective?"

She certainly liked to come to the point. So had Miss Clark. But I hoped I was man enough not to be afraid of a woman. "The best way to answer that," I told her, "is to explain why I came. You know what happened at that party and you know I was there. The idea seems to be that Faith Usher committed suicide. I have got the impression that the police may settle for that. But on account of what I saw, and what I didn't see, I doubt it. My personal opinion is that she was murdered, and if she was, I would hate to see whoever did it get away with it. But before I start howling about it in public I want to do a little checking, and I thought the best place to check on Faith Usher herself was here with you."

"I see." She sat straight and her eyes were straight. "Then you're a knight with a plume?"

"Not at all. I'd feel silly with a plume. My pride is hurt. I'm a professional detective and I try to be a good one, and I believe that someone committed murder right before my eyes, and how do you think I like that?"

"Why do you believe it was murder?"

"As I said, on account of what I saw and what I didn't see. A question of observation. I would prefer to let it go at that, if you don't mind."

She nodded. "The professional with his secrets. I have them too; I have a medical degree. Did Mrs. Robilotti send you here?"

That decision wasn't hard to make. Grantham House wasn't dependent on Mrs. Robilotti, since it had been provided for by Albert Grantham's will, and it was ten to one that I knew what Mrs. Irwin thought of Mrs. Robilotti. So I didn't hesitate.

"Good heavens, no. To have a suicide in her drawing room was bad enough. If she knew I was here looking for support for my belief that it was murder she'd have a fit."

"Mrs. Robilotti doesn't have fits, Mr. Goodwin."

"Well, you know her better than I do. If she ever did have a fit this would call for one. Of course, I may be sticking my neck out. If you prefer suicide to murder as much as she does I've wasted a lot of gas driving up here."

She looked at me, sizing me up. "I don't," she said bluntly.

"Good for you," I said.

She lifted her chin. "I see no reason why I shouldn't tell you what I have told the police. Of course, it's possible that Faith did kill herself, but I doubt it. I get to know my girls pretty well, and she was here nearly five months, and I doubt it. I knew about the bottle of poison she had—she didn't tell me, but one of the other girls did—and that was a problem, whether to get it away from her. I decided not to, because it would have been dangerous. As long as she had it and went on showing it and talking about using it, that was her outlet for her nerves, and if I took it away she would have to get some other outlet, and there was no telling what it might be. One reason I doubt if she killed herself is that she still had that bottle of poison."

I smiled. "The police would love that."

"They didn't, naturally. Another reason is that if she had finally decided to use the poison she wouldn't have done it there at that party, with all those people. She would have done it somewhere alone, in the dark, and she would have left a note for me. She knew how I felt about my girls, and she would have known it would hurt me, and she would have left a note. Still another reason is the fact that she was actually pretty tough. That bottle of poison was merely the enemy that she intended to defeat somehow—it was death, and she was going to conquer it. The spirit she had, down deep, showed sometimes in a flash in her eyes. You should have seen that flash."

"I did, Tuesday evening when I was dancing with her."

"Then she still had it, and she didn't kill herself. But how are you going to prove it?"

"I can't. I can't prove a negative. I would have to prove an affirmative, or at least open one up. If she didn't poison her champagne someone else did. Who? That's the target."

"Oh." Her eyes widened. "Good heavens! That's obvious, certainly, but if you'll believe me, Mr. Goodwin, it hadn't occurred to me. My only thought was that Faith had not killed herself. My mind had stopped there." Her lips tightened. She shook her head. "I can't help it," she said emphatically. "I wish you success, anyhow. I would help you if I could."

"You already have," I assured her, "and maybe you can more. If you don't mind a few questions. Since you've read the paper, you know who was there Tuesday evening. About the three girls—Helen Yarmis, Ethel Varr, and Rose Tuttle—they were all here at the time Faith Usher was, weren't they?"

"Yes. That is, the times overlapped. Helen and Ethel left a month before Faith did. Rose came six weeks before Faith left."

"Had any of them known her before?"

"No. I didn't ask them—I ask the girls as few questions as possible about their past—but there was no indication that they had, and there isn't much going on here that I don't know about."

"Did any trouble develop between any of them and her?"

She smiled. "Now, Mr. Goodwin. I said I would

help you if I could, but this is ridiculous. My girls have their squabbles and their peeves, naturally, but I assure you that nothing that happened here put murder into the heart of Helen or Ethel or Rose. If it had I would have known it, and I would have dealt with it."

"Okay. If it wasn't one of them I'll have to look elsewhere. Take the three male guests—Edwin Laidlaw, Paul Schuster, and Beverly Kent. Do you know any of them?"

"No. I had never heard their names before."

"You know nothing about them?"

"Nothing whatever."

"What about Cecil Grantham?"

"I haven't seen him for several years. His father brought him twice—no, three times—to our summer picnic, when Cecil was in his middle teens. After his father died he was on our Board of Directors for a year, but he resigned."

"You know of no possible connection between him and Faith Usher?"

"No."

"What about Robert Robilotti?"

"I have seen him only once, more than two years ago, when he came to our Thanksgiving dinner with Mrs. Robilotti. He played the piano for the girls and had them singing songs, and when Mrs. Robilotti was ready to leave, the girls didn't want him to go. My feelings were mixed."

"I'll bet they were. Faith Usher wasn't here then?"

"No."

"Well, we're all out of men. Celia Grantham?"

"I knew Celia fairly well at one time. For a year or so after she finished college she came here frequently,

three or four times a month, to teach the girls things
and talk with them; then suddenly she quit. She was a
real help and the girls liked her. She has fine qualities,
or had, but she is headstrong. I haven't seen her for
four years. I am tempted to add something."

"Go ahead."

"I wouldn't if I thought you would misunderstand.
You are looking for a murderer, and Celia would be
quite capable of murder if she thought the occasion
demanded it. The only discipline she recognizes is her
own. But I can't imagine an occasion that would have
led her to kill Faith Usher. I haven't seen her for four
years."

"Then if she had had contact with Faith Usher you
wouldn't know about it. Least but not last, Mrs.
Robilotti."

"Well." She smiled. "She is Mrs. Robilotti."

I smiled back. "I agree. You certainly have known
her. She was Mrs. Albert Grantham. I am tempted to
add something."

"You may."

"I wouldn't if I thought you would misunderstand.
I feel that if you knew anything that would indicate
that Mrs. Robilotti might have killed Faith Usher you
would think it was your duty to tell me about it. So I
can simply ask, do you?"

"That's rather cheeky, Mr. Goodwin. But I simply
answer, I do not. Ever since Mr. Grantham died Mrs.
Robilotti has been coming here about once a month
except when she was traveling, but she has never
been at ease with the girls, nor they with her. Of
course she came while Faith was here, but as far as I
know she never spoke with her except as one of a
group. So my answer to your question is no."

"Who picks the girls to be invited to the annual dinner on Grantham's birthday?"

"When Mr. Grantham was alive, I did. The first few years after he died, Mrs. Grantham did, on information I supplied. The last two years she has left it to Mr. Byne, and he consults me."

"Is that so? Dinky didn't mention that."

" 'Dinky'?"

"Mr. Byne. We call him that. I'll ask him about it. But if you don't mind telling me, how does he do it? Does he suggest names and ask you about them?"

"No, I make a list, chiefly of girls who have been here in the past year, with information and comments, and he chooses from that. I make the list with care. Some of my girls would not be comfortable in those surroundings. On what basis Mr. Byne makes his selections, I don't know."

"I'll ask him." I put a hand on her desk. "And now for the main point, what I was mostly counting on if you felt like helping me. It's very likely that the event or the situation, whatever it was, that led to Faith Usher's death dated from before she came here. It could have happened after she left, but you wouldn't know about that anyway. She was here nearly five months. You said you ask the girls as few questions as possible about their pasts, but they must tell you a lot, don't they?"

"Some of them do."

"Of course. And of course you keep it in confidence. But Faith is dead, and you said you'd help me if you could. She must have told you things. She may even have told you the name of the man who was responsible for her being here. Did she?"

I asked that because I had to. Mrs. Irwin was

much too smart not to realize that that was the first and foremost question a detective would want answered about Faith Usher's past, and if I hadn't asked it she would have wondered why and might even have been bright enough to suspect that I already knew. There wasn't much chance that she had the answer, in view of her tone and manner when she said that she had never heard of Edwin Laidlaw.

"No," she said. "She never said a word about him to me, and I doubt if she did to any of the girls."

"But she did tell you things?"

"Not very much. If you mean facts, people she had known and things she had done, really nothing. But she talked with me a good deal, and I formed two conclusions about her—I mean about her history. No, three. One was that she had had only one sexual relationship with a man, and a brief one. Another was that she had never known her father and probably didn't know who he was. The third was that her mother was still alive and that she hated her—no, hate is too strong a word. Faith was not a girl for hating. Perhaps the word is repugnance. I made those three conclusions, but she never stated any of them explicitly. Beyond that I know nothing about her past."

"Do you know her mother's name?"

"No. As I said, I have no facts."

"How did she get to Grantham House?"

"She came here one day in March, just a year ago. She was in her seventh month. No letter or phone call, she just came. She said she had once read about Grantham House in a magazine and she remembered it. Her baby was born on May eighteenth." She smiled. "I don't have on my tongue the dates of all the births here, but I looked it up for the police."

"Is there any possibility that the baby is involved? I mean in her death? Anything or anyone connected with it or its adoption?"

"Not the slightest. Absolutely none. I handle that. You may take my word for it."

"Did she ever have any visitors here?"

"No. Not one."

"You say she was here five months, so she left in August. Did someone come for her?"

"No. Usually the girls don't stay so long after the baby comes, but Faith had rather a bad time and had to get her strength back. Actually someone did come for her—Mrs. James Robbins, one of our directors, drove her to New York. Mrs. Robbins had got a job for her at Barwick's, the furniture store, and had arranged for her to share a room with another girl, Helen Yarmis. As you know, Helen was there Tuesday evening. Helen might know if anything— Yes, Dora?"

I turned my head. The woman who had opened the door—middle-aged and a little too plump for her blue uniform—stood holding the knob. She spoke. "I'm sorry to interrupt, Doctor, but Katherine may be going to rush things a bit. Four times since nine o'clock, and the last one was only twenty minutes."

Mrs. Irwin was out of her chair and moving. By the time she reached me I was up too, to take the hand she offered.

"It may be only a prelude," she said, "but I'd better go and see. I repeat, Mr. Goodwin, I wish you success, in spite of what success would mean. I don't

envy you your job, but I wish you success. You'll forgive me for rushing off."

I told her I would, and I could have added that I'd
rather have my job than hers, or Katherine's either.
As I got my coat from a chair and put it on I figured
that if she had been there fifteen years and had averaged one a week Katherine's would be the 780th, or
even at two a month it would be the 360th . . . On
my way out to the car I had a worry. If I met the girls
on their way back the maneuver would have to be
repeated with me headed downhill and them up, and I
didn't like the idea of them rubbing their fronts along
the side of the car again, with the door handles. But
luckily, as I started the engine, here they came, strag-
gling from the tunnel of the driveway into the cleared
space. Their faces were even pinker and they were
puffing. One of them sang out, "Oh, are you going?"
and another one called, "Why don't you stay for
lunch?" I told them some other time. I was glad I had
turned the car around on arrival. I had an impulse to
tell them Katherine was tuning up for her big act to
see how they would take it, but decided it wouldn't be
tactful, and when they had cleared the way I fed gas
and rolled. The only one who didn't tell me good-bye
was out of breath.

Chapter 8

When we have company in the office I like to
be there when they arrive, even if the matter being discussed isn't very important or
lucrative, but that time I missed it by five minutes.
When I got there at five past six that afternoon Wolfe
was behind his desk, Orrie Cather was in my chair,
and Helen Yarmis, Ethel Varr, and Rose Tuttle were
there in three of the yellow chairs facing Wolfe. As I
entered, Orrie got up and moved to the couch. He has
not entirely given up the idea that someday my desk
and chair will be his for good, and he liked to practice
sitting there when I am not present.

Not that it had taken me six hours to drive back
from Grantham House. I had got back in time to eat
my share of lunch, kept warm by Fritz, and then had
given Wolfe a verbatim report of my talk with Mrs.
Irwin. He was skeptical of my opinion that her mind
was sound and her heart was pure, since he is convinced that every woman alive has a screw loose
somewhere, but he had to agree that she had talked to
the point, she had furnished a few hints that might be
useful about some of our cast of characters, and she

had fed the possibility that Austin Byne might not be
guileless. Further discourse with Dinky was plainly
indicated. I dialed his number and got no answer, and,
since he might be giving his phone a recess, I took a
walk through the sunshine, first to the bank to deposit
Laidlaw's check and then down to 87 Bowdoin Street.

Pushing Byne's button in the vestibule got no response. I had suggested to Wolfe that I might take
along an assortment of keys so that if Byne wasn't
home I could go on in and pass the time by looking
around, but Wolfe had vetoed it, saying that Byne had
not yet aroused our interest quite to that point. So I
spent a long hour and a quarter in a doorway across
the street. That's one of the most tiresome chores in
the business, waiting for someone to show when you
have no idea how long it will be and you haven't much
more idea whether he has anything that will help.

It was twelve minutes past five when a taxi rolled
to a stop at the curb in front of 87 and Byne climbed
out. When he turned after paying the hackie, I was
there.

"We must share a beam," I told him. "I feel a desire to see you, and come, and here you are."

Something had happened to the brotherhood of
man. His eye was cold. "What the hell—" he began,
and stopped. "Not here," he said. "Come on up."

Even his manners were affected. He entered the
elevator ahead of me, and upstairs, though he let me
precede him into the apartment, I had to deal with my
coat and hat unaided. Inside, in the room that would
require only minor changes, my fanny was barely
touching the chair seat when he demanded, "What's
this crap about murder?"

"That word 'crap' bothers me," I said. "The way

we used it when I was a boy out in Ohio, we knew exactly what it meant. But I looked it up in the dictionary once, and there's no—"

"Nuts." He sat. "My aunt says that you're saying that Faith Usher was murdered, and that on account of you the police won't accept the fact that it was suicide. You know damn well it was suicide. What are you trying to pull?"

"No pull." I clasped my hands behind my head, showing it was just a pair of pals chatting free and easy, or ought to be. "Look, Dinky. You are neither a cop nor a district attorney. I have given them a statement of what I saw and heard at that party Tuesday evening, and if you want to know why that makes them go slow on their verdict you'll have to ask them. If I told them any lies they'll catch up with me and I'll be hooked. I'm not going to start an argument with you about it."

"What did you say in your statement?"

I shook my head. "Get the cops to tell you. I won't. I'll tell you this: if my statement is all that keeps them from calling it suicide, I'm the goat. I'll be responsible for a lot of trouble for that whole bunch, and I don't like it but can't help it. So I'm doing a little checking on my own. That's why I wanted to see Mrs. Irwin at Grantham House. I told you had been offered five hundred bucks for a story on Faith Usher, and I had, but what I was really after was information on whether anyone at that party might have had any reason to kill her. For example, if someone intended to kill her at that party he had to know she would be there. So I wanted to ask Mrs. Irwin how she had been picked to be invited and who had picked her."

I gave him a friendly grin. "And I asked her and

she told me, and that was certainly no help, since it was you, and you weren't at the party. You even faked a cold to get out of going—and by the way, I said I wouldn't broadcast that, and I haven't." I thought it wouldn't hurt to remind him that there was still a basis for brotherhood.

"I know," he said, "you've got that to shake at me. About my picking Faith Usher to be invited, I suppose Mrs. Irwin told you how it was done. I know she told the police. She gave me a list of names with comments, and I merely picked four of the names. I've just been down at the District Attorney's office telling them about it. As I explained to them, I had no personal knowledge of any of those girls. From Mrs. Irwin's comments I just picked the ones that seemed to be the most desirable."

"Did you keep the list? Have you got it?"

"I had it, but an assistant district attorney took it. One named Mandelbaum. No doubt he'll show it to you if you ask him."

I ignored the dig. "Anyway," I said, "even if the comments showed that you stretched a point to pick Faith Usher, that wouldn't cross any *T*s, since you skipped the party. Did anyone happen to be with you when you were making the selections? Someone who said something like, 'there's one with a nice name, Faith Usher, a nice unusual name, why don't you ask her?'"

"No one was with me. I was alone." He pointed. "At that desk."

"Then that's out." I was disappointed. "If you don't mind my asking, a little point occurred to me as I was driving back from Grantham House—that you were interested enough to take the trouble to pick the girls to be invited, but not enough to go to the party. You even went to a lot of trouble to stay away. That seemed a little inconsistent, but I suppose you can explain it."

"To you? Why should I?"

"Well, explain it to yourself and I'll listen."

"There's nothing to explain. I picked the girls because my aunt asked me to. I did it last year too. I told you last night why I skipped the party." He cocked his head, making the skin even tighter on his cheekbone. "What the hell are you driving at, anyhow? Do you know what I think?"

"No, but I'd like to. Tell me."

He hesitated. "I don't mean that, exactly, what I think. I mean what my aunt thinks—or I'll put it this way, an idea she's got in her mind. I guess she hasn't forgotten that remark you made once that she resented. Also she feels that Wolfe overcharged her for that job he did. The idea is that if you have sold the police and the District Attorney on your murder theory, and if they make things unpleasant enough for her and her guests you and Wolfe might figure that she would be willing to make a big contribution to have it stopped. A contribution that would make you remember something that would change their minds. What do you think of that?"

"It *is* an idea," I conceded, "but it has a flaw. If I remembered something now that I didn't put in my statement, no contribution from your aunt would replace my hide that the cops and the D.A. would peel off. Tell your aunt that I appreciate the compliment and her generous offer, but I can't—"

"I didn't say she made an offer. You keep harping on your damn statement. What's in it?"

That was what was biting him, naturally, as it had bit Celia Grantham and Edwin Laidlaw, and probably all of them. For ten minutes he did the harping on it. He didn't go so far as to make a cash offer, either on his own or on behalf of his aunt, but he appealed to everything from my herd instinct to my better nature. I would have let him go on as long as his breath lasted, on the chance that he might drop a word with a spark of light in it, if I hadn't known that company was expected at the office at six o'clock and I wanted to be there when they arrived. When I left he was so frustrated he didn't even go to the hall with me.

I had shaved it pretty close, and that was the worst time of day for uptown traffic, so I didn't quite make it. It was six-five when I climbed out of the taxi and headed for the stoop. If you think I was straining my nerves more than necessary, you don't know Wolfe as I do. I have seen him get up and march out and take to his elevator merely because a woman has burst into tears or started screaming at him, and the expected company, he had told me, was three females, Helen Yarmis, Ethel Varr, and Rose Tuttle, and there was no telling what shape they might be in after the sessions they had been having with various officers of the law.

Therefore I was relieved when I entered the office and found that everything was peaceful, with Wolfe at his desk, the girls in a row facing him, and Orrie in my chair. As I greeted the guests Orrie moved to the couch, and when I was where I belonged Wolfe addressed me.

"We have only exchanged civilities, Archie. Have you anything that should be reported?"

"Nothing that won't wait, no, sir. He is still afraid of a woman."

He went to the company. "As I was saying, ladies, I thank you for coming. You were under no obligation. Mr. Cather, asking you to come, explained that Mr. Goodwin's opinion, expressed in your hearing Tuesday evening, that Faith Usher was murdered, has produced some complications that are of concern to me, and that I wished to consult with you. Mr. Goodwin still believes—"

"I told him," Rose Tuttle blurted, "that Faith might take the poison right there, and he said he would see that nothing happened, but it did." Her blue eyes and round face weren't as cheerful as they had been at the party, in fact they weren't cheerful at all, but her curves were all in place and her pony tail made its jaunty arc.

Wolfe nodded. "He has told me of that. But he thinks that what happened was not what you feared. He still believes that someone else poisoned Miss Usher's champagne. Do you disagree with him, Miss Tuttle?"

"I don't know. I thought she might do it, but I didn't see her. I've answered so many questions about it that now I don't know what I think."

"Miss Varr?"

You may remember my remark that I would have picked Ethel Varr if I had been shopping. Since she was facing Wolfe and I had her in profile, and she was in daylight from the windows, her face wasn't ringing any of the changes in its repertory, but that was a good angle for it, and the way she carried her head would never change. Her lips parted and closed again before she answered.

"I don't think," she said in a voice that wanted to tremble but she wouldn't let it, "that Faith killed herself."

"You don't, Miss Varr? Why?"

"Because I was looking at her. When she took the champagne and drank it. I was standing talking with Mr. Goodwin, only just then we weren't saying anything because Rose had told me that she had told him about Faith having the poison, and he was watching Faith so I was watching her too, and I'm sure she didn't put anything in the champagne because I would have seen her. The police have been trying to get me to say that Mr. Goodwin told me to say that, but I keep telling them that he couldn't because he hasn't said anything to me at all. He hasn't had a chance to." Her head turned, changing her face, of course, as I had it straight on. "Have you, Mr. Goodwin?"

I wanted to go and give her a hug and a kiss, and then go and shoot Cramer and a few assistant district attorneys. Cramer hadn't seen fit to mention that my statement had had corroboration; in fact, he had said that if it wasn't for me suicide would be a reasonable assumption. The damn liar. After I shot him I would sue him for damages.

"Of course not," I told her. "If I may make a personal remark, you told me at the dinner table that you were only nineteen years old and hadn't learned how to take things, but you have certainly learned how to observe things, and how to take your ground and stand on it." I turned to Wolfe. "It wouldn't hurt any to tell her it's satisfactory."

"It is," he acknowledged. "Indeed, Miss Varr, quite satisfactory." That, if she had only known it, was a triumph. He gave me a satisfactory only when I hatched a masterpiece. His eyes moved. "Miss Yarmis?"

Helen Yarmis still had her dignity, but the corners of her wide, curved mouth were apparently down for good, and since that was her best feature she looked pretty hopeless. "All I can do," she said stiffly, "is say what I think. I think Faith killed herself. I told her it was dumb to take that poison along to a party where we were supposed to have a good time, but I saw it there in her bag. Why would she take it along to a party like that if she wasn't going to use it?"

Wolfe's understanding of women has some big gaps, but at least he knows enough not to try using logic on them. He merely ignored her appeal to unreason. "When," he asked, "did you tell her not to take the poison along?"

"When we were dressing to go to the party. We lived in an apartment together. Just a big bedroom with a kitchenette, and the bathroom down the hall, but I guess that's an apartment."

"How long had you and she been living together?"

"Seven months. Since August, when she left Grantham House. I can tell you anything you want to ask, after the way I've been over it the last two days. Mrs. Robbins brought her from Grantham House on a Friday so she could get settled to go to work at Barwick's on Monday. She didn't have many clothes—"

"If you please, Miss Yarmis. We must respect the convenience of Miss Varr and Miss Tuttle. During those seven months did Miss Usher have many callers?"

"She never had any."

"Neither men nor women?"

"No. Except once a month when Mrs. Robbins came to see how we were getting along, that was all."

"How did she spend her evenings?"

"She went to school four nights a week to learn typing and shorthand. She was going to be a secretary. I never saw how she could if she was as tired as I was. Fridays we often went to the movies. Sundays she would go for walks, that's what she said. I was too tired. Anyway, sometimes I had a date, and—"

"If you please. Did Miss Usher have no friends at all? Men or women?"

"I never saw any. She never had a date. I often told her that was no way to live, just crawl along like a worm—"

"Did she get any mail?"

"I don't know, but I don't think so. The mail was downstairs on a table in the hall. I never saw her write any letters."

"Did she get any telephone calls?"

"The phone was downstairs in the hall, but of course I would have known if she got a call when I was there. I don't remember she ever got one. This is kinda funny, Mr. Wolfe. I can answer your questions without even thinking because they're all the same questions the police have been asking, even the same words, so I don't have to stop to think."

I could have given her a hug and a kiss, too, though not in the same spirit as with Ethel Varr. Anyone who takes Wolfe down a peg renders a service to the balance of nature, and to tell him to his face that he was merely a carbon copy of the cops was enough to spoil his appetite for dinner.

He grunted. "Every investigator follows a routine up to a point, Miss Yarmis. Beyond that point comes the opportunity for talent if any is at hand. I find it a little difficult to accept your portfolio of negatives." Another grunt. "It may not be outside my capacity to contrive a question that will not parrot the police. I'll try. Do you mean to tell me that during the seven months you lived with Miss Usher you had no inkling of her having any social or personal contact—excluding her job and night school and the visits of Mrs. Robbins—with any of her fellow beings?"

Helen was frowning. The frown deepened. "Say it again," she commanded.

He did so, slower.

"They didn't ask that," she declared. "What's an inkling?"

"An intimation. A hint."

She still frowned. She shook her head. "I don't remember any hints."

"Did she never tell you that she had met a man that day that she used to know? Or a woman? Or that someone, perhaps a customer at Barwick's, had annoyed her? Or that she had been accosted on the street? Did she never account for a headache or a fit of ill humor by telling of an encounter she had had? An encounter is a meeting face to face. Did she never mention a single name in connection with some experience, either pleasant or disagreeable? In all your hours together, did nothing ever remind her— What is it?"

Helen's frown had gone suddenly, and the corners of her mouth had lifted a little. "Headache," she said. "Faith never had headaches, except only once, one day when she came home from work. She wouldn't eat anything and she didn't go to school that night, and I wanted her to take some aspirin but she said it wouldn't help any. Then she asked me if I had a mother, and I said my mother was dead and she said she wished hers was. That didn't sound like her and I said that was an awful thing to say, and she said she knew it was but I might say it too if I had a mother like hers, and she said she had met her on the street when she was out for lunch and there had been a scene, and she had to run to get away from her." Helen was looking pleased. "So that was a contact, wasn't it?"

"It was. What else did she say about it?"

"That was all. The next day—no, the day after— she said she was sorry she had said it and she hadn't really meant it, about wishing her mother was dead. I told her if all the people died that I had wished they were dead there wouldn't be room in the cemeteries. Of course that was exaggerated, but I thought it would do her good to know that people were wishing people were dead all the time."

"Did she ever mention her mother again?"

"No, just that once."

"Well. We have recalled one contact, perhaps we can recall another."

But they couldn't. He contrived other questions that didn't parrot the police, but all he got was a collection of blanks, and finally he gave it up.

He moved his eyes to include the others. "Perhaps I should have explained," he said, "exactly why I wanted to talk with you. First, since you had been in close association with Miss Usher, I wanted to know your attitude toward Mr. Goodwin's opinion that she did not kill herself. On the whole you have supported it. Miss Varr has upheld it on valid grounds, Miss

Yarmis has opposed it on ambiguous grounds, and Miss Tuttle is uncertain."

That was foxy and unfair. He knew damn well Helen Yarmis wouldn't know what "ambiguous" meant, and that was why he used it.

He was going on. "Second, since I am assuming that Mr. Goodwin is right, that Miss Usher did not poison her champagne and that therefore someone else did, I wanted to look at you and hear you talk. You are three of the eleven people who were there and are suspect; I exclude Mr. Goodwin. One of you might have taken that opportunity to use a lump of the poison that you all knew—"

"But we couldn't!" Rose Tuttle blurted. "Ethel was with Archie Goodwin. Helen was with that publisher, what's-his-name, Laidlaw, and I was with the one with big ears—Kent. So we couldn't!"

Wolfe nodded. "I know, Miss Tuttle. Evidentially, nobody could, so I must approach from another direction, and all eleven of you are suspect. I don't intend to harass you ladies in an effort to trick you into betraying some guarded secret of your relationship with Miss Usher; that's an interminable and laborious process and all night would only start it; and besides, it would probably be futile. If one of you has such a secret it will have to be exposed by other means. But I did want to look at you and hear you talk."

"I haven't talked much," Ethel Varr said.

"No," Wolfe agreed, "but you supported Mr. Goodwin, and that alone is suggestive. Third—and this was the main point—I wanted your help. I am assuming that if Miss Usher was murdered you would wish the culprit to be disclosed. I am also assuming that none of you has so deep an interest in any of the other eight people there that you would want to shield him from exposure if he is guilty."

"I certainly haven't," Ethel Varr declared. "Like I told you, I'm sure Faith didn't put anything in her champagne, and if she didn't, who did? I've been thinking about it. I know it wasn't me, and it wasn't Mr. Goodwin, and I'm sure it wasn't Helen or Rose. How many does that leave?"

"Eight. The three male guests, Laidlaw, Schuster, and Kent. The butler. Mr. Grantham and Miss Grantham. Mr. and Mrs. Robilotti."

"Well, I certainly don't want to shield any of *them.*"

"Neither do I," Rose Tuttle asserted, "if one of them did it."

"You couldn't shield them," Helen Yarmis told them, "if they *didn't* do it. There wouldn't be anything to shield them from."

"You don't understand, Helen," Rose told her. "He wants to find out who it was. Now, for instance, what if it was Cecil Grantham, and what if you saw him take the bottle out of Faith's bag and put it back, or something like that, would you want to shield him? That's what he wants to know."

"But that's just it," Helen objected. "If Faith did it herself, why would I want to shield him?"

"But Faith didn't do it. Ethel and Mr. Goodwin were both looking at her."

"Then why," Helen demanded, "did she take the bottle to the party when I told her not to?"

Rose shook her head, wiggling the pony tail. "You'd better explain it," she told Wolfe.

"I fear," he said, "that it's beyond my powers. It may clear the air a little if I say that a suspicious word

or action at the party, like Mr. Grantham's taking the
bottle from the bag, was not what I had in mind. I
meant, rather, to ask if you know anything about any
of those eight people that might suggest the possibility of a reason why one of them might have wanted
Miss Usher to die. Do you know of any connection
between one of them and Miss Usher—either her or
someone associated with her?"

"I don't," Rose said positively.

"Neither do I," Ethel declared.

"There's so many of them," Helen complained.
"Who are they again?"

Wolfe, patient under stress, pronounced the eight
names.

Helen was frowning again. "The only connection I
know about," she said, "is Mrs. Robilotti. When she
came to Grantham House to see us. Faith didn't like
her."

Rose snorted. "Who did?"

Wolfe asked, "Was there something definite, Miss
Yarmis? Something between Miss Usher and Mrs.
Robilotti?"

"I guess not," Helen conceded. "I guess it wasn't
any more definite with Faith than it was with the rest
of us."

"Did you have in mind something in particular
that Miss Usher and Mrs. Robilotti said to each
other?"

"Oh, no. I never heard Faith say anything to her
at all. Neither did I. She thought we were harlots."

"Did she use that word? Did she call you harlots?"

"Of course not. She tried to be nice but didn't
know how. One of the girls said that one day when she

had been there, she said that she thought we were harlots."

"Well." Wolfe took in air, in and clear down to his middle, and let it out again. "I thank you again, ladies, for coming." He pushed his chair back and rose. "We seem to have made little progress, but at least I have seen and talked with you, and I know where to reach you if the occasion arises."

"One thing I don't see," Rose Tuttle said as she left her chair. "Mr. Goodwin said he wasn't there as a detective, but he *is* a detective, and I had told him about Faith having the poison, and I should think he ought to know exactly what happened. I didn't think anyone could commit a murder with a detective right there."

A very superficial and half-baked way to look at it, I thought, as I got up to escort the ladies out.

Chapter 9

Paul Schuster, the promising young corporation lawyer with the thin nose and quick dark eyes, sat in the red leather chair at a quarter past eleven Friday morning, with the eyes focused on Wolfe. "We do not claim," he said, "to have evidence that you have done anything that is actionable. It should be clearly understood that we are not presenting a threat. But it is a fact that we are being injured, and if you are responsible for the injury it may become a question of law."

Wolfe moved his head to take the others in—Cecil Grantham, Beverly Kent, and Edwin Laidlaw, lined up on yellow chairs—and to include them. "I am not aware," he said dryly, "of having inflicted an injury on anyone."

Of course that wasn't true. What he meant was that he hadn't inflicted the injury he was trying to inflict. Forty-eight hours had passed since Laidlaw had written his check for twenty thousand dollars and put it on Wolfe's desk, and we hadn't earned a dime of it, and the prospect of ever earning it didn't look a bit brighter. Dinky Byne's cover, if he had anything to

cover, was intact. The three unmarried mothers had
supplied no crack to start a wedge. Orrie Cather, having delivered them at the office for consultation, had
been given another assignment, and had come Thursday evening after dinner, with Saul Panzer and Fred
Durkin, to report; and all it had added up to was an
assortment of blanks. If anyone had had any kind of
connection with Faith Usher, it had been buried good
and deep, and the trio had been told to keep digging.

When, a little after ten Friday morning, Paul
Schuster had phoned to say that he and Grantham
and Laidlaw and Kent wanted to see Wolfe, and the
sooner the better, I had broken two of the standing
rules: that I make no appointments without checking
with Wolfe, and that I disturb him in the plant rooms
only for emergencies. I had told Schuster to be there
at eleven, and I had buzzed the plant rooms on the
house phone to tell Wolfe that company was coming.
When he growled I told him that I had looked up
"emergency" in the dictionary, and it meant an un-
foreseen combination of circumstances which calls for
immediate action, and if he wanted to argue either
with the dictionary or with me I was willing to go
upstairs and have it out. He had hung up on me.

And was now telling Schuster that he was not
aware of having inflicted an injury on anyone.

"Oh, for God's sake," Cecil Grantham said.

"Facts are facts," Beverly Kent muttered. Unquestionably a diplomatic way of putting it, suitable
for a diplomat. When he got a little higher up the
ladder he might refine it by making it "A fact is a fact
is a fact."

"Do you deny," Schuster demanded, "that we owe
it to Goodwin that we are being embarrassed and

harassed by a homicide investigation? And he is your agent, employed by you. No doubt you know the legal axiom, *respondeat superior*. Isn't that an injury?"

"Not only that," Cecil charged, "but he goes up to Grantham House, sticking his nose in. And yesterday a man tried to pump my mother's butler, and he had no credentials, and I want to know if you sent him. And another man with no credentials is asking questions about me among my friends, and I want to know if you sent *him*."

"To me," Beverly Kent stated, "the most serious aspect is the scope of the police inquiry. My work on our Mission to the United Nations is in a sensitive field, very sensitive, and already I have been definitely injured. Merely to have been present when a sensational event occurred, the suicide of that young woman, would have been unfortunate. To be involved in an extended police inquiry, a murder investigation, could be disastrous for me. If in addition to that you are sending your private agents among my friends and associates to inquire about me, that is adding insult to injury. I have no information of that, as yet. But you have, Cece?"

Cecil nodded. "I sure have."

"So have I," Schuster said.

"Have you, Ed?"

Laidlaw cleared his throat. "No direct information, no. Nothing explicit. But I have reason to suspect it."

He handled it pretty well, I thought. Naturally he had to be with them, since if he had refused to join in the attack they would have wondered why, but he wanted Wolfe to understand that he was still his client.

"You haven't answered my question," Schuster

told Wolfe. "Do you deny that we owe this harassment to Goodwin, and therefore to you, since he is your agent?"

"No," Wolfe said. "But you owe it to me, through Mr. Goodwin, only secondarily. Primarily you owe it to the man or woman who murdered Faith Usher. So it's quite possible that one of you owes it to himself."

"I knew it," Cecil declared. "I told you, Paul."

Schuster ignored him. "As I said," he told Wolfe, "this may become a question of law."

"I expect it to, Mr. Schuster. A murder trial is commonly regarded as a matter of law." Wolfe leaned forward, flattened his palms on the desk, and sharpened his tone. "Gentlemen. Let's get to the point, if there is one. What are you here for? Not, I suppose, merely to grumble at me. To buy me off? To bully me? To dispute my ground? What are you after?"

"Goddammit," Cecil demanded, "what are *you* after? That's the point! What are you trying to pull? Why did you send—"

"Shut up, Cece," Beverly Kent ordered him, not diplomatic at all. "Let Paul tell him."

The lawyer did so. "Your insinuation," Schuster said, "that we have entered into a conspiracy to buy you off is totally unwarranted. Or to bully you. We came because we feel, with reason, that our rights of privacy are being violated without provocation or just cause, and that you are responsible. We doubt if you can justify that responsibility, but we thought you should have a chance to do so before we consider what steps may be taken legally in the matter."

"Pfui," Wolfe said.

"An expression of contempt is hardly an adequate justification, Mr. Wolfe."

"I didn't intend it to be, sir." Wolfe leaned back and clasped his fingers at the apex of his central mound. "This is futile, gentlemen, both for you and for me. Neither of us can possibly be gratified. You want a stop put to your involvement in a murder inquiry, and my concern is to involve you as deeply as possible—the innocent along with—"

"Why?" Schuster demanded. "Why are you concerned?"

"Because Mr. Goodwin's professional reputation and competence have been challenged, and by extension my own. You invoked *respondeat superior;* I will not only answer, I will act. That the innocent must be involved along with the guilty is regrettable but unavoidable. So you can't get what you want, but no more can I. What I want is a path to a fact. I want to know if one of you has buried in his past a fact that will account for his resort to murder to get rid of Faith Usher, and if so, which. Manifestly you are not going to sit here and submit to a day-long inquisition by me, and even if you did, the likelihood that one of you would betray the existence of such a fact is minute. So, as I say, this is futile both for you and for me. I wish you good day only as a matter of form."

But it wasn't quite that simple. They had come for a showdown, and they weren't going to be bowed out with a "good day" as a matter of form—at least, three of them weren't. They got pretty well worked up before they left. Schuster forgot all about saying that they hadn't come to present a threat. Kent went far beyond the bounds of what I would call diplomacy. Cecil Grantham blew his top, at one point even pounding the top of Wolfe's desk with his fist. I was on my feet, to be handy in case one of them lost control and picked up a chair to throw but my attention was mainly on our client. He was out of luck. For the sake of appearance he sort of tried to join in, but his heart wasn't in it, and all he could manage was a mumble now and then. He didn't leave his chair until Cecil headed for the door, followed by Kent, and then, not wanting to be the last one out, he jumped up and went. I stepped to the hall to see that no one took my new hat in the excitement, went and tried the door after they were out, and returned to the office.

I expected to see Wolfe leaning back with his eyes closed, but no. He was sitting up straight, glaring at space. He transferred the glare to me.

"This is grotesque," he growled.

"It certainly is," I agreed warmly. "Four of the suspects come to see you uninvited, all set for a good long heart-to-heart talk, and what do they get? Bounced. The trouble is, one of them was our client, and he may think we're loafing on the job."

"Bah. When the men phone, tell them to come in at three. No. At two-thirty. No. At two o'clock. We'll have lunch early. I'll tell Fritz." He got up and marched out.

I felt uplifted. That he was calling the men in for new instructions was promising. That he had changed it from three o'clock, when his lunch would have been settled, to two-thirty, when digestion would have barely started, was impressive. That he had advanced it again, to two, with an early lunch, was inspiring. And then to go to tell Fritz instead of ringing for him —all hell was popping.

Chapter 10

"How many times," Wolfe asked, "have you heard me confess that I am a witling?"

Fred Durkin grinned. A joke was a joke. Orrie Cather smiled. He was even handsomer when he smiled, but not necessarily braver. Saul Panzer said, "Three times when you meant it, and twice when you didn't."

"You never disappoint me, Saul." Wolfe was doing his best to be sociable. He had just crossed the hall from the dining room. With Fred and Orrie he wouldn't have strained himself, but Saul had his high regard. "This, then," he said, "makes four times that I have meant it and this time my fault was so egregious that I made myself pay for it. The only civilized way to spend the hour after lunch is with a book, but I have just swallowed my last bite of cheese cake, and here I am working. You must bear with me. I am paying a deserved penalty."

"Maybe it's our fault too," Saul suggested. "We had an order and we didn't fill it."

"No," Wolfe said emphatically. "I can't grab for the straw of your charity. I am an ass. If any share of

the fault is yours it lies in this, that when I explained
the situation to you Wednesday evening and gave you
your assignments none of you reminded me of my
maxim that nothing is to be expected of tagging the
footsteps of the police. That's what you've been doing,
at my direction, and it was folly. There are scores of
them, and only three of you. You have been merely
looking under stones that they have already turned. I
am an ass."

"Maybe there's no other stones to try," Orrie observed.

"Of course there are. There always are." Wolfe
took time to breathe. More oxygen was always
needed after a meal unless he relaxed with a book. "I
have an excuse, naturally, that one approach was
closed to my ingenuity. By Mr. Cramer's account, and
Archie didn't challenge it, no one could possibly have
poisoned that glass of champagne with any assurance
that it would get to Miss Usher. I could have tackled
that problem only by a minute examination of everyone who was there, and most of them were not available to me. Sooner or later it must be solved, but only
after disclosure of a motive. That was the only feasi-
ble approach open to me, to find the motive, and you
know what I did. I sent you men to flounder around
on ground that the police had already covered, or
were covering. Pfui."

"I saw four people," Fred protested, "that the cops
hadn't got to."

"And learned?"

"Well—nothing."

Wolfe nodded. "So. The quarry, as I told you
Wednesday evening, was evidence of some significant
association of one of those people with Miss Usher.

That was a legitimate line of inquiry, but it was precisely the one the police were following, and I offer my apologies. We shall now try another line, where you will at least be on fresh ground. I want to see Faith Usher's mother. You are to find her and bring her."

Fred and Orrie pulled out their notebooks. Saul had one but rarely used it. The one inside his skull was usually all he needed.

"You won't need notes," Wolfe said. "There is nothing to note except the bare fact that Miss Usher's mother is alive and must be somewhere. This may lead nowhere, but it is not a resort to desperation. Whatever circumstance in Miss Usher's life resulted in her death, she must have been emotionally involved, and I have been apprised of only two phenomena which importantly engaged her emotions. One was her experience with the man who begot her infant. A talk with him might be fruitful, but if he can be found the police will find him; of course they're trying to. The other was her relationship with her mother. Mrs. Irwin, of Grantham House, told Archie that she had formed the conclusion, from talking with Miss Usher, that her mother was alive and that she hated her. And yesterday Miss Helen Yarmis, with whom Miss Usher shared an apartment the last seven months of her life, told me that Miss Usher had come home from work one day with a headache and had said that she had encountered her mother on the street and there had been a scene, and she had had to run to get away from her; and that she wished her mother was dead. Miss Yarmis's choice of words."

Fred, writing in his notebook, looked up. "Does she spell Irwin with an *E* or an *I*?"

Wolfe always tried to be patient with Fred, but there was a limit. "As you prefer," he said. "Why spell it at all? I've told you all she said that is relevant, and all that I know. I will add that I doubt if either Mrs. Irwin or Miss Yarmis mentioned Miss Usher's mother to the police, so in looking for her you shouldn't be jostled."

"Is her name Usher?" Orrie asked. Of course Saul wouldn't have asked it, and neither would Fred.

"You should learn to listen, Orrie," Wolfe told him. "I said that's all I know. And no more is to be expected from either Mrs. Irwin or Miss Yarmis. They know no more." His eyes went to Saul. "You will direct the search, using Fred and Orrie as occasions arise."

"Do we keep covered?" Saul asked.

"Preferably, yes. But don't preserve your cover at the cost of missing your mark."

"I took a look," I said, "at the Manhattan phone book when I got back from Grantham House yesterday. A dozen Ushers are listed. Of course she doesn't have to be named Usher, and she doesn't have to live in Manhattan, and she doesn't have to have a phone. It wouldn't take Fred and Orrie long to check the dozen. I can call Lon Cohen at the *Gazette*. He might have gone after the mother for an exclusive and a picture."

"Sure," Saul agreed. "If it weren't for cover my first stop would be the morgue. Even if her daughter hated her, the mother may have claimed the body. But they know me there, and Fred and Orrie too, and of course they know Archie."

It was decided, by Wolfe naturally, that that risk should be taken only after other tries had failed, and that calling Lon Cohen should obviously come first, and I dialed and got him. It was a little complicated. He had rung me a couple of times to try to talk me into the eye-witness story, and now my calling to ask if he had dug up Faith Usher's mother aroused all his professional instincts. Was Wolfe working on the case, and if so, on behalf of whom? Had someone made me a better offer for a story, and did I want the mother so I could put her in, and who had offered me how much? I had to spread the salve thick, and assure him that I wouldn't dream of letting anyone but the *Gazette* get my by-line, and promise that if and when we had anything fit for publication he would get it, before he would answer my simple question.

I hung up and swiveled to report. "You can skip the morgue. A woman went there Wednesday afternoon to claim the body. Name, Marjorie Betz. B-E-T-Z. Address, Eight-twelve West Eighty-seventh Street, Manhattan. She had a letter signed by Elaine Usher, mother of Faith Usher, same address. By her instructions the body was delivered this morning to the Metropolitan Crematory on Thirty-ninth Street. A *Gazette* man has seen Marjorie Betz, but she clammed up and is staying clammed. She says Elaine Usher went somewhere Wednesday night and she doesn't know where she is. The *Gazette* hasn't been able to find her, and Lon thinks nobody else has. End of chapter."

"Fine," Saul said. "Nobody skips for nothing."

"Find her," Wolfe ordered. "Bring her. Use any inducement that seems likely to—"

The phone rang, and I swiveled and got it.

"Nero Wolfe's office, Arch—"

"Goodwin?"

"Yes."

"This is Laidlaw. I've got to see Wolfe. Quick."

"He's here. Come ahead."

"I'm afraid to. I just left the District Attorney's office and got a taxi, and I'm being followed. I was on my way to see Wolfe about what happened at the District Attorney's office but now I can't because they mustn't know I'm running to Wolfe. What do I do?"

"Any one of a dozen things. Shaking a tail is a cinch, but of course you haven't had any practice. Where are you?"

"In a booth in a drugstore on Seventh Avenue near Sixteenth Street."

"Have you dismissed your taxi?"

"Yes. I thought that was better."

"It was. How many men are in the taxi tailing you?"

"Two."

"Then they mean it. Okay, so do we. First, have a Coke or something to give me time to get a car—say, six or seven minutes. Then take a taxi to Two-fourteen East Twenty-eighth Street. The Perlman Paper Company is there on the ground floor." I spelled Perlman. "Got that?"

"Yes."

"Go in and ask for Abe and say to him, 'Archie wants some more candy.' What are you going to say to him?"

"Archie wants some more candy."

"Right. He'll take you on through to Twenty-seventh Street, and when you emerge I'll be there in front, either at the curb or double-parked, in a gray Heron sedan. Don't hand Abe anything, he wouldn't like it. This is part of our personalized service."

"What if Abe isn't there?"

"He will be, but if he isn't don't mention candy to anyone else. Find a booth and ring Mr. Wolfe."

I hung up, scribbled "Laidlaw" on my pad, tore the sheet off, and got up and handed it to Wolfe. "He wants to see you quick," I said, "and needs transportation. I'll be back with him in half an hour or less."

He nodded, crumpled the sheet, and dropped it in his wastebasket; and I wished the trio luck on their mother hunt and went.

At the garage, at the corner of Tenth Avenue, I used the three minutes while Hank was bringing the car down to go to the phone in the office and ring the Perlman Paper Company, and got Abe. He said he had been wondering when I would want more candy and would be glad to fill the order.

The de-tailing operation went fine, without a hitch. Going crosstown on Thirty-fourth Street, it was a temptation to swing down Park or Lexington to Twenty-eighth, so as to pass Number 214 and see if I recognized the two in the taxi, but since they might also recognize me I vetoed it and gave them plenty of room by continuing to Second Avenue before turning downtown, then west on Twenty-seventh. It was at the rear entrance on Twenty-seventh that the Perlman Paper Company did its loading and unloading, but no truck was there when I arrived, and I rolled to the curb at 2:49, just nineteen minutes since Laidlaw had phoned, and at 2:52 here he came trotting across the sidewalk. I opened the door and he piled in.

He looked upset. "Relax," I told him as I fed gas. "A tail is a trifle. They won't go in to ask about you for at least half an hour, if at all, and Abe will say he took you to the rear to show you some stock, and you left that way."

"It's not the tail. I want to see Wolfe." His tone indicated that his plan was to get him down and tramp on him, so I left him to his mood. Crossing town, I considered whether there was enough of a chance that the brownstone was under surveillance to warrant taking him in the back way, through the passage between buildings on Thirty-fourth Street, decided no, and went up Eighth Avenue to Thirty-fifth. As usual, there was no space open in front of the brownstone, so I went on to the garage and left the car, and walked back with him. When we entered the office I was at his heels. He didn't have the build to get Wolfe's bulk down and trample on it without help, but after all, he was the only one of the bunch, as it stood then, who had had dealings with Faith Usher that might have produced a motive for murder, and if a man has once murdered you never know what he'll do next.

He didn't move a finger. In fact, he didn't even move his tongue. He stood at the corner of Wolfe's desk looking down at him, and after five seconds I realized that he was too mad, or too scared, or both, to speak, and I took his elbow and eased him to the red leather chair and into it.

"Well, sir?" Wolfe asked.

The client pushed his hair back, though he must have known by then that it was a waste of energy. "I may be wrong," he croaked. "I hope to God I am. Did you send a note to the District Attorney telling him that I am the father of Faith Usher's child?"

"No." Wolfe's lips tightened. "I did not."

Laidlaw's head jerked to me. "Did you?"

"No. Of course not."

"Have you told anybody? Either of you?"

"Plainly," Wolfe said, "you are distressed and so must be indulged. But nothing has happened to release either Mr. Goodwin or me from our pledge of confidence. If and when it does you will first be notified. I suggest that you retire and cool off a little."

"Cool off, hell." The client rubbed the chair arms with his palms, eyeing Wolfe. "Then it wasn't you. All right. When I left here this morning I went to my office, and my secretary said the District Attorney's office had been trying to reach me, and I phoned and was told they wanted to see me immediately, and I went. I was taken in to Bowen, the District Attorney himself, and he asked if I wished to change my statement that I had never met Faith Usher before Tuesday evening, and I said no. Then he showed me a note that he said had come in the mail. It was typewritten. There wasn't any signature. It said, 'Have you found out yet that Edwin Laidlaw is the father of Faith Usher's baby? Ask him about his trip to Canada in August nineteen fifty-six.' Bowen didn't let me take it. He held on to it. I sat and stared at it."

Wolfe grunted. "It was worth a stare, even if it had been false. Did you collapse?"

"No! By God, I didn't! I don't think I decided what to do while I sat there staring at it; I think my subconscious mind had already decided what to do. Sitting there staring at it, I was too stunned to decide anything, so I must have already decided that the only thing to do was refuse to answer any questions about anything at all, and that's what I did. I said just one thing: that whoever sent that note had libeled me and I had a right to find out who it was, and to do that

I would have to have the note, but of course they wouldn't give it to me. They wouldn't even give me a copy. They kept at me for two hours, and when I left I was followed."

"You admitted nothing?"

"No."

"Not even that you had taken a trip to Canada in August of nineteen fifty-six?"

"No. I admitted *nothing*. I didn't answer a single question."

"Satisfactory," Wolfe said. "Highly satisfactory. This is indeed welcome, Mr. Laidlaw. We have—"

"Welcome!" the client squawked. *"Welcome!"*

"Certainly. We have at last goaded someone to action. I am gratified. If there was any small shadow of doubt that Miss Usher was murdered, this removes it. They have all claimed to have had no knowledge of Miss Usher prior to that party; one of them lied, and he has been driven to move. True, it is still possible that you yourself are the culprit, but I now think it extremely improbable. I prefer to take it that the murderer has felt compelled to create a diversion, and that is most gratifying. Now he is doomed."

"But good God! They know about—about me!"

"They know no more than they knew before. They get a dozen accusatory unsigned letters every day, and have learned that the charges in most of them are groundless. As for your refusal to answer questions, a man of your standing might be expected to take that position until he got legal advice. It's a neat situation, very neat. They will of course make every effort to find confirmation of that note, but it is a reasonable asumption that no one can supply it except the person who sent the note, and if he dares to do so we'll have

him. We'll challenge him, but we'll have him." He
glanced up at the wall clock. "However, we shall not
merely twiddle our thumbs and wait for that. I have
thirty minutes. You told me Wednesday morning that
no one on earth knew of your dalliance with Miss
Usher; now we know you were wrong. We must review every moment you spent in her company when
you might have been seen or heard. When I leave, at
four o'clock, Mr. Goodwin will continue with you.
Start with the day she first attracted your notice,
when she waited on you at Cordoni's. Was anyone you
knew present?"

When Wolfe undertakes that sort of thing, getting
someone to recall every detail of a past experience, he
is worse than a housewife bent on finding a speck of
dust that the maid overlooked. Once I sat for eight
straight hours, from nine in the evening until daylight
came, while he took a chauffeur over every second of
a drive, made six months before, to New Haven and
back. This time he wasn't quite that fussy, but he did
no skipping. When four o'clock came, time for him to
go up and play with the orchids, he had covered the
episode at Cordoni's, two dinners, one at the Wood-
bine in Westchester and one at Henke's on Long Island, and a lunch at Gaydo's on Sixty-ninth Street.

I carried on for more than an hour, following
Wolfe's *modus operandi* more or less, but my pulse
wasn't pounding from the thrill of it. It seemed to me
that it could have been handled just as well by putting
one question: "Did you at any time, anywhere, when
she was with you, including Canada, see or hear anyone who knew you?" and then make sure there were
no gaps in his memory. As for chances that they had
been seen but he hadn't known it, there had been

plenty. Aside from restaurants, he had had her in his car, in midtown, in daylight, seven times. The morning they left for Canada he had parked his car, with her in it, in front of his club, while he went in to leave a message for somebody.

But I carried on, and we were working on the third day in Canada, somewhere in Quebec, when the doorbell rang and I went to the hall for a look through the one-way glass and saw Inspector Cramer of Homicide.

I wasn't much surprised, since I knew there had been a pointer for them if they were interested enough; and just as Laidlaw's subconscious had made his decision in advance, mine had made mine. I went to the rack and got Laidlaw's hat and coat, stepped back into the office, and told the client, "Inspector Cramer is here looking for you. This way out. Come on, move—"

"But how did—"

"No matter how." The doorbell rang. "Damn it, move!"

He came, and followed me to the kitchen. Fritz was at the big table, doing something to a duck. I told him, "Mr. Laidlaw wants to leave the back way in a hurry, and I haven't time because Cramer wants in. Show him quick, and you haven't seen him."

Fritz headed for the back door, which opens on our private enclosed garden if you want to call it that, whose fence has a gate into the passage between buildings which leads to Thirty-fourth Street. As the door closed behind them and I turned, the doorbell rang. I went to the front, not in a hurry, put the chain bolt on, opened the door to the two-inch crack the chain allowed, and spoke through it politely.

"I suppose you want me? Since you know Mr. Wolfe won't be available until six o'clock."

"Open up, Goodwin."

"Under conditions. You know damn well what my orders are: no callers admitted between four and six unless it's just for me."

"I know. Open up."

I took that for a commitment, and he knew I did. Also it was conceivable that some character—Sergeant Stebbins, for instance—was on his way with a search warrant, and if so it would take the edge off to admit Cramer without one. So I said, "Okay, if it's me you want," removed the bolt, and swung the door wide; and he stepped in, marched down the hall, and entered the office.

I shut the door and went to join him, but by the time I arrived he wasn't there. The connecting door to the front room was open, and in a moment he came through and barked at me, "Where's Laidlaw?"

I was hurt. "I thought you wanted me. If I had—"

"Where's Laidlaw?"

"Search me. There's lot of Laidlaws, but I haven't got one. If you mean—"

He made for the door to the hall, passing within arm's length of me en route.

The rules for dealing with officers of the law are contradictory. Whether you may restrain them by force or not depends. It was okay to restrain Cramer from entering the house by the force of the chain bolt. It would have been okay to restrain him from going upstairs if there had been a locked door there and I had refused to open it, but I couldn't restrain him by standing on the first step and not letting him by, no matter how careful I was not to hurt him. That may make sense to lawyers, but not to me.

But that's the rule, and it didn't matter that he had said he knew *our* rules before I let him in. So when he crossed the hall to the stairs I didn't waste my breath to yell at him; I saved it for climbing the three flights, which I did, right behind him. Since he was proving that in a pinch he had no honor and no manners, it would have been no surprise if he had turned left at the first landing to invade Wolfe's room, or right at the second landing to invade mine, but he kept going to the top, and on in to the vestibule.

I don't know whether he is off orchids because Wolfe is on them, or is just color blind, but on the few occasions that I have seen him in the plant rooms he has never shown the slightest sign that he realizes that the benches are occupied. Of course in that house his mind is always occupied or he wouldn't be there, and that could account for it. That day, in the cool room, long panicles of Odontoglossums, yellow, rose, white with spots, crowded the aisle on both sides; in the tropical room, Miltonia hybrids and Phalaenopsis splashed pinks and greens and browns clear to the glass above; and in the intermediate room the Cattleyas were grandstanding all over the place as always. Cramer might have been edging his way between rows of dried-up cornstalks.

The door from the intermediate room to the potting room was closed as usual. When Cramer opened it and I followed him in, I didn't stop to shut it but circled around him and raised my voice to announce, "He said he came to see me. When I let him in he dashed past me to the office and then to the front room and started yapping, 'Where's Laidlaw?' and when I told him I had no Laidlaw he dashed past me again for the stairs. Apparently he has such a craving for someone named Laidlaw that his morals are shot."

Theodore Horstmann, at the sink washing pots, had twisted around for a look, but before I finished was twisted back again, washing pots. Wolfe, at the potting bench inspecting seedlings, had turned full around to glare. He had started the glare at me, but by the time I ended had transferred it to Cramer. "Are you demented?" he inquired icily.

Cramer stood in the middle of the room, returning the glare. "Someday," he said, and stopped.

"Someday what? You will recover your senses?"

Cramer advanced two paces. "So you're horning in again," he said. "Goodwin turns a suicide into a murder, and here you are. Yesterday you had those girls here. This morning you had those men here. This afternoon Laidlaw is called downtown to show him something which he refuses to discuss, and when he leaves he heads for you. So I know he has been here. So I come—"

"If you weren't an inspector," I cut in, "I'd say that's a lie. Since you are, make it a fib. You do not know he has been here."

"I know he hopped a taxi and gave the driver this address, and when he saw he was being followed he went to a booth and phoned, and took another taxi to a place that runs through the block, and left by the other street. Where would I suppose he went?"

"Correction. You *suppose* he has been here."

"All right, I do." He took another step, toward Wolfe. "Have you seen Edwin Laidlaw in the last three hours?"

"This is quite beyond belief," Wolfe declared. "You

know how rigidly I maintain my personal schedule. You know that I resent any attempt to interfere with these two hours of relaxation. But you get into my house by duplicity and then come charging up here to ask me a question to which you have no right to an answer. So you don't get one. Indeed, in these circumstances, I doubt if you could put a question about anything whatever that I *would* answer." He turned, giving us the broad expanse of his rear, and picked up a seedling.

"I guess," I told Cramer sympathetically, "your best bet would be to get a search warrant and send a gang to look for evidence, like cigarette ashes from the kind he smokes. I know where it hurts. You've never forgotten the day you did come with a warrant and a crew to look for a woman named Clara Fox and searched the whole house, including here, and didn't find her, and later you learned she had been in this room in a packing case, covered with osmundine that Wolfe was spraying water on. So you thought if you rushed up before I could give the alarm you'd find Laidlaw here, and now that he isn't you're stuck. You can't very well demand to know why Laidlaw rushed here to discuss something with Wolfe that he wouldn't discuss downtown. You ought to take your coat off when you're in the house or you'll catch cold when you leave. I'm just talking to be sociable while you collect yourself. Of course Laidlaw was here this morning with the others, but apparently you know that. Whoever told you should—"

He turned and was going. I followed.

Chapter 11

At five minutes past six Saul Panzer phoned. That was routine; when one or more of them are out on a chore they call at noon, and again shortly after six, to report progress or lack of it and to learn if there are new instructions. He said he was talking from a booth in a bar and grill on Broadway near Eighty-sixth Street. Wolfe, who had just come down from the plant rooms, did him the honor of reaching for the phone on his desk to listen in.

"So far," Saul reported, "we're only scouting. Marjorie Betz lives with Mrs. Elaine Usher at the address on Eighty-seventh Street. Mrs. Usher is the tenant. I got in to see Miss Betz by one of the standard lines, and got nowhere. Mrs. Usher left Wednesday night, and she doesn't know where she is or when she'll be back. We have seen two elevator men, the janitor, five neighbors, fourteen people in local shops and stores, and a hackie Mrs. Usher patronizes, and Orrie is now after the maid, who left at five-thirty. Do you want Mrs. Usher's description?"

Wolfe said no and I said yes simultaneously. "Very well," Wolfe said, "oblige him."

"Around forty. We got as low as thirty-three and as high as forty-five. Five feet six, hundred and twenty pounds, blue eyes set close, oval face, takes good care of good skin, hair was light brown two years ago, now blonde, wears it loose, medium cut. Dresses well but a little flashy. Gets up around noon. Hates to tip. I think that's fairly accurate, but this is a guess with nothing specific, that she has no job but is never short of money, and she likes men. She has lived in that apartment for eight years. Nobody ever saw a husband. Six of them knew the daughter, Faith, and liked her, but it has been four years since they last saw her and Mrs. Usher never mentions her."

Wolfe grunted. "Surely that will do."

"Yes, sir. Do we proceed?"

"Yes."

"Okay. I'll wait to see if Orrie gets anywhere with the maid, and if not I have a couple of ideas. Miss Betz may go out this evening, and the lock on the apartment door is only a Wyatt."

"The hackie she patronizes," I said. "She didn't patronize him Wednesday night?"

"According to him, no. Fred found him. I haven't seen him. Fred thinks he got it staight."

"You know," I said, "you say *only* a Wyatt, but you need more than a paper clip for a Wyatt. I could run up there with an assortment, and we could go into conference—"

"No," Wolfe said firmly. "You're needed here."

For what, he didn't say. After we hung up all he did was ask how I had disposed of Laidlaw and then ask for a report of the hour and a quarter I had spent with him, and I could have covered that in one sentence just by saying it had been a washout. But he

kept pecking at it until dinner time. I knew what the
idea was, and he knew I knew. It was simply that if I
had gone to help Saul with an illegal entry into Elaine
Usher's apartment there was a chance, say one in a
million, that I wouldn't be there to answer the phone
in the morning.

But back in the office after dinner he decided it
was about time he exerted himself a little, possibly
because he saw my expression when he picked up his
book as soon as Fritz had come for the coffee service.

He lowered the book. "Confound it," he said, "I
wait to see Mrs. Usher not merely because her daughter said she hated her. There is also the fact that she
has disappeared."

"Yes, sir. I didn't say anything."

"You looked something. I suppose you are reflecting that we have had two faint intimations of the
possible identity of the person who sent that communication to the District Attorney."

"I wasn't reflecting. That's your part. What are
the two intimations?"

"You know quite well. One, that Austin Byne told
Laidlaw that he had seen Faith Usher at Grantham
House. He didn't name her, and Laidlaw did not regard his tone or manner as suggestive, but it deserves
notice. Of course, you couldn't broach it with Byne,
since that would have betrayed our client's confidence. You still can't."

I nodded. "So we file it. What's the other one?"

"Miss Grantham. She gave Laidlaw a bizarre reason for refusing to marry him, that he didn't dance
well enough. It is true that women constantly give
fantastic reasons without knowing that they are fantastic, but Miss Grantham must have known that that

one was. If her real reason was merely that she didn't care enough for him, surely she would have made a better choice for her avowed one, unless she despises him. Does she despise him?"

"No."

"Then why insult him? It is an insult to decline a proposal of marriage, a man's supreme capitulation, with flippancy. She did that six months ago, in September. It is not idle to conjecture that her real reason was that she knew of his experience with Faith Usher. Is she capable of moral revulsion?"

"Probably, if it struck her fancy."

"I think you should see her. Apparently you do dance well enough. You should be able, without disclosing our engagement with Mr. Laidlaw—"

The phone rang, and I turned to get it, hoping it was Saul to say he needed some keys, but no. Saul is not a soprano. However, it was someone who wanted to see me, with no mention of keys. She just wanted me, she said, right away, and I told her to expect me in twenty minutes.

I hung up and swiveled. "The timing," I told Wolfe, "couldn't have been better. Satisfactory. I suppose you arranged it with her while I was out getting Laidlaw. That was Celia Grantham. She wants to see me. Urgently. Presumably to tell me why she insulted Laidlaw when he asked her to marry him, though she didn't say." I arose. "Marvelous timing."

"Where?" Wolfe growled.

"At her home." I was on my way, and turned to correct it. "I mean her mother's home. You have the number." I went.

Since there were at least twenty possible reasons, excluding personal ones, why Celia wanted to see me,

and she had given no hint which it was, and since I
would soon know anyhow, it would have been point-
less to try to guess, so on the way uptown in a taxi
that's what I did. When I pushed the button in the
vestibule of the Fifth Avenue mansion I had considered only half of them.

I was wondering which I would be for Hackett,
the hired detective or the guest, but he didn't have to
face the problem. Celia was there with him and took
my coat as I shed it and handed it to him, and then
fastened on my elbow and steered me to the door of a
room on the right that they called the hall room, and
on through it. She shut the door and turned to me.

"Mother wants to see you," she said.

"Oh?" I raised a brow. "You said you did."

"I do, but it only occurred to me after Mother got
me to decoy for her. The Police Commissioner is here,
and they wanted to see you but thought you might
not come, so she asked me to phone you, and I realized I wanted to see you too. They're up in the music
room but first I want to ask you something. What is it
about Edwin Laidlaw and that girl? Faith Usher."

That was turning the tables. Wolfe's idea had been
that I might manage, without showing any cards, to
find out if she was on to our client's secret, and here
she was popping it at me and I had to play ignorant.

"Laidlaw?" I shook my head. "Search me. Why?"

"You don't know about it?"

"No. Am I supposed to?"

"I thought you would, naturally, since it's you
that's making all the trouble. You see, I may marry
him someday. If he gets into a bad jam I'll marry him
now, since you've turned out to be a skunk. That's

based on inside information but is not guaranteed. Are you a skunk?"

"I'll think it over and let you know. What about Laidlaw and Faith Usher?"

"That's what I want to know. They're asking questions of all of us, whether we have any knowledge that Edwin ever knew her. Of course he didn't. I think they got an anonymous letter. The reason I think that, they wanted to type something on our typewriters, all four of them—no, five. Hackett has one, and Cece, and I have, and there are two in Mother's office. Are you thwarting me again? Don't you really know?"

"I do now, since you've told me." I patted her shoulder. "Any time you're hard up and need a job, ring me. You have the makings of a lady detective, figuring out why they wanted samples from the typewriters. Did they get them?"

"Yes. You can imagine how Mother liked it, but she let them."

I patted her shoulder again. "Don't let it wreck your marriage plans. Undoubtedly they got an anonymous letter, but they're a dime a dozen. Whatever the letter said about Laidlaw, even if it said he was the father of her baby, that proves nothing. People who send anonymous letters are never—"

"That's not it," she said. "If he was the father of her baby, that would show that if I married him we could have a family, and I want one. What I'm worried about is his getting in a jam, and you're no help."

Mrs. Irwin had certainly sized her up. She had her own way of looking at things. She was going on. "So now suit yourself. If you'd rather duck Mother and the Police Commissioner, you know where your hat

and coat are. I don't like being used for a decoy, and
I'll tell them you got mad and went."

It was a toss-up. The idea of chatting with Mrs.
Robilotti had attractions, since she might be stirred
up enough by now to say something interesting, but
with Police Commissioner Skinner present it would
probably be just some more ring-around-a-rosy. However, it might be helpful to know why they had gone
to the trouble of using Celia for bait, so I told her I
would hate to disappoint her mother, and she escorted
me out to the reception hall and on upstairs to the
music room, where we had joined the ladies Tuesday
evening after going without brandy.

The whole family was there—Cecil standing over
by a window, and Mr. and Mrs. Robilotti and Commissioner Skinner grouped on chairs at the far end, provided with drinks, not champagne. As Celia and I
approached, Robilotti and Skinner arose, but not to
offer hands. Mrs. Robilotti lifted her bony chin, but
not getting the effect she had in mind. You can't look
down your nose at someone when he is standing and
you are sitting.

"Mr. Goodwin came up on his own," Celia said. "I
warned him you were laying for him, but here he is.
Mr. Skinner, Mr. Goodwin."

"We've met," the Commissioner said. His tone indicated that it was not one of his treasured memories.
He had acquired more gray hairs above his ears and a
couple of new wrinkles since I had last seen him, a
year of so back.

"I wish to say," Mrs. Robilotti told me, "that I
would have preferred never to permit you in my
house again."

Skinner shook his head at her. "Now, Louise." He

sat down and aimed his eyes at me. "This is unofficial, Goodwin, and off the record. Albert Grantham was my close and valued friend. He would have hated to have a thing like this happen in his house, and I owe it to him—"

"Also," Celia cut in, "he would have hated to ask someone to come and see him and then not invite him to sit down."

"I agree," Robilotti said. "Be seated, Goodwin." I didn't know he had the spunk.

"It may not be worth the trouble." I looked down at Mrs. Robilotti. From that slant her angles were even sharper. "Your daughter said you wanted to see me. Just to tell me I'm not welcome?"

She couldn't look down her nose, but she could look. "I have just spent," she said, "the worst three days of my life, and you are responsible. I had had a previous experience with you, you and the man you work for, and I should have known better than to have you here. I think you are quite capable of blackmail, and I think that's what you have in mind. I want to tell you that I won't submit to it, and if you try—"

"Hold it, Mom," Cecil called over. "That's libelous."

"Also," Skinner said, "it's useless. As I said, Goodwin, this is unofficial and off the record. None of my colleagues know I'm here, including the District Attorney. Let's assume something, just an assumption. Let's assume that here Tuesday evening, when something happened that you had said you would prevent, you were exasperated—naturally you would be—and in the heat of the moment you blurted out that you thought Faith Usher had been murdered, and then you found that you had committed yourself. It carried along from the precinct men to the squad men, to Inspector Cramer, to the District Attorney, and by that time you *were* committed."

He smiled. I knew that smile, and so did a lot of other people. "Another assumption, merely an assumption. Somewhere along the line, probably fairly early, it occurred to you and Wolfe that some of the people who were involved were persons of wealth and high standing, and that the annoyance of a murder investigation might cause one of them to seek the services of a private detective. If that were a fact, instead of an assumption, it should be apparent to you and Wolfe by now that your expectation is vain. None of the people involved is going to be foolish enough to hire you. There will be no fee."

"Do I comment as you go along," I inquired, "or wait till you're through?"

"Please let me finish. I realize your position. I realize that it would be very difficult for you to go now to Inspector Cramer or the District Attorney and say that upon further consideration you have concluded that you were mistaken. So I have a suggestion. I suggest that you wanted to check, to make absolutely sure of your ground, and came here this evening to inspect the scene again, and found me here. And after a careful inspection—the distances, the positions, and so on—you found that, though you had nothing to apologize for, you had probably been unduly positive. You concede that it is possible that Faith Usher did poison her champagne, and that if the official conclusion is suicide you will not challenge it. I will of course be under an obligation to ensure that you will suffer no damage or inconvenience, that you will not be pestered. I will fulfill that obligation. I know you will probably have to consult with Wolfe before you can give me a definite answer, but I would like to have it as soon as possible. You can phone him from here, or go out to a booth if you prefer, or even go to him. I'll wait here for you. This has gone on long enough. I think my suggestion is reasonable and fair."

"Are you through?" I asked.

"Yes."

"Well. I could make some assumptions too, but what's the use? Besides, I'm at a disadvantage. My mother used to tell me never to stay where I wasn't wanted, and you heard Mrs. Robilotti. I guess I'm too sensitive, but I've stood it as long as I can."

I turned and went. Voices came—Skinner's and Celia's and Robilotti's—but I marched on.

Chapter 12

If, to pass the time, you tried to decide what was the most conceited statement you ever heard anybody make, or read or heard of anybody making, what would you pick? The other evening a friend of mine brought it up, and she settled for Louis XIV saying *L'état, c'est moi*. I didn't have to go so far back. Mine, I told her, was "They know me." Of course, she wanted to know who said it and when, and since the murderer of Faith Usher had been convicted by a jury just the day before and the matter was closed, I told her.

Wolfe said it that Friday night when I got home and reported. When I finished I made a comment. "You know," I said, "it's pretty damn silly. A police commissioner and a district attorney and an inspector of Homicide all biting nails just because if they say suicide one obscure citizen may let out a squeak."

"They know me," Wolfe said.

Beat that if you can. I admit it was justified by the record. They did know him. What if they officially called it suicide, and then, in a day or a week or a month, Wolfe phoned WA9-8241 to tell them to come and get the murderer and the evidence? Not that they were sure that would happen, but past experience had shown them that it was at least an even-money bet that it *might* happen. My point is not that it wasn't justified, but that it would have been more becoming just to describe the situation.

He saved his breath. He said, "They know me," and picked up his book.

The next day, Saturday, we had words. The explosion came right after lunch. Saul had phoned at eight-thirty, as I was on my second cup of breakfast coffee, to report no progress. Marjorie Betz had stayed put in the apartment all evening, so the Wyatt lock had not been tackled. At noon he phoned again; more items of assorted information, but still no progress. But at two-thirty, as we returned to the office after lunch, the phone rang and he had news. They had found her. A man from a messenger service had gone to the apartment, and when he came out he had a suitcase with a tag on it. Of course that was pie. Saul and Orrie had entered a subway car right behind him. The tag read: "Miss Edith Upson, Room 911, Hotel Christie, 523 Lexington Avenue." The initials "E.U." were stamped on the suitcase.

Getting a look at someone who is holed up in a hotel room can be a little tricky, but that situation was made to order. Saul, not encumbered with luggage, had got to the hotel first and gone to the ninth floor, and had been strolling past the door of Room 911 at the moment it opened to admit the messenger with the suitcase; and if descriptions are any good at all, Edith Upson was Elaine Usher. Of course, Saul had been tempted to tackle her then and there, but also of course, since it was Saul, he had retired to

think it over and to phone. He wanted to know, were
there instructions or was he to roll his own?

"You need a staff," I told him. "I'll be there in
twelve minutes. Where—"

"No," Wolfe said, at his phone. "Proceed, Saul, as
you think best. You have Orrie. For this sort of junc-
ture your talents are as good as mine. Get her here."

"Yes, sir."

"Preferably in a mood of compliance, but get her
here."

"Yes, sir."

That was when we had words. I cradled the receiver, not gently, and stood up. "This is Saturday," I
said, "and I've got my check for this week. I want a
month's severance pay."

"Pfui."

"No phooey. I am severing relations. It has been
eighty-eight hours since I saw that girl die, and your
one bright idea, granting that it was bright, was to
collect her mother, and I refuse to camp here on my
fanny while Saul collects her. Saul is not ten times as
smart as I am; he's only twice as smart. A month's
severance pay will be—"

"Shut up."

"Gladly." I went to the safe for the checkbook and
took it to my desk.

"Archie."

"I have shut up." I opened the checkbook.

"This is natural. That is, it is in us, and we are
alive, and whatever is in life is natural. You are headstrong and I am magisterial. Our tolerance of each
other is a constantly recurring miracle. I did not have
one idea, bright or not; I had two. We have neglected
Austin Byne. It has been two days and nights since

you saw him. Since he got you to that party, pretending an ailment he didn't have, and since he told Laidlaw he had seen Miss Usher at Grantham House, and since he chose Miss Usher as one of the dinner guests, he deserves better of us. I suggest that you attend to him."

I turned my head but kept the checkbook open. "How? Tell him we don't like his explanations and we want new ones?"

"Nonsense. You are not so ingenuous. Survey him. Explore him."

"I already have. You know what Laidlaw said. He has no visible means of support, but he has an apartment and a car and plays table-stakes poker and does not go naked. The apartment, by the way, hits my eye. If you hang this murder on him, and if our tolerance miracle runs out of gas, I'll probably take it over. Are you working yourself up to saying that you want to see him?"

"No. I have no lever to use on him. I only feel that he has been neglected. If you approach him again you too will be without a lever. Perhaps the best course would be to put him under surveillance."

"If I postpone writing this check is that an instruction?"

"Yes."

At least I would get out in the air and away from the miracle for a while. I returned the checkbook to the safe, took twenty tens from the expense drawer, told Wolfe he would see me when he saw me, and went to the hall for my coat and hat.

When starting to tail a man it is desirable to know where he is, so I was a little handicapped. For all I knew, Byne might be in Jersey City or Brooklyn, or

some other province, in a marathon poker game, or he
might be at home in bed with a cold, or walking in the
park. I got air by walking the two miles to Bowdoin
Street, and at the corner of Bowdoin and Arbor I
found a phone booth and dialed Byne's number. No
answer. So at least I knew where he wasn't, and again
I had to resist temptation. It is always a temptation to
monkey with locks, and one of the best ways to test
ears is to enter someone's castle uninvited and, while
you are looking here and there for something interesting, listen for footsteps on the stairs or the sound
of an elevator. If you don't hear them in time your
hearing is defective, and you should try some other
line of work when you are out and around again.

Having swallowed the temptation, I moved down
the block to a place of business I had noticed Thursday afternoon, with an artistic sign bordered with
sweet peas, I think, that said AMY'S NOOK. As I entered,
my wristwatch said 4:12. Between then and a quarter
past six, slightly over two hours, I ate five pieces of
pie, two rhubarb and one each of apple, green tomato,
and chocolate, and drank four glasses of milk and two
cups of coffee, while seated at a table by the front
window, from which I could see the entrance to 87,
across the street and up a few doors. To keep from
arousing curiosity by either my tenure or my diet, I
had my notebook and pencil out and made sketches of
a cat sleeping on a chair. In the Village that accounts
for anything. The pie, incidentally, was more than satisfactory. I would have liked to take a piece home to
Fritz. At six-fifteen the light outside was getting dim,
and I asked for my check and was putting my notebook in a pocket when a taxi drew up in front of 87
and Dinky Byne piled out and headed for the en-

trance. When my change came I added a quarter to the tip, saying, "For the cat," and vacated.

It was nothing like as comfortable in the doorway across from 87, the one I had patronized Thursday, but you have to be closer at night than in the daytime, no matter how good your eyes are. I could only hope that Dinky wasn't set to spend the evening curled up with a book, or even without one, but that didn't seem likely, since he would have to eat and I doubted if he did his own cooking. A light had shown at the fifth-floor windows, and that gave me something to do, bend my head back every half-minute or so to see if it had gone out. My neck was beginning to feel the strain when it finally did go out, at 7:02. In a couple of minutes the subject stepped out of the vestibule and turned right.

Tailing a man solo in Manhattan, even if he isn't wise, is a joke. If he suddenly decides to flag a taxi— There are a hundred ifs, and they are all on his side. But of course any game is more fun if the odds are against you, and if you win it's good for the ego. Naturally it's easier at night, especially if the subject knows you. On that occasion I claim no credit for keeping on Byne, for none of the ifs developed. It was merely a ten-minute walk. He turned left on Arbor, crossed Seventh Avenue, went three blocks west and one uptown, and entered a door where there was a sign on the window: TOM'S JOINT.

That's the sort of situation where being known to the subject cramps you; I couldn't go in. All I could do was hunt a post, and I found a perfect one: a narrow passage between two buildings almost directly across the street. I could go in a good ten feet from the building line, where no light came at all, and still see the front of Tom's Joint. There was even an iron thing to sit on if my feet needed a rest.

They didn't. I didn't last long enough. I hadn't been there more than five minutes when suddenly company came. I was alone, and then I wasn't. A man had slid in, caught sight of me, and was peering in the darkness. A question that had arisen on various occasions, which of us had better eyesight, was settled when we spoke simultaneously. He said, "Archie" and I said, "Saul."

"What the hell," I said.

"Are you on her too?" he asked. "You might have told me."

"I'm on a man. I'll be damned. Where is yours?"

"Across the street. Tom's Joint. She just came."

"This is fate," I said. "It is also a break in a thousand. Of course, it could be coincidence. Mr. Wolfe says that in a world that operates largely at random, coincidences are to be expected, but not this one. Have you spoken with her? Does she know you?"

"No."

"My man knows me. His name is Austin Byne. He is six feet one, hundred and seventy pounds, lanky, loose-jointed, early thirties, brown hair and eyes, skin tight on his bones. Go in and take a look. If you want to bet, one will get you ten that they're together."

"I never bet against fate," he said, and went. The five minutes that he was gone were five hours. I sat down on the iron thing and got up again three times, or maybe four.

He came, and said, "They're together in a booth in a rear corner. No one is with them. He's eating oysters."

"He'll soon be eating crow. What do you want for Christmas?"

"I have always wanted your autograph."

"You'll get it. I'll tattoo it on you. Now we have a problem. She's yours and he's mine. Now they're together. Who's in command?"

"That's easy, Archie. Mr. Wolfe."

"I suppose so, damn it. We could wrap it up by midnight. Take them to a basement, I know one, and peel their hides off. If he's eating oysters there's plenty of time to phone. You or me?"

"You. I'll stick here."

"Where's Orrie?"

"Lost. When she came out he was for feet and I was for wheels, and she took a taxi."

"I saw it pull up. Okay. Sit down and make yourself at home."

At the bar and grill at the corner the phone booth was occupied and I had to wait, and I was tired of waiting, having done too much of it in the last four days. But in a few minutes the customer emerged, and I entered, pulled the door shut, and dialed the number I knew best. When Fritz answered I told him I wanted to speak to Mr. Wolfe.

"But, Archie! He's at dinner!"

"I know. Tell him it's urgent." That was another unexpected pleasure, having a good excuse to call Wolfe from the table. He has too many rules. His voice came, or rather his roar.

"Well?"

"I have a report. Saul and I are having an argument. He thought—"

"What the devil are you doing with Saul?"

"I'm telling you. He thought I should phone you.

We have a problem of protocol. I tailed Byne to a restaurant, a joint, and Saul tailed Mrs. Usher to the same restaurant, and our two subjects are in there together in a booth. Byne is eating oysters. So the question is, who is in charge, Saul or me? The only way to settle it without violence was to call you."

"At meal time," he said. I didn't retort, knowing that his complaint was not that I had presumed to interrupt, but that his two bright ideas had picked that moment to rendezvous.

I said sympathetically, "They should have known better."

"Is anyone with them?" he asked.

"No."

"Do they know they have been seen?"

"No."

"Could you eavesdrop?"

"Possibly, but I doubt it."

"Very well, bring them. There's no hurry, since I have just started dinner. Give them no opportunity for a private exchange after they see you. Have you eaten?"

"I'm full of pie and milk. I don't know about Saul. I'll ask him."

"Do so. He could come and eat— No. You may need him."

I hung up, returned to our field headquarters, and told Saul, "He wants them. Naturally. In an hour will do, since he just started dinner. Do you know what a genius is? A genius is a guy who makes things happen without his having any idea that they are going to happen. It's quite a trick. Our genius wanted to know if you've had anything to eat."

"He would. Sure. Plenty."

"Okay. Now the m.o. Do we take them in there or wait till they come out?"

Both procedures had pros and cons, and after discussion it was decided that Saul should go in and see how their meal was coming along, and when he thought they had swallowed enough to hold them through the hours ahead, or when they showed signs of adjourning, he would come out and wigwag me, go back in, and be near their booth when I approached.

They must have been fast eaters, for Saul hadn't been gone more than ten minutes when he came out, lifted a hand, saw me move, and went back in. I crossed over, entered, took five seconds to adjust to the noise and the smoke screen from the mob, made it to the rear, and there they were. The first Byne knew, someone was crowding him on the narrow seat, and his head jerked around. He started to say something, saw who it was, and goggled at me.

"Hi, Dinky," I said. "Excuse me for butting in, but I want to introduce a friend. Mr. Panzer. Saul, Mrs. Usher. Mr. Byne. Sit down. Would you mind giving him room, Mrs. Usher?"

Byne had started to rise, by reflex, but it can't be done in a tight little booth without toppling the table. He sank back. His mouth opened, and closed. Liquid spilled on the table top from a glass Elaine Usher was holding, and Saul, squeezed in beside her, reached and took it.

"Let me out," Byne said. "Let us out or I'll go out over you. Her name is Upson. Edith Upson."

I shook my head. "If you start a row you'll only make it worse. Mr. Panzer knows Mrs. Usher, though she doesn't know him. Let's be calm and consider the situation. There must be—"

"What do you want?"

"I'm trying to tell you. There must be some good reason why you two arranged to meet in this out-of-the-way dump, and Mr. Panzer and I are curious to know what it is, and others will be too—the press, the public, the police, the District Attorney, and Nero Wolfe. I wouldn't expect you to explain it here in this din and smog. Either Mr. Panzer can phone Inspector Cramer while I sit and chat with you, and he can send a car for you, or we'll take you to talk it over with Mr. Wolfe, whichever you prefer."

He had recovered some. He had played a lot of poker. He put a hand on my arm. "Look, Archie, there's nothing to it. It looks funny, sure it does, us here together, but we didn't arrange it. I met Mrs. Usher about a year ago, I went to see her when her daughter went to Grantham House, and when I came in here this evening and saw her, after what's happened, naturally I spoke to her and we—"

"Save it, Dinky. Saul, phone Cramer."

Saul started to slide out. Byne reached and grabbed his sleeve. "Now wait a minute. Damn it, can't you listen? I'm—"

"No," I said. "No listening. You can have one minute to decide." I looked at my watch. "In one minute either you and Mrs. Usher come along to Nero Wolfe or we phone Cramer. One minute." I looked at my watch. "Go."

"Not the cops," Mrs. Usher said. "My God, not the cops."

Byne began, "If you'd only listen—"

"No. Forty seconds."

If you're playing stud, and there's only one card to come, and the man across has two jacks showing and all you have is a mess, it doesn't matter what his hole card is, or yours either. Byne didn't use up the forty seconds. Only ten of them had gone when he stretched his neck to look for a waiter and ask for his check.

Chapter 13

Surveying Elaine Usher from my desk as she sat in the red leather chair, I told myself that Saul's picture of her, pieced together from a dozen descriptions he had got, had been pretty accurate. Oval face, blue eyes set close, good skin, medium-cut blonde hair, around forty. I would have said a hundred and fifteen pounds instead of a hundred and twenty, but she might have lost a few in the last four days. I had put her in the red leather chair because I had thought it desirable to have Byne closer to me. He was between Saul and me, and Saul was between the two subjects. But my arrangement was soon changed.

"I prefer," Wolfe said, "to speak with you separately, but first I must make sure that there is no misunderstanding. I intend to badger you, but you don't have to submit to it. Before I start, or at any moment, you may get up and leave. If you do, you will be through with me; thenceforth you will deal with the police. I make that clear because I don't want you bouncing up and down. If you want to go now, go."

He took a deep breath. He had just come in from

the dining room, having had his coffee there while I reported on the summit conference at Tom's Joint.

"We were forced to come here by a threat," Byne said.

"Certainly you were. And I am detaining you by the same threat. When you prefer that to this, leave. Now, madam, I wish to speak privately with Mr. Byne. Saul, take Mrs. Usher to the front room."

"Don't go," Byne told her. "Stay here."

Wolfe turned to me. "You were right, Archie. He is incorrigible. It isn't worth it. Get Mr. Cramer."

"No," Elaine Usher said. She left the chair. "I'll go."

Saul was up. "This way," he said, and went and opened the door to the front room and held it for her. When she had passed through he followed and closed the door.

Wolfe leveled his eyes at Byne. "Now, sir. Don't bother to raise your voice; that wall and door are sound-proofed. Mr. Goodwin has told me how you explained being in that restaurant with Mrs. Usher. Do you expect me to accept it?"

"No," Dinky said.

Of course. He had had time to realize that it wouldn't do. If he had gone to see her because her daughter was at Grantham House, how had he learned that she was Faith's mother? Not from the records and not from Mrs. Irwin. From one of the other girls? It was too tricky.

"What do you substitute for it?" Wolfe asked.

"I told Goodwin that because the real explanation would have been embarrassing for Mrs. Usher. Now I can't help it. I met her some time ago, three years ago, and for about a year I was intimate with her.

She'll probably deny it. I'm pretty sure she will. Naturally she would."

"No doubt. And your meeting her this evening was accidental?"

"No," Dinky said. He had also had time to realize that that was too fishy. He went on, "She phoned me this morning and said she was at the Christie Hotel, registered as Edith Upson. She had known that I was Mrs. Robilotti's nephew, and she said she wanted to see me and ask me about her daughter who had died. I told her I hadn't been there Tuesday evening, and she said she knew that, but she wanted to see me. I agreed to see her because I didn't want to offend her. I didn't want it to get out that I had been intimate with Faith Usher's mother. We arranged to meet at that restaurant."

"Had you known previously that she was Faith Usher's mother?"

"I had known that she had a daughter, but not that her name was Faith. She had spoken of her daughter when we—when I had known her."

"What did she ask you about her daughter this evening?"

"She just wanted to know if I knew anything that hadn't been in the papers. Anything about the people there or exactly what had happened. I could tell her about the people, but I didn't know any more about what had happened than she did."

"Do you wish to elaborate on any of this? Or add anything?"

"There's nothing to add."

"Then I'll see Mrs. Usher. After I speak with her I'll ask you in again, with her present. Archie, take Mr. Byne and bring Mrs. Usher."

He came like a lamb. He had thrown away his discard and made his draw and his bets, and was ready for the show-down. I opened the door for him, held it for Mrs. Usher to enter, closed it, and returned to my desk. She went to the red leather chair, so Wolfe had to swivel to face her. Another item of Saul's report on her had been that she liked men, and there were indications that men probably liked her—the way she handled her hips when she walked, the tilt of her head, the hint of a suggestion in her eyes, even now, when she was under pressure and when the man she was looking at was not a likely candidate for a frolic. And she was forty. At twenty she must have been a treat.

Wolfe breathed deep again. Exertion right after a meal was pretty rugged. "Of course, madam," he said, "my reason for speaking with you and Mr. Byne separately is transparent: to see if your account will agree with his. Since you have had no opportunity for collusion, agreement would be, if not conclusive, at least persuasive."

She smiled. "You use big words, don't you?" Something in her tone and her look conveyed the notion that for years she had been wanting to meet a man who used big words.

Wolfe grunted. "I try to use words that say what I mean."

"So do I," she declared, "but sometimes it's hard to find the ones I want. I don't know what Mr. Byne told you, but all I can do is tell you the truth. You want to know how I happened to be with him there tonight, isn't that it?"

"That's it."

"Well, I phoned him this morning and said I

wanted to see him and he said he would meet me
there at Tom's Joint, I had never heard of it before, at
a quarter past seven. So I went. That's not very thrill-
ing, is it?"

"Only moderately. Have you known him long?"

"I don't really *know* him at all. I met him somewhere about a year ago, and I wish I could tell you
where, but I've been trying to remember and I simply
can't. It was a party somewhere, but I can't remember where. Anyhow, it doesn't matter. But yesterday
I was sitting at the window thinking about my daughter. My dear daughter Faith." She stopped to gulp,
but it wasn't very impressive. "And I remembered
meeting a man named Byne, Austin Byne, and someone telling me, maybe he told me himself, that he was
the nephew of the rich Mrs. Robilotti who used to be
Mrs. Albert Grantham. And my daughter had died at
Mrs. Robilotti's house, so maybe he could tell me
about her, and maybe he could get Mrs. Robilotti to
see me so I could ask her about her. I wanted to learn
all I could about my daughter." She gulped.

It didn't look good. In fact, it looked bad. Byne had
been smart enough to invent one that she couldn't be
expected to corroborate; he had even warned that she
would probably deny it; and what was worse, it was
even possible that he hadn't invented it. He might
have been telling the truth, like a gentleman. The
meeting of Wolfe's two bright ideas at Tom's Joint,
which had looked so rosy when Saul told me they
were together, might fizzle out entirely. Maybe he
wasn't a genius after all.

If he was sharing my gloom it didn't show. He
asked, "Since your rendezvous with Mr. Byne was in-

nocuous, why were you alarmed by his threat to call the police? What were her words, Archie?"

" 'Not the cops. My God, not the cops.' "

"Yes. Why, Mrs. Usher?"

"I don't like cops. I never have liked cops."

"Why did you leave your home and go to a hotel and register under another name?"

"Because of how I felt, what my daughter had done. I didn't want to see people. I knew newspapermen would come. And cops. I wanted to be alone. You would too if—"

The doorbell rang, and I went. Sometimes I let Fritz answer it when I am engaged, but with her there and Byne in the front room I thought I had better see who it was, and besides, I was having a come-down and felt like moving. It was only Orrie Cather. I opened up and greeted him, and he crossed the sill, and I shut the door. When he removed his coat there was disclosed a leather thing, a zippered case, that he had had under it.

"What's that?" I asked. "Your week-end bag?"

"No," he said. "It's Mrs. Usher's sec—"

My hand darted to clap on his mouth. He was startled, but he can take a hint, and when I headed down the hall and turned right to the dining room he followed.

I shut the door, moved away from it, and demanded, "Mrs. Usher's what?"

"Her secret sin." There was a gleam in his eye. "I want to give it to Mr. Wolfe myself."

"You can't. Mrs. Usher is in the office with him. Where did—"

"She's here? How come?"

"That can wait. Where did you get that thing?"

I may have sounded magisterial, but my nerves were a little raw. It put Orrie on his dignity. His chin went up. "It's a pleasure to report, Mr. Goodwin. Mr. Panzer and I were covering the Christie Hotel. When the subject appeared and hopped a taxi he followed in one before I could join him. That left me loose and I phoned in. Mr. Wolfe asked me if there had been any indication how long she would be gone, and I said yes, since she took a taxi it certainly wouldn't be less than half an hour and probably longer, and he said it would be desirable to take a look at her room, and I said fine. It took a while to get in. Do you want the details?"

"That can wait. What's in it?"

"It was in a locked suitcase—not the one the messenger took today, a smaller one. The suitcase was easy, but this thing had a trick lock and I had to bust it."

I put out a hand. He hated to give it up, but protocol is protocol. I took it to the table, unzipped it, and pulled out two envelopes, one nine by twelve and the other one smaller. Neither was sealed, and hadn't been. I slipped out the contents of the big one.

They were pictures that had been clipped from magazines and newspapers. I would have recognized him even if there had been no captions, since I had been old enough to read for some years, and you often run across a picture of a multi-millionaire philanthropist. The one on top was captioned: "Albert Grantham (left) receiving the annual award of the American Benevolent League." They were all of Grantham, twenty or more. I started to turn them over, one by one, to see if anything was written on them.

"To hell with that," Orrie said impatiently. "It's the other one."

It, not so big, held another envelope, smaller, of white rag bond. The engraved return in the corner said "Albert Grantham," with the Fifth Avenue address, and it was addressed in longhand to Mrs. Elaine Usher, 812 West 87th Street, New York, and below was written "By Messenger." Inside were folded sheets. I unfolded them and read:

6 June 1952

My dear Elaine:

In accordance with my promise, I am confirming in writing what I said to you recently.

I am not accepting the obligations, legal or moral, of paternity of your daughter, Faith. You have always maintained that I am her father, and for a time I believed you, and I now have no evidence to prove you are wrong but, as I told you, I have taken the trouble to inform myself of your method of life for the past ten years, and it is quite clear that chastity is not one of your virtues. It may have been, during that period fifteen years ago when I took advantage of your youth and enjoyed your favors—you say it was—but your subsequent conduct makes it doubtful. I shall not again express my regret for my own conduct during that period. I have done that and you know how I feel about it, and have always felt since I achieved maturity, and I have not been illiberal in supplying the material needs of your daughter and yourself. For a time that was not easy, but since my father's death I have given you

$2,000 each month, and you have paid no taxes on it.

But I am getting along in years, and you are quite right, I should make provision against contingencies. As I told you, I must reject your suggestion that I give you a large sum outright —large enough for you and your daughter to live on the income. I distrust your attitude toward money. I fear that in your hands the principal would soon be squandered, and you would again appeal to me. Nor can I provide for you through a trust fund, either now or in my will, for the reasons I gave you. I will not risk disclosure.

So I have taken steps that should meet the situation. I have given my nephew, Austin Byne, a portfolio of securities the income from which is tax exempt, amounting to slightly more than $2,000,000. The yield will be about $55,000 annually. My nephew is to remit half of it to you and keep the other half for himself.

This arrangement is recorded in an agreement signed by my nephew and myself. One provision is that if you make additional demands, if you disclose the relationship you and I once had, or if you make any claims on my estate or any member of my family, he is relieved of any obligation to share the income with you. Another provision is that if he fails to make the proper remittances to you with reasonable promptness you may claim the entire principal. In drafting that provision I would have liked to have legal advice, but could not. I am sure it is binding. I do not think my nephew will fail in his performance, but if he does you will know what to do. There is of course the possibility that *he* will squander the principal, but I have known him all his life and I am sure it is remote.

I have herewith kept my promise to confirm what I told you. I repeat that this letter is not to be taken as an acknowledgment by me that I am the father of your daughter, Faith. If you ever show it or use it as the basis of any claim, the remittances from my nephew will cease at once.

I close with all good wishes for the welfare and happiness of your daughter and yourself.

Yours sincerely,
Albert Grantham

As I finished and looked up Orrie said, "I want to give it to Mr. Wolfe myself."

"I don't blame you." I folded the sheets and put them in the envelope. "Quite a letter. *Quite* a letter. I saw a note in the paper the other day that some bozo is doing a biography of him. He would love to have this. You lucky stiff. I'd give a month's pay for the kick you got when you found it."

"It *was* nice. I want to give it to him."

"You will. Wait here. Help yourself to champagne."

I left, crossed to the office, stood until Wolfe finished a sentence, and told him, "Mr. Cather wants to show you something. He's in the dining room." He got up and went, and I sat down. Judging by the expression on Mrs. Usher's face, she had been doing fine. I really would rather not have looked at her, to see the cocky little tilt of her head, the light of satisfaction in her eyes, knowing as I did that she was about to be hit by a ton of brick. So I didn't. I turned to my desk and opened a drawer and got out papers, and did things with them. When she told my back that she was glad I had brought them to Wolfe, she didn't mind a bit explaining to him, I wasn't even polite enough to turn around when I answered her. I had taken my notebook from my pocket and was tearing sketches of cats from it when Wolfe's footsteps came.

As he sat down he spoke. "Bring Mr. Byne, Archie. And Saul."

I went and opened the door and said, "Come in, gentlemen."

As Byne entered his eyes went to Mrs. Usher and saw what I had seen, and then he too was satisfied. They took the seats they had had before. Wolfe looked from one to the other and back again.

"I don't want to prolong this beyond necessity," he said, "but I would like to congratulate you. You were taken in that place by surprise and brought here with no chance to confer, but you have both lied so cleverly that it would have taken a long and costly investigation to impeach you. It was an admirable performance—If you please, Mr. Byne. You may soon speak, and you will need to. Unfortunately, for you, the performance was wasted. Fresh ammunition has arrived. I have just finished reading a document that was not intended for me." He looked at Mrs. Usher. "It states, madam, that if you disclose its contents you will suffer a severe penalty, but you have not disclosed them. On

the contrary, you have done your best to safeguard
them."

Mrs. Usher had sat up. "What document? What
are you talking about?"

"The best way to identify it is to quote an ex-
cerpt—say, the fourth paragraph. It goes: 'So I have
taken steps that should meet the situation. I have
given my nephew, Austin Byne, a portfolio of securities the income from which is tax exempt, amounting
to slightly more than $2,000,000. The yield will be
about $55,000 annually. My nephew is to remit half.' "

Byne was on his feet. The next few seconds were a
little confused. I was up, to be between Byne and
Wolfe, but the fury in his eyes was for Mrs. Usher.
Then, as he moved toward her, Saul was there to
block him, so everything was under control. But then,
with Saul's back to her and me cut off by Saul and
Byne, Mrs. Usher shot out of her chair and streaked
for Wolfe. I might have beat her to it by diving across
Wolfe's desk, but maybe not, from where I was, and
anyway, I was too astonished to move—not by her,
but by him. He had been facing her, so his knees
weren't under the desk and he didn't have to swivel,
but even so, he had a lot of pounds to get in motion.
Back went his bulk, and up came his legs, and just as
she arrived his feet were there, and one of them
caught her smack on the chin. She staggered back
into Saul's arms and he eased her on to the chair. And
I'll be damned if she didn't put both hands to her jaw
and squawk at Wolfe, "You hit me!"

I had hold of Byne's arm, a good hold, and he
didn't even know it. When he realized it he tried to
jerk loose but couldn't, and for a second I thought he
was going to swing with the other fist, and so did he.

"Take it easy," I advised him. "You're going to need all the breath you've got."

"How did you get it?" Mrs. Usher demanded. "Where is it?" She was still clutching her jaw with both hands.

Wolfe was eyeing her, but not warily. Complacently, I would say. You might think that for a long time he had had a suppressed desire to kick a woman on the chin.

"It's in my pocket," he said. He tapped his chest. "I got it just now from the man who took it from your hotel room. You'll probably get it back in due course; that will depend; it may—"

"That's burglary," Byne said. "That's a felony."

Wolfe nodded. "By definition, yes. I doubt if Mrs. Usher will care to make the charge if the document is eventually returned to her. It may be an exhibit in evidence in a murder trial. If so—"

"There has been no murder."

"You are in error, Mr. Byne. Will you please sit down? This will take a while. Thank you. I'll cover that point decisively with a categorical statement: Faith Usher was murdered."

"No!" Mrs. Usher said. Her hands left her jaw but remained poised, the fingers curved. "Faith killed herself!"

"I'm not going to debate the point," Wolfe told her. "I say merely that I will stake my professional reputation on the statement that she was murdered—indeed, I have done so. That's why I am applying my resources and risking my credit. That's why I must explore the possibilities suggested by this letter." He tapped his chest and focused on Byne. "For instance, I shall insist on seeing the agreement between you and

Mr. Grantham. Does it provide that if Faith Usher should die your remittances to her mother are to be materially decreased, or even cease altogether?"

Byne wet his lips. "Since you've read the letter to Mrs. Usher you know what the agreement provides. It's a confidential agreement and you're not going to see it."

"Oh, but I am." Wolfe was assured. "When you came here my threat was only to tell the police of your rendezvous. Now my threat is more imperative and may even be mortal. Observe Mrs. Usher. Note her expression as she regards you. Have you seen the agreement, madam?"

"Yes," she said, "I have."

"Does it contain such a provision as I suggested?"

"Yes," she said, "it does. It says that if Faith dies he can pay me only half as much or even less. Are you telling the truth, that she was murdered?"

"Nuts," Byne said. "It's not the truth he's after. Anyhow, I wasn't even there. Don't look at me, Elaine, look at *him*."

"I thought," Wolfe said, "that it might save time to see the agreement now, so I sent Mr. Cather to your apartment to look for it. It will expedite matters if you phone him and tell him where it is. He is good with locks and should be inside by this time."

Byne was staring. "By God," he said.

"Do you want to phone him?"

"Not him. By God. You've been threatening to call the police. I'll call them myself. I'll tell them a man has broken into my apartment, and he's there now, and they'll get him."

I left my chair. "Here, Dinky, use my phone."

He ignored me. "It's not the agreement," he told

Wolfe. "It's your goddamn nerve. He won't find the agreement because it's not there. It's in a safe-deposit box and it's going to stay there."

"Then it must wait until Monday." Wolfe's shoulders went up an eighth of an inch and down again. "However, Mr. Cather will not have his trouble for nothing. Aside from the chance that he may turn up other interesting items, he will use your typewriter, if you have one. I told him if he found one there to write something with it. I even told him what to write. This: 'Have you found out yet that Edwin Laidlaw is the father of Faith Usher's baby? Ask him about his trip to Canada in August 1956.' He will type that and bring it to me. You smile. You are amused? Because you don't have a typewriter?"

"Sure I have a typewriter. Did I smile?" He smiled again, a poker smile. "At you dragging Laidlaw in all of a sudden. I don't get it, but I suppose you do."

"I didn't drag him in," Wolfe asserted. "Someone else did. The police received an unsigned typewritten communication which I have just quoted. And you were wrong to smile; that was a mistake. You couldn't possibly have been amused, so you must have been pleased, and by what? Not that you don't have a typewriter, because you have. I'll try a guess. Might it not have been that you were enjoying the idea of Mr. Cather bringing me a sample of typing from your machine when you know it is innocent, and that you know it is innocent because you know where the guilty machine is? I think that deserves exploration. Unfortunately tomorrow is Sunday; it will have to wait. Monday morning Mr. Goodwin, Mr. Panzer, and Mr. Cather will call at places where a machine might be easily and naturally available to you—for instance,

your club. Another is the bank vault where you have a
safe-deposit box. Archie. You go to my box regularly.
Would it be remarkable for a vault customer to ask to
use a typewriter?"

"Remarkable?" I shook my head. "No."

"Then that is one possibility. Actually," he told
Byne, "I am not sorry that this must wait until Monday, for it does have a drawback. The samples collected from the machines must be compared with the
communication received by the police, and it is in
their hands. I don't like that, but there's no other way.
At least, if my guess is good, I will have exposed the
sender of the communication, and that will be helpful.
On this point, sir, I do not threaten to go to the police;
I am forced to."

"You goddamn snoop," Byne said through his
teeth.

Wolfe's brows went up. "I must have made a lucky
guess. It's the machine at the vault?"

Byne's head jerked to Mrs. Usher. "Beat it,
Elaine. I want to talk to him."

Chapter 14

Austin Byne sat straight and stiff. When Saul had escorted Mrs. Usher to the front room, staying there with her, I had told Dinky he would be more comfortable in the red leather chair, but from the way he looked at me I suspected that he had forgotten what "comfortable" meant.

"You win," he told Wolfe. "So I spill my guts. Where do you want me to start?"

Wolfe was leaning back with his elbows on the chair arms and his palms together. "First, let's clear up a point or two. Why did you send that thing about Laidlaw to the police?"

"I haven't said I sent it."

"Pfui." Wolfe was disgusted. "Either you've submitted or you haven't. I don't intend to squeeze it out drop by drop. Why did you send it?"

Byne did had to squeeze it out. His lips didn't want to part. "Because," he finally managed, "they were going on with the investigation and there was no telling what they might dig up. They might find out that I knew Faith's mother, and about my—about the arrangement. I still thought Faith had killed herself,

and I still do, but if she *had* been murdered I thought
Laidlaw must have done it and I wanted them to
know about him and Faith."

"Why must he have done it? You invented that,
didn't you? About him and Miss Usher?"

"I did not. I sort of kept an eye on Faith, naturally.
I don't mean I was with her, I just kept an eye on her.
I saw her with Laidlaw twice, and the day he left for
Canada I saw her in his car. I knew he went to Canada because a friend got a card from him. I didn't
have to invent it."

Wolfe grunted. "You realize, Mr. Byne, that everything you say is now suspect. Assuming that you
knew that Laidlaw and Miss Usher had in fact been
intimate, why did you surmise that he had killed her?
Was she menacing him?"

"Not that I know of. If he had a reason for killing
her I didn't know what it was. But he was the only
one of the people there that night who had had anything to do with her."

"No. You had."

"Damn it, I wasn't there!"

"That's true, but those who were there can also
plead lack of opportunity. In the circumstances as I
have heard them described, no one could have
poisoned Miss Usher's champagne with any assurance
that it would get to her. And you alone, of all those
involved, had a motive, and not a puny one. An increase in annual income of $27,000 or more, tax exempt, is an alluring prospect. If I were you I would
accept almost any alternative to a disclosure of that
agreement to the District Attorney."

"I am. I'm sitting here while you pile it on."

"So you are." Wolfe looked at his palms and put

them on the chair arms. "Now. Did you know that Miss Usher kept a bottle of poison on her person?"

No hesitation. "I knew that she said she did. I never saw it. Her mother told me, and Mrs. Irwin at Grantham House mentioned it to me once."

"Did you know what kind of poison it was?"

"No."

"Was it Mrs. Usher's own idea to seclude herself in a hotel under another name, or did you suggest it?"

"Neither one. I mean I don't remember. She phoned me Thursday—no, Wednesday—and we decided she ought to do that. I don't remember who suggested it."

"Who suggested your meeting this evening?"

"She did. She phoned me this morning. I told you that."

"What did she want?"

"She wanted to know what I was going to do about payments, with Faith dead. She knew that by the agreement it was left to my discretion. I told her that for the present I would continue to send her half."

"Had she been using any of the money you sent her to support her daughter?"

"I don't think so. Not for the last four or five years, but it wasn't her fault. Faith wouldn't take anything from her. Faith wouldn't live with her. They couldn't get along. Mrs. Usher is very—unconventional. Faith left when she was sixteen, and for over a year we didn't know where she was. When I found her she was working in a restaurant. A waitress."

"But you continued to pay Mrs. Usher her full share?"

"Yes."

"Is that fund in your possession and control without supervision?"

"Certainly."

"It has never been audited?"

"Certainly not. Who would audit it?"

"I couldn't say. Would you object to an audit by an accountant of my selection? Now that I know of the agreement?"

"I certainly would. The fund is my property and I am accountable to no one but myself, as long as I pay Mrs. Usher her share."

"I must see that agreement." Wolfe pursed his lips and slowly shook his head. "It is extremely difficult," he said, "to circumvent the finality of death. Mr. Grantham made a gallant try, but he was hobbled by his vain desire to guard his secret even after he became food for worms. He protected you and Mrs. Usher, each against the frailty or knavery of the other, but what if you joined forces in a threat to his repute? He couldn't preclude that." He lifted a hand to brush it aside. "A desire to defeat death makes any man a fool. I must see that agreement. Meanwhile, a few points remain. You told Mr. Goodwin that your selection of Miss Usher to be invited to that party was fortuitous, but now that won't do. Then why?"

"Of course," Byne said. "I knew that was coming."

"Then you've had time to devise an answer."

"I don't have to devise it. I was a damn fool. When I got the list from Mrs. Irwin and saw Faith's name on it—well, there it was. The idea of having Faith as a guest at my aunt's house—it just appealed to me. Mrs. Robilotti is only my aunt by marriage, you know. My mother was Albert Grantham's sister. You've got

to admit there was a kick in the idea of having Faith
sitting at my aunt's table. And then . . ."

He left it hanging. Wolfe prodded him. "Then?"

"That suggested another idea, to have Laidlaw
there too. I know I was a damn fool, but there it was.
Laidlaw seeing Faith there, and Faith seeing him. Of
course, my aunt could cross Faith off and tell Mrs.
Irwin—" He stopped. In a second he went on, "I mean
you never knew what Faith would do, she might refuse to go, but Laidlaw wouldn't know she had been
asked, so what the hell. So I suggested that to my
aunt, to invite Laidlaw, and she did."

"Did Miss Usher know that Albert Grantham had
fathered her?"

"My God, no. She thought her father had been a
man named Usher who had died before she was
born."

"Did she know you were the source of her
mother's income?"

"No. I think— No, I don't think, I know. She suspected that her mother's income came from friends.
From men she knew. That was why she left. About
my picking Faith to be invited to that party and suggesting Laidlaw, after I had done that I got cold feet.
I realized something might happen. At least Faith
might walk out when she saw him, and it might be
something worse, and I didn't want to be there, so I
decided to get someone to go in my place. The first
four or five I tried couldn't make it, and I thought of
Archie Goodwin."

Wolfe leaned back and closed his eyes, and his lips
started to work. They pushed out and went back in,
out and in, out and in . . . Sooner or later he always
does that, and I really should have a sign made, GENIUS

AT WORK, and put it on his desk when he starts it. Usually I have some sort of idea as to what genius is working on, but that time not a glimmer. He had cleared away some underbrush, for instance who had sicked the cops on Laidlaw and how Faith and Laidlaw had both got invited to the party, but he had got only one thing to chew on, that he had at last found somebody who had had a healthy motive to kill Faith Usher, and Byne, as he liked to point out himself, hadn't even been at the party. Of course, that could have been what genius was at, doping out how Byne could have poisoned the champagne by remote control, but I doubted it.

Wolfe opened his eyes and aimed them at Dinky. "I'm not going to wait until Monday," he said. "If I haven't enough now, I never will have. One thing you have told me, or at least implied, will have to be my peg. If I asked you about it now, you would only wriggle out with lies, so I won't bother. The time has come to attack the central question: if someone had decided to kill Faith Usher, how did he manage it?" He turned. "Archie, get Mr. Cramer."

"No!" Byne was on his feet. "Damn you, after I've spilled—"

I had lifted the receiver, but Byne was there, jostling and reaching. Wolfe's voice, with a snap, turned him. "Mr. Byne! Don't squeal until you're hurt. I've got you and I intend to keep you. Must I call Mr. Panzer in?"

He didn't have to. Dinky backed away a step, giving me elbow room to dial, but close enough, he thought, to pounce. Getting Inspector Cramer at twenty minutes past ten on a Saturday evening can be anything from quick and simple to practically impossible. That time I had luck. He was at Homicide on Twentieth Street, and after a short wait I had him, and Wolfe got on, and Cramer greeted him with a growl, and Wolfe said he would need three minutes.

"I'll take all I can stand," Cramer said. "What is it?"

"About Faith Usher. I am being pestered beyond endurance. Take yesterday. In the morning those four men insisted on seeing me. In the afternoon you barged in. In the evening Mr. Goodwin and I were interrupted by a phone call summoning him to Mrs. Robilotti's house, and when he goes he finds Mr. Skinner there, and he—"

"Do you mean the Commissioner?"

"Yes. He said it was unofficial and off the record, and made an offensive proposal which Mr. Goodwin was to refer to me. I don't complain of that to you, since he is your superior and you presumably didn't know about it."

"I didn't."

"But it was another thorn for me, and I have had enough. I would like to put an end to it. All this hullabaloo has been caused by Mr. Goodwin's conviction, as an eye-witness, that Faith Usher did not kill herself, and I intend to satisfy myself on the point independently. If I decide he is wrong I will deal with him. If I decide he is right it will be because I will have uncovered evidence that may have escaped you. I notify you of my intention because in order to proceed I must see all of the people involved, I must invite them to my office, and I thought you should know about it. Also I thought you might choose to be present, and if so you will be welcome, but in that case you should get them here. I will not ask people to my office for a conference and then confront them with a police inspector. Tomorrow morning at eleven o'clock would be a good time."

Cramer made a noise, something like "Wmgzwmzg." Then he found words. "So you've got your teeth in something. What?"

"It's other people's teeth that are in something. In me. And I'm annoyed. The situation is precisely as I have described it and I have nothing to add."

"You wouldn't have. Tomorrow is Sunday."

"Yes. Since three of them are girls with jobs that is just as well."

"You want all of them?"

"Yes."

"Are any of them with you now?"

"No."

"Is Commissioner Skinner in this?"

"No."

"I'll call you back in an hour."

"That won't do," Wolfe objected. "If I am to invite them I must start at once, and it's late."

Not only that, but he knew darned well that if he gave him an hour Cramer would probably ring our bell in about ten minutes and want in. Anyway, it was a cinch that Cramer would buy it, and after a few more foolish questions he did.

We hung up, and Wolfe turned to Byne, who had returned to his chair. "Now for you," he said, "and Mrs. Usher. I do not intend to let you communicate with anyone, and there is only one way to insure against it. She will spend the night here; there is a spare room with a good bed. It is a male household, but that shouldn't disconcert her. There is another room you may use, or, if you prefer, Mr. Panzer will accompany you home and sleep there, and bring you here in the morning. Mr. Cramer will have the others here at eleven o'clock."

"You can go to hell," Byne said. He stood up. "I'm taking Mrs. Usher to her hotel."

Wolfe shook his head. "I know your mind is in disorder, but surely you must see that that is out of the question. I can't possibly allow you an opportunity to repair any of the gaps I have made in your fences. If you scoot I shall move at once, and you'll find you have no fences left at all. Only by my sufferance can you hope to get out of this mess without disfigurement, and you know it. Archie, bring Saul and Mrs. Usher—no. First ring Mr. Byne's apartment and tell Orrie to come. Also tell him not to be disappointed at not finding the agreement; it isn't there. If he has found any items that seem significant he might as well bring them."

"You goddamn snoop," Dinky said, merely repeating himself.

I turned to the phone.

Chapter 15

For an hour and a half Sunday morning Fritz and I worked like beavers, setting the stage. The idea was—that is, Wolfe's idea—to reproduce as nearly as possible the scene of the crime, and it was a damn silly idea, since you could have put seven or eight of that office into Mrs. Robilotti's drawing room. Taking the globe and the couch and the television cabinet and a few other items to the dining room helped a little, but it was still hopeless. I wanted to go up to the plant rooms and tell Wolfe so, and add that if a playback was essential to his program he had better break his rule never to leave the house on business and move the whole performance uptown to Mrs. Robilotti's, but Fritz talked me out of it. To get fourteen chairs we had to bring some down from upstairs, and then it developed later that some of them weren't really necessary. The bar was a table over in the far corner, but it couldn't be against the wall because there had to be room for Hackett behind it. One small satisfaction I got was that the red leather chair had been taken to the dining room with the other stuff, and Cramer wouldn't like that a bit.

Furniture-moving wasn't all. Mrs. Usher kept buzzing on the house phone from the South Room, for more coffee, for more towels, though she had a full supply, for a section she said was missing from the Sunday paper I had taken her, and for an additional list of items I had to get from the drugstore. Then at ten-fifteen here came Austin Byne, escorted by Saul, demanding a private audience with Wolfe immediately, and to get him off my neck I had Saul take him up the three flights to the vestibule of the plant rooms, where they found the door locked, and then Saul had to get physical with him when he wanted to open doors on the upper floors trying to find Mrs. Usher.

I expected more turmoil when, at ten-forty, the bell rang and Inspector Cramer was on the stoop, but it wasn't Wolfe he had come early for. He merely asked if Mrs. Robilotti had arrived, and, when I told him no, stayed outside. Theoretically, in a democracy, a police inspector should react just the same to a dame with a Fifth Avenue mansion as to an unmarried mother, but a job is a job, and facts are facts and one fact was that the Commissioner himself had taken the trouble to make a trip to the mansion. So I didn't chalk it up against Cramer that he waited out on the sidewalk for the Robilotti limousine; and anyway, he was there to greet the three unmarried mothers when Sergeant Purley Stebbins arrived with them in a police car. The three chevaliers, Paul Schuster, Beverly Kent, and Edwin Laidlaw, came singly, on their own.

I had promised myself a certain pleasure, and I didn't let Cramer's one-man reception committee interfere with it. When the limousine finally rolled to the curb, a few minutes late, and he convoyed Mrs.

Robilotti up the stoop steps, followed by her husband,
son, daughter, and butler, I held the door for them as
they entered and then left them to Fritz. My objective was the last one in, Hackett. When he had
crossed the sill I put my hands ready for his coat and
hat, in the proper manner exactly.

"Good morning, sir," I said. "A pleasant day. Mr.
Wolfe will be down shortly."

It got him. He darted a glance at the others, saw
that no eye was on him, handed me his hat, and said,
"Quite. Thank you, Goodwin."

That made the day for me personally, no matter
how it turned out professionally. I took him to the
office and then went to the kitchen, buzzed the plant
rooms on the house phone, and told Wolfe the cast had
arrived.

"Mrs. Usher?" he asked.

"Okay. In her room. She'll stay put."

"Mr. Byne?"

"Also okay. In the office with the others, with Saul
glued to him."

"Very well. I'll be down."

I went and joined the mob. They were scattered
around, some seated and some standing. I permitted
myself a private grin when I saw that Cramer, finding
the red leather chair gone, had moved one of the yellow ones to its exact position and put Mrs. Robilotti in
it, and was on his feet beside it, bending down to her.
As I threaded my way through to my desk the sound
of the elevator came, and in a moment Wolfe entered.

No pronouncing of names was required, since he
had met the Robilottis and the Grantham twins at the
time of the jewelry hunt. He made it to his desk, sent
his eyes around, and sat. He looked at Cramer.

"You have explained the purpose of this gathering, Mr. Cramer?"

"Yes. You're going to prove that Goodwin is either wrong or right."

"I didn't say 'prove.' I said I intend to satisfy myself and deal with him accordingly." He surveyed the audience. "Ladies and gentlemen. I will not keep you long—at least, not most of you. I have no exhortation for you and no questions to ask. To form an opinion of Mr. Goodwin's competence as an eye-witness, I need to see, not what he saw, since these quarters are too cramped for that, but an approximation of it. You cannot take your positions precisely as they were last Tuesday evening, or re-enact the scene with complete fidelity, but we'll do the best we can. Archie?"

I left my chair to stage-manage. Thinking that Mrs. Robilotti and her Robert were the most likely to balk, I left them till the last. First I put Hackett behind the table, which was the bar, and Laidlaw and Helen Yarmis at one end of it. Then Rose Tuttle and Beverly Kent, on chairs over where the globe had stood. Then Celia Grantham and Paul Schuster by the wall to the right of Wolfe's desk, with her sitting and him standing. Then I put Saul Panzer on a chair near the door to the hall, and told the audience, "Mr. Panzer here is Faith Usher. The distance is wrong and so are the others, but the relative positions are about right." Then I put an ashtray on a chair to the right of the safe, and told them, "This is Faith Usher's bag, containing the bottle of poison." With all that arranged, I didn't think Mrs. Robilotti would protest when I asked her and her husband to take their places in front of the bar, and she didn't.

That was all, except for Ethel Varr and me, and I

got her and stood with her at a corner of my desk, and told Wolfe, "All set."

"Miss Tuttle and I were much farther away," Beverly Kent objected.

"Yes, sir," Wolfe agreed. "It is not presumed that this is identical. Now." His eyes went to the group at the bar. "Mr. Hackett, I understand that when Mr. Grantham went to the bar for champagne for himself and Miss Usher, two glasses were there in readiness. You had poured one of them a few minutes previously, and the other just before he arrived. Is that correct?"

"Yes, sir." Hackett had fully recovered from our brush in the hall and was back in character. "I have stated to the police that one of the glasses had been standing there three or four minutes."

"Please pour a glass now and put it in place."

The bottles in the cooler on the table were champagne, and good champagne; Wolfe had insisted on it. Fritz had opened two of them. Pouring champagne is always nice to watch, but I doubt if any pourer ever had as attentive an audience as Hackett had, as he took a bottle from the cooler and filled a glass.

"Keep the bottle in your hand," Wolfe directed him. "I'll explain what I'm after and then you may proceed. I want to see it from various angles. You will pour another glass, and Mr. Grantham will come and get the two glasses and go with them to Mr. Panzer— that is to say, to Miss Usher. He will hand him one, and Mr. Goodwin will be there and take the other one. Meanwhile you will be pouring two more glasses, and Mr. Grantham will come and get them and go with them to Miss Tuttle, and hand her one, and again Mr. Goodwin will be there and take the other one. You will do the same with Miss Varr and Miss Grantham. Not

with Miss Yarmis and Mrs. Robilotti, since they are
there at the bar. That way I shall see it from all sides.
Is that clear, Mr. Hackett?"

"Yes, sir."

"It's not clear to me," Cecil said. "What's the idea?
I didn't do that. All I did was get two glasses and take
one to Miss Usher."

"I'm aware of that," Wolfe told him. "As I said, I
want to get various angles on it. If you prefer, Mr.
Panzer can move to the different positions, but this is
simpler. I only request your cooperation. Do you find
my request unreasonable?"

"I find it pretty damn nutty. But it's all nutty, in
my opinion, so a little more won't hurt, if I can keep a
glass for myself when I've performed." He moved,
then turned. "What's the order again?"

"The order is unimportant. After Mr. Panzer,
Misses Tuttle, Varr, and Grantham, in any order you
please."

"Right. Start pouring, Hackett. Here I come."

The show started. It did seem fairly nutty, at that,
especially my part. Hackett pouring, and Cecil carrying, and the girls taking—there was nothing odd
about that; but me racing around, taking the second
glass, deciding what to do with it, doing it, and getting
to the next one in time to be there waiting when Cecil
arrived—of all the miscellaneous chores I had performed at Wolfe's direction over the years, that took
the prize. At the fourth and last one, for Celia Grantham, by the wall to the right of Wolfe's desk, Cecil
cheated. After he had handed his sister hers he ignored my outstretched hand, raised his glass, said,
"Here's to crime," and took a mouthful of the bubbles.

He lowered the glass and told Wolfe, "I hope that didn't spoil it."

"It was in bad taste," Celia said.

"I meant it to be," he retorted. "This whole thing has been in bad taste from the beginning."

Wolfe, who had straightened up to watch the performance, let his shoulders down. "You didn't spoil it," he said. His eyes went around. "I invite comment. Did anyone notice anything worthy of remark?"

"I don't know whether it's worthy of remark or not," Paul Schuster, the lawyer, said, "but this exhibition can't possibly be made the basis for any conclusion. The conditions were not the same at all."

"I must disagree," Wolfe disagreed. "I did get a basis for a conclusion, and for the specific conclusion I had hoped for. I need support for it, but would rather not suggest it. I appeal to all of you: did anything about Mr. Grantham's performance strike your eye?"

A growl came from the door to the hall. Sergeant Purley Stebbins was standing there on the sill, his big frame half filling the rectangle. "I don't know about a conclusion," he said, "but I noticed that he carried the glasses the same every time. The one in his right hand, his thumb and two fingers were on the bowl, and the one in his left hand, he held that lower down, by the stem. And he kept the one in his right hand and handed them the one in his left hand. Every time."

I had never before seen Wolfe look at Purley with unqualified admiration. "Thank you, Mr. Stebbins," he said. "You not only have eyes but know what they're for. Will anyone corroborate him?"

"I will," Saul Panzer said. "I do." He was still holding the glass Cecil had handed him.

"Will you, Mr. Cramer?"

"I reserve it." Cramer's eyes were narrowed at him. "What's your conclusion?"

"Surely that's obvious." Wolfe turned a hand over. "What I hoped to get was ground for a conclusion that anyone who was sufficiently familiar with Mr. Grantham's habits, and who saw him pick up the glasses and start off with them, would know which one he would hand to Miss Usher. And I got it, and I have two competent witnesses, Mr. Stebbins and Mr. Panzer." His head turned. "That is all, ladies and gentlemen. I wish to continue, but only to Mrs. Robilotti, Mr. Byne, and Mr. Laidlaw—and Mr. Robilotti by courtesy, if he chooses to stay. The rest of you may go. I needed your help for this demonstration and I thank you for coming. It would be a pleasure to serve you champagne on some happier occasion."

"You mean we have to go?" Rose Tuttle piped. "I want to stay."

Judging from the expressions on most of the faces, the others did too, except Helen Yarmis, who was standing by the bar with Laidlaw. She said, "Come on, Ethel," to Ethel Varr, who was standing by my desk, and they headed for the door. Cecil emptied his glass and put it on Wolfe's desk and announced that he was staying, and Celia said she was too. Beverly Kent, the diplomat, showed that he had picked the right career by handling Rose Tuttle, who was seated beside him. She let him escort her out. Paul Schuster approached to listen a moment to the twins arguing with Wolfe, and then turned and went. Seeing Cramer cross to Mrs. Robilotti, at the bar with her husband, I noted that Hackett wasn't there and then found that he wasn't anywhere. He had gone without my knowing it, one more proof that a detective is no match for a butler.

It was Mrs. Robilotti who settled the issue with the twins. She came to Wolfe's desk, followed by Cramer and her husband, and told them to go, and then turned to her husband and told him to go too. Her pale gray eyes, back under her angled brows, were little circles of tinted ice. It was Celia she looked at.

"This man needs a lesson," she said, "and I'll give it to him. I never have needed you, and I don't need you now. You're being absurd. I do things better alone, and I'll do this alone."

Celia opened her mouth, closed it again, turned to look at Laidlaw, and went, and Cecil followed. Robilotti started to speak, met the pale gray eyes, shrugged like a polished and civilized Italian, and quit. When her eyes had seen him to the door, she walked to the chair Cramer had placed for her when she arrived, sat, aimed the eyes at Wolfe, and spoke.

"You said you wished to continue. Well?"

He was polite. "In a moment, madam. Another person is expected. If you gentlemen will be seated? Archie?"

Saul was already seated, still in Faith Usher's place, sipping champagne. Leaving it to the other four, Laidlaw, Byne, Cramer, and Stebbins to do their own seating, I went to the hall, mounted the two flights to the South Room, knocked on the door, was told to come in, and did so.

Elaine Usher, in a chair by a window with sections of the Sunday paper scattered on the floor, had a mean look ready for me.

"Okay," I said. "Your cue."

"It's about time." She kicked the papers away from her feet and got up. "Who's there?"

"As expected. Mr. Wolfe. Byne, Laidlaw, Panzer. Inspector Cramer and Sergeant Stebbins. Mrs. Robilotti. She sent her husband home. I take you straight to her."

"I know. I'll enjoy that, I really will, no matter what happens. My hair's a mess. I'll be with you in a minute."

She went to the bathroom and closed the door. I wasn't impatient, since Wolfe would use the time to get Mrs. Robilotti into a proper mood. Mrs. Usher used it too. When she emerged her hair was very nice and her lips were the color that excites a bull. I asked her if she preferred the elevator, and she said no, and I followed her down the two flights. As we entered the office I was at her elbow.

It came out so perfect that you might have thought it had been rehearsed. I crossed with her, passing between Cramer and Byne, turned so we were facing Mrs. Robilotti, right in front of her, and said, "Mrs. Robilotti, let me present Mrs. Usher, the mother of Faith Usher." Mrs. Usher bent at the waist, put out a hand, and said, "It's a pleasure, a great pleasure." Mrs. Robilotti stared a second, shot a hand out, and slapped Mrs. Usher's face. Perfect.

Chapter 16

Your guess is as good as mine, whether Wolfe would have been able to crash through anyway if the confrontation stunt hadn't worked—if Mrs. Robilotti had been quick enough and tough enough to take Mrs. Usher's offered hand and respond according to protocol. He maintains that he would have, but that the question is academic, since with Mrs. Robilotti's nerves already on edge the sudden appearance of that woman, without warning, bending to her and offering a hand, was sure to break her.

I didn't pull Mrs. Usher back in time to dodge the slap, though I might have, but after it landed I acted. After all she was a house guest, and a kick on the chin by the host and a smack in the face by another guest were no credit to our hospitality; and besides, she might try to return the compliment. So I gripped her arm and pulled her back out of range, bumping into Cramer, who had bounced out of his chair. Mrs. Robilotti had jerked back and sat stiff, her teeth pinning her lower lip.

"It might be well," Wolfe told me, "to seat Mrs.

Usher near you. Madam, I regret the indignity you have suffered under my roof." He gestured. "That is Mr. Laidlaw. Mr. Cramer, of the police. Mr. Stebbins, also of the police. You know Mr. Byne."

As I was convoying her to the chair Saul had brought, putting her between Laidlaw and me, Cramer was saying, "You stage it and then you regret it." To his right: "I do regret it, Mrs. Robilotti. I had no hand in it." Back to Wolfe: "All right, let's hear it."

"You have seen it," Wolfe told him. "Certainly I staged it. You heard me deliberately bait Mrs. Robilotti, to ensure the desired reaction to Mrs. Usher's appearance. Before commenting on that reaction, I must explain Mr. Laidlaw's presence. I asked him to stay because he has a legitimate concern. As you know, someone sent an anonymous communication making certain statements about him, and that entitles him to hear disclosure of the truth. Why Mr. Byne is here will soon be apparent. It was something he said last evening that informed me that Mrs. Robilotti had known that her former husband, Albert Grantham, was the father of Faith Usher. However—"

"That's a lie," Byne said. "That's a damn lie."

Wolfe's tone sharpened. "I choose my words, Mr. Byne. I didn't say you told me that, but that something you said informed me. Speaking of the people invited to that gathering, you said, 'Of course, my aunt could cross Faith off and tell Mrs. Irwin'—and stopped, realizing that you had slipped. When I let it pass, you thought I had missed it, but I hadn't. It was merely that if I had tried to pin you down you would have wriggled out by denying the implication. Now that—"

"There was no implication!"

"Nonsense. Why should your aunt 'cross Faith off'? Why should she refuse to have Miss Usher in her house? Granting that there were many possible explanations, there was one suggested by the known facts: that she would not receive as a guest the natural daughter of her former husband. And I had just learned that Faith Usher was Albert Grantham's natural daughter, and that you were aware of it. So I had the implication, and I arranged to test it. If Mrs. Robilotti, suddenly confronted by Faith Usher's mother extending a friendly hand, took the hand and betrayed no reluctance, the implication would be discredited. I expected her to shrink from it, and I was wrong. I may learn someday that what a woman will do is beyond conjecture. Instead of shrinking, she struck. I repeat, Mrs. Usher, I regret it. I did not foresee it."

"You can't have it both ways," Byne said. "You say my aunt wouldn't have Faith Usher in her house because she knew she was her former husband's natural daughter. But she did have her in her house. She knew she had been invited, and she let her come."

Wolfe nodded. "I know. That's the point. That's my main reason for assuming that your aunt killed her. There are other—"

"Hold it," Cramer snapped. His head turned. "Mrs. Robilotti, I want you to know that this is as shocking to me as it is to you."

Her pale gray eyes were on Wolfe and she didn't move them. "I doubt it," she said. "I didn't know any man could go as low as *this*. This is incredible."

"I agree," Wolfe told her. "Murder is always incredible. I have now committed myself, madam, be-

fore witnesses, and if I am wrong I shall be at your
mercy. I wouldn't like that. Mr. Cramer. You are
shocked. I can expound, or you can attack. Which do
you prefer?"

"Neither one." Cramer's fists were on his knees. "I
just want to know. What evidence have you that
Faith Usher was Albert Grantham's daughter?"

"Well." Wolfe cocked his head. "That is a ticklish
point. My sole concern in this is the murder of Faith
Usher, and I have no desire to make unnecessary
trouble for people not implicated in it. For example, I
know where you can find evidence that the death of
Faith Usher meant substantial financial profit for a
certain man, but since he wasn't there and couldn't
have killed her, I'll tell you about it only if it becomes
requisite. To answer your question: I have statements
of two people, Mrs. Elaine Usher and Mr. Austin
Byne." His eyes moved. "And, Mr. Byne, you have
trimmed long enough. Did your aunt know that Faith
Usher was the daughter of Albert Grantham?"

Dinky's jaw worked. He looked left, at Mrs.
Usher, but not right, at his aunt. Wolfe had made it
plain: if he came through, Wolfe would not tell Cramer
about the agreement and where it was. Probably
what decided him was the fact that Mrs. Robilotti had
already given it away by slapping Mrs. Usher.

"Yes," he said. "I told her."

"When?"

"A couple of months ago."

"Why?"

"Because—something she said. She had said it before, that I was a parasite because I was living on
money my uncle had given me before he died. When
she said it again that day I lost my temper and told

her that my uncle had given me the money so I could provide for his illegitimate daughter. She wouldn't believe me, and I told her the name of the daughter and her mother. Afterwards I was sorry I had told her, and I told her so—"

A noise, an explosive noise, came from his aunt. "You liar," she said, a glint of hate in the pale gray eyes. "You sit there and lie. You told me so you could blackmail me, to get more millions out of me. The millions Albert had given you weren't enough. You weren't satisfied—"

"Stop it!" Wolfe's voice was a whip. He was scowling at her. "You are in mortal peril, madam. I have put you there, so I have a responsibility, and I advise you to hold your tongue. Mr. Cramer. Do you want more from Mr. Byne, or more from me?"

"You." Cramer was so shocked he was hoarse. "You say that Mrs. Robilotti deliberately let Faith Usher come to that party so she could kill her. Is that right?"

"Yes."

"And that her motive was that she knew that Faith Usher was the illegitimate child of Albert Grantham?"

"It could have been. With her character and temperament that could have been sufficient motive. But she has herself just suggested an additional one. Her nephew may have been using Faith Usher as a fulcrum to pry a fortune out of her. You will explore that."

"I certainly will. That show you put on. You say that proved that Mrs. Robilotti could have done it?"

"Yes. You saw it. She could have dropped the poison into the glass that had been standing there for

three or four minutes. She stayed there at the bar. If
someone else had started to take that glass she could
have said it was hers. When her son came and picked
up the two glasses, if he had taken the poisoned one in
his right hand, which would have meant—to her, since
she knew his habits—that he would drink it himself,
again she could have said it was hers and told him to
get another one. Or she could even have handed it to
him, have seen to it that he took the poisoned one in
his left hand; but you can't hope to establish that,
since neither she nor her son would admit it. The moment he left the bar with the poisoned glass in his left
hand Faith Usher was doomed; and the risk was
slight, since an ample supply of cyanide was there on
a chair in Miss Usher's bag. It would unquestionably
be assumed that she had committed suicide; indeed, it
was assumed, and the assumption would have pre-
vailed if Mr. Goodwin hadn't been there and kept his
eyes open."

"Who told Mrs. Robilotti that Miss Usher had the
poison? And when?"

"I don't know." Wolfe gestured. "Confound it,
must I shine your shoes for you?"

"No, I'll manage. You've shined enough. You say
the risk was slight. It wasn't slight when she got Miss
Usher's bag and took out the bottle and took some of
the poison."

"I doubt if she did that. I doubt if she ever went
near that bag. If she knew that the poison Miss Usher
carried around was cyanide, and several people did,
she probably got some somewhere else, which isn't
difficult, and had it at hand. I suggest that that is
worth inquiry, whether she recently had access to a
supply of cyanide. You might even find that she had

actually procured some." Wolfe gestured again. "I do not pretend that I am showing you a ripened fruit which you need only to pick. I undertook merely to satisfy myself whether Mr. Goodwin was right or wrong. I am satisfied. Are you?"

Cramer never said. Mrs. Robilotti was on her feet. I had the idea then that what moved her was Wolfe's mentioning the possibility that she had got hold of cyanide somewhere else, and learned a few days later that I had been right, when Purley Stebbins told me that they had found out where she got it, and could prove it. Anyhow, she was on her feet, and moving, but had taken only three steps when she had to stop. Cramer and Purley were both there blocking the way, and together they weigh four hundred pounds and are over four feet wide.

"Let me pass," she said. "I'm going home."

I have seldom felt sorry for that pair, but I did then, especially Cramer.

"Not right now," he said gruffly. "I'm afraid you'll have to answer some questions."

Chapter 17

O ne item. You may remember my mentioning that one day, the day after the murderer of Faith Usher was convicted, I was discussing with a friend what was the most conceited remark we had ever heard? It was that same day that I caught sight of Edwin Laidlaw in the men's bar at the Churchill and decided to do a good deed. Besides, I had felt that the amount on the bill we had sent him, which he had paid promptly without a murmur, had been pretty stiff, and he had something coming. So I approached him, and after greetings had been exchanged I performed the deed.

"I didn't want to mention it," I said, "while her mother was on trial for murder, but now I can tell you, in case you're interested. One day during that commotion I was talking with Celia Grantham, and your name came up, and she said, 'I may marry him someday. If he gets into a bad jam I'll marry him now.' I report it only because I thought you might want to take some dancing lessons."

"I don't have to," he said. "I appreciate it, and many thanks, but we're getting married next week. On the quiet. We put it off until the trial was over. Let me buy you a drink."

There you are. I'm one good deed shy.

The World of
Rex Stout

Enjoy a peek into the life of Nero Wolfe's creator, Rex Stout, courtesy of the Stout Estate. Pulled from Rex Stout's own archives, here are rarely seen memorabilia.

Champagne for One

Authors and editors often rely on one another when deciding on a title for a novel. Fortunately for Marshall Best, Stout's longtime editor, his author was able to come up with something that worked perfectly without the help of his "title department." Could you imagine this classic story titled *Champagne for Faith Usher*?

July 16 1958

Dear Marshall:

My title department seems to be
on vacation. I suggest either CHAMPAGNE
FOR FAITH USHER ~~of~~ or CHAMPAGNE FOR ONE.
Please let me know as soon as you decide
which one to use; or if you think neither
will do I'll try again.

                         Yours.....

THE VIKING PRESS INC · PUBLISHERS

625 MADISON AVENUE · NEW YORK 22 · NY

Cable: Vikpress   Telephone: PL 5-4330

July 23, 1958

Mr. Rex Stout
High Meadow
Brewster, New York

Dear Rex:

Your title department does pretty well in
absentia. We are all, including the difficult
Alan Green, quite satisfied with CHAMPAGNE
FOR ONE, and Bill English is going ahead with
his jacket.

Sincerely,

M. Marshall

MAB/vs

*Publication date November. No magazine
complications this time, I trust*

Not for publication
Confidential Memo
From Rex Stout
September 15 1949

DESCRIPTION OF NERO WOLFE

Height 5 ft. 11 in. Weight 272 lbs. Age 56.
Mass of dark brown hair, very little greying, is not
parted but sweeps off to the right because he brushes
with his right hand. Dark brown eyes are average in
size, but look smaller because they are mostly half
closed. They always are aimed straight at the person
he is talking to. Forehead is high. Head and face
are big but do not seem so in proportion to the whole.
Ears rather small. Nose long and narrow, slightly
aquiline. Mouth mobile and extremely variable; lips
when pursed are full and thick, but in tense moments
they are thin and their line is long. Cheeks full but
not pudgy; the high point of the cheekbone can be seen
from straight front. Complexion varies from some
floridity after meals to an ivory pallor late at night
when he has spent six hard hours working on someone.
He breathes smoothly and without sound except when he
is eating; then he takes in and lets out great gusts of
air. His massive shoulders never slump; when he stands
up at all he stands straight. He shaves every day. He
has a small brown mole just above his right jawbone,
halfway between the chin and the ear.

DESCRIPTION OF ARCHIE GOODWIN

Height 6 feet. Weight 180 lbs. Age 32. Hair is
light rather than dark, but just barely decided not to
be red; he gets it cut every two weeks, rather short,
and brushes it straight back, but it keeps standing up.
He shaves four times a week and grasps at every excuse
to make it only three times. His features are all reg-
ular, well-modeled and well-proportioned, except the
nose. He escapes the curse of being the movie actor
type only through the nose. It is not a true pug and
is by no means a deformity, but it is a little short
and the ridge is broad, and the tip has continued on
its own, beyond the cartilage, giving the impression
of startling and quite independent initiative. The eyes
are grey, and are inquisitive and quick to move. He is
muscular both in appearance and in movement, and upright
in posture, but his shoulders stoop a little in unconscious
reaction to Wolfe's repeated criticism that he is too
self-assertive.

DESCRIPTION OF WOLFE'S OFFICE

The old brownstone on West 35th Street is a double-
width house. Entering at the front door, which is seven
steps up from the sidewalk, you are facing the length of

a wide carpeted hall. At the right is an enormous coat
rack, eight feet wide, then the stairs, and beyond the
stairs the door to the dining room. There were origi-
nally two rooms on that side of the hall, but Wolfe had
the partition removed and turned it into a dining room
forty feet long, with a table large enough for six (but
extensible) square in the middle. It (and all other
rooms) are carpeted; Wolfe hates bare floors. At the
far end of the big hall is the kitchen. At the left of the
big hall are two doors; the first one is to what Archie calls
the front room, and the second is to the office. The front
room is used chiefly as an anteroom; Nero and Archie do
no living there. It is rather small, and the furniture
is a random mixture without any special character.

The office is large and nearly square. In the far
corner to the left (as you enter from the hall) a small
rectangle has been walled off to make a place for a
john and a washbowl — to save steps for Wolfe. The door
leading to it faces you, and around the corner, along its
other wall, is a wide and well-cushioned couch.

SKETCH OF OFFICE

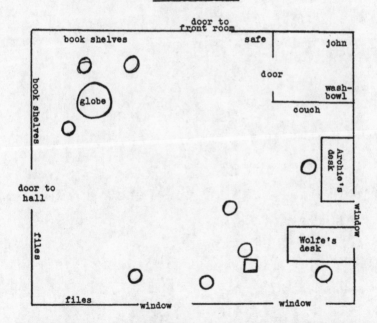

In furnishings the room has no apparent unity
but it has plenty of character. Wolfe permits nothing
to be in it that he doesn't enjoy looking at, and that
has been the only criterion for admission. The globe
is three feet in diameter. Wolfe's chair was made by
Meyer of cardato. His desk is of cherry, which of
course clashes with the cardato, but Wolfe likes it.
The couch is upholstered in bright yellow material
which has to go to the cleaners every three months.
The carpet was woven in Montenegro in the early nine-
teenth century and has been extensively patched. The
only wall decorations are three pictures: a Manet, a
copy of a Corregio, and a genuine Leonardo sketch. The
chairs are all shapes, colors, materials, and sizes.
The total effect makes you blink with bewilderment at
the first visit, but if you had Archie's job and lived
there you would probably learn to like it.

Rex Stout

REX STOUT, the creator of Nero Wolfe, was born in Nobles-
ville, Indiana, in 1886, the sixth of nine children of John and
Lucetta Todhunter Stout, both Quakers. Shortly after his
birth the family moved to Wakarusa, Kansas. He was educated in a country school, but by the age of nine he was
recognized throughout the state as a prodigy in arithmetic.
Mr. Stout briefly attended the University of Kansas but left
to enlist in the Navy and spent the next two years as a warrant officer on board President Theodore Roosevelt's yacht.
When he left the Navy in 1908, Rex Stout began to write
freelance articles and worked as a sight-seeing guide and
itinerant bookkeeper. Later he devised and implemented a
school banking system that was installed in four hundred
cities and towns throughout the country. In 1927 Mr. Stout
retired from the world of finance and, with the proceeds
from his banking scheme, left for Paris to write serious fiction. He wrote three novels that received favorable reviews
before turning to detective fiction. His first Nero Wolfe
novel, *Fer-de-Lance*, appeared in 1934. It was followed by
many others, among them *Too Many Cooks*, *The Silent
Speaker*, *If Death Ever Slept*, *The Doorbell Rang*, and *Please
Pass the Guilt*, which established Nero Wolfe as a leading
character on a par with Erle Stanley Gardner's famous pro-
tagonist, Perry Mason. During World War II Rex Stout waged
a personal campaign against Nazism as chairman of the War
Writers' Board, master of ceremonies of the radio program
Speaking of Liberty, and member of several national com-
mittees. After the war he turned his attention to mobilizing
public opinion against the wartime use of thermonuclear devices, was an active leader in the Authors Guild, and resumed writing his Nero Wolfe novels. Rex Stout died in 1975
at the age of eighty-eight. A month before his death he published his seventy-second Nero Wolfe mystery, *A Family Affair*. Ten years later a seventy-third Nero Wolfe mystery was
discovered and published in *Death Times Three*.